A
WORLD
ELSEWHERE

A
WORLD
ELSEWHERE

SHANTA ACHARYA

A World Elsewhere

iUniverse books may be ordered through booksellers or by contacting:

iUniverse
1663 Liberty Drive
Bloomington, IN 47403
www.iuniverse.com
1-800-Authors (1-800-288-4677)

This is a work of fiction. All of the characters, names, incidents,
organizations, and dialogue in this novel are either the products
of the author's imagination or are used fictitiously.

ISBN: 978-1-4917-4364-5 (sc)
ISBN: 978-1-4917-4365- 2 (e)

Library of Congress Control Number: 2014915358

Printed in the United States of America

iUniverse rev. date: 02/13/2015

For my family

'I am growing up,' she thought... 'I am losing my illusions, perhaps to acquire new ones' ...

Orlando, **Virginia Woolf**

Happiness in marriage is entirely a matter of chance.

Pride and Prejudice, **Jane Austen**

She did not know that loneliness can be an unnoticed cramping of the spirit for lack of companionship.

The Grass is Singing, **Doris Lessing**

She was no longer struggling against the perception of facts, but adjusting herself to their clearest perception.

Middlemarch, **George Eliot**

CHAPTER 1

"How much longer do you plan to stay in here?" Karuna whispered as she circled her right palm over her stomach. It had grown larger than the largest pumpkin she had seen. She felt the foetus move as if in reply. Tight as a drum, her skin was stretched thin. She could see the veins branching out like a map of the Deccan delta. Karuna was getting dressed after her morning bath. She wiped the sweat off her forehead with the anchal of her cotton, pasapalli sari. Woven in red, white, black and yellow, they represented the colours of Lord Jagannath. She sighed in sympathy, knowing why her child had chosen to spend a little bit longer inside her.

Why do I sweat after a bath? Karuna wondered, powdering under her full breasts and armpits that smelt of sandalwood soap. The sultry weather weighed her down. Mid-July in Cuttack, the sun's rays penetrated each pore of the skin like tiny flaming arrows. Being heavily pregnant intensified everything—colour, sound, smell, taste—especially the heat and dust. The monsoon storms quenched the parched earth, cooling things down. But the thunder and lightning left Karuna in one of her moods. Life rushed past, puffing and whistling like a train, each day a different compartment with its special spell.

"Who are you talking to?" Aditya, her husband, enquired.

He noticed his wife had recently started talking to herself. So preoccupied was she conversing with her child she did not see him until he appeared right before her.

Karuna exclaimed, "She moved!"

"She?" Aditya teased. "How do you know the baby is a *she*?"

"I know—women know these things," she said. They already had a son, Vikram. Karuna wanted a daughter. "We'll call her Armita!"

"Armita Guru!" said Aditya, as if announcing the arrival of someone important at an august gathering. Nodding with approval, he added, "The universe was created out of Divine desire—all children are God's gift expressed through our desire. I do like the conjunction of Desire and the one who teaches, enlightens! But if we have a boy, what will you call him?"

"It's a girl. We'll call her Asha at home. But, we can decide all that later. Don't you have to go to your convocation? You'll be late," Karuna reminded him.

"I don't think I can accompany you to the hospital tonight. This convocation has taken up more of my time than I expected," he apologised.

Aditya doted on his wife, who was twelve years younger. Soon after completing his masters from Calcutta University in 1950, the year India became an independent, democratic republic, he joined Harrison College in Cuttack as a lecturer. Established in the 1870s by the British, it was the premier educational institution of the East Indian state of Orissa. Marriage followed, and now six years later he was a householder expecting their second child.

"Everything takes time when you do it with care. But if you want perfection, you must be prepared to pay the price," Karuna said, appreciating her husband's dilemma.

"We are born the way we are! What can I do if I was born meticulous? The chief minister, governor, and the education minister will be there. Bapa will also be attending," Aditya replied, referring to his father-in-law, Siddhartha Mishra, who was the secretary of state for education. "But what puzzles me is your expected date of delivery. It is long past. Yet no one seems to know when Armita, our Asha, will be born?" he added, pausing the moment he realised he, too, had referred to their unborn child as a girl.

"Asha will arrive when she is ready. She is preparing to face the world. How can doctors predict these things? Don't worry. Bapa will drop me off at the hospital this evening," Karuna replied, inspecting her husband's attire.

With his jet-black, wavy hair brushed back, he looked handsome yet dignified in his white chudidar and black sherwani. The tight chudidar, its rings gracefully clasping the ankles, with the sherwani hugging the body from his waist up, enhanced his height and slender build. His smile revealed a perfect set of white, gleaming teeth. As a student in Calcutta, his looks and manners, his thoughtfulness and generosity had earned Aditya the title 'Prince of Mayurbhanj'. Now he was the 'Prince of Harrison College', and they were the 'royal couple'. Karuna was well known for her beauty, poise and grace. At this late stage of her pregnancy, she had lost none of her charm and allure. She was positively glowing.

Karuna preferred the comfort of a ride in her father's Chevrolet to being ferried around in a rickshaw. As they made their way to the hospital, the incipient pain she had been nursing all day, which incidentally started not long after her little chat with her daughter, got worse. Normally Karuna enjoyed sitting in the back seat of the car, resting her body against the soft leather, which was specially waxed by the driver. Daily he polished the body of the car until it reflected the world around it like a mirror that represented everybody according to the goodness of their heart. Karuna would settle herself in the car as if occupying a comfortable seat in a theatre. She loved watching the grand ceremony of life unfold as they drove through the bustling streets of Cuttack. Today, she felt restless.

Siddhartha had booked one of the maternity cabins in the local medical college and hospital founded by the Maharaja of Mayurbhanj. Built in the days of the Raj, the self-contained accommodation was private and comfortable. Located in the sprawling acres of leafy, deodar-lined grounds of the hospital, it was within easy reach of the best medical assistance one could get in Orissa. The hospital campus was almost as well maintained as the college grounds that Aditya was in charge of. Karuna felt gratified that the immaculate grounds and throughways of Harrison College beat that of the hospital on every count.

Siddhartha had accompanied his daughter to the hospital the day before her due date. When nothing much happened after a couple of days, during which time Karuna enjoyed a much-needed rest, she began to spend her days at her father's home. Her elder sister, Saswati, had also temporarily lodged herself there with her daughter, Sadhana. In the evenings, after the family dinner, Aditya would accompany Karuna to the hospital, where they spent the night, in case she gave birth and needed urgent medical attention. This ritual had been going on for almost a month.

Vikram, their firstborn, was completely at home at his grandfather's, where all his needs were met better than they were at his parents'. For a start, at home he was not pampered so much. They did not have as many servants to spoil him, nor did their house have an uninterrupted supply of electricity. Aja's bungalow, on the other hand, was a magical place where darkness vanished with the flick of a switch. There were other attractions too—the children could play games and hide in its many secret nooks and niches. The house was fenced off by a forest of trees. There was a majestic guava tree, which Vikram loved to climb, disappearing within its buxom branches. The tree was like a grandmother feeding the children with her sweet guavas, soothing them when tempers flared and egos got bruised.

The colonial-style bungalow was separated from the kitchen and the servants' quarters by an open corridor. It was so long that at night the children sprinted across its length, screaming, frightened to death by ghost stories and tales of horror depicting supernatural creatures lurking in the wings in the dark to carry away unsuspecting persons. During the day, they listened carefully for the sound of Aja's wooden sandals striding across the corridor. It signalled any number of things—from the arrival of fresh food from the kitchen to a warning that they should put a stop to whatever practical joke they were planning to execute. Sometimes, they got their coded messages mixed up. It led to the inevitable inquisition until they confessed their misdemeanours in a bewildering babble of tears.

There was also the river at the edge of the sprawling backyard, offering a place of retreat, its beauty unparalleled at sunrise and sunset. Vikram would sit there mesmerised by the currents in the river gliding effortlessly by like snakes in grass. Besides, there was his cousin to play with. He had no objection to staying at his Aja's while his mother spent the night in hospital.

After dropping off his daughter, Siddhartha spoke to the chowkidar and the midwife. They, too, were patiently awaiting the new arrival. By then Karuna's pregnancy was a topic of conversation; even passers-by began to enquire if the child had arrived. Everyone had a theory why it was taking so long, why the baby was not coming out. What kind of 'special' child was Karuna carrying? Her overlarge belly ensured no one doubted she was with child. But speculations about the nature of the child kept mounting with each passing day.

The one good thing about Karuna's extended pregnancy was the much-needed break she got from housework. "This one," the midwife observed as she massaged Karuna's body with herbal oil, "is definitely a girl. She is thinking of you already, giving you a rest even before she is born! You'll need all your strength when you return home to look after two young children and your family."

That night Karuna lay in bed, unable to sleep. It was not just the stomach cramps that kept her awake. The raga of croaking frogs and the spirited singing of the cicadas, coupled with the chorus of street dogs in the neighbourhood, disturbed her. She had dozed off briefly, but was awakened by a flash of pain that ran through her body like lightning. For a moment she thought she was dreaming. The full moon reminded her of the polished brass plate carved with an image of Nataraja dancing in the centre, which hung in her parents' home. The craftsmanship was so unique it had the pride of place on the wall of their sitting room. The memory transported her to her childhood in Puri, when her mother was alive and the world was a different place.

Karuna was six when her mother died. Since then her life had taken on an element of unreality. Married at fourteen, she was a mother by sixteen. Before she was twenty, she was ready to give birth to her second child. Her life stretched ahead like a long, dirt road into the unknown. She paused, lingering on the memory of her last walk on Puri beach with her family. On their way back from the Jagannath Temple, in one of the filigree shops along the Bada Danda, her mother had spotted the exquisite workmanship lavished on that decorative brass plate.

Arranging the folds of her sari, Karuna tried not to think about her mother's death at the age of twenty-six from childbirth, during her fifth delivery, the one that went horribly wrong. Both mother and child died. Penicillin was not available in Orissa, not even in an emergency in the State's best hospital. Looking at the moon through the open window, Karuna walked to the toilet, cushioning her protruding stomach with both hands. She whispered, "How are you, ma?"

She could hear someone playing a familiar piece of music on a flute. The scene in the film flashed past in her mind's eye. But the name of the film escaped her—the one with Nargis pining for Raj Kapoor—*Awara? Chori Chori? Shree 420?* When Karuna switched on the bathroom light, the spasms of pain gripped her body like electric shock waves, as if that act had triggered the final stages of her labour.

"Nurse, nurse!" cried Karuna when her waters broke. By the time the nurse alerted the medical staff and they got their act together, Asha, impatient to make an appearance, had struggled her way out. She had been preparing a long time! When Asha was born, surprised that no family member apart from her mother was there to greet her, celebrate the joint achievement of mother and daughter, or commiserate with them, she cried without anyone having to spank her on the bottom.

⁘⁘⁘⁘⁘

Aditya had taken the day off. He had drafted a letter to the principal of Harrison College, requesting a leave of absence from his duties. This letter, written over a month ago, was signed and ready to be delivered to the principal's office. Only the date had to be inserted. The moment Aditya heard the news, he woke up his younger brother, Abhay, who lived with them. The two brothers were so excited they could not stop smiling as they attended to their chores. Aditya asked Abhay to submit the letter at the principal's office. Then he instructed Ramesh, the manservant who also lived under the same roof, to prepare a flask of special masala chai for his wife.

When Aditya reached the hospital, the chowkidar informed him with a smile displaying his full set of buckteeth, "Sahib, namaskar! The little girl arrived safely at dawn even before the sun appeared. Karunama and baby are both sleeping."

Thanking him profusely, making a mental note to give him bakshish, Aditya tiptoed up the stairs and gently opened the wire-gauze door. He was breathless as if he had been flying, which may have been the case. He had cycled as fast as he could when he heard the news from a college peon of all people. The peon had taken the trouble to deliver the message to him at home. *But how did he know?* Aditya could not help wondering as he dodged the traffic all the way to the hospital.

There are moments in life when ordinary people do extraordinary things. Fathers feel like gods after the birth of a child. If there was any doubt how he felt about having a daughter, when this little creature curled her tiny fingers round his thumb in her sleep, he was smitten for life. It was not until much later, when he went to fetch the family doctor, he thought of her marriage and her dowry. How could he not as a father, that too on a lecturer's salary?

Aditya was in the kitchen when Siddhartha arrived with Saswati and the children. Having lost his wife in childbirth, Siddhartha was not only devoted to his children, but was involved in the lives, including the births, of his grandchildren. His wife's last words had been, "Look after her," referring to their youngest daughter. Perhaps she knew her newborn would not make it. He had since dedicated his life to his children and their children. Young and healthy, he never remarried in case his new wife, unable or unwilling to take on another woman's children, would not love them as much as her own.

Siddhartha, too, was at home when he got the message from his driver, who in turn had received the news from someone he barely knew. Siddhartha's bungalow in the Cantonment area was at one end of Cuttack. Aditya's house, near Harrison College at the opposite end of town, was perhaps slightly closer to the hospital. News of the birth had travelled at equal speed in opposite directions. But thanks to the slow-moving traffic of rickshaws, bullock carts, buses, itinerant cows and pedestrians, Aditya's Raleigh bicycle beat his father-in-law's Chevrolet hands down.

Karuna stirred the moment she heard car doors banging shut and her front door creaking open. On seeing her father, she smiled and half got up.

"No, no. You rest, no need to get up. Saswati and the children have also come. Has Aditya babu been informed?" Siddhartha asked as he smiled and made faces at his granddaughter, who lay in a cot like a miniature Sleeping Buddha, next to her mother, smiling. Then realising his granddaughter was fast asleep, turning to Karuna, he said, "Today is Ratha Jatra."

"May the Lord Jagannath's blessings be with her," said Karuna. "Yes, he too just arrived," she added, referring to Aditya.

"What about Amitava babu, does he know?" Siddhartha enquired.

Aditya's father, Amitava Guru, a historian and archaeologist, lived in Bhubaneswar, where he was in charge of the State Museum. His son, Viswajit, universally known as Vishu, was the first to arrive that morning. Though he no longer lived with Aditya and his family, Vishu was so often there that everyone assumed he still did. Delighted with the birth of his niece, he had taken on the task of spreading the good news.

"Yes, our daughter was born on a holy day. Vishu has gone to send a message to bapa," Aditya answered from the kitchen.

He was poised to pour the tea, specially brewed with ginger, cloves and cardamom, when he heard his father-in-law's voice. Hastily bottling up the flask, Aditya emerged to greet him. The tea ceremony had to be postponed. It would have been disrespectful to drink tea in Siddhartha's presence. He never drank tea, nor did he know that his children and their spouses secretly drank anything as detrimental to the body and mind as tea.

In fact, Siddhartha Mishra was an unusual man—his self-denial and discipline beyond compare. A vegetarian, he ate only sattvik food, as was the practice in traditional Brahmin households. Tea was included in the long list of drinks he had never tasted. He ate food cooked without onions, garlic or other spices that excited the senses and were deemed harmful to one's physical and spiritual wellbeing.

He did yoga and meditation every day. In his mid-forties, he was a picture of good health. Though his dark, straight hair was already thinning, leaving a clear bald patch on his head, it only added to his gravitas. His tall figure, bright eyes, fair complexion, and simple yet elegant clothes ensured that people noticed him. His intelligence, fair disposition and quiet manners meant that when he spoke, everyone listened. His opinion was universally sought, especially in times of crises.

He was rare in other ways too. For example, he bought a car because sitting in a rickshaw reminded him of the many things that were wrong with his country. It degraded him; he did not think it fair that one man should bear the burden of another—sometimes a lean, half-starved, old man would be carrying a well-fed family of four. How could a few rupees compensate for such injustice? His entire life was based on such awareness of and thought for others.

A mathematician by education and inclination, he charted the horoscopes of his children and grandchildren. Thanks to him, the exact time, date, and year of Asha's birth was recorded for posterity. Nobody ever consulted the horoscope when deciding anything. It had no bearing on what they did or did not do. Even Siddhartha did not trust in them, though he was always ready to concede there were things in our universe that human beings knew nothing about. For the family, however, the fact that their horoscopes existed was not to be sneered at, such things mattered.

Before they got out of the car, Saswati cautioned Sadhana and Vikram to be good. They looked at each other with surprise, wondering what she meant. Were they not always good, always trying to be better? Vikram dragged his feet until his grandfather and aunt disappeared inside the cabin, and they were left trailing behind like two cygnets separated from the rest of the brood.

"What does mausi mean—be good?" he asked.

"She means we mustn't cry, shout or scream, make a fuss, ask for food, run around, or in general be a nuisance. We can always come out here and play!" Sadhana explained, trying to demonstrate her superior knowledge of the world. She was barely a month older.

"How long will ma be in hospital?" Vikram knew his mother

had been coming here every night. He also thought hospitals meant only one thing, illness.

"Now that Karuna mausi has given birth, she will come home. But the good news is I now have a sister to play with," Sadhana replied.

Unsure if his cousin preferred playing with girls, Vikram said, "We can both play with her."

"Sadhana, Vikram—what are you doing outside?" Saswati called out.

On seeing the two of them enter, Karuna opened her arms wide and said, "Come here, Vikram; you too, Sadhana. You have a sister—look, she is asleep!"

Vikram shuffled close up to his mother and stood there holding her hand. He glared at this doll-like creature that did not do much, not even acknowledge his presence. It annoyed him that everyone was beaming with admiration and wonder as if no one had seen a newborn child before. When his uncles joined them—his paternal uncles, Vishu and Abhay, and his maternal uncle, Madhav—Vikram could no longer bear the cooing and babbling, the gurgling and other infantile noises the elders made. Asha carried on smiling, her eyes closed, oblivious of the world. Vikram, who was struggling with his contrary emotions, was palpably relieved when Aja said he had to go to work and Karuna needed to rest.

Siddhartha added, "I'll come in the evening. Saswati will send you lunch."

Turning to Aditya, he asked, "I assume you'll be staying here for the rest of the day?"

"Yes, I've taken the day off now that the convocation is over." He nodded.

Vikram could not make up his mind if he should stay with his mother or leave with his cousin and aunt. He did not wish to miss out on imagined treats this intruder, his sister, might receive in his absence.

"You'd better come with us," Sadhana whispered in his ear.

He was persuaded only after Karuna said, "Asha will sleep most of the day, or she will cry when she wakes up—it's what babies do. You did that too."

To be told at that precise moment, in front of everyone, that he had been a cry-baby was not what he had anticipated. *Did I really cry or sleep all the time after I was born?* Vikram wondered for a moment before agreeing. "I'll go now. Sleeping Beauty here will not get up, it seems." He had overheard the phrase recently and thought this was as good a time as any to use it. Besides, lunch would certainly be better at Aja's.

Karuna was quite mistaken about Asha—she barely cried, at least during the first few years of her life. The crying was to come later. In the first year Asha mostly slept, smiled, waved her limbs about when awake, and told her family things they did not understand. It was Karuna who began worrying about the fate of her daughter the moment she was born. So concerned was she, her milk dried up. When her son was born, she was bursting with milk. Now, she was dry as a river in summer.

Born prematurely, Vikram had looked tiny and frail. Karuna could hold him in her palms like Gangajal. He looked so fragile, helpless and vulnerable, she felt utterly protective as he suckled hungrily at her breasts, nestling in her arms. She could not take her eyes off this delicate, miniature human being! Having given birth to a son, she had fulfilled her duty as wife and daughter-in-law, secured her position in the world, and preserved the family line. Sons mattered. A daughter was welcome, too, but did not have the same cachet. Asha's birth had not been a difficult delivery, just an interminable pregnancy with the hours singing their lullabies for a whole month. As if the female child, knowing the perils of the world, was delaying her arrival.

A strange thing happened the evening Karuna was due to leave the hospital. A raggle-taggle crowd gathered outside. As she packed her belongings, she kept humming a tune from the *Gita Govinda*. The song had somehow lodged itself in her head since morning. It had arrived from nowhere like some migratory bird and built a nest in her head. She was still humming it when Aditya arrived and observed, "Is anything the matter? You've been humming that song all day. Have you seen the people waiting outside? The chowkidar said they've come for darshan, to pay their respects!"

"Yes, I noticed the crowd. But why have they come? This is a hospital, not a museum or a temple. How did they find out about our Asha?"

"Perhaps your father will know what to do," Aditya replied.

When Siddhartha arrived he, too, was puzzled, but asked the chowkidar to give them some alms as one gave money to beggars after visiting a temple.

"I'm afraid more people will come when they hear of alms," said Aditya.

"Well, we are leaving now. But this is most unusual," Karuna added.

When the driver began to load the car, the crowd slowly began to disperse. They left as they had come, quietly, leaving their gifts, which they referred to as offerings, dakshina, for the newborn child.

"They would not take any money, said they had come to see the child. They left their dakshina with me," the chowkidar reported back.

"You keep them," Karuna said.

Aditya and Siddhartha nodded in agreement.

"I can't. It's for your child," the chowkidar pointed out.

As he spoke, he thrust forward both his hands laden with an overwhelming assortment of handmade gifts—embroidered pieces of cloth, trinkets made of beads that looked like amber, a mirror decorated with shells arranged in an exquisite design, a bouquet of dried, wild, brightly coloured flowers among other curios. On top of it all lay a rag doll with a painted face that uncannily resembled Asha's.

13

CHAPTER 2

Durga Puja, the ten-day festival marking the victory of good over evil, began with Aditya tuning in to All India Radio—Akashvani, literally the voice from heaven—at the crack of dawn on Mahalaya day. The hypnotic chanting of the Mahamantras, inviting the Goddess Durga to descend on earth, lulled the family back to sleep.

Later, after breakfast, Asha began to recite the slokas as she settled down to her puja in front of the altar of the holy tulsi. Praying was how she spent her time playing. She preferred the tulsi altar in the inner courtyard. In summer, she retreated to the puja room, savouring its unique mix of fragrances—of incense, wicks dipped in ghee, camphor, joss sticks, sandalwood and flowers.

"Can you hear her singing?" Karuna whispered to Aditya as they watched her through the window of his study-cum-office.

"Yes, but how did she pick up the words and the music? Was she not asleep?" Aditya whispered back, not wanting to draw Asha's attention.

"She must've been half awake. But you are right; she is barely four. Girls grow up so fast; they have to. Not like boys," she said.

"Yes, Asha was speaking fluently by the time she was a year old," he added.

While they were admiring their daughter, astonished at her many gifts, Vikram came and sat down next to his sister and started to sing along. When she paused, he said, "Are you done; can we go and play now, mataji?"

"Wonders will never cease," Karuna observed. She thought her two children did not play together enough. "Childhood is for playing," she added.

"He should be playing with boys of his own age, not with Asha and Sadhana. He follows you around like a puppy. Hope he does not turn out to be an excellent cook, who practices yoga and keeps the house spick and span!" Aditya joked.

"What's wrong with that? Is that what you think of me?" Karuna asked.

"Absolutely not. Women are extraordinary. What would I do without you? But Vikram is a boy. We must teach him to become a good man. You know what I mean."

"Then you must spend more time with him. Vikram spends a lot of time with bapa and your father, not to mention all his uncles," Karuna said. "You were brought up by your mother and aunts. Your father was a busy man and had to travel a lot. If God wanted children to be brought up by men, he'd have created a different world."

"But see how I turned out!" Aditya said with a smile.

Though their upbringing and backgrounds could not have been more different, Aditya and Karuna both aspired for their children to be better and have better lives. Perhaps it was something in the air—everyone they knew believed in better.

"If you feel that way, you must find time for Vikram, do more things with him the way I do with Asha. Why don't you start doing yoga? Then you can ask Vikram to join you. Asha learnt yoga because I keep her locked up with me in the room every morning when I do yoga. Even Vikram learnt yoga from me the same way. It is not just their bodies that are supple at this age!" Karuna explained.

"Perhaps I should take him shopping with me?" Aditya said.

Most mornings Aditya went shopping, returning home with

milk, vegetables and whatever he thought was fresh, sometimes still alive, from the open market. He was as likely to return with bags bursting with greens as much as live fish or crabs. The crabs were especially skilled at crawling out of whatever container they were placed in to explore the kitchen, sometimes wandering into other parts of the house. All this shopping necessitated hours of patient weeding, soaking, cudgelling, cleaning.

It would also happen to be the only day in the week that the maidservant would report ill or Karuna would have unexpected guests. When she complained about the intelligent and superactive crabs that would not stay still, or the time it took to shell the prawns, or fillet the fish, Aditya would say apologetically, "I'll give you a hand. They are fresh and were going cheap; I could not resist." Or he would reply, regretfully, if he too did not have the time, "Give it to the maid if you can't use it."

"Well, try the yoga. He's perhaps a bit young to be your shopping assistant," suggested Karuna. Then remembering the big family get-together in a few days' time, she reminded him, "Listen, you need to get the Petromax lamp ready. I'll ask Ramesh to polish the lanterns, but you need to supervise the cleaning of the Petromax. Wish we had electricity in our house and did not have to worry about lanterns and lamps."

"Don't worry about the Petromax. I'll clean it myself. Maybe we should think of moving to the new quarters in the college campus when they are ready. They'll have electricity," Aditya said, still thinking how best to bond with his son.

"Now you must pay your respects to all your elders, not a namaskar, but a proper juhar," Karuna instructed Asha.

Karuna had just dressed her daughter up in a new pink, silk frock that hung loosely on her, even after the belt was tied in an elegant knot at the back of her waist. The dress was a gift from

Aditya's parents. Karuna made two trips to her favourite textile merchant in Choudhury Bazaar before she found one that seemed just right for Asha. The layers of frills, laced with zari embroidery, made her look like the heavenly creatures that hover among gods and goddesses in religious paintings.

"Do I look like a pari, a fairy?" Asha asked.

"You'll soon grow into this frock. It looks beautiful—yes, you look like an angel! But first we must go and offer our prayers to Ma Durga," replied Karuna.

She led Asha to the shrine where the household gods and goddesses were consecrated. Mother and daughter sat down in lotus pose and prayed. The puja room was spotlessly clean, no footwear was allowed there. Aditya and Vikram had already lighted the diya and joss sticks, and said their prayers. It was a family custom that on wearing new clothes one sought the blessing of one's elders as much as of the gods. Wearing new clothes symbolised a new beginning. And in any case, one always needed the protection of gods. There was no way of knowing what surprises the future might hold. "Sarba mangala mangaley..." mother and daughter chanted.

It was Nabami, the ninth day of Dussehra, one of the most celebrated festivals in the Hindu calendar. Aditya being the eldest, the entire family gathered in his home to observe the puja. As everyone was also older than Asha, it took a long time to pay her respects to all her elders. She would kneel or bend to touch their feet, which seemed like the simplest part of the ritual. Before she could slip away, they insisted on blessing her, which they did first by placing their right hand on her head.

As it would be disrespectful to leave in the middle of the blessing, Asha resisted the urge to do so. The elders would be engrossed in conversation as if they were reciting a mantra, their palms stuck to her head. Asha was convinced her elders were spellbound as long as their conversation lasted. It was only after it ended they would be able to remove their hand. If Asha moved, she would be held back before being kissed on both cheeks, sometimes on her forehead as well. She would be inspected from head to toe and told what a beautiful child she was before being released. A juhar could last a long time depending on the person and the mood they were in.

When it was her grandmother's turn, her father's mother, who sat cross-legged on a low divan-like bed preparing paan for her husband, she was left waiting for Asha to rise from her genuflection so she could bless her. Asha, in the meanwhile, having forgotten her original purpose, failed to make an appearance. She remained in that curled-up foetal position with her forehead resting on the new jute carpet. Unable to stretch her body forward to find out what exactly had happened to Asha, her jejema hollered for help. Subhalakshmi was accustomed to Asha's long sessions in front of the tulsi altar. She would proudly tell others, "Don't disturb Asha. She is praying, doing her puja." While all the time Asha was simply having a conversation with herself as she had no one else to talk to. But that day, as Subhalakshmi could not see what her granddaughter was up to, she needed to borrow a pair of eyes.

"What's the matter?" Karuna rushed in to her mother-in-law's assistance.

Vikram and Sadhana appeared alongside like minor deities flanking the images of major gods and goddesses on temple walls. Asha, woken from her trance by her jejema's yelling, slowly raised her head like a baby cobra disturbed in its journey.

"Ah, there she is! God knows where she disappeared," Subhalakshmi said, looking at Karuna with her finger pointing at Asha. Then she asked Asha, "What were you doing down there? Come, let me look at you in your new dress before I bless you! No need for such a long juhar, my child."

However, Subhalakshmi was secretly pleased with her granddaughter's public display of devotion. Turning to Karuna, she added, "Asha is a lovely girl, really!"

"What happened?" Vikram whispered in his sister's ear.

"Nothing," Asha whispered back. "I forgot I was supposed to be doing just a down-and-up juhar, not saying a prayer. I thought I was in a temple praying to God. I closed my eyes and forgot I was at home!"

Sadhana was also listening in. "Out of sight, out of mind," she said.

"I don't know what you are talking about, but I am not up to any more juhars today—not even a simple down-and-up one," Asha confessed.

"Okay, we'll let it pass this time," Vikram said magnanimously. Sadhana nodded. "But you owe us two juhars each," she said.

"Agreed. One for not paying your respects to us now, and the other is our reward for being so understanding," Vikram confirmed.

"I can do as many juhars as you wish. Ma says it's a kind of yoga, good for you. But not now," Asha panted wearily.

She could not help wondering why indulging briefly in her favourite pastime, talking to herself, created such a ruckus. She could sit for hours in front of the tulsi altar, sharing her innermost thoughts with a dark, polished, round stone that would fit snugly in the palm of a male adult. She had picked up the smooth, granite pebble on the beach in Puri during their last visit. It now nestled at the foot of the tulsi tree, a shrine where images of gods, who were far from complete or perfect themselves, vied for attention with fragments from the natural world. That stone was to become Asha's childhood confidante.

Karuna knew her daughter was different. How else could one explain her staying inside the womb for an extra month? But she did not have the time, energy, or the awareness to consider how to channel her daughter's long, meditative silences. Aditya certainly had no time for such things. He was at work during the day and busy organising events on campus in the evenings, or he was out visiting the various members of his extended family. Vikram was in school or at his Aja's. When at home, he followed his mother around. If Karuna suggested, "Go and play with Asha," pat came the reply, "How can I? She is already playing with God!" No one had the time to worry about Asha's preoccupation with a stone. As every cloud has a silver lining, every silver lining has a cloud. Asha never learnt how to be heard or be noticed, never learnt the child that cried the most, received the most attention.

The last three days of Durga Puja were the best, especially for the children. The days were filled with fun and games. It was open house, but the women congregated in the kitchen and the inner veranda, where they cooked, gossiped, shared their problems, and laughed at each other's jokes. The ritual of preparing and sharing sumptuous meals marked the victory of good over evil, the season of joy and peace. The aroma of spices, with the promise of delicious dishes and desserts, left the children salivating. The men, gathered in the sitting room and the outer veranda, also thought of food as they discussed weighty matters of the world, bursting forth unexpectedly into loud guffaws and applauses, as if they were watching a nail-biting cricket match.

The children conspired to overhear the adult conversations, one half creating a distraction while the other eavesdropped, strictly taking turns in such espionage. The only snag was their inability to interpret the many muffled whispers bordering on silence that interspersed both sets of adult conversations. It was indeed a hindrance, there being no access to facial expressions guiding them through the morass, not unlike pigs sniffing their way through quicksand.

Bored with that game, the children soon gathered to play in one room. It suited the elders, easier to keep watch if the children were all in one place, not dispersed in different rooms. The Laughing Game practically invented itself when they sat in a circle sharing jokes. The tipping point came when Ava, Asha's cousin, could not stop laughing. Seeing her hysterical with giggles, another cousin joined in. Soon laughter spread like wildfire; just looking at each other spurred the children to more laughter.

The adults ignored it, knowing as long as there was laughter, all was well. Usually the children laughed till they could laugh no more, holding on to their aching bellies. Sometimes, they were reprimanded if they laughed loudly and hiccupped at the same time. "You'll choke yourself if you don't stop this tamasha. What are you laughing about, anyway? Share the joke with us, so we too can laugh with you," the most stressed-out family elder would enquire sharply. The children, of course, had no answers, for by then they had forgotten why they were laughing.

Playing games was what all the children looked forward to when the different branches of the family got together. Asha liked the Laughing Game best. It was more fun than Blind-Man's Buff, when one was expected to move around the crowded room with arms outstretched like a devotee in blindfold searching for God! Invariably the game of Blind Man's Buff led seamlessly to the Laughing Game. Someone would stumble, bump into a wall or furniture, lose their balance, or do something silly, invoking ridicule and mirth that rippled like wind in a field of corn.

For Asha, both games were infinitely superior to the one where they enacted scenes from the Indian epics. Vikram and Sadhana, thick as thieves, took on the role of casting directors, giving themselves the best parts, playing the royal couple, king and queen, or god and goddess. Asha was assigned the roles they did not want. In those golden days, kings and queens always won, as did gods and goddesses. The evil one lost and suffered a terrible end. Shaitan did not have the best lines or the best tunes. In Asha's world, good and bad knew their place and never upset the status quo.

It was not fashionable, original or revolutionary dressing up as the evil queen, a rakhyasuni, witch or a diabolical demon terrorising the world. Asha was hopeless at enacting those roles, failing even to lift the mace or whatever homemade theatrical prop was given to her. Her feeble attempts at depicting evil drew no fear, never left anyone quaking in terror except herself. On the contrary,

Asha made evil appear powerless, even endearing, leaving everyone smiling if not collapsing in an irrepressible fit of laughter. *One day I will show my mettle, but first I need the right part*, she thought.

Later in the evening, after the guests were gone, preparations began for the annual visit to the images of Ma Durga in town. Each neighbourhood had its own ensemble for the celebration.

Aditya suggested Asha and Sadhana accompany Karuna, Saswati, and Aja in his Chevrolet for the grand tour. Wishing to take every opportunity to spend time with his son, he said, "Vikram, you come with me and Vishu kaku in the rickshaw."

Normally Vikram did as he was told. But that evening, perhaps he was too tired, or had been denied that extra rasogola, he threw an almighty tantrum.

"Ever since you've had your precious daughter, she gets the best of everything. Why can't I go in the car? I can stand at the back with ma, mausi and Sadhana nani," he screamed.

"There is not enough room, not even to sit on anyone's lap." Aditya tried to explain as affectionately and patiently as he could.

"I will go with Aja," Vikram insisted, stamping his foot.

"You mustn't be so disobedient," Vishu intervened.

But Vikram was not budging. "I will not go with you," he snarled at Vishu.

Observing her son's unprecedented act of rebellion, Karuna told Aditya, "You take Asha; let Vikram come with us. We can't take all three children in the car."

Asha was sorely disappointed with this sudden reversal of fortune, but did not think she could match her brother's tantrum. She was on the verge of tears when Aja said, "Asha, you know what good girls get? When we return home, you will get not one, not two, but three Threptin biscuits!" He clapped his hands jubilantly as if he had just given her a full packet. Aja's biscuits were sought after badges of honour, the children got one if they stopped crying or did something worthy. To get three seemed like a big deal. Asha nodded her approval.

Once enthroned on her father's lap in an open rickshaw with Vishu uncle by her side, Asha was soon distracted. The streets were alive with song and dance to the accompaniment of music. She was enthralled, caught up in the wild abandonment of the moment. She could have climbed the moon as their rickshaw-wallah cycled off to give them a tour of the Durga images in town. When they approached a medha, they got off their burnished pedestal to cast a more discerning look. Perched on the shoulders of her uncle, who was over six feet in height, Asha was assured a safe and unrestricted view. She could also see the beggars, lepers and cripples, who wheeled themselves around with dexterity. So giddy was she with excitement and terror, Asha hugged her uncle's head and held on to his thick mat of hair, with both hands.

"Asha, are you all right?" Vishu asked, craning his neck upwards, holding his niece's legs to stop them moving about wildly.

Nodding her head, she said, "Was that asura not listening to his parents, not even God? Ma Durga has so many hands..." Asha could not find the words to express her sense of wonder.

Durga's face was supremely calm, filled with serenity as she speared the demon Mahisha. Her fish-shaped eyes, black and beautiful, shone from within, lit by a smile. Ma Durga looked even more beautiful than her mother. Asha thought of all the gods and goddesses as members of her family. Sometimes, she thought her elders were also divine creatures.

"Yes, Mahisasura was not listening to anyone. So the gods created Durga, the invincible one. In each of her ten hands she holds a weapon given to her by them—spear, trident, sword, chakra, bow and arrow, gada..." explained Vishu.

Overwhelmed with the whole spectacle, Asha was no longer listening to what her uncle was saying. It was difficult for her to hear him—what with all the chanting, singing, drumming, dancing and shouting going on around them. Traditional religious music competed with the latest Hindi film songs, both blaring from loudspeakers within hearing distance of each other in the street.

After returning home, Asha was too excited to sleep. Like a wound-up toy, she spelled out her enthrallment at having seen the many images of the goddess. "Durga's eyes were like this!" Asha declared, straining to open her eyes as wide as she could. She entertained the family late into the night, demonstrating the poses of all the gods and goddesses. There was no stopping her. "She has ten arms and sits on a lion!" she said, mounting her rocking horse to show exactly how Durga sat on her lion, holding up both her hands as if smiting the invisible demons around her.

Asha's song and dance soon woke up Vikram. "See what you've done; you've woken up your brother," Karuna complained. "It's late. You must both go to bed."

"Nana is awake. That's good." Asha clapped jubilantly. "Nana, in the Chandi medha, Durga looked like this. In the Suna medha..." On she went, re-enacting all over again for her brother's benefit the various poses in which Durga was depicted.

"But we only saw the medhas in College Square and Mangalabag," Vikram complained. "We did not even get out of the car!"

"Why did you go in the car?" Asha squealed with pleasure. "You should've listened to bapa. You know what happened to Mahisasura; he did not listen to his elders. You should've come with us in the rickshaw; then you, too, would've seen everything!" Asha declared ecstatically. No one could argue with her impeccable logic. Even Vikram felt vanquished.

"We invited you to come with us," said Vishu.

Abhay and Karuna nodded in agreement.

Taking his daughter in his arms, Aditya said, "Mahisasura was a bad, cruel man, a demon, Asha. You and Vikram are both good children, are you not?"

Asha nodded her head vigorously in agreement as if to say, 'Yes, of course we are good children; what else can we be?'

"So you go to sleep now. Tomorrow we have to attend the bhasana."

"What is bhasana?" Vikram asked as they both lay down in bed, exhausted.

Before Aditya finished explaining, they were fast asleep.

The next day, the last day of Dussehra, the huge clay images of Durga and her entourage were taken for the immersion ceremony on the banks of Mahanadi. As the family approached the river, they walked past rows of beggars, who called out loudly for alms. Asha clung to her father when she saw a boy with no legs or arms swivel by on a wooden board, grinning at her. The drums beat a hypnotic rhythm as the priests' chants gathered momentum. The hawkers advertised their wares with greater frenzy, their voices rising to a crescendo as the crowd thickened to a standstill. The sand, dust and heat, the smell of sweat and other bodily odours, including that of urine and faeces, combined with the pungent smell of food assaulted their senses.

On the dusky banks of the Mahanadi, the grand spectacle of Dussehra ended with the Durga effigies being immersed in the river that flowed undisturbed on its journey like the soul through its various incarnations until it was home. Asha counted the river lamps that made their way downstream. Open, human pyres blazed in the distant crematorium. Hypnotised by the tongues of fire that leaped around like fire-eaters, she clung to Vikram's arm.

"Bhasana is getting more and more crowded every year, almost like Ratha Jatra," Karuna remarked as they made their way to Aja's.

"Ma, why are there so many beggars? I saw a beggar boy without any arms or legs," Asha observed, her brows furrowed in thought.

She remembered the time she was taken into the inner sanctum of the Jagannath temple in Puri, where she saw the deities with stumps for arms. Their faces were not human either. *Why are they not as beautiful, serene and perfect as our other gods?* Asha had wondered. She had looked at the gods—Jagannath, his sister Subhadra, and his brother Balabhadra—with astonishment until they began to look normal, and she bowed down in prayer.

"I don't know why there are so many beggars or why there is so much poverty and disease. It is sad and shocking. People no longer care enough for each other," Karuna replied as she instinctively put her arm around her daughter.

"Is that why we give food and money to the beggars who come to our house?" Asha asked. "What about his parents? Did they die? Will I lose my hands and legs if–?" She stopped. She also wanted to ask her parents about Jagannath and his deformed body, but did not think it was the right time. It was never the right time.

"Nothing of the sort will happen to you," Karuna and Aditya said together.

They were almost home. True to his word, without anyone having to remind him, Aja gave Asha three Threptin biscuits. Then he asked her, conspiratorially, "Can we give just one each to Vikram nana and Sadhana nani?"

Asha was too well brought up to say no to anyone, certainly not to her Aja.

While Asha and Sadhana slowly licked their biscuits till they melted in the mouth, Vikram munched through his first. Approaching Asha, with a grand flourish of his hand, he said, "I can do magic. Do you want to see?"

"What magic? You are not a magician! Liar," Asha teased.

Extending his right hand, with his eyes closed, he chanted, "Om namoh to all the gods in the universe. Let a piece of Threptin biscuit appear in my hand!"

Asha dropped a small piece on his palm.

Vikram opened his eyes and said with another dramatic flourish, "Look. God gave me this piece!"

"No, *I* gave it to you," she said, laughing.

"Certainly not," Vikram retorted after eating it. "If you don't believe me, I can do it again."

Asha did not mind; she let Vikram have more of her biscuit. She would have given it to him anyway, if he had just asked her affectionately.

CHAPTER 3

"What will I do in school that I can't do at home?" Asha complained, shoving her bottom all the way back on the shiny, slippery seat of the rickshaw. One of its rear wheels had just hurtled over a pothole, practically throwing her overboard.

Karuna repositioned herself, sitting with her arm firmly strapped across Asha. Karuna did not say anything apart from appealing to the rickshaw-wallah to drive carefully. "Aare baba, please drive more carefully. You know what the roads are like," said Karuna.

Vikram, a few years older and as many pounds heavier, did not bounce around as much as his sister. "You will learn how to read and write," he told Asha.

"I already read and write," Asha corrected her brother. "If you love school so much, you go. Why must I? I know A, B, C, D, E, F, H ... I can also count from 1, 2, 3 to one hundred! I know A for apple, B for banana and C for cabbage—"

"A for aeroplane," said Vikram. "Can you spell aeroplane?"

"A-R-O-P-L-A-N," Asha said, enunciating each letter clearly.

"You can't even spell aeroplane, and you think you know everything. If you go to school, you'll at least learn to spell," Vikram teased.

"That's enough, both of you," said Karuna. "Ma, you have to

go to school, Sadhana nani, Ava nani, Vikram nana and all your nanas and nanis do. You don't want to remain uneducated, do you?"

"Will I be unducated if I don't go to school?" Asha asked.

"Yes, you'll remain an idiot!" Vikram laughed.

"Ma, will I have to go to school forever? What will happen after I finish school?" Asha asked, ignoring Vikram's remark.

"You will go to college like Abhay uncle and Madhav uncle," said Karuna.

"What will happen after college?" Asha asked as if listening to a story. She always asked at the end of every story what happened next.

"What will happen after college? You'll be married, of course. Then you'll have children. And then they'll grow up and go to school!" Vikram declared, anticipating his sister's chain of questions.

"Will you also marry after college and have children?" Asha asked Vikram. "I don't want to go to school, nor do I want to marry," she declared.

"Asha, can you keep quiet for a moment—you are both driving me mad! You too, Vikram—no talking till we reach school, not a–"

Before Karuna could finish, a dark, heavy-built man, with a pockmarked face, approached on a bicycle at full speed. With a powerful forward stroke, he hit Karuna hard on her right shoulder as he groped and squeezed her breast with his fleshy fingers. She fell back with the force of the blow, flabbergasted with what had just happened. She had never experienced this sort of an attack before.

Asha clung with all her strength to her mother's handbag, but Karuna did not think it was the handbag he was after. If he had managed to snatch the bag, that would have been a bonus.

Vikram screamed at the top of his voice, "Catch that badmash! He is cycling away in that direction."

It all happened so fast that by the time Raghu, the rickshaw-wallah, stopped to take stock of the situation, there was no sign of the culprit. Raghu swore the country had gone to the dogs. Things were better under the British; there was no decency left in

Independent India. He could not redress the situation as the cyclist had disappeared in the city's maze of alleyways.

"I should have put the hood on, ma. It is a cool and fresh morning. I did not think," Raghu said apologetically.

"I will become a policeman when I grow up," a frustrated Vikram declared.

Karuna was shaken beyond belief. She could not conceive of such a thing happening in College Square. This neighbourhood was their home.

A traumatised Asha declared, "Ma Durga will punish that badmash!"

⚜

It was Asha's first day at school, the same primary school Vikram went to. Cambridge School was close to Harrison College. Aditya had already met with the headmaster, and everything had been arranged. That morning he was unable to accompany the children to school; he had several meetings to attend at the college. It was settled that Karuna would go with Asha and Vikram. Aditya also engaged Raghu to take them to school and bring them back home.

Feeling flustered, her heart beating so fast she could barely breathe, Karuna gathered her composure as she walked through the wrought-iron gates of the school. Asha clasped her mother's hand. Once inside, wondering which way to turn, Karuna noticed the headmaster, Mr Harrison, hurrying towards her.

"Good morning, Mrs Guru," he said jubilantly. "Welcome! I'll introduce you and your daughter to Miss Webster. She looks after the children in kindergarten."

Older than Karuna, Miss Webster was as tall as her. But unlike Karuna, she had short, russet-coloured hair. Miss Webster wore a short-sleeved, sea-green dress, which enhanced the colour of her eyes. Her skin reminded Asha of roses in their garden. The only time Asha had visited Vikram's school before, she had met his teacher, who looked as ruddy as an apple. Asha wondered if all the teachers in the school were gora foreigners. Her Miss was fairer than her mother and everyone else she could think of, including herself.

"Ah, here she is!" sighed the headmaster. "Miss Webster, may I introduce you to Mrs Guru, the wife of our esteemed Professor Guru, whom you've already met. This is their eldest son, Vikram, who is a pupil here, and this is his sister..." He faltered, hoping someone would fill in the gap.

"Armita, this is my daughter, Armita," Karuna repeated her daughter's name.

"Very nice to meet you both." Miss Webster nodded with a smile.

Instead of greeting Miss Webster or Mr Harrison, Asha turned to her mother and whispered, "I want to go home."

Karuna had a brief word with Miss Webster and Mr Harrison, explaining how the unfortunate incident on the way to school had upset them all.

"It's shocking you were subjected to such a horrendous experience! This eve-teasing must be made illegal. It happens to decent women all over the country, yet the government does nothing," said Mr Harrison, shaking his head with deep disapproval.

"But how do you catch the scallywags? You can't punish the miscreants if you can't catch them! Men who behave like that are all cowards. Hope you are all right, Mrs Guru?" Miss Webster asked sympathetically.

Karuna wondered if Miss Webster had been through a similar experience. Returning to the matter at hand, Karuna said, "Yes, we are all right, thank God. May I take my daughter home after a couple of hours? It's her first day, and she's not had a good start. I don't want her to end up disliking school as a result."

"Yes, of course. I see no reason why you cannot take her home early," Mr Harrison said, looking at Miss Webster, who nodded in agreement.

Vikram, who had been talking to Asha mostly to distract her, excused himself. "I'll come and see you when we have a break. Don't worry," he told Asha as he left.

Before Karuna left, accompanied by Mr Harrison and Miss Webster, she told Asha she'd be back soon. But Asha needed reassurance. She whispered in Karuna's ear, "Ma, you *will* come back *soon*? What if the badmash also comes back?"

"No, he won't be able to enter the school. I'll try to bring Abhay kaku or Madhav mamu with me," Karuna replied.

Asha sat silently in her corner of the classroom. The din in the corridor outside soon died down. As her teacher was nowhere to be seen, Asha wondered if going to school meant sitting quietly, uncomfortably, in a not very attractive room. There was an open window not far from her seat. It let in a cool breeze along with an uninterrupted cacophony of traffic, frenetic honking, people talking at the top of their voices, spitting, clearing their throats. Asha wished she was at home with her stone.

She turned to survey the pandemonium that had suddenly erupted in the class. It began with whispers and sniggers, which she had initially ignored. Then all hell broke loose as some of the boys began to hurl abuse at each other. Soon they were attacking one another as they wrestled on the floor. The two girls who were caught in the middle joined in the fracas and, screaming like banshees, gave as good as they got. While this hullaballoo was going on, Asha noted that among the sixteen pupils in her class, four were girls. And the two girls not involved in the fight sat flanking the front row like guardian angels.

Miss Webster's high heels could be heard click-clack-click-clacking down the corridor, reminding Asha of a hoofed animal's approach. The class went quiet as abruptly as it had exploded into chaos. On entering, Miss Webster clapped her hands and said in a stern voice, "Children, this is no way to behave. I could hear you at the other end of the corridor! Anyone would think you were a bunch of hooligans. Let's begin our first day in school properly, learn some good manners. I want each one of you to introduce yourself."

Then placing her right palm over her heart, she continued, "I am Miss Webster, your teacher. I want you to tell me your names." At this point, she waved her hand from left to right, taking in the whole class. Then she added, "I also want you to tell me a little bit about yourself—the names of your parents, your brothers and sisters, where you live, what you like doing, anything you feel like sharing. Now, who wants to begin?"

Instantly, a few hands shot up. But Asha did not think it was appropriate to tell complete strangers, particularly after their rowdy performance, anything about herself or her family. When it was her turn, she disclosed the minimum information possible.

"My name is Asha," she whispered and clammed up.

"Yes, Asha is what they call you at home—that's very good. And your parents' names are...?" Mrs Webster encouraged her to say more.

But Asha looked down at her desk and refused to open her mouth.

"Perhaps Armita will tell us more about herself later." And Miss Webster moved on to the next child in her charge.

During the break, when Asha needed to use the bathroom, she also felt too self-conscious to ask Miss Webster where the lavatory was, particularly after having refused to answer her question in front of the entire class. This level of disobedience was totally uncharacteristic; even she could not figure out why she had acted that way. Nor did she feel confident enough to ask the other girls. None of them raised the matter. Asha sat there holding herself back, wondering when her ma would come.

By the time Vikram arrived, Asha was practically in tears. "I want to go home," she pleaded. All this time she had refrained from crying or laughing as that would exert pressure on her bladder. Then the game would truly be over.

"What's wrong, Asha?" Vikram asked, kneeling by her side.

Miss Webster bent down and, gently stroking Asha's back, said, "I am so sorry about what happened on the way to school. It does not happen always, you know. You've been out with your family many times before without this happening. Next time you hit him back. You are a smart girl—you can read, write, recite, sing and dance. You are good at sums. But you must overcome your shyness and talk to me and the others in class. We are not the kind of strangers you should not talk to."

Asha looked at her Miss, who smelled like a fragrant lily flower, wondering how she knew so much about her. Did her mother tell her?

"I need to go to the bathroom," Asha confessed.

"Why did you not say so before?" Miss Webster led the way to the bathroom.

Asha took one look and rushed out. She could not bear the smell or the sight of the place. All the cubicles in the toilet were filthy. She waited until she could no longer see the back of her Miss. Then she returned to the class.

When Karuna finally appeared at the door, Asha heaved a sigh of relief.

Miss Webster had a word with Karuna and, turning to Asha, said, "You go home now, Armita. I look forward to seeing you tomorrow. Remember, tomorrow everything will seem different."

"I'll see you later," Vikram told Asha. "Ma, I'll walk home," he added.

"Raghu can come to pick you up," Karuna suggested.

"I've been walking to school all this time with Prashant. Today I came with you and Asha in the rickshaw, and see what happened! I could not do anything. Bapa could not have done anything either, that bas–bad man was on a bicycle," Vikram explained calmly.

Karuna thought her children were growing up much too fast.

Aditya had found his chance to spend more time with Vikram when he started school. He took his son to school and picked him up from school. It was the perfect opportunity for father and son to talk man to man. After a few months, Aditya had to go away on a training course. Vikram said it was fine; he could walk to school with his friend Prashant, who also lived in the same street.

The moment mother and daughter stepped out of the school gates, Asha asked, "Ma, who is going to accompany us back? There is no one here."

"There was not enough time to find anyone. The hood of the rickshaw is up, and I don't have a handbag. We'll look out for any badmash," Karuna explained.

She noticed Asha was walking in a peculiar way, taking tiny steps forward. It took them a while to cross the road and get to the rickshaw. Far from being her usual bouncy self, Asha stood by the rickshaw, hesitating, raising a leg as if to climb up and then bringing it down. That surprised Karuna. Normally Asha jumped up and took her seat. Raghu then lifted Asha, placing her gently on the seat.

"Are you not eating anything? You are light as a feather," he remarked.

"What's the matter, Asha? Is everything all right?" Karuna asked, putting her arm over Asha.

Asha looked at her mother as if to say, 'Do you even have to ask after the day I've had?' Then she whispered, "I'll tell you when we get home."

As home was just a few minutes away, Karuna was content to wait. Moments later she enquired, "Did you make any new friends today, Asha?"

"No," Asha replied. "If you knew how badly most of them behaved in class today, you would not ask."

"Why, what happened?" Just then Raghu turned the rickshaw into the lane where their house was located. Giving Asha a sideways hug, Karuna said, "We are almost home. Tell me what happened?"

"I need to go to the bathroom urgently. I haven't since I left home," Asha whispered, not wishing Raghu to hear her private business.

"Why not—does the school not have a toilet?"

Rushing down the sloping road, the tricycle rickshaw gathered momentum. Trying to make up for the morning's disaster and wishing to give Asha an exhilarating end to her ride back home, Raghu did not brake but let the wheels roll. The road was empty as far as one could see. As they sped past the first house, a dog ran out barking ferociously, almost biting Raghu's left calf. In his effort to save himself from the angry dog, he swerved and drove the rickshaw first over a large pothole and then over a concrete slab. The road was in dire need of repair; mounds of loose earth and boulders lay next to potholes. The work never seemed to progress.

The unexpected jerking movements ended badly for Asha. She lost control of her bladder. And once it started, she could not stop. By the time the rickshaw came to a halt in front of their home, her humiliation was complete. When Raghu got off his seat and looked fondly at Asha and Karuna, instead of being rewarded with smiles and applause for his skill and control, he was surprised to see a tearful Asha.

"Can't you even drive the rickshaw properly?" Asha wailed.

Karuna discreetly indicated the floor of the rickshaw.

On seeing what had happened, Raghu said, both his hands up in the air as if praying, "Gangajal! Ma, I'll clean it up. Children are children..."

Karuna tipped Raghu generously for his trouble. She also instructed Ramesh, who was all packed to go to his village to see his ailing mother, to give Raghu a hand to clean his rickshaw.

Asha was still crying when Karuna locked the door after Ramesh's departure. Then heaving a sigh of relief, she said, "Asha, take off your clothes. We'll have a nice bath, have lunch and a nap! I am exhausted."

"I'm *not* going to school any more," Asha declared in between sobs. "I did not know where the bathroom was! How am I supposed to know everything? When Miss showed me where it was, I could not use it. It was filthy. You would not have used it, not bapa or nana. I don't know how the other girls use it. The boys in my class don't know how to behave—they shout and fight for no reason. If you really loved me, you would not send me to school. Then Miss wanted to know everything about our family. And that badmash who hit you—when will Ma Durga punish him?"

"Asha, please don't cry. We are tired, dirty and hungry. You say I don't love you; the other day Vikram nana said no one loves him. Then who do we love—your bapa and I?" Karuna pulled her daughter onto her lap.

Now that she had her mother's undivided attention, Asha said, "Why don't you complain no one loves you? Bapa can also complain no one loves him…" Asha found the idea so ludicrous she began to laugh, and then she could not stop laughing.

Hugging her daughter, Karuna said, "How thin you are! You must eat properly, even Raghu kaku said so. How will you get strong if you don't eat enough?"

"If I become too heavy, no one can lift me—what will I do then? I can't play ringa-ringa roses with Vishu kaku, nor can I sit on his shoulders when I go to visit Ma Durga!" Asha pointed out the pitfalls of putting on weight. Then she added, "I have a lot of mental strength…just like you!"

<hr />

There was no water in the bathroom. In fact, there was no water in the house except for an earthenware pot of drinking water in the kitchen. Karuna realised Ramesh had given Raghu the only supply of water there was in the house. The storage tank in the bathroom was empty. She had forgotten to remind Ramesh to fill it up that morning. He clearly had other things on his mind. The next supply of water was not till later in the afternoon, and they needed a bath now.

As work never ceased for Karuna, there were days when she never got around to having a proper breakfast or lunch. It was turning out to be one of those days. But after her gall bladder flared up a year ago, she resolved to look after herself. She did not want her children growing up without a mother. Never did Karuna complain or think it unfair having to do the housework. If she did not look after her home, who would? She had help, but demand far exceeded supply. And at the most critical of moments, like now, she was left to her own devices. There was no option but to draw water out of the well in the inner courtyard.

Asha did not have the strength to draw water out of the well. But she was always eager to help, to prove she was an adult. "I can help you," she cried as she loosened the rope, letting the bucket fall all the way down. Her body tingled with pleasure when the balti hit the water with a splash. "Ha! Ha!" She clapped excitedly.

As the bucket filled up, Asha heaved and sighed, pulling the rope up only to lose control halfway, letting go of her heavy load. This ritual was repeated till she pulled out an empty bucket that kept hitting the inside walls of the well, making a terrific din. A wet and naked Asha danced and clapped with delight.

Karuna did not have the heart to reprimand her. Letting the bucket fall back into the well, she began to sing, "Our lives are mysteries, my dear girl, like buckets at the bottom of the well. It's hard to tell which bucket will hold water and which one will spill. The bucket is no better at controlling its destiny—the same bucket draws water for a wedding or a funeral."

Asha liked her mother's singing. She sensed they were words of wisdom although she could hear the sadness in her mother's voice. When her ma turned and smiled at her, she went and gave her a big hug.

In the evening when Aditya came home, he did not have to ask Asha about her first day in school. "It was the worst day of my life," Asha announced the moment she saw her father. Hearing her talk like her mother made him smile.

"Why are you smiling? Have you no heart at all? I've had such a miserable day!" Asha complained.

It made Aditya laugh out loud. Taking Asha in his arms, he said, "Let me get out of these clothes, and you can tell me why it was the worst day of your life."

As he changed into something more casual and comfortable, Karuna told him about the incident on the way to school.

"That man appeared from nowhere, and before I realised what had happened, he was gone. I saw his face, but I did not observe it carefully. Why should I? Suddenly he hit me hard like this." Karuna demonstrated how she had been attacked.

"Did Raghu manage to identify the rascal, chase him? I don't think it was a student. It must be a good-for-nothing lafanga on the way to chatra-bazaar," Aditya said, referring to the open market where he went to buy fruits and vegetables. "Young men these days have no respect. They don't work, they don't do anything constructive—just behave like rogues! The country is really falling apart. People have no values."

"That's what Raghu said. He did not take a good look at that rascal either. Why would you unless you were expecting this to happen? The goonda sped off on his bike—how could Raghu chase him on foot?" Karuna explained.

"Someone must've seen that chor's face. People these days don't believe in doing their civic duty. All the men on that road would have seen him. Someone could've given chase. How can we live in a society if no one cares?" he said.

"It happened fast, and the man disappeared down an alley. It's difficult to react so fast. What I don't understand is what he got out of it? One can't even report it to the police; they do nothing. Remember the policeman who came when you reported that theft?" Karuna reminded him.

"How can I forget? That idiot asked why the thief had not taken all our other belongings with him! With such men protecting us, what can one expect?" he lamented.

The post-mortem into the incident continued into the night as various family members came and left. Karuna served freshly fried pakoras and bhajees made from wedges of cauliflower, aubergine and potato dipped in spicy batter. When it was time for Asha to go to bed, she tiptoed upstairs to the balcony, which served as a lounge in the evenings. Normally, everyone sat on mats, leaning on cushions as they gossiped, laughed, sang and listened to music. Hugging her pillow, Asha loved half-listening to whatever conversations the adults were having while she lay on her mother's lap. She would let her thoughts drift in the cool breeze of a slow summer's night, tracing the pattern of the constellations in the sky. Falling asleep in such a manner was bliss.

Asha was looking forward to doing the same that evening. Approaching Karuna from behind, she rested her hand on her mother's right shoulder, having forgotten it was the same shoulder where she had been hit that morning. Karuna swerved her head instantly as if in grave danger. Then she screamed and screamed; nothing could silence her. Asha had triggered her mother's delayed reaction. Unable to understand why her mother was so upset, Asha joined in the screaming. Embracing each other, they could not hold back their tears.

CHAPTER 4

The discussion went on for days if it would be possible to visit Simlipal National Park during the summer vacation. There were many factors to consider. For a start, Aditya was concerned whether it would be safe to leave the house unattended.

Abhay said, "Nana, aren't you forgetting I will be here. I have no plans to travel. Then there is Ramesh. If you're still worried, Madhav can stay here too."

Madhav, Karuna's younger brother, stayed with them during the week. He was studying for his master's at Harrison College. It saved him the hassle of travelling from one end of the city to the other during the semesters. Abhay was also residing there for the same reason. So did Vishu before him.

"What about bapa, not to mention your parents?" Karuna asked.

"What about them?" Abhay enquired.

"I mean what if they fall ill while we're gone?" Karuna spelt it out for him.

Abhay offered to keep an eye on them. "I can call on your father every other day. He's just a cycle ride away. He'll end up looking after me, feeding me! It won't be practical to see my parents. But you don't see them every day either. If they fall ill—well, we'll cross that bridge when we get there. You are going to Baripada to see

41

Savitri nani. This is the perfect opportunity to visit Simlipal. Vishu nana wants to take you there. What difference does a couple more days make? I'll look after the house."

The concept of a holiday was alien to Karuna and the family. It was work that necessitated travel and provided a reason for abandoning the comfort of one's home. They were going to Baripada to see the person who had played an important role in Aditya's childhood. When Subhalakshmi had to accompany her husband on his excavation trips, it was not possible to take their young son with them. Savitri, Amitava's older sister, a spinster, looked after Aditya. Now old and ailing, she had expressed a keen desire to see him and his family 'for the last time in my life' she had written in an unsteady hand, barely legible. Aditya felt the need to fulfil her wish.

Once in Baripada, the matter was settled when Vishu said he had already made the arrangements. They left for Simlipal early one morning. Until lunchtime, everyone was excited. After lunch, energy levels flagged. Karuna and Aditya dozed off only to wake up with a jolt every time the jeep swerved, which was far too often for their comfort. Before long, Sujata, Vishu's wife, said she needed to go to the bathroom. Everyone agreed it was time to have a break and stretch their legs.

Vishu parked the jeep and the trailer, which was filled with provisions, including live chickens, supplies of food, drinking water, petrol, blankets, bed sheets, towels, and all sorts of things deemed essential by city dwellers for a few days in the jungle. He led the way to locate a space safe and private enough for the women and children to relieve themselves. The spot he chose was overgrown with grass. Vishu stamped on it with his boots to flatten the area.

Holding him back, Sujata said, "That's enough. May God forgive us for killing all the insects and creatures that lived here."

A row of ancient sal trees in full bloom provided the privacy that the women sought. Asha was wary of squatting on her haunches in case something attacked her. She had overheard some girls in school gossiping about germs that were capable of climbing up one's stream of urine. She squatted to a safe point and was peeing and stopping, peeing and stopping, making sure nothing could enter her body while she was doing so. This required a level of concentration way above normal. So, when she saw a deer looking straight at her, albeit from a distance, she lost all control. But the deer disappeared with such speed, Asha wondered if she had imagined it. Returning to the main road, where the rest of the family were enjoying the water of green coconuts, Asha enquired with great excitement, "Did anyone see the deer?"

Vikram burst out laughing. Then looking up at the sky, he said, "The wind is really blowing hard today!" It was an unusually still and sultry day.

"Promise, I saw a deer!" said Asha.

When she turned to her parents, Karuna nodded in affirmation. But Asha got the distinct impression that no one believed her.

"I don't care if none of you believe me. I know what I saw, and I know what a deer looks like." Asha knew she saw things others said they did not. This was not the first time. *One day, I'll get to the bottom of this illusion thing,* she promised herself.

"I believe you," said Kalpana, Vishu's daughter, who was a couple of years younger than Asha.

While Vikram doubled up with laughter, the girls held hands in solidarity and walked back to the jeep.

The final leg of the journey got harder. Vishu steered the jeep and the trailer up the steep and sharp bends of the road as it snaked upwards. The trees were so tall, broad and thick, they blotted out the sun.

Thankfully, Asha could barely see the steep precipice at every bend in the road. It would have made her nausea worse. While the trailer had a tarpaulin sheltering its contents, the children sitting in the back had no such cover. Every time the jeep scaled up a gradient, it groaned, emitting masses of fumes that choked them. Asha spluttered and coughed between bouts of retching. After the third time she threw up, Vishu did not stop.

"At this rate, we'll never reach our destination," he complained and drove on. "We must get there before it gets dark."

The soot along with the red dust that blew off the mountain soil began to settle on their hair, faces and bodies. The roads were being carved out of the vast belly of the mountain. There were mounds of red soil everywhere. When a vehicle passed, it left a trail of sandstorms and whirlwinds behind. The children sitting in the back got caught in the fat tail of the dust storm. Vikram and Kalpana turned part of their clothing into a mask and looked like fresh recruits for a guerrilla war.

Asha tried to cover her face. As she needed to breathe and throw up at regular intervals, her mask was far from effective. She felt like a whale that needed to come up to the surface of the ocean to breathe, spouting gallons of water, except in her case it was vomit. She had no idea where it all came from. She could hear the chickens cackling away to high heaven, though the protests of the poor birds were drowned by the groaning jeep crawling up the steep mountain.

By the time they arrived at the mountain lodge, their faces were painted black and red from the soot and iron-rich dust. Asha also smelled of vomit; the wind had blown her vomit back onto various parts of her body. She was so tired, all she wanted to do was to get out of her soiled, stinking clothes, wash herself clean, eat and sleep.

When Vikram, Asha and Kalpana got out of the jeep, they were greeted with utter astonishment by the villagers, especially the half-naked Adivasi children, who had dressed up for the occasion. They stood there in a semicircle like a welcoming committee unsure of its purpose. It had been a long time since any children had come to stay at the lodge, especially ones looking as unkempt and smelly as these!

The lodge, consisting of four large wooden cabins balanced on stilts, resembled a tree that sprouted these boxed structures instead of leaves and flowers. One had to climb up a ladder made of thick planks of wood held together by rope. The children felt dizzy climbing up the ladder as it swung under their weight. Asha could feel the entire edifice gently heaving as they walked up and down the creaking wooden floors.

"Why is the lodge not built on the ground?" Kalpana asked.

"Elephants, bears, tigers cannot enter lodge," replied Mr Parida, the local government official.

The caretaker of the lodge had clearly gone to a lot of trouble to prepare for their visit. Everything looked clean. There was enough space—four rooms and two bathrooms—but no electricity or water supply. The furnishings were minimal, too. There were just a couple of buckets of water in each bathroom.

Seeing the scandalised looks on their faces, Mr Parida ordered more water be delivered. "The problem is, we don't have enough buckets," he apologised.

"Parida babu, it's not a problem," said Karuna. "Let the children wash up first. Then the buckets can be refilled. Unfortunately, after this long journey we all need a proper wash. The roads are full of dust, as you know."

"Yes, yes. Madam, I understand," said Parida, nodding sympathetically.

Aditya, Vishu and Vikram made their way to the well for a bath.

Vishu said, "Asha and Kalpana, you can come with us, or you can wait for a bath in the river tomorrow."

Asha's need for a bath being paramount, she followed the men to the well. Kalpana joined her. It was after the bathing ceremony that Asha felt able to take in the beauty of the place. She observed the rich colours of the orchids and the tall sal trees that surrounded them like sentries. The sighing of the wind as it caressed the leaves was haunting. She could see patches of grassy meadows at a distance, beyond the lush, thick, green forest.

By dusk the clouds came home, descending low enough for the

children to think they were in heaven! After supper, they sat on the balcony admiring the crescent moon and the iridescent stars that never twinkled as brightly back home, even during power cuts. The fireflies sparkled like illuminated jewels flying in the night. The jungle sounds, from the howling of wild dogs to occasional trumpeting of elephants in the distance, gave it an eerie, scary appeal.

"Do you know why this place is called Simlipal?" Vishu asked the children.

When the children looked at each other for answers, he explained, "Simlipal derives its name from the simul tree, the red silk cotton tree. Tomorrow we will see the blazing red flowers of the simul tree."

Apurva Parida nodded as he laid out the plans for the next day. Soon it was time for jungle stories, and he recounted a true incident about a village boy who was swallowed by a python. But the boy had the presence of mind to wedge his large, sharp woodcutter's knife in the mouth of the snake.

"As python suck boy"—Parida demonstrated with his hands— "knife cut into snake. Boy saved. But boy not walk; stay six months in hospital. Python killed by Adivasis. They take boy to witch doctor, herbal medicine doctor. Boy still not walk!" He went on to add how much the villagers had enjoyed feasting on python meat.

At this point, when everyone was feeling terribly sorry for the crippled but brave boy, Vishu whispered he had just noticed a pair of luminous eyes among the bushes not far from the lodge. They all withdrew into the largest room, which happened to be located at the centre of the lodge.

"Parida babu, are there any man-eaters in Simlipal?" asked Aditya.

"Not recently. There was one—an old tigress turned man-eater." Trying to reassure everyone, he added, "Just foxes looking for food, I think. I'll wait until the night watchmen arrive."

Aditya and Vishu thought it was no bad thing to have a third male adult with them, especially one who knew the jungle. Soon the chowkidars arrived, and they went off to ensure there were no dangerous animals lurking in the vicinity.

Vishu suggested Aditya and Karuna retire to their room.

"The rest of us will sleep here," he said. "You don't have to worry about the children. But please don't leave your room at night. Under no circumstance should you open the door. Just call me if you need anything. I will come to you."

"How will you all sleep in one room?" Karuna asked.

"We'll manage," Sujata replied. "It's safer this way. If the children sleep in separate rooms, and there is enough room as you can see, what if they wake up at night and accidentally walk out of the room? And God forbid, what if some wild animal tries to get into their room? If we all sleep in one room, it'll be safe."

"What will happen if some animal tries to get into our room?" Karuna gasped.

"Nothing of the sort will happen," Vishu reassured her. "The chowkidars are here. If you need anything, just knock on the wall, three loud knocks, like this." He demonstrated. "I'll be with you in no time."

Vishu accompanied Karuna and Aditya to their room to make sure they securely bolted their door from inside. By the time he returned, the chowkidars had lighted a fire outside the lodge, where they sat warming their hands, talking, singing and sharing jungle stories.

Asha fell asleep listening to tales about life in the jungle, dreaming of tigers, elephants, leopards and other wild beasts. She woke up the next morning to more stories, but could not decide if they were true or not.

"Last night a tiger came near our lodge," Kalpana said.

"There are paw marks and droppings," Vikram confirmed. "Bapa, ma, kaku and I—we heard the tiger growling and prowling outside. I was so scared; his growl sounded like the roar of a large family of tigers!"

Asha was not sure Vikram was speaking the truth, not pulling her leg. "Why did you not wake me up? What happened to the chowkidars?" she asked.

"We didn't want you to be frightened," Vikram whispered as if the tiger was still patrolling the neighbourhood. "The chowkidars woke us up. What else could you have done except pray for your life?"

Then Kalpana said, "Badama woke up at dawn and opened the door!"

Asha's face distorted in panic. "Did she forget what Vishu kaku told us last night?" She ran to make sure her mother was all right and had not been mauled by the tiger. Arriving in her parents' room, she cried, "What happened?"

"I saw a family of snakes, a king cobra couple and their children, dancing at the edge of the well. I must have disturbed them. When they saw me, they stopped dancing and turned their hoods towards me like this," Karuna replied, raising her hand imitating the hood of a snake.

Asha recoiled as if she was being attacked.

"I shut the door immediately, remembering what Vishu kaku had said," Karuna added.

"Did you forget before—when you opened the door?" Asha asked, concerned.

"I did." Karuna sighed with a guilty face.

"Were you frightened?" Asha gave her mother a hug. "Where was bapa?"

"He was asleep," replied Karuna.

"And then what happened?" Asha wanted to know.

"Vishu kaku came, but the snakes had gone by then," said Karuna.

"Bapa snake and ma snake and Vikram snake and Asha snake had all gone?" A palpable sense of relief appeared on Asha's face.

Parida had appointed an Adivasi family to look after the Guru family. Adivasis, the primitive hill tribes, were reputed to be the original settlers of the land, even before the days of the *Mahabharata* or the *Ramayana*. Unlike other parts of India, Orissa had ancient and liberal tribal customs and traditions that played a significant role in shaping the political structures and cultural practices of its people. The Adivasis depended on the forest for their sustenance. They not only respected nature, they worshipped it by emulating its rich and pluralistic ways. They adhered to its sacred laws and knew the forest like the back of their hands.

When asked his age, the wizened old man, the head of his household, nodded and replied, "Very old." Then moving his right thumb, as if he was counting, he declared confidently, "Twenty!"

He looked about eighty, his face a land of many rivers, many conquests, decorated with lines that ran down his features like badges of honour. But when he led the family into the forest, he was indeed a nimble twenty-year-old, a young spirit dancing in an ancient, ageless soul. His son, who could count, confessed he was eighteen, but was not sure of his father's age.

"What should we call your father and you?" Vishu asked.

"We call him Father," the son replied, trying to conceal his puzzlement.

The father, who had been following the conversation, laughed and said, "We used to call him Fatboy, but he is no longer fat. You can call me Buddhu."

As Buddhu translated to stupid, Aditya said, "How can we call you Buddhu if you are going to be our guide, our guru, as it were?"

A surprised Buddhu said, "Then call me Budha."

Aditya was also called Budha; it was traditionally the nickname given to the eldest son. The Guru family members looked at each other for answers.

Vishu asked Fatboy, "What is your family name?"

Fatboy looked at his father.

Then an inspired Vishu said, pointing at Buddhu, "We'll call you Valmiki."

This made Aditya, Karuna and Sujata smile in a way that Vishu immediately recognized. "What did I say now? Was Valmiki not an Adivasi?" he asked.

"Yes, but Valmiki also wrote the *Ramayana*," Karuna pointed out.

"Buddhu will learn to write in his next incarnation, right?" Aditya said.

Buddhu nodded vigorously.

"And what do we call him?" Sujata enquired, referring to Fatboy.

"What about Valmiki's son?" Vishu suggested.

"No, there'll be confusion. When you call one they'll both come running, or you call one and the other will appear," Sujata pointed out.

"They won't respond to whatever new name we call them. We have to call them by the names they are used to," said Aditya.

Parida, who had been standing there silently, confused with the bewildering exchange, finally said, "I agree. They will not respond to any of these new names, even one as great as Valmiki."

"Fine, we'll call them by whatever names they are accustomed to," Vishu said.

It was settled the father would be called Buddhu and the son Fatboy.

❧

After breakfast, the family ventured forth with four of the Adivasis into the jungle.

"What do we call the other two?" Asha asked.

"If you need something ask me, bapa, kaku or khudi," said Karuna.

They were well guarded as they walked wedged between the guides, who led the way and followed after them. Parida was in the middle, flanked by Asha in front and Kalpana behind. The group of twelve walked single file in an orderly queue. The guides cleared the path through the thick undergrowth, scything their way across with knives and then flattening the grass with thick, rounded sticks.

"If there are snakes, they will escape, not bite us," explained Parida.

"I'm scared!" whispered Kalpana when a worried Asha looked back at her.

"What will happen if a snake attacks us?" Kalpana asked.

"Buddhu is very skilled at catching snakes," Parida reassured her.

"A family of snakes came near the lodge this morning. Ma saw them. Wish Buddhu was at the lodge then." Asha volunteered the information.

"Yes, I heard," Parida said as the queue slowly snaked forward.

After walking for almost an hour, they came across a clearing with trees trampled by large feet. All along the way, their eyes feasted on the beauty of the forest, the rich hues of brightly coloured orchids that highlighted the many shades of green. And now a precipitous waterfall sparkling in the distance beckoned them.

But their attention was drawn to a baby elephant that lay not far from where they stood, somewhat hidden behind a tree, seemingly asleep. One of the guides went closer, confirmed the baby elephant was dead, and declared the jungle tour had ended for the day. He ululated, and everyone heard a similar wailing reply.

"When will the baby hathi's soul go to heaven? Can't we stay and watch?" Asha pleaded, excited with the prospect of more jungle magic.

One of the guides muttered something to Parida, and he explained in a low but urgent tone, "We must return to lodge now. Elephant family mourning death of baby, mauling man. Man dead. We must leave before elephant family return."

"The hathi's soul will go to swarga, not the body," Karuna explained.

"Can't we stay and see the soul go to heaven, then?" Asha begged.

"Didn't you hear what Parida babu said?" Vikram gulped his words; he was practically running on the spot. "You can't see the soul." He pooh-poohed the idea.

"No need to run," Parida said, holding Vikram's hand. "That will also alert the elephants. They are good listeners. Let's all walk calmly, quietly, as fast as we can."

Asha thought she could hear the elephants' low growl from a distance. It reminded her of the time when she, Vikram and Sadhana were so frightened to see a severely disfigured and crippled beggar approaching Aja's house, they screamed at the top of their voices while running as fast as they could. It was not till Aja appeared on the scene did they realise they had been running in the same spot. Their screams were also muted. Aja sent the driver to pay the beggar and to ask him not to come all the way to the house. The gate was practically a quarter mile from the house. Aja gave them their favourite Threptin biscuits to comfort them.

Keeping pace with the adults, a breathless Asha said, "Nana, do you remember the day at Aja's when that beggar came?"

"Shh," said Parida. "Please keep quiet. No talking till we reach lodge."

Vikram nodded vigorously, as if to say, 'How could I ever forget?'

Karuna whispered it was a big mistake to have ventured on foot so deep into the jungle with the children. Asha wanted to tell her mother she could hear the elephants, but decided it was not worth the risk. To banish her fears, she began to pray to Ganesh, the remover of all obstacles. Everyone heaved a sigh of relief when they reached the lodge.

It was past noon by the time the Adivasi guides thought it safe to escort the family to the river. The river was freezing cold, but after the initial shock, Asha was surprised how invigorating it felt. Refreshed, they prepared to walk back to the lodge, hungry as lions. It was then that Kalpana screamed. *My God, has she been attacked by a crocodile; is a leopard carrying her off?* Asha wondered as she swerved round, her head spinning with possibilities. Kalpana stood there pointing at dark, fat, wormlike things hanging from her calf.

Buddhu picked some leaves that grew along the path. He squashed them between his fingers. As he applied the pack to her calf, he said, "Nature very intelligent—everything useful. Nature create leech, also create leaf. Leeches, the rascals, jump on you." He demonstrated. "Leaf make them fall. But bastards drunk with blood already, will drop off any minute," he added.

Everyone checked their bodies to make sure the rascals had not attached themselves to them. As if that was not enough excitement for the day, lunch consisted of chicken curry, which Asha refused to touch. The poor creatures had travelled with her. How could she eat them?

"Don't be stupid," said Vikram. "Why can't you eat the chicken curry? If Parida babu's wife had cooked chicken curry, you would've eaten it, right? So why can't you eat this? Chicken is chicken; doesn't matter if they travelled with us!"

Karuna intervened. "If she doesn't want to eat the chicken curry, she doesn't have to. Don't force her."

The matter was settled. After a brief nap and afternoon tea, there was talk of driving to see the wild animals that come in the evening to have a drink in the river. Parida suggested the children stay back. Karuna agreed. Asha was disappointed yet relieved. In the end, everyone went to Parida's for dinner before going to the local Adivasi festival, where they were delighted with the gracefully athletic tribal dances accompanied by music. They had not seen or heard anything like it before.

The following day, it was decided it would be safer to go on a drive in the jungle. Asha did not think it was possible to cram the jeep with more people. But Parida, Buddha and Fatboy climbed in with them at the back. Every few miles they stopped and got off the crowded vehicle to admire the verdant mountains, dazzling waterfalls, and herds of grazing deer. Occasionally, they perched on fallen trunks of trees, dipping their feet in cool streams and watching flying squirrels or dancing peacocks. Driving back, they heard the wild trumpeting of elephants. Buddhu said they were mourning the death of their baby.

"Just like humans," said Aditya.

That evening, before dinner at Parida's, the men went for a brief stroll in the nearby woods. The children and women stayed in, listening to Fatboy's stories. Soon the men were back, their faces drained of colour.

"What happened?" Mrs Parida asked her husband.

"Bha-bhalloo!" He could barely speak. His ashen face spoke instead.

"We saw the bear's back and retreated as quietly as we could. God help us if the bear, or bears, follows us here," said Aditya.

Having bolted the door, they huddled quietly in the room. It took a while for the face of fear to disappear.

When dinner was finally served, Asha said, "Maybe bear was also hungry."

On the way back to Baripada, they stopped at the chief forest ranger's house. Vishu wanted to thank him for organising their visit. There were two other compelling reasons—one to buy honey from the forest shop. The other was a surprise treat for the children. When the ranger called out peremptorily, "Rani, come here," everyone thought a bitch would come running, wagging her tail. When a tiger cub made a majestic entrance, there was a collective gasp. Karuna and Kalpana immediately jumped up and followed Sujata and the ranger's wife out of the room.

"I'm afraid of cats and dogs, let alone a tiger! The little devil knows it, and she teases me. Poor thing, she lost her mother. Who will look after her if we don't?" The ranger's wife commiserated as she led the exodus.

Rani snuggled up to Vishu, demanding to be cuddled. Seeing Aditya and Vishu lavishing their attention on Rani, Vikram and Asha plucked up the courage to come closer. When they touched Rani, they felt her strong heart beating wildly against her soft, beautifully spotted fur. They could feel the fragility of their bodies against hers.

Then Vishu called out for Kalpana, but she would have nothing to do with Rani, who, sensing Kalpana's fear, started to tease her, boxing Kalpana with her paws. Kalpana screamed and ran to her father, hoping that would teach Rani a lesson. But Rani kept endearing herself to Vishu, and when he began to play with Rani, she climbed on his lap, displacing Kalpana from her perch. Then Rani yawned, opening her mouth wide as if smiling, lapping up all the attention.

"When will you take her back to the jungle?" Vishu asked.

"Very soon," the ranger said, his voice tinged with sadness.

"The longer you keep her, the less able she'll be to adapt to life in the jungle," said Aditya.

"I know, and I'll miss her terribly. She is just like a child, only wilder. Sometimes she jumps into bed with me. My wife is fond of Rani, but this little bitch lords it over her like her master."

CHAPTER 5

One of Aditya's self-appointed chores every morning was to open all the windows and unlock the doors in their home. At night, before going to bed, he did the opposite—making sure all potential entrances were secured. The struggle for the country's independence had left an indelible mark. As a student in Calcutta, he had seen enough madness—killing of innocents, looting and mindless destruction of property. However, he only started locking up doors and securing the windows in his home after they were burgled twice and the police did nothing. On the contrary, the police wanted to know why the burglar did not help himself to the other items in the vicinity as if doubting Aditya's version of events.

It was a colleague who gave him the idea. "Aditya babu," he said, "I started locking my doors and windows after I was burgled three times! What is it they say—vigilance is the price of freedom. Even freedom does not come free!" And he had shaken his head sadly, as if freedom was an illusion like everything else in life.

Aditya invested in a full set of padlocks that were burglar-proof; it was an expensive decision. When he explained the situation to the locksmith, he said, "Babu, you and your neighbours should get together and hire a night watchman."

"We already have one. Now we have to put up with this

additional expense. The price of safety has gone up with the price of everything else," Aditya complained.

"Perhaps the watchman is in cahoots with the burglar—telling him when you are out, in? These days you can't trust anyone," the locksmith had pointed out.

When Aditya flung open the windows and doors of his home each morning, it was as if he was also opening his heart to the universe. He welcomed the day as a sunflower might greet the sun. Equally, he expressed his discontentment with life if, for example, the morning newspaper had not been delivered or a window was stubbornly stuck, both of which happened on a regular basis for completely unconnected reasons. To be born methodical and organized was a curse in India.

It was natural to feel indignant about the state of the nation and the fate of human beings facing such a dire situation. As the day progressed, opportunities to feel angry, confused and depressed mounted with precision, like walking on a treadmill. Aditya's frustrations and complaints were epitomised in one word, *dhet*, expressed with the right mix of disgust and despair spiced with a hint of acceptance, if not self-realization. It translated loosely to: What can one possibly do when people no longer believed in doing their duty except learn to accept calmly such calamity? It was to become the Guru family password for life's many unexpected trials.

Asha was also used to hearing her mother instructing the maids every morning. They seemed to possess terribly poor memories, as Karuna greeted them daily with the same pep talk and set of instructions as she served them breakfast and tea. Karuna told them more or less the same things each morning, inspiring them to do their best because any job worth doing was worth doing well. Yet they never seemed to master simple tasks! Perhaps their minds were on higher things, or they did not heed her words, knowing they would hear it again the following day.

When Asha woke up that morning, she knew she was back at home the moment she heard her mother instructing the maids, and her father saying, *"Dhet,"* twice in a matter of minutes. However, she was completely surprised when he said, "Asha, get up. We have work to do. Your school opens in a fortnight. You need to prepare. Remember, life is all about being prepared."

During the summer vacation, Asha had forgotten all about school. Now it hit her, she had been promoted, at her own request, to Standard One. After two months in kindergarten she had asked Vikram, "Do you learn anything in school? I learn more at home where no one teaches me!"

Vikram reported the conversation to his parents.

Aditya spoke to Miss Webster, who explained, "Asha is very bright, better than her classmates. We thought you tutored her. After all, she comes from an educated family; you are a professor!"

It was agreed Asha would be promoted to Standard One. Karuna was pleased her daughter had automatically moved up a class. If Asha was to complete her bachelor's degree before marrying, she needed to work her way through school and college like a game of Moksha Patam, avoiding the snakes and finding the ladders. For Karuna, life was all about finding the ladders and carefully avoiding the snakes. As there was no way of knowing where the ladders might be hidden, or if they were snakes in disguise, the only responsible thing was to hold on to the right path, which she had scrupulously adhered to. But she never understood why God let her mother die so young or what she could possibly have done wrong to have earned such a fate.

After spending half an hour with Asha, going through her books, Aditya said, "Now you read the first two chapters of all your books and then come back to me."

Nodding absentmindedly, Asha murmured, "Bapa, do you think they'd have already taken Rani back to the jungle?"

"Rani's home is the jungle," Aditya replied.

"What if the other animals attack her?" Asha asked.

"Don't worry. They'll look after her—until Rani can look after herself."

"Just the way you and ma look after me—until I can look after myself?"

Aditya nodded and said, "We'll look after you always. It's what parents do."

"I will look after you too when I'm grown up," Asha said, hugging her knees and rocking on her bottom. She looked as if she would lose her balance, but never did.

"Asha, go and study now. This is not the time to do yoga," Aditya said, thinking she was practicing her yoga exercises.

Just at that moment Karuna called out from the kitchen, "Asha, have you finished your homework? Can you come and give me a hand?"

Asha looked at her father and said, as if their roles had suddenly been reversed, "Better go and find out what she needs. Ma always needs a hand."

<hr>

Studying was what Asha did when there was nothing else to be done. As she was asked to attend to a multitude of tasks by her elders, studying was something she ended up doing between chores. She was just beginning her apprenticeship with Karuna, though she had been Vikram's secret apprentice for years. In the afternoons, for example, while the rest of the household took a nap, Vikram taught her how to roll up dried rose petals in wafer-thin paper. They would light up the home-made biddis and inhale. Asha never mastered the art of inhaling deeply or blowing out elegantly looped rings of smoke. She coughed violently, and Vikram despaired when she did so.

"Shu...shush... If you make such a racket, you'll only wake up everyone," he would whisper, gesturing threateningly as if he was going to strangle her.

Asha never relished their secret smoking sessions. If truth be told, nor did Vikram. In fact, they disliked it so much that neither was tempted to smoke anything later in life—no cigarettes, cigars, pipes, biddis, cheroots, drugs, or pot.

Not all their afternoon pranks were as innocent. Sometimes, they made mud balls, which they dropped into Ramesh's mouth. He usually slept with his mouth wide open. As he also snored the moment he dozed off, it served as a signal for Vikram to spring into action. Ramesh would wake up spluttering, spitting mud and complaining, "Ma, Vikram babu is getting naughtier every day. See what he has done now." He would spit the mud out of his mouth, coughing loudly for everyone to hear.

"Vikram, come here immediately," Karuna would call out to Vikram.

"Why don't you sleep with your mouth closed?" Vikram would mock Ramesh before dashing off to his mother.

Sometimes, the mud dried up while they waited for Ramesh to fall asleep. Sometimes, they fell asleep before he did. There were days, too, when Asha found herself with nothing to do, especially in the afternoons when Karuna took a nap, and Vikram pretended to sleep if he did not want to play with her. Occasionally, Ramesh told her a story. Often she got bored with his narration and wandered off to find her own entertainment, talking to her stone or her imaginary friends. Sometimes, she, too, curled up in bed and let her mind retrace the Bible stories they read in school. These stories were as fantastic as the ancient Indian epics.

One afternoon, while Ramesh regaled her with his version of tales from the *Mahabharata*, he sat on the floor with his half-pant splayed open. Asha sat at a safe distance on a kitchen stool. When he suggested she come closer, she declined, shaking her head. Then she stood up, startled, when the front of his pant billowed up as if a snake had suddenly raised its hood beneath it. Eyes wide open, she ran to share her concern with Vikram, her best friend. But he was in one of his surly moods.

He snapped, "Get lost, you moron. What rubbish are you talking about?"

Instead of being rewarded for her honest reportage, for sharing sensitive inside information, she received several blows on her bottom. Asha was howling by the time Karuna arrived on the scene.

"Vikram nana hit me," she complained to Karuna.

"What's the matter with you two? Can't you play without fighting for just an hour while I rest? Is it that difficult to keep quiet?" Karuna asked.

Before she could investigate matters further, Abhay walked in, his eyebrows raised like two horizontal question marks.

"The children have become very disobedient; they quarrel and never listen to me," she appealed to him.

Instead of forgetting about the children's squabbles and moving on to adult concerns, as they usually did, Asha was surprised when her mother turned to Vikram and asked him why he hit her.

Vikram hesitated for a moment before coming clean. "Asha was talking dirty."

"You must have taught her to talk like that!" Karuna insisted.

"No, I did not. She was with Ramesh. He did," he added in self-defence.

"What has Ramesh got to do with your fight?" Karuna asked, dragging him into her bedroom.

Abhay and Asha followed them. Vikram patiently explained why he had behaved the way he did. Karuna turned to Asha for her version of events. The moment she finished recounting what had happened earlier, all hell broke loose. Karuna ordered Ramesh to leave the house. Ramesh kept pleading he would never repeat his mistake.

"I don't know what came over me. Please forgive me," Ramesh begged Karuna and Abhay, falling at their feet. He even pleaded with Vikram and Asha to forgive him. Asha had never seen her mother in such a rage.

"We treated you like family, and this is how you reward our trust? Get out of my home right now!" Karuna was shaking like a leaf in a storm, her hands raised to strike Ramesh. As she cursed him, she struck a blow to his face, breaking the coloured glass bangles on her right hand and cutting herself in the process.

"Bohu, look, you've hurt yourself. Let's wait till nana gets home. Ramesh is repentant. But first that cut needs to be attended to. It's bleeding," Abhay said.

A furious Karuna lashed out. "Abhay, what more damage do you want him to inflict on us? My mother died, but Asha has a mother to protect her."

By the time Aditya returned, Ramesh was gone. Karuna complained that apart from Ramesh's utterly unacceptable behaviour towards Asha, his recent demeanour towards her had not been respectful enough.

"I don't know what changed. But of late he was disobedient and did exactly as he pleased. He went to his village far too often, saying his mother was ill. But was his mother really ill? What's the point of keeping such a namak-haram?" Karuna said.

"Ramesh had been with us for such a long time," Aditya remarked, shaking his head in disbelief. "You can't depend on servants these days. Servants will always remain servants, however well you treat them. Hope we find someone trustworthy soon. It's just that you are expecting. You need more rest, not more work."

Asha could not understand what her father meant when he said her mother was expecting. Expecting what? Nor did she know what Karuna told Vikram when they had a long heart-to-heart later and she was asked to go and play, which seemed rather silly as she had no one to play with. So Asha sat silently with her stone, hoping to find some answers. But from that afternoon Vikram behaved differently. He stopped demonstrating the long arc of his pee or chatting to her while he peed.

What is the purpose of our lives; why are we here? These were *not* the sort of questions that consumed Asha. The *how* bit was fascinating; *how* a child is born. The *why* bit made no sense at all. Things are as they were. She was curious about death, not hers, but of her parents more than that of her grandparents, uncles and aunts. The most worrying thing, however, was marriage, as marriage resulted in children, and she knew all too well how women died in childbirth. Had her grandmother not died in childbirth? If her ma also died in childbirth, would she be married off?

These were among the many questions that bothered Asha when she heard her aunts talking excitedly about Karuna having a baby. Her mother put on weight, and soon her stomach grew larger than the melons and gourds her father brought home from the bazaar. Asha was worried her ma's stomach might burst open one day.

By the time Karuna got round to telling her—"Asha, you are going to have a brother, maybe a sister."—Asha already had a pretty good idea.

"Why didn't you tell me before? I'll have a brother. You'll have a son."

Karuna assumed her daughter wanted a brother. But Asha did not want a brother or a sister. She was perfectly happy with the way things were. She may have wanted a new dress, a toy or a treat at Calcutta Sweets, but not another brother, not even a doll-like sister. Remembering how Angel Gabriel had made an announcement to Mary about the birth of Jesus, Asha asked, "When did you get the message? Why did you not tell me before? What did Gabriel look like?"

"What are you talking about? Stop daydreaming. Come, help me lay the table," said Karuna, despairing of her daughter's inability to focus on matters at hand.

"God knows which world Asha lives in—always daydreaming, lost in her world! How will I manage when the baby arrives?" Karuna complained to Aditya.

He ignored her remark about Asha; she was just a child. He agreed with his wife about her need for help at home.

Aditya said, "Vishu wrote he has found a suitable servant boy for us in the village. Let's hope he arrives soon."

"Hope this one proves to be more reliable. Perhaps we need an older man. A good woman is hard to find, and young men are untrustworthy," said Karuna.

That summer the heat was no less oppressive. One afternoon, when the entire world had a siesta and even birds and animals took shelter from the heat, Asha was unable to sleep. The ceiling fan's somnolent whirring distracted her. But something else was also disturbing her. A few days ago, Vikram had shown her some pot-bellied guppies swimming in the glass aquarium. He had also mentioned casually they were pregnant, hence their bloated shape. Later, he was practically in tears when he found two of his precious guppies dead.

Unable to keep her worries to herself, Asha turned to Vikram. "Nana, what will happen if ma dies?" she asked.

"Why will ma die, you idiot?" Vikram snapped.

"Women die in childbirth," said Asha. "You seem to know nothing."

<hr/>

It was also the year of the Cuban Missile Crisis, which somehow got lost in translation and circulated as an end-of-the-world story. Schools and colleges were closed till the danger passed. It was not clear exactly what the danger was, though there was talk of a flood that would wipe away cities. It was decided the family would move to Aja's bungalow. Asha could not figure out if they were going to Aja's on account of the flood or because the world was coming to an end. Maybe the world would end with an almighty flood? Would God send a Noah's Ark? If they were going to die, reasoned Asha, it made sense to spend their last days together at Aja's.

They could bathe in the river at the edge of the orchard, climb trees, and spend entire afternoons eating guavas, star fruit, sapetta and mango, coiled around sturdy branches of trees like pythons, until the end of the world. Asha was also partial to the unmistakable fragrance of khus-khus tatties that hung in Aja's kutcherry and along the long, open corridors and windows. The mellow richness of the scent triggered a sense of well-being like the smell of parched earth after the first monsoon shower. It made her body tingle just the way it did when they visited the temple in Konarka and she first saw the sculptures of gods and goddesses locked in deep embrace.

"If the world is really coming to an end, does it matter where we are? All that matters is who we are with."

Asha made that profound observation when the children assembled in one corner of the veranda at the back of the bungalow facing the river. They were having a discussion similar to the one their parents were having in the adjacent room. Freshly made bhajees and samosas with raita, pickles and chutneys were doing the rounds.

"How will the world end? Could it be due to the Chinese? They have been attacking us," Vikram said before licking the chutney off his fingers.

"I think so too," said Asha, pleased they agreed on such important matters.

The tension between China and India had not gone unnoticed by her, especially as her father often raged against people she did not know about when he read the newspapers. Aditya would tell Karuna, "At least the Chinese have sense enough to build roads. Our politicians talk of Hindi-Chini Bhai-Bhai and pocket the money! *Dhet*, this country has lost its way."

The Chinese threatened to march straight into India, calling her bluff. Failing to welcome the prodigal bhai, India flexed its muscles, barely managing to defend her territory, thanks to the politicians and generals who did not build the roads they were supposed to, but divided the spoils among themselves. India almost lost the war in 1962. When the Chinese saw the state of the Indian roads, they called it a day. It was not possible for their soldiers to keep marching on.

When Asha heard about the Forbidden City, she wondered why there was no mention of it in the Bible. She thought the Garden of Eden, with its Forbidden Fruit, was in England, thanks to the nuns at her school, who in her view were all English—though in reality they came from Wales, Scotland and Ireland. She read the Bible, King James Version, which the nuns gave to all the girls. If the Garden of Eden is actually located in China and not in England, Asha reasoned, should the Bible not say so? As many things were forbidden in China, the Forbidden Fruit could easily have come from the Forbidden Garden in the Forbidden City? Many things were forbidden in India too—even after the British left, when, of course, just about everything was forbidden. No wonder the British had to go!

Caught in a state of high uncertainty, the children, aware of the severity of the situation, felt unable to indulge in their usual games and charades.

"We can listen to what the adults are discussing," Sadhana suggested.

When they overheard phrases and words like the Bay of Pigs, Fidel Castro, Cuba, Kennedy, Khrushchev, arms race, they completely lost the plot. Bored, they resumed their own entertainment. After all, there was not enough time left, though no one seemed to know exactly when the world would end.

When the world did not end and the promise of a normal life appeared as a rainbow, Asha asked Sadhana about the Forbidden Fruit in the Forbidden City. Sadhana laughed, mentioning something about how curiosity killed the cat. Asha was not amused. "What does it have to do with cats?" she snapped. But she could no longer look at cats without wondering how many died of curiosity. Asha despaired of her limited knowledge about most things. As cats have nine lives, even more than Brahmins, who are born twice as

human beings, she hoped she might learn more in her life. 1
of knowledge made her *curiouser and curiouser. If I am going to die of
curiosity*, she thought, *perhaps I should be as curious as a cat.*

She would not forget the day; in fact, it was the day after the day
the world did not come to an end, when one of the peons reported
to Aja, "Sahib, a sahib owl is in your kutcherry!"

A large snow-white owl had perched itself on the highest shelf
in Aja's office. Asha had never seen a creature as beautiful. The owl
stayed there all day. Aja used the drawing room for his kutcherry.
The children took turns guarding the bird. When it was her turn,
Asha swore she had a vision of the Goddess Lakshmi warning her
against distrust. The next morning their visitor had disappeared as
mysteriously as it had appeared. The same day they all returned to
their respective homes.

⚬⚬⚬

Three months later her younger brother Vijay was born. Asha
was split in her loyalty—part of her was pleased she had a younger
sibling to play with. Yet she envied the attention lavished on him.
It was terribly confusing and upsetting when she heard her aunts
talking excitedly about her mother having another baby not long
after the arrival of Vijay! She was worried how many more might
arrive as Karuna's stomach began to grow all over again. Nine
months later, Vivek was born.

Asha's life changed irrevocably after the birth of the third son.
When Vijay was born, she lost her special status as the youngest.
When Vivek arrived, she became a surrogate mother to her younger
brothers without accruing any of the benefits. A child herself, she
was no longer treated as one. She was the *older* sister, expected
to be responsible, look after her *younger* brothers, and help her
mother with the household chores. Asha was no longer the centre
of anyone's world. She had not changed, yet everything around
her had.

Karuna, too, was getting to grips with the changes in her life. Asha, being a good helper, got landed with more and more chores, but felt she received less and less of her mother's affection. Love may be limitless, human beings are not. Karuna may have had enough love for all her children, but she did not demonstrate it adequately to Asha. On the contrary, Karuna's need to ensure Asha was well-trained for her life to come meant that whenever she forgot to do something, or failed to do it to Karuna's satisfaction, Asha's lapses were recounted in minute detail before the family elders. Karuna knew that however special her daughter may be, she was still a girl, expected to have an arranged marriage and look after her family and home. She only wanted the very best for her daughter.

Asha could not understand why she was being treated differently. The distinction the family made between her and Vikram palpably grated on her sense of fairness. If her parents had treated her and Vikram differently, she had not noticed it before. Perhaps she had received enough attention not to worry about it. But when the two younger sons arrived, the family dynamics changed completely. More was always expected of her, but she received less and less in return. That was how it appeared to Asha. The injustice of it all made her desperately unhappy.

It was certainly a time of change for all the family. Aditya needed to supplement his income, and he took on more responsibilities at the college. He, too, had less time for his family, and that included his daughter. They moved to a smaller but more modern house with electricity in the college campus. Asha lost her best friend, her stone, in the move. Barely had they settled in their new home, Vikram and Asha moved to Rutherford School, which was at the opposite end of town. Then Abhay got married, so did Madhav— just about everything she was accustomed to altered. Asha tried hard to change as fast as she could, but somehow the more she tried, the less she succeeded. She was back to running in the same spot, scared out of her wits of all the changes that were buffeting her. But this time she was on her own; there was no one to comfort her and tell her all would be well.

Then one day news arrived that Subhalakshmi had died. Her jejema went to bed the previous night and never woke up. She did not look young, nor did she appear old. She lay in bed, eyes closed, seemingly fast asleep. As far as Asha could recall, her grandmother looked exactly the same as she always did. Asha wondered if her grandmother's appearance might change after her soul left for heaven, where her atma would rest in peace. It was not possible to ask anyone. Everyone—especially her parents, her jejebapa, Vishu uncle, Abhay uncle and all her aunts—was weeping uncontrollably. Their tears conveyed to Asha the gravity of the situation. Something terrible had happened. Even Vikram was crying. She began to weep, and once she started, she could not stop. Too much had changed recently, and she did not understand why.

CHAPTER 6

Rutherford School was a good forty minutes' ride by rickshaw. Raghu, who had peddled the Guru family all over the city in all kinds of weather and shared all sorts of experiences with them, was by then part of the family. Vikram and Asha called him Raghu kaku. He was accustomed to every mood, whim, wish and command of the children. When they quarrelled, he reprimanded them as he would his own.

On the first day, on their way back from school, Vikram and Asha started to hurl abuse at each other. Each word was delivered with a kick or closed-fist punch.

"Rakhyasuni," said Vikram.

"Asura," Asha retorted.

"Leper."

"Beggar."

"Choroni."

"Daku."

"Namak-haram!"

"Lafanga!"

"You ignominious cretin," growled Vikram.

"You pathetic liar," Asha screamed.

"Wait till I report you both," Raghu cried, stopping the rickshaw, unable to comprehend what had triggered such an outburst. Turning to face them, he said, "What will Karuna ma and Aditya babu think? They send you to good schools, love you, provide for you, yet you behave like this!"

Realising they had stepped beyond an invisible boundary, Asha and Vikram cried in unison, "Sorry, Raghu kaku, we'll be good. Promise."

"We were just joking," Vikram added.

After a moment's silence, Asha said calmly, "Let's play stories. Once upon a time there was a king. Your turn…"

"The king wanted to know how his subjects lived, what they thought of him. So he went disguised for a walk in the city," said Vikram.

"You added two sentences," Asha protested. "I have to add two sentences now. He saw beggars and ill people. When he came home, he sent food and money for the beggars, and he built a hospital for the ill people."

"The next day he went to a football match," said Vikram, dismissing his urge to complain that she, too, had exceeded her limit by making her sentences too long.

"'I didn't know my kingdom was so poor,' cried the king, 'so many people running after one ball!' He asked his minister to give each player a football," she said.

"Why can you add two or three sentences, but I can't? The next day the king went disguised to a school," Vikram said. "Just one sentence, remember!"

Asha paused for a moment and then said, "A badmash came and hit him hard on his chest. The king's soldiers pursued the man and put him in jail, to teach other badmashes like him not to attack innocent people."

"It is impossible to play any game with you," Vikram complained. "You keep breaking all the rules, adding as many sentences as you please. I can't play with you."

"How can you say so? I only added two sentences," Asha pleaded.

"We're almost home," he said. "I need some peace and quiet to think!"

"And...?" She was waiting for him to complete the sentence. It's not as if Asha did not want games or stories to end, she was simply sceptical of ones that ended with and-so-they-lived-happily-ever-after. Even in her own not-very-long life, she knew that just as night follows day and day follows night, bad follows good and good follows bad. Nothing seemed to last forever, not even stories.

"There was a boy who had a sister who did not stop talking," Vikram said. They both laughed as Raghu brought the rickshaw to a halt in front of their house.

Karuna was at the door, waiting for them. "How was your first day in your new school? Do you like it more than the old one, Asha? What about you, Vikram?"

Vikram shrugged his shoulders. "It was all right," he mumbled.

"How did you know when we would return home?" Asha asked, surprised.

Taking her daughter in her arms, Karuna said, "Mothers know these things because they love their children and worry about them. But tell me how was school?"

"I don't know. A girl in my class wanted a strand of my hair. She said it resembled a thread of gold. Is my hair golden? When I refused to give her my hair, she offered me money. Look, she gave me two paisas for one hair!" Asha confessed.

"She bought your hair, and you sold it?" Karuna grimaced.

"I didn't want her money, promise! *She* gave it to me. Here it is; you can have it. What could I have done? She insisted, practically begged," Asha explained.

Taking the coin, Karuna said, "No more selling of hair or any other body part. If she or anyone asks for anything, say you have to talk to your mother first."

"Or to your older brother," Vikram added. "School was fine for me—no one wanted anything from me. It was pretty much as expected, really!"

Asha was no more enamoured of her new school than she was of her old one. On the contrary, after a few months, a fat slob of a bully, his face covered with pimples, began to terrorise her. On one occasion while they were out in the field playing, the boy, called Jayanta, threw a cricket ball at her with a ferocity that astonished her. It hit Asha hard on her chest. She experienced a momentary blackout. She knew it was no accident, but had no idea what he was capable of until another day when he cornered her and gave her a slap that made everything around her go dark again. Still Asha did not report the assault to anyone, not even to Vikram, who failed to notice the redness of her right cheek.

The next morning Karuna informed Aditya, "Asha's face looks red and swollen. Hope she isn't coming down with mumps or something."

"Does she have a fever?" Aditya asked.

"No," replied Karuna. She asked Asha if she felt well enough to go to school.

Asha nodded. Her face was still sore when she returned from school, but the redness and swelling was barely visible.

Usually, Asha foiled Jayanta's attacks by surrounding herself with her classmates, always moving with the crowd. If she was on her own, she ran as fast as her legs would carry her the moment she saw him. She turned into an excellent short-distance sprinter and even excelled at a game the older boys played in school.

There was a moat—now dry and overgrown with shrubs, wild grass, and filled with rubbish—right at the edge of the playing field. During the morning break, it was a common sight to see the boys charging across the field like a herd of bison. The challenge, however, was to jump across the moat. Most of the boys stopped before they fell into the moat. Asha along with a few of the older boys found themselves safely on the other side. The first time she jumped it was by accident. She was running at such speed she could not stop herself, the momentum carried her across. Thinking she would land inside the moat, Asha closed her eyes. Finding herself on the other side, albeit squatting precariously near the edge, she was exhilarated as if she had been flying. The boys on either side of the moat gave her a standing ovation, except for Jayanta who glowered at her. Despite such a public display of physical fitness, Asha was far from being strong, and she had no stamina.

One morning, on her way to general assembly a little later than usual, as Raghu had overslept, she found herself alone in a deserted corridor with Jayanta approaching from the opposite direction with a confident grin on his face. Before Asha could retreat, he pounced on her like a tiger descending on its prey. When Asha fell, he began to kick her viciously. She curled up to save her face, chest and stomach. He kept kicking her mercilessly. She tried not to cry out loud, not wishing to give him the pleasure of knowing the excruciating pain he was inflicting on her. But she could not stop screaming at the top of her voice. Incredibly, the moment she began to scream, she could not feel the pain. "Help, help!" she yelled as loudly as she could.

As luck would have it, Vikram and his friends, Shankar and Pratap, were on their way to assembly too. Hearing a girl screaming, they ran to the rescue. Seeing it was none other than Asha, they fell upon Jayanta and gave him a sound thrashing. So upset they were at what they had witnessed, they could not stop swearing as they laid into him. They made him promise he would never touch anyone again in school.

"You'll have to deal with us," they said, panting in unison after their exertions.

"How many times has he hit you?" Vikram asked Asha, who stood there shivering with the shock of being so severely roughed up.

"This is the third time," she replied, though in reality Asha had lost count. It was perhaps the third time he had hit her hard enough to make her cry.

"I remember," Pratap said, "he hit you with that cricket ball. I did not suspect anything then and thought it was an unfortunate accident. His behaviour is appalling! We'll have to report the matter to the principal, of course."

"This is the last time you touch her or anyone else. Do you understand? Look at me," said Shankar, holding Jayanta's face firmly in the palm of his right hand.

"Let us know if he even looks at you," the three musketeers said in chorus.

Asha knew that was the end of Jayanta's bullying.

❦

On their way home from school that afternoon, Vikram asked, "Asha, why did you not say anything about that boy bullying you before?"

"I thought he would stop. The first time he beat me, I told him good boys don't go around beating up girls. Ma had told me the day before that being good, doing the right thing, is like wearing armour—if people do bad things, it will hurt them and not you. The next time he hit me, I told him that you and your friends knew about his bullying, and that you'd make mincemeat of him if he touched me again! See, that's how it turned out," Asha replied, thinking goodness works, albeit slowly.

"Bewakoof, you should have told me the moment the bullying started. Boys like Jayanta only understand one language. We could have warned him off before. You don't have to fight your battles alone," he said.

"How can I tell anyone anything when no one listens to me any more? We don't gossip, not the kind of gup-shup we used to have. You don't share any secrets with me. These days your adda is with boys. How am I the bewakoof?" she asked.

"That's not true. We came to help even without knowing it was you. Anyone would've done so," Vikram said, after giving the matter some thought.

"That's exactly what I mean! As you say, you would've done it for anyone. Did you ever ask *me* if I was being bullied in school? What do you know; you're a boy. No one bullies *you*. You did not even notice the first time he hit me—my face was red and swollen!" Asha said, with tear-filled eyes.

"What do you mean no one noticed? You didn't say anything when ma pointed out your face looked red and swollen. Give me one example when, as you claim, we did not listen to you?" Vikram asked, confident his sister would fail to cite any. Then he added as an afterthought, "By the way, boys get bullied too!"

"I can give you many examples when no one thought of me," Asha replied. "Remember the time Abhay uncle had that party at our College Square house?"

"What about it—it was years ago! Who bullied you then?" asked Vikram.

"No one bullied me, but it proves my point—no one cared enough for me then, either. You were at home, and I was at Aja's," Asha explained.

"Yes, I remember. Vishu kaku went to fetch you, but you didn't want to come," he said in a tone of voice as if to say how can you blame anyone for that?

"Vishu kaku never told me there was a big bhoji that evening for Abhay kaku. How was I to know? Kaku just said, 'Asha, do you want to stay here or come home?' Sadhana nani asked me to stay, so I did. No one told me there was a celebration that evening at home. Someone should've told me," Asha replied, crying.

"I didn't know that's what happened. Don't think ma or bapa did either. You can't blame us for what Vishu kaku did? He probably thought you'd like to stay at Aja's with Sadhana nani," Vikram explained.

"Why did you, ma or bapa not tell me about the party? How would you have felt if it had happened to you?" Asha could barely speak in between sobs.

"Now, don't cry. It must've been very hurtful. It was a lovely party. So many people were invited!" Vikram reminisced. "We all went to see *Ben-Hur* because you cried so much when you returned home the next day."

"Yes, how can I forget? It was my first film and my last," Asha reminded him. "Tell me, how many films have you seen since, and how many have I? Being a girl is a punishment, and *you* want examples. *Bekaar katha guda kahibuni*, you speak such rubbish! You will never know what it is to be a girl. You are treated preferentially just because you are a boy and the eldest. How will you know how *I* feel? On the contrary, everyone thinks I am pampered because I am the only girl! People are so..." Asha could not think of a word to describe her feelings at that precise moment.

"It can't be that bad?" Vikram observed.

"You try being a girl for some time and then tell me how it is," Asha said.

When they reached home, Vikram told his parents about the bullying, and that the principal was going to write to Jayanta's parents about it.

Asha's body was so sore that Karuna gave her a dose of Arnica. Tipping the medication into her mouth, she asked, "Why did you not tell us before, Asha?"

"I never expected him to attack me like this. I thought he would stop," Asha explained. "How can I say anything to anyone any more when no one talks to me—not you, bapa or nana. No one has the time these days; everyone is always busy."

"We'll find the time to deal with problems, but if you do not tell us, how can we know?" Aditya replied. Then he asked Karuna, "Should I take her to the hospital?"

"Bibhuti babu will be coming this evening. He is a doctor and can see her," Karuna said. "If he says we need to take her to the hospital, you can do so."

"I must talk to the principal. How come this boy has been bullying her for so long? The boy needs to be punished. How will he learn otherwise?"

"It's just like that man who attacked me in the rickshaw. And they call it eve-teasing. How ludicrous is that? Women in our society simply do not count—it's all lip service," Karuna said, sensing Asha's inability to communicate her plight.

Asha felt like saying her experience had been a lot worse than her mother's.

"It takes a long time for society to change. Unfortunately, the world is full of men and women who never seem to do the right thing," said Aditya.

On the rare occasions when Asha spent an afternoon with Devika, whose family were neighbours of the Gurus, it widened her horizons no end. But listening to the older women in Devika's family gossip about marriage and childbirth, the fate of women appeared pretty dire to Asha. The first time she heard about a young bride committing suicide because her in-laws harassed her for not bringing enough dowry, Asha was distraught. Nobody knew for sure if one of her in-laws set her on fire or if she did it herself. Asha knew about women dying in childbirth, which she thought was bad enough. But this was beyond comprehension. *How many women*, she wondered, *die for the lack of a dowry?*

Devika's father, Buddhadeb Chatterjee, a professor of philosophy at Harrison, left East Bengal at the time of India's Partition. The Chatterjee household was unusual. He had two wives and several children—their ages ranged from a daughter of three to a son in his mid-twenties. The professor sat in his armchair reading and stroking his flowing beard. Sometimes, he would sit in the veranda, staring into space. Occasionally, he scratched his beard as if it was lice-infested. When he left his beard alone and did not open his mouth, he resembled Rabindranath Tagore.

During the afternoons, Devika and Asha climbed trees in

the backyard of the Chatterjee house. They clung to the sturdy branches like lizards, with their eyes closed, licking chaat while Devika shared her endless knowledge of the world with Asha. One afternoon, sprawled on the thickest branch of the guava tree, Devika was unusually quiet, lost in her reveries. Asha did not mind the silence, but was curious to find out what was on her friend's mind. A simple way of distracting Devika was to ask a question, any question. For someone who was not terribly curious, Devika could not resist questions.

"Would you like to be a tree?" Asha was, for no particular reason, thinking of her cousin's remark recently that they had grown up like trees without needing much care or attention. Personally, she thought it was no bad thing, and fancied being among the tallest, looking at the stars.

"Of course not, why would anyone want to be a tree? Even a tree given a choice would not want to be a tree, stuck in one place!" Devika yelled back, adding, "With snot-nosed children climbing over you, breaking your branches, dogs peeing on you! Even a brick on that wall wants to be something else!"

Asha was not ready to abandon her position. "Some trees live for over a hundred years; they can renew themselves year after year. They breathe in the poison of the world and breathe out purity, oxygen. Trees are worshipped—" she said.

Interrupting her impatiently, Devika snapped, "So many trees are cut down every day—living to over a hundred! In your dreams... What use is the ability to breathe out oxygen, foxygen, if you are burnt as firewood? I'd prefer to be *free* as a bird." She pronounced free with an infinite number of *es*, her face resembling a joker's with her mouth stretched across the face.

Asha laughed as she found Devika's face quite ridiculous. "Birds are eaten all the time—by human beings, snakes. Their eggs get stolen," Asha said.

"This is boring, depressing talk. I would like to be a man, but I don't mind being a woman either. Let's talk about something different," Devika said, flipping her coin. She decided a lot of things by flipping her coin.

"What shall we talk about?" Asha asked as they both watched the coin spinning dizzyingly in mid-air. When Asha had questions that no one in her family had the time to respond to, she turned to Devika. Having heard about the bride in Calcutta committing suicide for not bringing enough dowry, Asha asked, "What is a dowry? Why do women marry and leave home?"

Devika was in her oracle mode. Besides, the coin landed on its head, which meant Devika did not have the advantage. She replied, nonchalantly, "To have children, of course. Dowry is what a girl's parents give her when she marries."

"Can't you have children without getting married? Can't you marry without dowry?" Asha asked, none too pleased at the prospect of marriage, leaving home, having children, and running the risk of dying. Mary's husband was old, though she did not die, but her son was crucified. Women did not get a good deal in life; it was self-evident. Even the mother of the son of God faced such suffering! Thankfully, the Hindu goddesses did not end up with such difficult lives.

"Maybe," Devika whispered, "there is another reason."

"What?" Asha purred with satisfaction, as if the secret of everything was finally within her reach. Also, Devika's mood appeared to have improved.

"Do you really want to know?" teased Devika.

Thinking her friend was being unnecessarily obtuse, Asha replied in Bengali to please Devika, "Of course I want to know! Do you even have to ask?"

"Come with me, then," Devika said in Bengali, sliding off the branch with the speed of a panther.

"Wait, wait," Asha cried, trying to catch up with her friend.

Asha may have been lithe, but Devika was strong. She beat everyone at kabbadi, except that one time when Asha ran like the wind breathing out fire. Asha also worried about not ripping her clothes or getting them dirty. Nor did she wish to get scratched or fall ignominiously, break her bones, go to hospital—where she might catch an infection and, God forbid, die.

By the time Asha reached the room at the far end of the house, Devika was closing the windows. Turning to Asha, she whispered, "Shut the door."

Afternoon siestas were common at Asha's home too. By the time she lay down beside Devika on the cool coir mattress, she had forgotten why they had jumped off the tree and come running into that room, which had no furniture, only an array of boxes and suitcases piled along the walls. The ceiling fan moved so imperceptibly Asha thought the wind was pushing it half-heartedly, like some disgruntled slave waving a flywhisk for his master smoking a hookah, swallowing time.

She was lost in her thoughts when Devika whispered, "Are you ready?"

Demonstrating her eternal readiness, Asha turned towards Devika, who lay beside her with her eyes closed. Noticing Devika's left hand moving gently over her crotch, Asha lay on her back and closed her eyes, unsure of what was expected of her.

"You can go back to sleep, or you can feel like a married woman," said Devika as if her eyelids were transparent and she could see Asha's every movement.

"What do you mean—feel like a married woman? Are you feeling itchy?" Asha thought the entire Chatterjee family needed a full body scrub with neem soap.

Devika heaved and sighed. "You have to find out for yourself," she gasped.

Asha touched various parts of her body, from the small hills of her breasts, the concave crater of her stomach down to the smooth, silky plains of her thighs. While stroking herself was relaxing, she did not arch over with what appeared more like pain as her friend did, writhing next to her. Asha could not help wondering what the fuss was all about as she looked at Devika, who lay there flushed, smiling.

Later that evening, helping her mother in the kitchen, Asha asked, "Ma, what is dowry, can you die if you do not have a dowry when you marry? Did you bring a large dowry with you when you married?"

"I wish I knew what goes on inside that head of yours!" Karuna said.

"They were talking today at Devika's about a young bride who was killed by her in-laws because she did not bring a big enough dowry. I don't want to be burnt alive like her. I don't want to marry." Asha's eyes were brimming with tears; she was chopping an onion.

"How can you even think of such a thing?" Karuna looked at Asha, thinking she was crying. Hugging her daughter, she said, "God willing, your husband will be good, loving and generous. Don't worry about dowry and marriage. You are far too young to think of such things."

"But you were married young," Asha reminded her mother.

"Yes, my mother died. But with God's grace, I am here for you," said Karuna.

But she was not taking any chances with Asha's future. Karuna had been working away at what she perceived as her daughter's weaknesses. Karuna knew the world was an unforgiving place, especially for women. She never applauded Asha, never said how good she was at household chores, nor did she praise her for coming first in her class. It was Asha's outspokenness, her intelligence and curiosity, qualities that were deemed undesirable in a woman, which caused concern. However, such a mindset spurred Asha to apply herself harder at activities she did not excel in.

It was not just the family that thought everything you did could be done better. Asha and Vikram had a private maths tutor who also belonged to the same school of thought—self-improvement. He told them off even after they answered correctly all the sums assigned to them overnight as homework.

"Vaat is there to be praood of?" Masterji would begin matter-of-factly, chewing his paan and taking the time to spit carefully into the bidri spittoon that was reserved for his use. "If you haad ahttempted sum moor of the haarder questeeons, aand nat gat them wrang, Iai maight haave been praoud!" Masterji's English pronunciation may have been atrocious, but he was an excellent maths teacher.

Karuna liked Masterji for his cleanliness, which she believed was next to godliness, and Aditya admired him for his sense of discipline. They both agreed what a fine teacher he was. The fact he had given the children one hundred equations to solve overnight did not elicit a smile. More was always expected. It was the sign of the times; doing one's best was taken for granted. There was no reward for doing what was expected. Unsurprisingly, on the day they heard about the assassination of President Kennedy, Masterji reminded them of what they can do for their country, not what their country can do for them.

Granted, focusing on one's duties and weaknesses was not a bad strategy in life. If you knew your weaknesses, you learned to protect yourself. Asha worked away at her weaknesses. No one taught her how to protect herself from her strengths.

It was not that her parents did not consider the wishes of their children. As all close-knit families do, they did what their parents, families and friends did—built on tradition. Asha's academic abilities did not alter their plans, it did not influence hers either. They thought it was their responsibility to give Asha the best education she needed to fulfil her ordained role in life as a wife, mother, and housekeeper. So Asha was engaged in myriad household chores, which she was expected to deliver to the best of her ability, if not to perfection. That her rotis came out in all shapes but round, or she consistently forgot to pour the tea after brewing it for four minutes in the pot, which needed to be rinsed first with hot water, were minor impediments.

The first time Asha cooked a full meal for the family was the day Karuna could not get out of bed. She woke up with excruciating stomach pains. While attending to her mother's needs and making tea for family and friends who came to see her ma, Asha managed to cook two vegetable curries. The maid helped with the washing, chopping and grinding. Vijay and Vivek appointed themselves helpers at large, as well as unofficial tasters, and declared the food was 'first class'.

They prepared the salad, helping themselves to whatever took their fancy, taking turns in grating the cucumber and carrot, chopping the tomatoes, spring onions and fresh coriander leaves, confessing that cooking was a lot of fun. After squeezing the juice out of a green lime and sprinkling some ground pepper, they invited Asha to do the honour of adding the right amount of salt. The problem arose when it was time to make the rotis. The first one came out with flying colours—it was almost round and puffed up handsomely like a balloon. Beginner's luck, there was great jubilation. Luck ran out with the second roti, it resembled a mangled star and refused to puff up. The third was a rectangle, but it was nicely bloated.

"Can I have a go?" Vijay wanted to try his hand.

Vivek could not let it pass without giving it a try. It was difficult for the young boys to will the rotis into shape.

The maid intervened. "See my rotis—how perfectly round they are!" She took a round tin container with sharp edges and pressed it on the flattened dough, leaving a perfect roti in place. They agreed it was nothing short of a miracle that rotis came out *sooo* round when their ma made them, without having to resort to any such device.

Asha was a good cook certainly for her age, but Karuna was a perfectionist. Doing one's best translated to doing everything better than you did the last time. It was all part of Asha's education—building her character. Just as Gandhi directed his wife to clean the latrines in his ashram, no work was considered menial for Asha. Servants were there to help, but Asha swept, scrubbed, wiped floors, cleaned bathrooms, washed and ironed clothes, cooked and looked after her younger brothers.

They were far from rich. How could anyone be with an academic's salary and without any other source of income? Yet Karuna ensured the family ate well—four meals a day, breakfast, lunch, tea and dinner—at least three of which were freshly cooked and served hot. She got help with the shopping, chopping, grinding. But she did all the work and took pride in looking after her family. That was the least she could do for her children, having lost her ma when she was a child.

As far as cooking was concerned, Karuna's view was, 'If you cannot cook for your family, what's the point of having a family?' It was far too important a task to leave to an outsider. 'If the cook or servant served defiled food—sneezed or coughed while cooking, God forbid if he spat on your food, or tasted it first, ignoring the rules. How would you know you were not eating aintha? You are what you eat. How can we call ourselves brahmanas if we ignore the basic principles of life and the universe?'

Just as Karuna believed it was her job to prepare the family meals, she also thought it was her job to teach her daughter everything she knew. After all, did she not have to learn everything the hard way, having lost her mother? Their father loved them and looked after them—no father could have done more. They had so many servants at home that Karuna did not have to do anything. But no one taught her how to cook. The children never had to step inside the kitchen.

When she married and her sister-in-law led her to the kitchen, leaving her there to cook, Karuna sat down on the floor and wept. She had absolutely no idea what to do, where to begin. She was not going to leave her daughter in the lurch. Karuna made a good cook of Asha and also taught her to sew, sing, be the perfect hostess, and execute household chores to perfection—making her daughter fit for a royal alliance. "You will have an arranged marriage," she said, looking at Asha with great pride and affection, as one would at one's masterpiece. "You will make a happy home for your family and teach your daughter all the things you know."

Asha's life was mapped out for her—marriage, children, looking after the family. And when she was old, she would be looked after by her family. The idea that a woman could be anything other was not worth considering unless she had the misfortune of being born so unattractive that no eligible man would have her. This worldview was not embodied in any single person; the family shared it like the tributaries of the mighty Ganges merging in a grand confluence. Home is not just bricks and mortar, it's a vision of the world, a way of living, of finding one's place in the universe.

CHAPTER 7

Asha's love affair with books began the year her parents decided it was time for her to attend St Joseph's Convent School, an educational institution for girls. Karuna wanted her daughter married at eighteen. She reckoned it was essential Asha should also be a graduate by then. Naturally, Karuna explained to Sister St Mary, headmistress of the school, with all the passion and reason she could muster, the importance of education and marriage in a woman's life.

"I was married very young," said Karuna. "It was the custom then. My mother died in childbirth; what could my father do? He had to move with his job, and the education of his daughters suffered. I am studying now, privately, of course. But with a family to look after, it is hard. There is a time for everything, as you know. I would not like my daughter to struggle like me, later in life. With the grace of God, I am alive, and so is Armita's father. We would like her to have the best possible start in life. Everything, of course, is God's will. We can only try to do our best.

"We would like our Asha, I mean Armita, to be a graduate when she marries. But we cannot delay her marriage just for the sake of education. Society will not permit us to do so. We will not be able to find a good husband for her if we delay her marriage beyond her eighteenth birthday. As God has been kind to bless our daughter with many gifts, we must play our part. We must give her the best education we can afford. One never knows what life has in store. Please understand our dilemma." Karuna appealed to Sister St Mary, who was a few years older and who sat listening intently to the long and fervent request as if hearing a confession.

Asha sat quietly while Karuna delivered her petition to Sister St Mary, who understood Karuna's dilemma and admitted Asha to Standard VII straight from Standard V. Asha, accustomed to coming first in her class at Rutherford School, lost her top ranking when she received her first quarterly report. What held her back were algebra and geometry, subjects not included in the Standard V curriculum in her previous school. They dragged Asha's overall ranking down to fifth in a class of forty-five. Surekha, who came first, got better marks in precisely those subjects.

At the end of term, the girls huddled together with their report cards and began to compare grades.

"The teachers, especially the masters, favour her," Surekha declared after scrutinising Asha's report. "Men get carried away with those attractive, doe eyes of hers. See, she's got a hundred percent in arithmetic—just because she's so beautiful."

The girls lapped up her sugar-coated bile, relishing every moment of it. There was one girl sitting in the back who did not join in the ragging. She looked at Asha as if to say, 'I wouldn't worry about this lot of nincompoops!' Later, she opened her mouth and said, "Thank God you're such a whizz-kid that you got a double promotion. We wouldn't have become classmates, otherwise. I'm Rashmi."

The two girls had connected instantly. Asha was searching for the right words when Rashmi added, "I've also heard that you, with your family, stand on your head first thing in the morning, walk on your hands, and drink water through your nose!"

As Asha's eyebrows furrowed, Rashmi winked and said, "I tell them that is exactly what we do, too. But first we come down from a spaceship where we sleep and drink our own urine!"

"They obviously don't know me well. I have so many faults they could've mentioned. That is why I never gossip. I don't seem to know the failings of others," Asha replied with a smile.

"I haven't told you some of the truly fantastic things I've heard. Beware the green-eyed monster!" Rashmi rolled her eyes round as she spoke. They both burst out laughing, and that is how their friendship began.

Seeing her school report, Asha's parents were delighted. To be placed fifth in class after her second double-promotion felt like a vindication of their decision.

"Maybe we should've requested a triple promotion—our daughter is indeed very bright!" Vishu remarked on hearing how well his niece had fared in school.

But no one asked Asha how she felt. The family had clearly not taken into account the years of training that had instilled in her the uncompromising need to succeed. Being placed fifth in class seemed like a terrible climb-down, although everyone at home applauded how well she had done. And it was definitely a first for Karuna—to acknowledge how well her daughter had done in school.

Aditya was in the porch seeing off Abhay when a lean, half-naked man with a wild look in his eyes ran past shouting, "Neula is dead; Neula is dead." As neula means mongoose in Oriya, the brothers looked at each other somewhat puzzled, but carried on with their conversation. After Abhay left, Aditya noticed the same man running back delivering the same message, except this time he came closer and said, "Neula is dead, babu. Neula is dead!"

"Which neula?" Aditya asked, wondering if the man was in full possession of his mental faculties.

"The famous neula in Dilli," he replied and kept repeating, "Neula is dead."

He kept prancing around as if he was standing on a hotplate.

"What is he saying? What does he want?" enquired Karuna when she heard the kerfuffle outside. Within moments, Vikram, Asha, Vijay and Vivek arrived.

"The famous neula—in Dilli—died," repeated the stranger.

When Karuna offered him some money, thinking he might be a beggar out of his wits, he declined and ran off crying loudly, "Neula is dead!"

"He keeps saying neula is dead, but what does that mean? Is this just some hocus-pocus, or is there something more to his words?" Aditya asked.

"He looks like a ghost, half-starved. Yet he declined food or money!" Karuna said, surprised.

"If it's someone famous, then it'll be in the news," Aditya said as he went to switch on the radio. In a few moments, the death of Jawaharlal Nehru was announced.

"How on earth did he hear of it?" both Karuna and Aditya remarked.

"How did Nehru die? Was he killed?" Asha asked.

"What a strange idea, Asha! What makes you think so?" Karuna asked.

"Ma, Gandhi was shot, so were Kennedy and Abraham Lincoln—are not all great leaders assassinated?" She could barely manage to pronounce assassinated, so caught up was she in that moment of national loss.

"Well, Nehru was not assassinated," said Aditya. He meant to add that he did not consider Nehru to be as great a leader as she seemed to think. Did he not end up agreeing to partition the country? Was he not the man carrying on with that Mountbatten woman? Did he not rule over the country when the Chinese practically invaded India? But he decided his daughter was a bit too young for such enlightenment. Forgiving her her naivety, he said, "Yes, Gandhi, Kennedy and Lincoln were all assassinated and so was Martin Luther King, and yes, great thinkers are often misunderstood—Socrates had to drink poison for holding on to his views, and Christ was crucified. But Nehru died of natural causes."

"You can read his autobiography," Karuna said.

"His letters to his daughter is better. I'll get that book for you," Aditya added.

<hr />

Before a copy of *Letters from a Father to His Daughter* arrived, one afternoon during the summer vacation when the family was having a siesta, Asha began to browse through *Pride and Prejudice*. Rashmi had given it to her, preoccupied as she was with her older brother's wedding. She had no time to read anything. Handing the book to Asha, she had observed, "Interesting title, let me know what you think?" Once Asha began to read, intrigued by the title and the first sentence, she lost track of time.

"It's half past four, Asha. Why did you not wake me up before?" a puzzled Karuna asked. Seeing Asha with a book in her hand and a surprised look on her face annoyed Karuna. "I told you to wake me up at 4pm. Reading is not going to get the housework done. It's my karma to have given birth to such an alakhani. Even the servants understand my plight better. What can I do if my daughter does not?"

Asha winced, thinking such accusations were uncalled for. "Ma, I did not realise it was half past four," she said.

When Amitava overheard his daughter-in-law complaining to her husband about Asha, he pleaded, "Asha was reading a book, and she forgot the time."

Karuna was not pleased. "Bapa," she said, "however gifted and special Asha may be, she is still a girl. And she will have an arranged marriage, look after her husband and family, and do all the things that women are expected to do. She can't lead a life of her own choosing. If she is self-willed and independent in her ways, she will suffer and be miserable all her life. I don't wish to encourage that. How will she learn to be responsible unless she starts young?"

"Karuna, your daughter is still a child. Her job is to dream, to forget the time. She will become responsible when it is time for her to be so. Be patient with her; her childish ways will not last forever," Amitava said.

Since his wife died, Amitava spent most of his time in Baripada, where he had built a house. He was born and grew up in a village not far from Baripada. Vishu and his family lived with him. He came and stayed with his eldest son when he had some work in Cuttack or Bhubaneswar. Deeply committed to intellectual pursuits himself, he did not fail to notice his granddaughter's interest in books. The previous summer on seeing her leafing through his copy of *The Bhagavad Gitā* when she was clearly too young to understand it, he had not dissuaded her from reading, nor had he admonished her for borrowing his books. When she persisted in her efforts, he presented the book to her, saying, "One day you will understand its true meaning."

Asha secretly devoured novels that summer—she lost count as she read one book after another, voracious as a caterpillar, working her way through as many as she could lay her hands on. The magical world of literature opened its doors to her. Books became her trusted friends. She had finally, quite unconsciously, replaced her stone with the written word, albeit in English. Whenever she felt dejected, she read a book. It propped up her sagging spirits.

When the new school term began, Asha started submitting short stories for her weekly assignments. Interestingly, her grades in English shot up. Getting to grips with algebra and geometry was not a major problem. During the vacation, Asha did as many sums as she could. She had not forgotten Masterji, she had learnt from him that the way to succeed at anything was by doing it—"practice makes perfect" was his motto. She was placed third in class at the end of the second term. By the end of the year, she was top of her class. Surekha never forgave Asha for usurping her position.

It was the last class for the day, moral studies, and Sister had not turned up. After patiently waiting for five minutes, the girls started gossiping. The conversation lapsed into what they wanted to be. Various options were bandied about. "I want to marry a rich man," "I want to marry an IAS," "I want to marry a tall, handsome man," "I want a big house with servants and lots of children," "I want ..."

Asha was reading *Sense and Sensibility*. The girls ganged up and demanded a confession. "What do you want, Armita?" they asked in a chorus.

She could have lied, said something to get them off her back. But Asha confessed, "I want to be a nun."

The girls roared with laughter and hooted at the idea, even Rashmi could not suppress a smile.

"You mean a devadasi? Become a nun and break the hearts of all those poor men out there?" Surekha teased the loudest.

"Why do you always rag her the most, Surekha?" Rashmi protested.

The girls suddenly turned on her. "So, tell us, Rashmi, what is *your heart's* desire? Why are *you* defending Armita? Do *you* also want to be a *nun*? You *two* would make a fine pair! Some of the priests are so handsome, aren't they? God knows what goes on between nuns and priests!"

Their hysterical laughter reverberated down the entire length of the school corridor. Sister St Mary, who was on her way back to her office from a rather stressful meeting, stepped into the class and enquired loudly, "Who said that?"

The girls fell silent and looked at each other. Sister was in no mood for fun and games, the truth came out in fragments and half-truths.

Then Sister said, "Rashmi and Armita, go home. If they repeat such deplorable behaviour in the future, let me know." Then turning to the rest of the class, she announced, "Brother John will now take your moral studies class."

Brother John was the oldest among the priests who taught at

both Rutherford and Convent schools. He had lived in India for so long he had long forgotten how he got there in the first place. The girls gasped in horror; they had never been taught by him. Brother John had a reputation for being fiercely strict, the degree of his severity hovering at the highest end of the austerity scale. He was well known for being the worst person to be saddled with for one's detention, his classes lasted significantly longer. With his long beard and fiery eyes almost piercing through his round glasses, he looked formidable in his flowing robes. The girls froze every time they saw him approaching like a tornado clearing everything along his path. Now he was coming for them.

"Do you want to come home with me to play badminton?" Rashmi asked as they left the class. Rashmi had a badminton court in her backyard.

"Not today," Asha said, not entirely sure why she said so.

"Okay, another day, your loss!" Rashmi said as she boarded the rickshaw.

When Asha reached home, finding her mother in a foul mood, she wished she had gone with Rashmi. Though that was not the sort of thing she ever did, going away with friends without asking her mother's permission first.

A harassed Karuna, who had her period, instructed Asha to wash the clothes that had been soaking all day. The maid had not come. The timings of the maids and chakara boys were complicated—they came and went as they pleased. And every day one or more members of the home-help team failed to turn up. Besides, one could not ask the gardener to wash clothes, or the maid who swept the floor and cleaned the bathrooms to chop vegetables and grind masala. The caste system was worse than trade unions. One could easily end up with a mutiny.

Karuna had also entrusted Asha with the task of looking after her younger brothers. This was like a permanent assignment when she was at home. Unable to decide which task needed to be done first, Asha yielded to her brothers' fervent pleas to take them out to play in the field located near their house. Considering Asha forgot to pour tea after brewing it for a few minutes, it was no surprise she forgot all about washing the clothes while keeping an eye on Vijay and Vivek.

When Aditya came home, Karuna complained how difficult it was to do everything—what with the maids not turning up, the servant Krushna away in his village, and she herself not well. It must have been one of those days for Aditya too. No one asked him how his day had fared.

He just said, frustrated, "Dhet, maids these days are useless. You can't depend on servants any longer—everyone is now swadhin and act as they please! No responsibility, no sense of duty."

He went to his study, left his leather buckled briefcase in its place, and got out of his suit into something more comfortable. Perhaps because he saw his daughter was looking after her two younger brothers while still wearing her school uniform, he did not have the heart to scold her for not washing the clothes.

Maybe that was exactly why Karuna was irritated. She went on about Asha's disobedience. "Why does my daughter not listen to anything I say? Why am I so unfortunate?" she complained, loud enough for everyone to hear.

Asha had just walked in, followed by Vivek and Vijay. Stung by her mother's accusations, she said, "How can you say that, ma? When you were ill, who did all the work? Even now, I am the one who helps you always."

"She answers back, has no respect for elders." Karuna sighed. "I was ill, who else would've helped me if not my daughter? I don't know what she expects. I am not yet recovered from my illness, and here she is so unsympathetic."

Aditya suddenly turned towards Asha. Slapping her on one cheek, he said, "Why can't you listen to your ma?"

Asha reeled from the blow, utterly shocked.

But that was not the end of the matter. Karuna did not end her litany of complaints. "How am I to do everything—the housework, the children, then there is this examination I have to study for. Where is the time for everything?"

Asha was trying to figure out what her mother was talking about—what illness, what exams? Then Aditya grabbed her by the shoulders with both hands, without realising how hard he was shaking her. Asha began to gasp. But what she felt inside her was significantly worse. When Aditya saw her face turning pale, it dawned on him that Asha was short of breath. Cradling her in his arms, he rocked her gently, worried sick at the hurt he had caused.

But the damage was done. When Asha recovered and began to breathe normally, unable to control her tears, howling with indignation and pain, she went to wash the wretched clothes that had caused her so much grief. She was trembling with rage, with the unfairness of it all. It was not her fault. She was always working, helping. Why not ask Vikram to help? He was never there when help was needed.

Asha locked the bathroom door, opened the tap, and as the water fell noisily in the balti, she sat on the wet floor and wept her heart out. Wishing she was never born, she cursed an unjust world. She did not understand what her mother was talking about. When she could cry no more, Asha turned to the clothes in the bucket and tried to pick out the end of what she thought was a bed sheet. But like Draupadi's sari, she could not find the other end. The piece was a double bedspread that weighed more than her. As she attempted to lift it again, Asha felt something drop inside her body, in the pelvic area. She heaved, but could not haul the mass out of the bucket onto the bathroom floor to give it a scrub. Given the unpleasant atmosphere at home, she did not think anyone would listen to her if she told them how impossibly heavy the bedspread was. Confused, tired and angry, Asha sat there sobbing until her father knocked on the door.

Aditya had meant to wash the clothes himself when Karuna first complained about the maid. He had never meant to scold or punish Asha. It was not her fault the clothes were left unwashed. He deeply regretted his actions. *Why did I lose my calm?* Aditya chided himself as he got round to the washing. Stroking his daughter's back, he said, "Asha, I am sorry. It was not your fault. I lost my temper."

Though her father had never struck her before, and nothing like that was to happen again, Asha could not help feeling abandoned by her family. Her world was transformed into a dark, lonely place. *They do not understand me; how can they find the right husband for me!* She poured out her disappointment, anger, and frustration in her diary, which she started writing around this time.

Every time the question of her marriage came up, Asha panicked that her parents would find someone unsuitable. It was evident she would have to find someone herself, someone who would love and understand her. It seemed like an impossible task; where and how would she find such a man? All she was left with was a strong faith that God would lead her to him.

As a kind of backup plan, Asha held on to a phial of mercury she found in the waste-paper basket after a chemistry class. It was a small amount, enough to cause damage if ingested. When life appeared too bleak, she would take out the glass phial from its secret place and look at it in a kind of trance. Just knowing there was a way out made her feel better. Like God, she thought. As long as there is God, love, hope—everything seemed possible.

Nobody knew about her suicidal thoughts, she did not share them with anyone—not Vikram, Sadhana, Rashmi or Devika. No one was there when those black moods visited her. The feeling would pass, and she would carry on with whatever she was doing. But loneliness kept growing inside her. Knowing she was no longer the centre of her parents' world, or of anyone else's in her family, kept gnawing away at her injured pride, feeding the emptiness inside her.

Not that Vikram had a host of friends, but as the eldest son, he had a special status. Everyone knew Aja and Karuna doted on him. While Aditya loved his daughter, he also loved his sons. But after that incident, Asha no longer felt she was the apple of her father's eye. It had been so long since Asha felt her mother loved her as much as her sons that she could not fall back on her memories. Asha yearned to be loved now.

Karuna loved her daughter, but her manner of expression was such that it got lost in translation. Perhaps she would have learnt the language of love from her mother had she not died so young. Karuna made things worse by announcing periodically that things were different for Asha because *she* was a girl, as if Asha had a choice in the matter. If Karuna was trying to explain the harsh realities of a woman's life to her daughter, she simply ended up alienating her. Not to be valued equally as her brothers was for Asha the greatest betrayal, especially as she thought that they, she and her ma, had a special bond.

Asha needed someone in her corner fighting for her, protecting her. Finding herself alone, she concluded no one cared for her. By the time she was fourteen, she had turned into a troubled and lonely teenager. Every time a sentence escaped Karuna's lips that seemed unkind or unfair to Asha, she erected another wall around her, so great was her need to be loved and appreciated. Asha did not know how many walls were needed to protect her, how much detachment was required not to be miserable. Highly sensitive, Asha was responsive to each nuance, vibration or change around her. She could sense things others missed, understood what was left unsaid. Sometimes, she would look at a family member and read their thoughts. Her intuitiveness even surprised her.

Maybe Karuna knew that her daughter knew, and punished her for the intrusion into her private grief. On their twentieth wedding anniversary, for example, the atmosphere at home was so frosty it did not require Asha's extraordinary abilities to detect the chill factor. Vikram, Vijay and Vivek made their excuses after breakfast, went out, and did not return home till dinner time. That evening when Aditya remarked, unaware that his daughter was in the adjacent room with her mother, "Today, I am really dead; my life's over," Asha looked at her ma for an explanation.

Karuna brushed her off with "Nothing. Nothing that concerns you."

It did concern Asha. Her parents' unhappiness touched them all. She needed to know why her parents were at the edge of the world, unequipped as she was to see the world through her mother's eyes. It was Karuna, crushed with the weight of her own life, who had forgotten to see the world through the eyes of her young daughter. Having been brought up in a quarantined world, Karuna thought it was the best way to bring up her own beloved daughter. Obliged to spend their time at home, the ebb and flow of feelings, of happiness as much as pain, among the various family members affected mother and daughter the most.

Asha's diary entries during that time recorded her wish never to have been born, her suffering blotting out the happiness like an eclipse of the sun. During these moments of distress, she thought her birth mother was dead, that she was adopted. Vishu used to tease her, saying they had found her abandoned in the local hospital! While Asha laughed when he joked, in her moments of quiet desperation she wondered if he spoke the truth. Her insecurities took many disguises.

Karuna and Aditya were the worst victims, as they watched each other grow into different versions of themselves. Growing apart together into strangers was heart-breaking. Like two mighty rivers, they were meandering away from each other, succumbing to forces beyond their control.

Though Asha knew of things others did not know, she knew there were many things she did not know. Life was a giant jigsaw puzzle, except most of the pieces were missing. The games got more complex as she grew older. She was always asked to wait for the answers to come to her, but no one seemed to know how long this waiting game might last.

One afternoon, she was with her cousin Sadhana at Aja's, learning how to swim. They thrashed their legs, practising to stay afloat in the river. The undercurrents felt strong; they held on to the sturdy wooden poles dug deep into the riverbed. It was not the best moment to ask, but Asha felt she could not wait a moment longer to ask her cousin about the Forbidden Fruit.

"You must wait till you marry to find out about it," said Sadhana.

Not wishing her mother and aunt, who sat chatting on the riverbank on boulders, to overhear their conversation, Asha whispered, "Why must a woman wait for everything until marriage? No wonder child marriage was common before. Think about it, if your life began with marriage and everything depended on it, would you not marry as early as possible?"

Sadhana dismissed her with a laugh. The girls in her class in school, where girls from orthodox Hindu families read the King James Version of the Bible, also seemed to know of things that remained a mystery to Asha. She loved the Bible stories but was deeply disappointed with Eve. Asha proceeded to interpret for the benefit of her cousin the significance of the Forbidden Fruit.

"Nani, you know about this business of the Forbidden Fruit in the Bible? If God asked them not to do something, why did *she* not listen? Adam, being a boy, inevitably did not know any better. But what was Eve's problem? Why eat the fruit from the tree of knowledge if God asked them not to? Why not talk to God about it? Had they eaten from the tree of life that would perhaps have been different; maybe God would not have expelled them!" Asha explained.

"I can't imagine not listening to my parents!" said Sadhana.

"I know. I try, I really do. But I also do things my own way. Perhaps that's why I get into trouble all the time?" Asha observed.

But what bothered her most about the Christian God was His powerlessness. Why did an all-powerful Being permit such injustice and suffering? What sort of a God would let his *only son* be crucified? She understood gods had to go to war to establish the reign of truth and justice. Rama had to overcome all kinds of adversity, though there was no need to treat Sita so harshly later. She got her own back, returned to her mother—Mother Earth! Arjuna went to war against his cousins. What could he do but face up to injustice, live through reversals of fortune? But humiliation and death as Jesus Christ experienced was hard to stomach.

"Can you imagine our Hindu gods being stripped naked, whipped, mocked, spat upon, dragged through the streets carrying the heavy cross on which you were to be nailed, judged by people who are not even fit to wipe your feet, and then be crucified alongside common thieves?" Asha asked, astonished, as if it was happening in front of her.

In fact, she found it curious that everything had happened long ago or would happen in some distant future. *What about now? Why are good things not happening now? Have the gods abandoned us?* Asha wondered.

"Even Draupadi was rescued from abject humiliation. Our gods are there to help us in the nick of time," said Sadhana, disturbing Asha's reverie.

"Exactly!" Asha nodded, thinking they were indeed branches of the same tree. "When our parents ask us not to do something, don't we obey?"

"We do, though sometimes, I wish we didn't," said Sadhana.

"Now don't go thinking I'm a dari on which anyone can walk," Asha added defensively. "I think it's important to take everyone with you when you want things to change, you know, like a glacier moving through a mountain."

"When I am denied something on which my mind is set, I

appeal to my parents. After all, they look after me and care enough to warn me not to do something. I wait till I get their permission," Sadhana said.

It was a lesson they learnt early in life—*all good things come to those who wait*. They were good at waiting. Asha worked hard at being happy with what she had while she waited for things to change. If talking and reasoning failed, she waited for a change of heart. If everything failed, Asha did what Gandhi did—non-violent non-cooperation. The problem was time—there was never enough of it.

<hr />

Unfortunately, non-violent non-cooperation failed Asha in times of greatest need, when self-preservation demanded extraordinary presence of thought and action.

"I used to think doing one's duty and believing in God was enough," she made an undated entry in her diary. "Two things happened this summer that have shaken my firm belief. The first incident was in Chandipur. The beach stretched for miles when the tide went out as if the sea was on holiday. Abhay kaku, Vikram nana and I were walking towards the sunset, holding hands. I felt safe in the middle. The wet beach caught the sunset as if sky and earth were playing Holi.

"Then we heard bapa and Vishu kaku screaming, 'Come back; run back.' I did not know the sea was such a fast sprinter. It came rushing towards us, rising above us. However fast we ran, we could not keep pace with the waves that started playing with us—first tickling our feet and then pouncing from above. One huge wave split us like a giant chopping axe. I was thrown off course, saw water everywhere, could barely breathe, nor could I swim. I was drowning, thought I was going to die.

"I saw kaku swimming towards me. I stretched out my hand. He caught hold of me and lifted me above the water. I was gasping for air, choking. Nana was not far from us, bobbing up and down in neck-deep water. Exhausted, I could not wrestle with the powerful waves. The next wave swept the three of us back to the beach. I felt the strong arms of the waves carrying us. We held on to each other's hands for support. Nature is powerful, worthy of our worship.

"The second incident was in Puri at Ratha Jatra, where something equally terrifying happened. Bapa, ma, nana and I had gone with Aja. Vivek and Vijay stayed with Abhay kaku. It was meant to be a birthday treat for me. As Collector of the State, Aja was on duty. We were taken for darshan by one of the high priests. Jejebapa and Vishu kaku also joined us for the darshan. Ma was holding my left hand and bapa my right as we headed for Jagannath's chariot. Suddenly, we heard shouting; some goondas started fighting. In the ensuing melee and stampede, I was separated from both bapa and ma.

"Then someone pulled me from behind. I thought it was Vikram nana trying to protect me from the marauding crowd. But when I saw two black, hairy hands around me, I yelled while wrestling to be free. Luckily, my screams drew the attention of the pilgrims. Vishu kaku also heard me. Thank God, being so tall, he towered above the crowd, spotted me immediately, and he called for help. His voice was like a loudspeaker. 'Catch that badmash. He is kidnapping our daughter!'

"I did not realise I was being kidnapped. I kept on screaming and kicking. Before kaku or bapa could rescue me, the thug, looking more ferocious than Mahisasura, was pinned securely to the ground by the pilgrims. By the time the police arrived, the pilgrims had administered their own justice—beaten up the kidnapper. Aja had to intervene and explain to the pilgrims that both God and the law will punish him and his gang. I could not help thinking of the beggar children in the streets. How many of them were kidnapped? Would I have suffered the same fate?

"During the brief darshan, I asked Jagannath why bad things happen, why He let them happen. I don't think He heard me. If He did and replied, why could I not hear Him? Have I lost my ability to listen to God? The temple was very noisy—not a calm and quiet place like the tulsi altar at home. Perhaps I was not paying attention. Why does God not talk to us the way we talk to Him?

"My body kept trembling for the rest of the day. I could not sleep that night as I kept seeing the face of that badmash man when I closed my eyes."

CHAPTER 8

The collective sex education that Asha received—from the biology classes at school, gossip among her classmates, hints, innuendoes and more from her cousins—had provided her with a rudimentary idea of reproduction. She had progressed far enough in configuring that babies arrived after marriage. Her classmates referred to the sexual act graphically enough, but Asha was not entirely sure what it translated to. Until one morning she noticed a bull in the field outside their house chasing a cow and then mounting her. Asha stood there, shocked, thinking the poor cow could not possibly enjoy such an assault.

At home they had a cow whose milk was so thick and creamy that Karuna had to add water to make it digestible. Asha could not imagine their cow, the meek and docile Dhira, having such an unpleasant experience. Dhira smiled, or so Asha used to think when younger, every time she offered her pails full of her favourite bites—banana skins and peeled skins of fresh vegetables and fruits that were discarded in the kitchen. Asha had seen Dhira giving birth, licking the calf, urging her newborn to suck milk from her udders. Asha marvelled how quickly animals could grow up.

She had also heard of girls having sex before marriage, thus ruining their chances of finding a decent husband. "It's like putting the cart before the horse," Surekha had pointed out. "Why place yourself at the mercy of circumstances beyond your control, especially when there is a high probability of getting pregnant, which is of course the worst possible outcome for an unmarried woman?"

But no one had prepared Asha for menstruation. She had not failed to notice her mother hanging out pieces of cloth, segregated from the rest of the clothes, on the line in the inner courtyard. Asha thought of them as a caste apart, the untouchables, but could not quite place them in the grand scheme of things, nor decipher where they fitted in the manifold applications of linen in the efficient management of the household. It was not the type of cloth used to dry dishes or to clean shelves. It was certainly not chamois that one used to clean and polish glass, silver, brass and other delicate surfaces. Nor was it the kind used to wipe floors. There was never enough time to solve that puzzle.

One afternoon she picked up all the clothes hanging out on the line as an almighty storm was gathering in the horizon. Karuna took the pile from her hands with unseemly haste, and separated those pieces.

"What are they for?" asked Asha.

"Not now," replied Karuna.

Asha assumed it was the imminent storm that prevented further discussion. Mother and daughter flew in different directions to bolt all the windows and doors of the house. The servants were not yet back from their afternoon expeditions into town.

The next day, while Karuna was taking her bath, Asha noticed the water rushing out of the bathroom looked rusty as if it had seeped through the iron-rich, fertile soil of Orissa. She never gave it much thought; dyes in India were constantly running. Her mother looked normal, albeit somewhat flushed, when she emerged from her ablutions. But that is how she normally looked when she appeared after her bath carrying a bucket full of hand-washed clothes.

As Asha helped her mother to hang the items out in the sun, the smell of the water trickling out of the open drain reminded her of fish left to dry in the sun, or of slightly rotten eggs. So many things had the smell of decaying meat, dried fish or stinking garlic, it was difficult even for all-knowing Asha to guess.

Seeing her mother clip those unfamiliar pieces of cloth on the line, Asha took the opportunity to ask. "Ma, what are they for?"

"Later, we'll have a chat later," said Karuna. But later never materialised.

***

The morning she woke up and discovered her pee had turned red, Asha never thought anything was seriously wrong. *Perhaps I ate something?* was her initial reaction. But she could not fathom what it might have been. When she wiped herself and saw red, she concluded she had hurt herself. *How on earth did I do that in my sleep?* Asha wondered, feeling no aches or pains, just a slight feverishness. Her body felt warm as if she'd been out in the sun, although she was safely tucked in bed all night. The more she wiped, the more rust-coloured stains appeared.

Luckily, it was the last day of the cultural tour. The Kala Mandap, or performing arts institute where Asha went to learn Indian classical vocal music, had been selected to participate in a major cultural festival in Orissa. Her parents, needless to mention, did not want her to go. As it happened, Ava, the daughter of Aditya's youngest sister, was part of this troupe. And Nirmal, the husband of Jayasree, the eldest of Aditya's three sisters, was in charge of the cultural delegation. Nirmal was also a trustee of the institution, and it was his turn to escort the artistes on tour. He reasoned with Aditya and Karuna to let Asha go. After all, she was well chaperoned.

Though Asha attended the institute to train as a singer, she was also part of the dance delegation. In fact, she was one of the lead dancers in the Karama dance, a tribal dance performed to worship the God of Fate. As she spent a fair bit of time sitting in the dance class, after her singing lessons were done, waiting to be given a lift home by the institute's rickshaw-wallah, Asha was familiar with the dance routines. At home, she practised the dance movements as assiduously as the classical ragas. Secretly she yearned to be a dancer, but her family would have none of it. Girls from respectable families did not give dance performances in public.

Saswati and Karuna were both good singers. Madhav played the sarangi. Saswati even employed professional musicians who gave her lessons at home. They had musical soirees, inviting the men in the family to join them. But it was strictly a celebration with family and close friends in the privacy of their home. To go out and dance or sing on a stage in public, being ogled at by men who were not part of your family, was beyond contemplation. So, when offered a lead role, albeit in a folk dance, with established dancers in the school, Asha's joy knew no bounds.

The night before there had been a lot of teasing and joking among the girls. Asha never understood the half of it. Ava, who was sharing the bed with another girl, laughed so much she wet herself. Asha was pleased her cousin was not sleeping in her bed at the time. Though curious about the cause of their collective mirth, a tired Asha fell asleep amid the hullabaloo. When she woke up the next morning and her body ached all over, she attributed it to the uncomfortable beds. Rourkela was also colder than Cuttack, being higher in altitude and further away from the coast. *Maybe I caught a chill having kicked off my blanket while I slept, or it could be all that vigorous dancing?* Asha wondered.

When the steady trickle of blood did not stop by lunchtime, she was concerned. It felt like the magical Blood of India. She kept hoping the bleeding would stop, but, like P.C. Sorcar's Water of India, the blood kept appearing. Asha had not forgotten the occasion when her parents had taken her to a performance by the famous magician. To a five-year-old, his illusions appeared more than fantastic. He placed an empty jug on a table, and every few moments poured water from it—the water accumulating in the jug as if by magic. He kept repeating that process, and each time he emptied the jug, he called it the 'Water of India!'

Asha, too, went to the toilet every half hour to wipe herself. There was no toilet paper, of course—lucky if there was a supply of water. She used the two large cotton handkerchiefs she had with her and then started to wipe herself with her slip. She wore a cream, silk salwar kameez suit with a cotton slip beneath. By the end of the morning she had soiled the entire lower portion of the slip. Thankfully, the silk dress did not absorb the blood from the cotton lining, leaving no telltale signs. A casual observer would never have guessed her plight.

When the bleeding did not stop, she worried if it might go on for the rest of her life. Finally, it dawned on her she was now a *real* woman. *Is this what it feels like to be one—utterly disconsolate?* Asha could not contain her disappointment.

Unable to deal with the matter on her own any longer, she confided in her cousin. "Avani, I am bleeding down there. It doesn't stop," she confessed.

"You mean you've just had your first period?" Ava squealed. She normally spoke in a high-pitched voice. This was like broadcasting to the world. Ava was so thrilled, she embraced her cousin and informed the girls in the dormitory, "Asha is now one of us. We can share all our jokes with her!"

Wondering what the girls were laughing about the night before, it dawned on Asha that all the girls there had already experienced *It!* Standing in a circle around her, they sympathized with her and warned her that life's problems had just begun. Childhood was lost forever! Kissing, embracing and congratulating her, they enlightened Asha with what they called 'the facts of life'.

"You can get pregnant if a man just looks at you," one of them teased, eyeing Asha lustfully, imitating a man's lascivious gaze. Everyone giggled.

Her cousin Ava handed her a piece of cloth that resembled

the ones Asha had seen her mother hang out to dry. Ava took an oblong pad of cotton from her bag, wrapped the cloth around it and proceeded to demonstrate how to wear it.

"I've seen it all," Ava said when Asha resisted. "This will take care of you till we reach home. Don't run around or go on the swings. Eat something. You can have a cup of tea, now that you *are* a grown-up."

Ava gave her cousin a hug and pinched her cheek with great pride and affection. Asha winced.

Rita, an accomplished dancer, tall and slender, brought Asha delicious samosas and masala chai. While Asha ate the samosas and drank the tea, Rita kept stroking the small of her back, giving her a gentle massage. Walking with a pad between her legs reminded Asha of penguins. *Even penguins look more elegant*, she thought, convinced the pad would slip and fall, embarrassing her in front of everyone. She waddled around unsteadily, covering short distances.

In the bus Asha was offered a seat, right in the front, thanks to her travel sickness. But she slept through the entire journey, waking up only when they reached Cuttack. Ava decided it was her duty to tell her aunt about Asha's rite of passage.

Asha did not *feel* any different—except for the next few days blood continued to trickle out of her vagina, and the indefinable pain in the small of her back persisted.

Karuna still had no idea how to explain to her daughter the intricacies of sex. She sent Asha off to bed with a hot water bottle. "Tomorrow, we'll talk about bras," she said, tucking the mosquito net under the mattress.

After officially becoming a woman, Asha found herself even more vexed about the question of marriage. But she felt she had no choice but to wait for her destiny to manifest itself, for the 'right' man to appear. She never had any great expectations or grand plan, only make-believe ones. Her parents did the real planning, though life's propensity to alter their plans was not lost on her. As she interpreted her place in the world, Asha altered her parents' plan marginally—no grand revolution or declaration of independence, just a marginal amendment. Asha subscribed to the overarching idea of marriage and family, only not an 'arranged' one. She wanted to choose her partner, a swayamvara. Marriages were traditionally arranged, but a girl 'falling in love' and marrying was not unheard of. Besides, Jane Austen was filling her head with unrealistic notions of romance, love and marriage.

During family discussions about marriage, mostly of her cousins, Asha's marriage, though unmentioned, loomed like a ghostly presence in the background. Then one evening, Ava's parents arrived with their two daughters. Ava was to be introduced to a prospective match, who also arrived with his family. There were six of them—the nondescript groom-to-be, his short and plump sister, and their not-tall, not-short, not-fat, not-thin parents. Then there was a younger brother, who did not look like he belonged to the family as he was quite tall and slim, and an uncle who also did not look like an uncle at all. "Are they all really related?" the girls asked each other.

"So good looking—the younger brother and that other man, isn't he the uncle?" asked Rashmi, who was spying through the window with Asha and Ava's younger sister, hiding behind the thick chintz curtains.

They had received strict instructions not to show their faces in the drawing room. "Your turn will come," Ava's mother said. "I trust the three of you, *Teen Devian*, won't make an appearance today. They're coming to see Ava. We've been given this opportunity after a lot of puja. God is kind. Their horoscopes match; the family belongs to the right gotra. We can only pray they will choose our Ava."

The boy's family did not explicitly turn down the vivacious Ava on account of the lack of a sizeable dowry. They left without making a commitment, which spoke louder than words.

Later, Asha heard her aunt say, "After all, the boy is an IAS officer. They can get as much of a dowry as they want. Our dowry is our daughter."

The acceptance and resignation in her voice upset Asha.

"How can that be fair? I'm not going through this tamasha; it's worse than an auction," Asha complained bitterly.

"How will you get married to an Indian Administrative Services' officer without such a farce?" Rashmi remarked, adding that one of her cousins had married an IAS who was noticeably shorter than her. "He's not as bright as his wife, either."

"Swayamvara and no dowry, am I worse than the man I'll marry? Why does the boy not give the girl a dowry? What's so special about the Indian Adulterated Service? I'd pass if I sat for the IAS," Asha said.

"Not just pass, I'm sure you'd pass with flying colours. Why don't you become an IAS officer yourself and demand a dowry? In some parts of India, the girl's family receive a dowry," Rashmi pointed out. After a brief pause, she asked, "But what is gotra?"

"I'm not a hundred percent sure, but I think our gotra identifies our ancestors. If two people with the same gotra marry, it's like marrying within the family—it's a bit incestuous. Better to marry someone from a different gotra. That's why marriage within the same gotra is prohibited among Hindus," explained Asha.

"But what difference does it make if people have no judgement, decency, or common sense?" said Rashmi.

"I couldn't agree more. The man I marry has to be my equal, if not better than me, in every way—how can you accept an unequal alliance? I am not settling for a short, plump, balding IAS officer with no culture, values and clearly no class! Money is not everything in life," declared the idealistic Asha.

"I agree with both of you," said Ava, who had been stunned into silence, wondering how many more rejections she would have to face. "Why would a decent man want a dowry? He's not good looking anyway," she consoled herself.

"Good riddance!" Rashmi chipped in.

They embraced Ava and consoled her, saying good men were hard to find, but not impossible. Good things come to those who suffer and wait. After all, their mothers had married without any dowry. Where there was faith, there was hope. "The right man will come for you, just have faith," they reassured her and each other.

The day Asha heard about Devika's wedding, she felt as if the sky had fallen on her, the finger of fate had finally touched her. Until then marriage was something that happened to others who were older. She herself was not on the front line. Devika was a couple of years older, but her friend's marriage reminded Asha that she was getting closer to the firing line. She felt as if someone had arbitrarily changed the goalposts. She was simply not ready to marry, not yet anyway. She had things to do before having babies and looking after a large household.

"How long have you known?" Asha asked, concealing her sense of betrayal. "Did they come to see you? When did all this happen? Why did you not say anything before? I thought we were good friends." Questions and accusations flew out of her mouth like bees whose hive had been disturbed.

"Hold on to your horses!" cried Devika. "I knew my parents were looking, but didn't realise it all began such a long time ago!"

"What do you mean?" Asha enquired, worried her parents might have done something similar.

"You know when I went to Calcutta?" Devika began.

"Yes, yes—but that was over two years ago, almost three now. You said some older man was interested in you. I thought that had blown over!" Asha interrupted her.

"That's what I thought, too! He saw me at the wedding; nothing had been arranged previously. He was a guest, like us. Then he approached my parents. As he is a bit older and was going away to study in America, my parents were not sure what to do. They told him I was too young to marry. He came back recently, said he had good prospects now in America, and wants to marry me without a dowry. Everybody was so pleased that my parents agreed. Such a good match, they said." Devika was practically in tears by the time she finished.

"Are *you* not happy, then?" Asha asked.

"I don't know. Sometimes I feel excited, at other times I worry. Going abroad with a man I don't know. What if things don't work out? Also he is older than I expected." Devika tried to smile, trying to see the bright side of things.

"He's been interested in you all these years," Asha reminded her. "Surely, that's a good thing? How much older is he?"

"He's almost twelve years older, but he doesn't look his age," said Devika.

"There you go. You've answered your own question. If he treats you kindly and loves you—that's ultimately what matters, eh?" Asha said, consoling her friend.

But she couldn't help wondering how she would feel if her parents found someone twelve years her senior. Remembering that her father was also twelve years older than her mother, she wondered if there was something more to that number? *Did Christ not have twelve disciples, are there not twelve signs of the zodiac, not to mention twelve months in a year?* Asha thought.

"I will not be able to see my family and friends," Devika said.

"Be realistic, we haven't seen each other recently, have we? That's life. We can always write to each other. But I think you'll get busy with your new life, your family, and forget your friends!" Asha teased.

On the night of Devika's wedding, lying in bed, Asha had no difficulty imagining her own wedding. She had attended many and played major supporting roles in several. She had been the official make-up artist, preparing her cousins, brides-to-be, for the ceremony. Asha applied kohl to their eyes, painted nails and decorated their feet, though traditionally a lady was hired for the pedicure, to apply nail polish and the vermilion-coloured paint along the edges of the feet. Asha hennaed hands and chignoned hair, adorning it with delicate braids of jasmine. She went shopping with her aunts and cousins for jewellery, saris, and the bridal trousseau. Asha had picked up invaluable experience through such an extended apprenticeship.

Late that night in bed, she could almost hear the music of shehnai and sarangi, tabla and sitar greeting the guests at her own wedding. Hundreds arrived through grand floral gates with WELCOME neon signs flashing on the arch above, decorated with flowers and lanterns, adorned with tiny, multicoloured electric bulbs wrapped around the borders of bougainvillea bushes, rose shrubs, and hibiscus trees. Exotic lampshades from Pipli swung from palm trees resembling tall, turbaned waiters in the silhouette of the night. The shamiana was heady with the perfume of rajnigandha, lilies and jasmine. She imagined herself sitting on a mandap decorated with traditional artwork, elegantly draped in a red Benarasi silk sari embroidered with gold thread, glittering with ornaments from head to toe, looking breathtakingly beautiful.

The guests, arriving in their finest attire, were received by her father in the finest cotton dhoti and a silk Punjabi top, and her mother in a shimmering silk sari the colour of a peacock's throat, with an ornate, embroidered border. Asha never completed this scene, especially the image of the man she was to marry. Sometimes, she imagined him carrying her off on a horse like Prithviraj. At other times, he came riding an elephant. Though in Orissa, the groom traditionally arrived in a car, the staid-looking Ambassador, manufactured by the Hindustan Motor Company. As long as the groom was tall, slim, handsome, and passionately in love with her, Asha did not have an image in her mind of what his face looked like. Driven to near ecstasy at this point in her fantasies, she would heave and climax with pleasure.

Having lost her mother at an early age, Karuna grew up more or less a novice in the elaborate religious rituals observed by women in traditional Hindu families. Her father, a deeply spiritual man, did not believe in such practices. Karuna learnt such ceremonies after her marriage. Karuna's mother-in-law, named after the Goddess Lakshmi, was also the reason why Karuna celebrated Lakshmi Puja, offering prayers and inviting the goddess into her heart, not just her home. It was the time for cleansing both home and heart, and opening them up to the service of Lakshmi. She was not only the Goddess of wealth, Lakshmi was the Supreme Goddess.

It was also the time when Karuna's skill in the intricate calligraphic art of chitta, which involved squatting or kneeling on the floor and using the tips of the fingers as a brush and applying rice paste as paint, was brilliantly displayed. When dry, the whiteness of the rice paste stood out on the floor. Karuna scattered marigold petals on the decorations before going to bed. In the morning, Asha would skip and dance from one chitta to another, admiring the previous night's artwork, inhaling the fragrance of marigold petals, golden as the morning sunlight that had woken her.

Ever since Asha could squat on her haunches and draw a straight line with her fingers, she took pride in joining her mother every Thursday night during the month of Kartika, decorating the house with intricate floral patterns. She followed every movement of Karuna's hand, the way her mother painted the Goddess's feet, balanced on Hindu swastikas, at all the entrances. Each room had several entrances, and Lakshmi's feet appeared at each doorway. It would be unthinkable if Lakshmi arrived at one door and found no welcome there!

Now that Asha was a woman in her own right and had years of experience drawing Lakshmi's feet, mother and daughter were immersed in applying chitta. They could hear refrains of Oriya bhajans wafting from their neighbour's house. Aditya was inside supervising the homework of his two younger sons. Vikram, too, was absorbed in his studies. The Guru home was a hive of mental activity. Apart from the younger boys periodically asking their father for help with their homework, everyone was engrossed in their own work. Time passed as unobtrusively as the sky that watched over them, in meditative silence.

Then from nowhere without any notice, Vishu vroomed-vroomed in on his motorbike. As he roared to a standstill and entered the house, his hands laden with Indian cakes and gifts, he whispered, "Why is everyone so quiet? What's the matter?"

A surprised Karuna said, "I didn't know you were coming. What do you mean everyone is so quiet? What else did you expect? We don't normally sing and dance, do we? Let me complete this chitta; I'll make tea and also create some noise for you!"

"I had no idea I was coming; how could I let you know? Carry on with your chitta. I need a wash first. You have no idea what a haven of peace this home of yours is!" Vishu said as he went in carrying his bags. He was back within minutes, and seeing them still engrossed in their artwork, he joined in.

Having completed decorating the inside of the house, mother and daughter were outside painting the porch and entrance. The lights were on; they needed to see what they were doing. So could every passer-by from the street.

Turning to Vishu, Karuna said, "What will the neighbours think? Please don't apply chitta. Keep us company while we complete this; then we can all go in."

Vishu disappeared without saying a word. They thought he went in to make himself a cup of tea. He was quite adept in the kitchen. The journey was a good six to seven hours, though he was well known for driving his motorbike at around 90mph, regardless of potholes, the terrible condition of the roads, and the sclerotic traffic. Moments later he appeared, but this time he had one of Karuna's saris draped over his trouser and shirt. He squatted with his back to the road, the anchal of the sari covering his head like a bride's, and carried on with his handiwork.

"Bohu, shall I paint one here?" asked Vishu, pointing to a blank spot.

Bohu means bride; it also translates to daughter-in-law. Karuna came as a bride to her in-laws' and the appellation stuck. Her in-laws called her 'bohu'.

On seeing Vishu in one of her saris, Karuna said, convulsing with laughter, "What are you wearing? See, now I can't keep my hands steady, nor complete the rest of the chitta."

Vishu ignored her comments and continued with his floral and paisley patterns that came out better than Asha's.

The house was a five-minute walk from the new men's hostel, where Aditya served as the warden. The traffic on the circular road inside the campus consisted of students, most of whom thought they were in love with Asha. She was the cynosure of all eyes. Some of these young men felt compelled to sing their appreciation aloud if they saw her as they cycled by. Sometimes they sang even when they could not see her—thinking that, like God, she could hear their hearts' prayer.

They sang out lines from Hindi films—*Choundvi ka chand ho, khula asaman ho, jo bhi ho tum khuda ki kasam, lajavab ho...; Roop tera mastana, pyar mera diwana...; Tumse achcha kaun hai...; Meri sapno ki rani kab aayegi tu...*—praising her many worthy attributes and highlighting their devotion to her. There was no shortage of such romance; each film enriched the repertoire. The list of lyricists who gave hope to youthful hearts was long. They had a fine measure of the Indian soul, its bottomless need for romance.

Sometimes, the students mistook Karuna for Asha. Karuna was not only a young mother, she looked considerably younger than her age. Realising their mistake, they would cycle off, hoping not to be recognized. On this occasion, the cyclist yelled, "ASHA, MY DARLING," his gaze fixed on the porch as he slowed down.

Vishu turned his head towards the cyclist, revealing not only his face but a resplendent moustache resembling that of Lord Kitchener's. Then he stood up, his full six feet and two inches of his well-built body, and marched ahead, bellowing, "What did you say, you sala, MY DARLING? What is your name, you sala, MY DARLING?" He made a dash as if giving chase, though dressed as he was he had no such plan.

The poor chap almost fell off his bike as he cycled crazily into the night, unable to figure out how he could have been so deceived. Karuna and Asha could not stop laughing. They laughed so much the rest of the family came to investigate the matter. On seeing Vishu draped in a sari, the entire family was in stitches.

CHAPTER 9

By the time Asha was in her penultimate year in school, she had fallen into the habit of staying up late after the family retired for the day. Studying was what the family thought she was doing. For Asha, it was precious time to think, dream—be herself. She never seemed to have enough time or space. The presence of others disturbed her world, even when they were not physically present. Her need to be loved and appreciated grew stronger as she got older. As no one seemed to understand her, she settled for the next best thing—she tried to understand herself. *Did the ancient texts not recommend 'know thyself' as the path to enlightenment and happiness?* She reasoned, not knowing where exactly to begin.

It was another hot and sultry summer. The windows were open, but the curtains were drawn. Asha was revising for her physics exam, her favourite subject, when she heard footsteps outside. A piece of folded A4 was carefully dropped in; the curtain did not stir. She sat frozen in her chair until she heard the footsteps receding. Finally, she plucked up the courage to approach the window. While her heart was pounding furiously, she drew in the shutters without lifting the curtain, and managed to lock the window. Then she opened the A4; it was a love letter.

She had so many admirers it was difficult for her to guess who the author might be of that particular epistle. The suitor confessed how besotted he was with her, and went on to add how a single look of hers left him devastated, how her fair and glowing skin and her black, lustrous hair drove him to imagine what heaven would be like, how with her by his side he could change the world, even change himself.

The following night she received another note apologising for perhaps frightening her the night before, but not for the flickering hope a drowning man may hold on to of being rescued, of winning her love. These letters, praising her beauty and expressing his deep passion and dedication to her, arrived every other night. So scared was Asha that the letters might fall into the wrong hands, she started to read late most nights with the window open. Which, in turn, may have sent out the wrong message, as every letter sounded more fervent than the one before.

Unable to deal with the matter by herself any longer, Asha confessed to Rashmi about the billets-doux saga. Rashmi resolved to find out who the Majnoo might be and arranged to sleep over one night. Serendipitously, a letter was dropped in that night. Rashmi lifted the curtain with the greeting, *"Pyar kiya to darna kya?"* Astonished to see her brother's friend, she cried, "Prashant bhai, what on earth are *you* doing here?"

A male voice replied, "May I ask *you* the same question? My letter is for Asha, not *you*. Can I please talk to her?"

Seeing an embarrassed and surprised Asha shaking her head and waving her hands signalling a definitive no, Rashmi said calmly, "Prashant bhai, if Asha is willing, you can talk to her at our place sometime. But you *must* leave now. If uncle wakes up, I'll be in real trouble." Rashmi shut the window in his face.

"How do you know him? Do you know all the men in Cuttack?" a surprised Asha asked.

"Prashant bhai is a friend of my brother's. We've known his family for a long time. I had no idea *he* was sending you these letters! So what do you want to do, Leila—are you interested in Majnoo?" Rashmi winked with a mischievous smile.

"I barely know him," replied Asha.

What she did not tell Rashmi was that from the brief glimpse she had of her suitor in the dark, she was not smitten. Asha acknowledged it was an unfair decision. How could she dismiss any man on such a flimsy ground?

"No, no, no—he's not right for you. I'll let him know," Rashmi said.

"Why do you say that? You sound just like my parents. No one is good enough for me!" Asha protested.

"Too many barriers—it's not just his caste as he happens to be a Kshatriya. And his height, you are probably the same height. Or his looks—he is not handsome enough. Nor is he an IAS. I can't see your parents, or you, for that matter, choosing him. Will you go against the wishes of your family?" Rashmi asked.

"How can I? I barely know him. But what sort of a human being—"

Rashmi could not wait for Asha to finish her sentence. "Believe it or not, his older brother is also in love with a Brahmin girl. Her father has kept that poor girl under house arrest. Prashant bhai's parents are distraught. But what can they do? Their son is determined to marry her. And now if the younger son gets involved with you, another Brahmin girl, it will really be the talk of the town and cause a lot of grief all round. I know we all want to create a new India, but it's not as if you've fallen head over heals for him, have you? Best not to think about it. I'll talk to Prashant bhai," Rashmi concluded.

Asha was surprised. She would not have let caste or any similar consideration stand in the way of love. In matters of the heart she was uncompromising. If the letters had kept arriving and she had fallen for the man who wrote them without knowing who he was, who knows where things would have led?

Prashant, however, never entirely gave up hope. Every morning he could be seen standing on the front porch of the men's hostel, reading a newspaper, waiting for Asha's school bus to pick her up.

There were other students also hanging about, doing pretty much the same thing. It was not clear if they were simply taking in the morning sun, having a smoke, waiting for a glimpse of Asha, or just had the time to stand and stare! Asha was relieved when the letters stopped arriving, though she also missed the waiting, the not-knowing, and the slow unfurling of warm declarations of love.

⚜

Asha and her mother were in the kitchen in the middle of preparing arisa pitha, a cake that is the speciality of Orissa, especially in the Jagannath temple in Baripada.

Aditya arrived and said, "Can we have some cha?"

Cha was a euphemism for snacks and tea. Rarely did cha mean just a cup of tea. Karuna was teaching Asha how to make this delicious, but also the most demanding of Orissan cakes. Mother and daughter were both taken aback at Aditya's sudden need for cha. They had cha just before they began the elaborate ritual of making the pitha.

"Don't stop stirring, Asha," Karuna warned. Then turning to Aditya, she said, "We're in the middle of preparing the dough. The arisa won't bind properly, otherwise. You just have to wait. But why do you need cha again?"

"What can I do? Bibhuti babu's daughter and son-in-law have come to invite us to the wedding of his youngest sister. They're in a hurry," Aditya replied.

"Then why offer them cha?" said Karuna. "If they're in a hurry, let them go." As Karuna spoke, she pointed to the state of the kitchen, which was in disarray.

"She wants to see you. Radha was following me here, but I said you were in the bathroom!" he whispered, hoping his wife would appreciate his diplomatic skills.

"Oof!" Karuna sighed, annoyed for being disturbed in the middle of cooking.

Aditya followed her out of the kitchen, pleased with the prospect of arisa pitha later. He smiled and nodded appreciatively at Asha before he left.

Closing the kitchen door behind her, Karuna instructed Asha, "Keep stirring. I don't want them to come here. I'll be back in a moment."

Asha kept stirring the contents of the karai, which was coming together nicely. As the dough thickened, it also became more difficult for her to keep stirring, what with her left leg having gone to sleep as she sat on it and her right hand dreaming in sympathy. When the door opened, Asha was relieved, thinking her mother was back.

But she was surprised to see Radha.

"So this is where you've been hiding. Where's your ma?" she asked.

Behind her peered a young man with an angelic face, who kept making faces at Asha. Some of his gestures were plainly rude. It dawned on Asha that this person, who looked more like a boy than a man, had the mental age of a child. Even a child, thought Asha, would not make such faces.

"Ma went to see you, Radha mausi," Asha replied, trying to keep a straight face. The boy was gesticulating wildly. Though she could not understand his gestures, they appeared rude to Asha.

"Wish I had time to taste your pitha. Karuna has trained you well, I see. Good cook, good looks! But where on earth is your ma? We have to leave. Many more people to invite," said Radha.

Soon Karuna returned to the kitchen, and on seeing Radha, said, "I've been looking all over for you!"

"I've been waiting for you here, of course. We came to invite you to the wedding. You must come, all of you. You too, Asha. Next time I'll have cha. Your arisa pitha smells delicious!" she said, smiling indulgently at Asha.

Radha's father and Karuna's were good friends. But Asha wasn't sure if her ma and Radha were as close, though both had lost their mothers young.

Before Karuna was back, Abhay arrived. He sat down on one of the kitchen stools without a word or a smile. He had a tired, dazed look. Asha had never seen her uncle like this; he was always cheerful and had a kind word for her. Yet, here he was sitting with his eyes closed. He remained in that meditative state. Sensing something was deeply wrong, Asha kept quiet. They both sat in companionable silence.

"When did you arrive?" Karuna asked when she returned, puzzled to see Abhay. "We were in the veranda outside, but never saw you come in. Radha and Bibhu were here to invite us to his sister's wedding."

"Ah! On seeing you and nana with your guests, I came in through the side gate. Couldn't recognize Radha, she's put on weight," he replied in a hoarse voice.

Aditya arrived in the kitchen a moment later and, on seeing Abhay, exclaimed, "When did you arrive?" Turning to Karuna, he said, "Perhaps we can have some cha now?" Then he added, "Pity about the boy, such a misfortune, really!"

"Yes, very sad..." Karuna was still searching for the right words when Abhay said, "Nana, bohu—bapa died..." He looked and sounded totally gutted.

There followed a stunned silence. Karuna and Aditya looked at each other.

Aditya said, "But I got a letter from him today. He said he's fine, is coming here in a few days." Then his face distorted as he began to weep.

Abhay and Karuna also burst forth into tears; soon Asha joined them. Vikram, Vivek and Vijay rushed in when they heard the cries from the kitchen. Vikram barely managed to ask, "What happened?" The sight of their parents, uncle and sister weeping was unbearable. They all began to weep loudly.

"Your jejebapa died," Aditya explained.

"Bapa did not suffer," Abhay added. "He was writing an article for *Samaj*. He was having his afternoon tea. When Vishu nana came to ask him something fifteen minutes later, he was gone."

"How did *you* hear about it?" Karuna asked.

"Vishu nana called the principal's office. He was sending a peon to nana with the message. I was on my way to see the finance officer when the principal called me to deliver the message personally. He has granted us leave already. He knows we'll be going to Baripada tonight for bapa's kriya," Abhay replied.

All through the journey Asha kept thinking about life after death. *If there is reincarnation,* she thought, *surely there is some kind of life after death before one is reborn? Does God look after such matters— how each soul receives its just desserts? Do we get to meet God? Why does God not give us better evidence of his existence? Does God shape our lives by making us the way we are? But with so many of us, surely it's an impossible task? Perhaps that's why God has no time for me? Is that why he created all the other gods to help him? Or is it that when we are born, there is a bit of God in each one of us? If that's the case, is God there in all the evil people as well?* She would have liked to ask someone. However, no one was speaking in the hired car as they drove to Baripada, where the cremation was to take place.

Asha was struck by the look on the faces of her parents. They looked so lost and sad she felt like giving them a big hug. Vikram, who was asleep, looked as if he had just stopped crying his heart out. There were many questions she had no answers to, including why Radha aunt's boy was born handicapped. Life seemed incredibly unfair; things simply happened and one was left to deal with the consequences. It sent a shiver down her spine. The fact that she would never be able to talk to her grandfather ever again left her devastated. Death's finality was almost as difficult to accept as life's many injustices.

By the time they arrived in Baripada, jejebapa's body was ready for cremation. A large crowd of family and friends, who had come to pay their respects, were already gathered outside the house, waiting to accompany the body to the crematorium. On the arrival of the eldest and youngest sons, with their families, heart-rending cries could be heard from inside the house. The women started to wail loudly, and the children, tired and confused, joined in. One by one, the latest arrivals took the dust from jejebapa's feet and said a prayer for his soul to rest in peace. Then they joined the other family members who sat around the bier.

When it was Asha's turn, she had no trouble praying. She simply could not touch her jejebapa's feet to bid him farewell. She looked fondly at his face and was reminded of her jejema's face after she had died. Both looked as if they were asleep. Jejebapa's face had the look of someone who had seen the world and was content to leave it a better place than he had found it. The serene look on his face seemed incongruous against the other faces distorted with grief.

The priests soon arrived and conducted the final puja—there was not a single dry eye in that large gathering. The entire town had turned up to bid him farewell. Asha broke down when her father and uncles raised the bier on which jejebapa's inert body lay, and the men began to chant, *Ram nam satya hai*, as they carried him away. The women and children were left behind, standing in front of the house, crying.

***

Something inexplicable happened to Asha after they returned to Cuttack. Having been a fluent, colourful, and dramatic speaker of several languages, Asha started to stammer. There was no clear pattern to her stuttering. Nor did she know which words would get stuck in her throat or cling to the tip of her tongue, refusing to come out, reminding her of self-willed children who could not be commanded to do anything. The words could not be cajoled out with love either, as if she was divinely charged to hold the unhappiness of the world in her throat. She could not swallow nor spit it out.

Her repertoire of synonyms enlarged considerably. If she could not pronounce one word, she replaced it with another she could utter. Sometimes, all her attempts were foiled. She simply had to stop mid-sentence, leaving the listener puzzled. Occasionally, she said whatever came out of her mouth, not what she meant to say. The strangest thing is that anyone listening to her wouldn't have guessed. She was never left with her mouth half-open, struggling to get the words out. Her lips were sealed unless she was sure of delivery. People who did not know her might have thought she was rude, stupid, forgetful, or any combination of such human failings. Some of her classmates were cruel enough to suggest she had gone deaf and dumb. In the beginning, even her family did not fully appreciate what was going on.

Having asked her to do some chores, Karuna was expecting a reply. When Asha nodded absent-mindedly, Karuna said somewhat harshly, "Can't you speak, a big ox sitting on your tongue? Children these days have no manners."

It took Asha a good few minutes to explain why she had nodded. "N-n-now you kn-kn-know!" Asha stammered as tears slid down her cheeks.

An astonished Karuna blamed one of Aditya's students, Prafulla Indra Kumar Chandra Senapati, better known as PIKCS. He had a terrible speech impediment.

"Look how Asha has started to speak, just like Prafulla!" Karuna complained to Aditya.

"What can I do?" Aditya scratched his head in despair. "I can't ask him not to come to our house because Asha has started to stammer! Let's hope she'll recover from it just the way she lapsed into it."

Vikram had this theory that PIKCS ended up stammering because he could not remember his own name. It was just too long. But Vikram was kind enough not to tease Asha about her stutter, which kept disappearing and then reappearing just as mysteriously. Her classmates told each other endless jokes about people with speech impediments. One of the jokes even made Asha laugh out loud.

"Have you heard this one?" Surekha began, her friends gathered around her. "There was this man on a train, a well-dressed man wearing a gold watch, reading a newspaper. A vendor selling peanuts came up to him and asked, 'Babu, wha-wha-what is the t-t-time?'"

The girls smirked.

"The well-dressed man never said anything. He kept on reading the newspaper and did not even look at the vendor. Thinking the gentleman had not heard the question, the vendor repeated, 'Hey, babu, wha-wha-what is the t-t-time?'

"When he received no answer again, he was annoyed and said, 'Wh-why wear a wa-watch if you ca-can't t-tell the t-t-time?' Then he got off at the next stop, still grumbling at the babu's rude behaviour."

By this time the girls were giggling.

Surekha carried on, "Another man who was travelling in the same compartment, and who had witnessed the whole episode, asked the gentleman wearing the gold watch, 'Sir, why did you not tell that man the time when he asked? Has your watch stopped—you could've told him so?'"

The girls paused, waiting eagerly for the punchline.

Carefully delivering her words, Surekha said, "The man replied, 'Wh-wh-what, and g-g-get b-b-beaten up again?'"

The whole class was hysterical by then.

"'What do you mean?' The man who'd asked the question wanted to know." Surekha had not quite finished. "The gentleman explained. 'I had tr-tried to he-help an-another man once, and wh-when I opened my big m-mouth, he th-thought I was mi-mi-micking him, and he sl-slapped me.'"

At this point the girls begged her to stop, they could laugh no more. That was when Asha chuckled loud enough for the girls to hear. Since that day the girls stopped teasing Asha about her stammer of unknown origin.

The day Sister St Mary invited Asha to deliver the welcome address to the guests at the school's Annual Day she was still suffering from unexpected attacks of the stammer bug. When Sister first announced that Asha had been chosen to deliver the address, Asha was as surprised as the other girls in her class. Some were ungracious enough to let out a loud gasp—*Ahhh!* A member of the graduating class was normally elected to deliver this prestigious address. It was considered an honour to be asked. Taking her stutter into account, Asha never thought she would be chosen, although she had been awarded the Best All-Round Student's prize that year. The canny headmistress knew exactly what she was doing. Later she asked Asha to come to her office, where she asked her privately if she did not wish to deliver the address.

Asha replied without any hesitation or hint of a stutter, "Sister, I'd be delighted and honoured, but I need a bit of help from you."

It was also the year the decorative shield was not awarded. "The school's finances will not permit the distribution of such prizes," Sister announced during assembly in a voice that conveyed regret, sympathy, even an element of contrition. "The ceremony will be held, everything will be the same, more or less, except the prizes, the silver cups and the shield. These are hard times; we must all make sacrifices. I am grateful to all the prize-winners, especially to our Best All-Rounder, Armita Guru, for stoically rising to the occasion!" She clapped enthusiastically, encouraging everyone else to give the winners a rousing ovation.

Asha practised delivering her speech. After the ceremony, she was complimented for having given one of the most inspired and inspiring addresses.

"Armita, you were sensational," Sister cried, clapping her hands like a child, her face beaming. Sister had even chosen the light-pink silk sari Asha wore that evening. "Just look around you; see how impressed everyone is!"

Asha looked around her and surveyed a gallery of admiring faces. All the guests trooped up to Sister and congratulated both of them. Soon Asha was cordoned off by strangers who reminded her how unfortunate it was that *she* was *not* getting the Best All-Round Shield that year. "But the important thing is it was awarded to you!" they said, shaking her hand.

Later at home, her mother noted why nothing in her life had worked out as expected. "Once you arrive late, you never catch up—for the rest of your life. Everything seems to happen before or after—never at the right time." Karuna's words seemed prescient. Asha spent most of her life waiting for things to happen, while things magically fell into place for Vikram. Things worked out for him just the way they did not for her. As she mastered the art of waiting for things to happen, or not, life passed, changing so imperceptibly it gave the impression of remaining the same. Asha could not help wondering if the delay in her birth had anything to do with the many-a-slip-between-the-cup-and-the-lip experiences in her life.

Like any mother, Karuna had expectations, though nothing extraordinary. Yet it took mother and daughter a lifetime to be reconciled to the way things turned out. Connected like deep underground springs, on the surface the misunderstandings, the years of frustration, and even consternation at life's many unexpected turns, disillusioned both. Each felt the ache of letting the other down, of being let down. Yet the subterranean connection could never be severed as one did with the umbilical cord. From the moment of her daughter's birth, the fear of dying, losing a child, the fate of women in society, and the uncertainty of not being able to direct one's destiny haunted Karuna as much as her daughter.

CHAPTER 10

During the six months after leaving school and before starting college, Asha wrote a story, which turned out to be too long for a short story and too short for a novel. It was about a young woman who refuses to marry the man chosen by her family, deciding instead to wed someone of her own choosing. The point at which her protagonist's decision crystallised, she declared, '*That's one small step for a woman, one giant leap for womankind.*' This declaration of independence Asha inserted the day after the Americans landed Neil Armstrong and Buzz Aldrin on the moon. The *Hindustan Times* and *Samaj*, the local newspaper in Oriya, carried the iconic pictures of the moon landing. Asha found the expedition to the moon strangely liberating—all she needed was somewhere to stand so she, too, could move the earth.

She did not tell anyone about her novel. Once, she mentioned it in passing to Rashmi, rather it accidentally slipped out, and Rashmi teased a confession out of her.

"Can I read it, please?" Rashmi pleaded.

"No," Asha replied firmly.

"Writing a story, long or short, and not letting others read it is pointless. Why write? You may as well keep a diary," Rashmi remarked.

"Well, some people's diaries get published posthumously," Asha pointed out.

"Do I then have to kill you first to read it?" Rashmi joked. Then she said, feeling let down, "Why can't I read your story? I thought we were good friends."

"You can read my story if you tell me honestly what you think," said Asha.

"Are you suggesting I don't always tell you what I think? But, tell me, is it autobiographical? You really should write a novel," said Rashmi.

"The problem with novels is they take forever to write—you can say the same things in a few lines in a poem. Who has the time to write or, for that matter, read novels?" replied Asha.

"I have all the time in the world to read novels. They are easier to read; poems can be difficult. As far as I know, you have plenty of time to read novels. Surely you can find the time to write one? Tell me, what's your story about? It must be autobiographical, most are!" said Rashmi.

"A novel is too explicit—it stands there naked. A poem beckons you to first get to know her, spend time with her, before she undresses herself. What difference does it make if it is autobiographical, magical, philosophical or delusional? The main thing is if the story is worth reading, if the characters are alive, and the words breathe," said Asha, taking a deep breath.

"I get it—your story is autobiographical. I agree it makes no difference—as long as what you've written is worth reading. As I like spending time with you, I look forward to reading your story. And I will tell you what I think," Rashmi promised.

"Novels can be difficult too. I tried to read one recently, called *Ulysses*. The writer is very famous, actually supposed to be great. But I found it difficult. He's written another novel, which is incomprehensible. Hope my humble story will not put you off. I'm afraid you may not like it, but it will be a real tragedy if you don't understand it. But then, as they say, we barely understand ourselves," said Asha.

"Isn't that why they also say *know thyself*? I'll come to you if I can't understand something. But what about the reader's license to interpret the text? It'll mean whatever it means to me. I might change my mind, but that is my prerogative. But, Asha, I don't want anyone to understand me fully—that would be shockingly intrusive. Better to be misunderstood—at least by a few. Life would be so dull otherwise!" Rashmi said, making a face.

Asha was so lost in her thoughts that she failed to respond. Rashmi gave her a poke and asked, "Have you heard a word of what I just said?"

"Yes, but I feel sorry for Michael Collins, who merely orbited the moon in the mother ship," Asha replied.

"They also serve who sit and observe," Rashmi remarked. "Don't try to divert my attention. Just as well you ignored what I said. *When* can I read your novel?"

"Yes, soon… Do you know most people in China have no idea about the moon landing," said Asha.

"How do you know?"

"I read in the newspaper that in China people only get to read about things that Chairman Mao wants them to know. It has not been reported in their newspapers."

Asha was glad in her country they could learn about everything. She needed to believe in miracles—the flags planted on the moon were as good as her personal prayer flags. The first manned landing and walk on the moon on 20 July 1969 was front-page news. The Apollo 11 mission was proof the world was changing, albeit slowly. A woman on the moon alongside the men would have been better. It was only a matter of time; in time everything will change. If only one had enough time!

As such thoughts occupied her, Asha felt catapulted into a space bubble where she could manage time. An arranged marriage was not far off, now that she was at the threshold of her new life in college. Besides, her Sadhana nani's marriage was to take place that winter. They were marrying her into a wealthy family. The groom was several years her senior, just like Devika's husband.

Some things were changing, and others stayed the same. Asha wondered how the dice would roll out for her.

In her perfect world, Asha gave herself the freedom to choose her husband! In spite of her graduating at the top of her class, a loving home and family were the stuff of her dreams, not a career or financial independence. It was not surprising it failed to register with her that on the day the Americans landed a man on the moon, the Indian economy was in such a dire state that the government nationalized the fourteen major commercial banks! No one mentioned it in the family, not even in passing. The event was certainly not discussed among her friends. Perhaps the government timed it in such a way that no one would notice.

The preoccupation with marriage was of such magnitude that Asha observed all the relevant religious festivals in the Hindu calendar. On the day of Kumarapurnima, unmarried girls worshipped the autumnal full moon for the gift of a good husband. The moment a sliver of a moon made an appearance, Asha started blowing the conch shell and said her prayers. Devika had once remarked, "If you want a young husband, you have to pray to a young moon. If you delay, do your puja even fifteen minutes late, you'll be saddled with an old man." Asha never forgot that statement. She often wondered if Devika did not heed her own advice. Asha was not taking any chances. She knew that by the time the family puja would be done, it would be late.

Asha also fasted with her mother on the day Karuna observed the Savitri Brata, though that puja was for married women. As Savitri had rescued her husband, Satyavan, Asha thought it would be essential to enlist her help in finding a suitable husband. Savitri's story was as formidable as Durga's. So firm was Savitri's devotion to her husband that when Satyavan died, she asked Yama, no other than the Lord of Death himself, for the gift of Satyavan's life. Yama offered Savitri any boon except the life of her husband. Savitri asked for the restoration of her father-in-law's eyesight and his throne, sons for herself and a life in all its fullness.

When Yama happily granted Savitri all her wishes, she reminded him that she needed her husband to fulfil her wishes. So impressed was Yama with her intelligence and devotion to her husband that he relented and released Satyavan to return to her. She was henceforth known as 'Sati Savitri', the pure one. Asha could only hope to emulate such love. Her mother did not object to her fasting; she saw no harm in it. If anything, Karuna thought fasting was good for one's health.

In her search for the ideal swami, Asha did not leave any stone unturned. On reading John Keats' *The Eve of St Agnes*, in her first year in college, she determined to discover the identity of the man destined for her. Asha had read "how, upon St Agnes' Eve, young virgins might have visions of delight, if ceremonies due they did right; as, supper less to bed they must retire and couch supine their beauties, lily white; nor look behind nor sideways, but require of Heaven with upward eyes for all that they desire." It did not seem too difficult to comply. Her life already involved several fasts. Lying in bed with hands under the pillow and looking up to heaven was what she did normally. If she could find out about her future husband by observing those rituals, it was certainly worth a try.

On the eve of the feast of St Agnes, Asha was already committed to attending a wedding ceremony with Rashmi. Not wishing to let her friend down, Asha went to the reception, but resolved not to eat anything. Rashmi kept on repeating how very *delicious* every item was as she tucked in mouth-watering morsels. Asha's resolution was firm. She allowed herself a glass of water. It would have been difficult to come up with a credible excuse for her mother had she been there. There was no need to hide matters from Rashmi, who was rather curious about her friend's experiment. As far as explaining her fast to other friends at the wedding was concerned, it was simple. As a Brahmin, one could find religious justification for all of one's dietary aberrations. You could eat anything on any day of the week. Equally, you could opt not to eat the same things on the same days of the week.

Officially there were no caste barriers in India; unofficially, they existed everywhere. The marriage they were attending was as good as 'arranged'—the couple were of the same caste and class, and had known each other since childhood. Prashant, a good friend of the groom's, was also at the wedding. When he saw Asha and Rashmi, he approached them.

A panic-stricken Rashmi muttered under her breath, "Prashant bhai is coming. What do you want me to do?"

Asha's heart was not fluttering at all, just the usual *tu-dumb-tu-dumb*. She replied, "I don't want you to do anything. As long as your Prashant bhai doesn't think I'm giving him false hope. How can I even appear to do so if I feel nothing in here? Isn't your heart supposed to go *thump-thump-thump* like mad when you're in love?"

"I have no idea. My heart does that most of the time!"

"Maybe you need to get it examined."

Asha's need to find out something, anything about her future partner dominated her thoughts. The horoscope was no help; rather the family did not believe in horoscopes in spite of their faith in arranged marriages. Marriage proposals arrived with horoscopes. As far as Asha knew, her parents had not shown a real interest in any. There was no suitable suitor hovering in the background. If only St Agnes would send her a message.

Returning home after the reception, Asha did not have to speak to anyone. Vijay informed her that Karuna, feeling unwell, had gone to bed. Asha tiptoed to her room and followed the due ceremonies. She lay in bed, her eyes raised heavenwards, her heart intent on all it desired. She prayed for the vision to appear—settling for a fleeting vision, not the long-lasting, kissing, feasting experience that Madeline seemed to have been blessed with in Keats' poem. Close to midnight, Asha's mind was focussed on one thing, like Madeline she sighed for St Agnes' dream. The brutal fact was she had none, no vision—it was a blank, tabula rasa, a dark nothing. No visions, dreams, hallucinations, NOTHING. She lay there all through the night wide awake, feeling ravenously hungry.

When Rashmi enquired the next day about her vision, Asha replied sheepishly, "Perhaps I was punished for not staying at home and praying all evening. Must've broken some rule, defiled my fast by looking at the food. I had no vision at all!"

"That's a real shame. You saw nothing at all?" Rashmi sighed, disappointed. Then, as if she had a moment of clarity, she said, "If I told you the message is there is no such thing, no ideal man, and that you should settle for an arranged marriage, what would you say? I think a man in hand is worth ten in your dreams, that most men are mostly 'unsuitable'. Would you dismiss me with my wild yet very sensible ideas?"

"Probably," said Asha.

"Such is the recklessness of youth." Rashmi laughed.

Though Asha felt utterly crushed, she remembered her Aja's words when she had mentioned the shortcomings of arranged marriages. Aja had said, "From where will I find that 'special' man for you, Asha ma?"

The possibility of not finding Mr Right did not cross Asha's mind. She did not know much about love, even less about men. If you asked her what a successful marriage was, she did not have a clue. She knew what an unhappy marriage was. Why she believed her own *love* marriage would turn out to be happy is anybody's guess.

⚜

Asha's determination to find someone 'special' got stronger after her St Agnes' Eve fiasco, though the prospect of finding that treasure of a husband seemed as bleak and empty as her dream. The lack of a vision did not prevent her from dreaming of love that overcame all barriers: *Amor vincit Omnia*. She found the lack of a sign baffling, not to mention a serious blow to her self-esteem. Why had God dismissed her prayer so completely when she was prepared to sacrifice everything for love? *What more is expected of me?* Asha could not help asking God.

When there was talk of Rashmi's marriage, an astonished Asha asked, "Surely you can't just marry anyone? Have you been introduced to someone already? Why haven't you told me? I thought you were my best friend!"

"Don't get so excited. My parents are probably looking. But they haven't told me anything. These days a man can see a woman in college, at a wedding or in some public place. There's no need for formal introductions; that happens later if both parties wish to proceed." Rashmi outlined the latest trends in matrimonial viewings.

"You mean to say we are constantly on show like film stars in cinema posters? Anyone can see us anytime without our knowledge?" The thought had not crossed Asha's mind. She couldn't help wondering if her parents had found someone and not bothered to tell her.

"Isn't that what's been happening anyway? All these men mad about you—because they keep seeing you day after day, and dream of winning your hand one day! You are *sooo* naïve!" Rashmi said, shaking her head with disapproval.

"Okay, I admit sometimes I cannot see what is so obvious to you—why do you think I have you as my friend? You're supposed to be my eyes and ears, and me yours. Believe me, I can see things you can't," Asha pointed out.

It also occurred to her that she might lose Rashmi after her marriage the way Devika had disappeared from her life. Devika had written a couple of letters from Texas during the first two years of her marriage. Her last letter said she was pregnant, and then everything had gone quiet. Devika's father had long retired, and the family had moved away from the college campus. And just like that Devika vanished from her life. Asha could not bear the prospect of losing Rashmi in such a manner.

"Wake up. You are an idealist. The world is not." Rashmi's words shook her.

Feeling as if she had just received a mild electric shock, Asha said, "Idealists are the best pragmatists, the most practical of human beings."

Rashmi smiled and said, "Words are just words. Look inside yourself."

"What if I am idealistic? As you say, words are words; they can mean different things to different people. What are you—idealist, realist or romanticist?" Asha asked.

Asha did not for a moment think she herself was the kind of pragmatic idealist that, for example, her father's youngest sister's husband, Suresh Tripathy, was. When his eldest daughter reached marriageable age, Suresh informed Aditya and Karuna that he was looking for a son-in-law. When Karuna enquired what sort of son-in-law he had in mind, Suresh's reply was, "It doesn't really matter!" Then he had gone on to elaborate, "No one would choose me as a son-in-law. I smoke, drink, eat meat, and do not believe in God. But I am not so bad, eh? The only thing is the boy's family should not have any hereditary disease, and he must have a source of reasonable income. Everything else is negotiable."

With a flourishing law practice in Midnapur, Suresh was a member of the Communist Party in West Bengal. He was a chain smoker who also drank alcohol (both taboo in the Guru family). His long, oval-shaped face and twinkling eyes made him look like Satyajit Ray, and his deep, thundering voice was that of an orator. Asha could well imagine her uncle in court presenting his case with panache. Suresh wanted all three of his daughters to live in Orissa. "West Bengal is rife with Naxalites wishing to change the world, but they only make it worse," he said.

The marriage 'introductions' and 'viewings' took place in Aditya's home. Asha was convinced of her unsuitability for such charades. Nor could she imagine marrying any of the men chosen for her cousins. *I really have to find a suitable man myself.* Her resolution became more firm with every introduction her cousins had to go through. Asha was so put off with the idea, not to mention the rituals that accompanied such practices, she felt compelled to take matters into her own hands.

"I am a realist," Rashmi said, bringing Asha back to the present.

"What do you mean—define realist?" demanded Asha, knowing how words mean different things to different people.

"Well, I will marry the man my parents choose," explained Rashmi.

"Not the one you love?" Asha wanted to be doubly sure.

"As far as I know, I don't love any man apart from my father and my brother, and as far as I know, nor do you. So I cannot understand your obsession with love!"

"I accept you have not met your Prince Charming, nor have I. But we are very young. Marrying someone when you are young is not always a good thing. Wasn't that what child marriages were all about? Better to meet someone when you know what you want. Then you might meet someone tomorrow, and so may I!" said Asha.

"Tell me, will you consider sex before marriage?" Rashmi asked.

"Yes, if you deeply love each other—why not?" Asha replied, after a moment's thought.

"How will you know you love him for sure, and he loves you?" Rashmi asked, hoping her friend would see how flawed her love-marriage project really was.

"If you are in love, you know; you don't have to ask. I agree it's difficult to know if *he* loves you. You just have to trust him," Asha replied, searching in her mind for better proof of love. Then she added, "You never really know, do you? Maybe that's why one needs to trust in God. But then first you need to believe in God!"

"This is your problem—why bring God into everything? Where does God say that sex, love, marriage are all connected?" Rashmi asked. "You can be sure that God does not demand from us what we cannot be. Even Hinduism does not ask for such impossible things from mere mortals. Yet you do. How ridiculous and insane is that!

Mind you, I am not even raising the fundamental question of the nature and existence of God!" Rashmi pointed out.

"What do you mean? What does Hinduism advocate?" asked Asha.

"What do I know? You are the intellectual," Rashmi said. "Six centuries of foreign rule—first the Muslims, then the British—corrupted Hinduism. Its life-affirming, my-creator-has-infinite-mansions approach was compromised."

"What about the Arya Samaj movement and men like Tagore, Gandhi, and Bhave? Did they not try to change things?" asked Asha.

"Well, they had other pressing concerns—the status of women was not high on their agenda," replied Rashmi.

"This is all very interesting, I mean, what you say about Hinduism. But is it fair to say Hindus were blameless? Surely, they, too, were culpable?" Asha asked.

"Yes, we are all culpable—some more than others. The way powerful men have interpreted the ancient scriptures and passed on their understanding of ethical behaviour, particularly with regards to women, leaves a lot to be desired. There is no limit to human hypocrisy. The worst thing that can happen to a woman in our society is for her to get pregnant outside marriage. So, if you sleep with the man you love and then get pregnant, a likely outcome, it is *your* fault, not his. The man simply carries on with his life. Like Hester Prynne, it's the woman who goes around wearing her 'A' badge of shame. The man does not. It's the same everywhere," Rashmi complained.

"Yes, life is hard for a woman everywhere."

"Having an affair is far too risky for a woman. If the affair does not end in marriage, the woman's life is ruined. Even after marriage, if the husband dies, it is the wife's fault. *Sati* may have been banned, but life as a widow is miserable. She may as well join her husband in the funeral pyre," said Rashmi, her eyes shining with anger.

Asha held her hand and said, "Let's not talk about all this, eh?

We cannot change the past. Maybe we can try to change the future, in our own small way?"

Rashmi was not done. Having caught her breath, she carried on, "Even within marriage, sex is rarely the heavenly state of fulfilment it is made out to be..."

"Particularly for women..." Asha added as Rashmi paused for breath.

"Yes," said Rashmi. "The ancient Hindus recognized the importance of sex. The *Kama Sutra* is amazing. People who are sexually fulfilled are happier."

"I didn't know you were an expert on the *Kama Sutra!*" Asha smiled mischievously. "Do you secretly read your parents' copy?"

"What if I do, don't you? But tell me, what do you think? Do you think I'm talking rubbish?" Rashmi asked.

"Well, what do I think? How much time have you got? I think Hinduism is pragmatic enough to acknowledge sex as a positive thing. It's so different from Christianity, where it is the 'original sin', an act of disobedience. Then Mary has an immaculate conception. And Christ, who was born to redeem mankind, is asexual! Our gods have families and occasionally indulge in behaviour that is not very godlike. Hinduism is perhaps more down to earth, offers more choice—many gods and many paths to nirvana," said Asha.

"I agree entirely. Hinduism offers so much more. Self-knowledge comes with sex as being an integral part of the self," Rashmi said. "Ironically, the search for self, truth drove Gandhi into celibacy later in his marriage! It was not necessarily the Hindu way, it was Gandhi's way. Perhaps, a reflection of his Western education and Christian-induced guilt that he was making love to his wife when his father died. Hinduism is open enough to include Gandhi's way. But was his wife a party to that decision? The sort of sexual restraint Gandhi confesses to in his autobiography is no revelation. There are any number of women who lead celibate lives with their husbands. Equally, there are wives who enjoy sex with their husbands. It takes all sorts," Rashmi added.

Asha remembered Rashmi saying that one of her aunts had sex precisely twice in her life. The lady had clearly conceived on both occasions, for she had a son and a daughter. Much like their mother's generation, Asha knew little of the sexual liberation that was changing lives in the West. In Asha's world, good girls refrained from sex before marriage. Once married, they refrained from having sex outside marriage. If a woman was adventurous or foolish enough to have sex outside marriage, albeit with the man she loved and was engaged to wed, it was a risk. What if the man had all the fun and then married someone else?

After the family moved to a larger house within the campus, it appeared to Asha as if everything was getting bigger—from her breasts to her problems. Differences of opinion had also grown between her and her mother. Karuna was tired, irritable, angry or depressed most of the time. She felt her council went unheeded. Asha felt exactly the same; she wished her mother would listen to her. Mother and daughter could not find a way of connecting with each other.

Asha felt unable to share her deep sense of injustice with anyone, not even with Sadhana or Rashmi. They never complained about their families, though both regularly protested about any number of things. It would have been a travesty if Asha confessed her problems to them. Besides, her mother kept saying she knew of no other daughter who gave her parents so much grief. How could Asha mention her own failings to anyone except God? Even God, she was beginning to think, did not have the time to concern Himself with her problems. Balanced on the edge, Asha did not wish to do anything that might tip her into the abyss.

Karuna vented her frustration mostly in the presence of Vishu or Abhay. They listened to her patiently, and from time to time they encouraged Asha to mend her ways. This did not serve its purpose, as it alienated Asha further. When Karuna felt Aditya was not being supportive enough, he too became a reason for her unhappiness. "He supports her. Why should Asha listen to me? She is too outspoken, like her father. God knows who will marry her—she is so stubborn," Karuna would moan.

When Karuna was happy, the atmosphere at home brightened up beyond recognition, as if the sun had come out, driving away the clouds and mists of doubt. Asha would sing *Jan pehachan ho, jina aasan ho*....joyously, carrying on with all the chores Karuna wanted her to do.

One day, finding her mother in a good mood, Asha enquired, "Ma, you haven't by any chance arranged my marriage without telling me?"

"I will never understand you—you say the most incredible things. How can you think we would do something like that?" Karuna replied.

Asha kept quiet, silence seemed golden. She did not wish the dark clouds to appear on her mother's brow. She liked to see her ma happy.

Then Karuna said, "You are doing well in your studies. Both bapa and I think it will be good if you carried on with your education. There is time to find a suitable husband for you."

Asha would have liked to have asked her ma why she was so unhappy and angry these days, why she could not be happy like she was now. But she did not think it was the right moment. It was never the right moment.

Life had been one long haul for Karuna too. The previous winter her gall bladder had to be removed in an emergency operation. She had fallen ill every summer for almost ten years. Yet no doctor had diagnosed the cause of her illness. When she was rushed to hospital, writhing in pain, and they opened her up, they found thirty-six pieces of gall stones inside her.

As if that had not been herculean enough, Karuna had successfully completed the Bachelor of Arts degree as a private student, without attending any lectures or classes in college, and had passed her exams with flying colours. She had not completed her school-leaving exams when she got married. Since then, she had steadily worked her way through the alternative educational system until finally she could call herself a graduate. She had battled on valiantly on all fronts.

Yet life has a way of changing our perspective, making us see things differently—the more she knew, the more she realised how little she knew. Unknown pastures beckoned. Karuna now wanted to study for her master's. Asha, fearing she was no longer important in her mother's life, was certain of complete oblivion.

CHAPTER 11

Arriving at her first undergraduate Eng Lit Hons class, Asha was surprised to find the lecture theatre empty. Normally, the corridors were packed with young men, half of whom did not have a class, but turned up to ogle at the women, who were unwitting participants in a campus-wide beauty pageant as they cat walked to class in their colourful saris and shalwar-kameezes. The women considered it a privilege to be able to walk demurely down the corridors without the men commenting audibly on their looks or demeanour. Most of the remarks were flattering, though from time to time some home truths were thrown in. An empty corridor, however, was a true anomaly.

Thinking she got her information mixed up, Asha went to the English department's staff common room, which was located on the same floor. The SCR was empty except for an older member of staff, who did not even cast a glance in her direction. She did not have the courage to intrude. There was no information on the notice board about a change of venue or cancellation of any class. A puzzled Asha walked back to the lecture theatre while she considered her next move.

On seeing a young man standing near the classroom, who she assumed was a student like her waiting for the professor to turn up, Asha asked, "Are you also waiting for the English Honours class? I thought it was to be held in this lecture theatre, but there's no one here. The staff common room is also empty."

The man, nodding in a noncommittal sort of way, as if he was not sure himself, mumbled, "Better go and find out." Then he, too, disappeared. A baffled Asha went home after waiting for a further ten minutes.

The following week, at the same class, she noticed the same guy sitting in the back row. He flashed a smile as if to say, 'Remember me!' Asha could not figure out what there was to smile about, considering he had walked away leaving her in the lurch, in a manner of speaking. She thought of putting on one of her Mona Lisa smiles—a smile that was also not a smile—but decided against it. Instead, she pretended she had not seen him, that she was simply looking at the imposing tamarind tree outside. A few days later, the episode was repeated. He smiled, and she ignored him.

The women normally occupied the benches on either side of the platform where the teacher's desk was located. Such a configuration meant the facial expressions of the women, especially those in the front row, were visible to the men who sat on the opposite side. Thus, a smile that was not a smile could easily be misconstrued as a declaration of love. In a society where exchanging glances with someone of the opposite sex acquired significance, Asha had learnt to put on a mask when she stepped out of her home, a mask that made her appear serious, unapproachable, not someone to be trifled with. If simply looking at a man makes him fall in love with you, then what choice does one have but to exude gravitas? Only her close friends and family were familiar with her wild and wicked sense of humour.

About a month later, one afternoon, walking home with Shakti, a classmate who shared a room with two others in the overcrowded ladies' hostel, Asha heard a male voice calling out after her, "Wait, Armita. I have a book for you."

When Asha turned round, she was puzzled to see the same man running towards them. He handed her a copy of *Keats' Letters*.

She had not asked him for the book. They had barely exchanged a few words on the afternoon he disappeared. Without wishing to be rude, Asha said, "I'm sorry, but I'm too busy to read this now."

"No rush," he said, thrusting the book into her hand.

A voracious reader, Asha browsed through any book she could lay her hands on. If she liked what she read, she gave the book her full attention.

"When do you want it back?" she asked, automatically.

"No rush," he repeated. "You can keep it for as long as you wish."

He turned and walked away. Asha could not see his face beaming with joy.

Noticing the book's title, Shakti said, "Wasn't Keats that Romantic poet who died of love?"

"He died of TB, maybe of love too," Asha replied. Then she said, "You know, I never asked him for the book! What gave him the idea? I've never even spoken to him. How very strange!"

"Yes, I've noticed you never talk to the men in our class or any man in college—apart from members of your family, of course. But all these men are dying to talk to you. This one fancies you!" Shakti winked. "Isn't that evident? How else can he approach you? You must agree Anand is very good looking—like a film star."

"How do you know his name?" Asha asked.

She couldn't help wondering if she was the only ignoramus around. Anand seemed to know her name, Shakti his. What was going on! Until that point she had not considered his looks. Now that Shakti mentioned it, it dawned on Asha that he was not bad looking at all. He would blend in rather well with the men in her family, who were tall and good looking.

"I heard someone call him by that name!" Shakti replied. "If I was not already hitched, I'd be jealous. Did you notice? He didn't even look at me! He had eyes only for you. He's fallen for you in a big way."

Asha didn't know what to say. She found the entire episode

mildly absurd. But Shakti's confession that she was 'already hitched' intrigued her.

"What do you mean you're already hitched? Are you engaged?" Asha asked.

"Yes!" Shakti smiled.

Thinking the engagement was an arranged one, Asha said, "I take it, then, you're happy with the man your family have chosen for you?"

"No, you silly, we love each other. I chose him; we chose each other. My parents don't know anything about it. They would not approve," Shakti replied.

"When did this happen? I mean, where did you meet him?"

"I met him a year ago, in college, like you've just met Anand."

Asha was not pleased with the comparison. Nor did she like the implication that something might happen between her and Anand in the future.

"I barely know this Anand and don't think I'm interested in him," said Asha.

"Maybe so, but he seems very interested in you. Anyway, see you tomorrow." They had reached the hostel. "Do you want some tea?" Shakti asked.

"I need to go home now, but thanks for the invitation—we'll have tea another day when I'm not feeling so tired. You must come for tea at our place," said Asha.

As she walked home, Asha became conscious not only of the smell of paper that new books possess, but also a faint smell of sweat. She was familiar with the smell of her father and Vikram when she ironed their clothes. She could tell which belonged to whom. The younger ones were not men yet, and smelt as children do. She loved the smell of freshly bathed babies and missed the way Vijay and Vivek used to smell. She was also familiar with the smell of her uncles. When they were children, Vishu uncle's punishments extended to having to smell his armpits if they didn't obey his bidding—such as being quiet in the afternoons or pressing his feet while he slept and snored. He would be snoring away loudly, but if they moved, he would immediately roar, "Where do you think you're going?" Asha never fathomed how anyone could both sleep and be awake at the same time.

Karuna smelled mostly of whatever it was she was last doing— spices if she was cooking, of soap when washing clothes, of sweat when dusting and sweeping, sandalwood talcum-powder fresh out of her bath, or of jasmine when she wrapped a garland on her plait before the family settled in the garden sipping sherbet in the long summer evenings. On rare occasions Karuna dabbed herself with attar of rose.

Asha was curious about the smell of this book. She may not have been wild about it, but she didn't dislike it. She could not recall the name of the person who'd said that souls know one another by smell, like horses. When she opened the book, a letter dropped out. It had the hint of a fragrance she could not decipher. The note was not very original, nor did it contain any declarations of undying love. He did not resort to Hindi film songs to woo her, nor did he quote Keats or any of the Romantic poets. His initial approach was tentative, uncertain of success.

When Asha saw him next, she continued to ignore him. The thought of Anand presuming there might be something going on between them felt intrusive. She did not respond to his letter. But when she returned the book, he gave her another with a letter inside. He kept giving her books every time she returned one. She found it difficult to say no, and the letters got longer and bolder.

The two people Asha could have spoken to about Anand had little time to spare. Sadhana was adjusting to married life and preparing for motherhood. The first three months after her wedding, which included a honeymoon, something unheard of in the family, were rapturously idyllic. But after that, from what Asha could glean from the brief conversations she had with her cousin, life was not as blissful or carefree. As far as Asha could make out, this is what marriage was all about, except in Sadhana's case, her in-laws' family was larger than normal. Which meant she was perennially busy, always at the beck and call of her in-laws. When Asha went to visit her, she never found those moments private enough to talk about anything, let alone Anand, who was sending her love letters. There were constant intrusions; Asha could hardly complete a sentence before someone would walk in needing Sadhana's intervention.

Rashmi's life, too, underwent changes that were totally unexpected. One fine morning, her father, who had never been ill, collapsed in his office in the middle of a meeting. They rushed him to hospital but could not revive him; he succumbed to a massive heart attack. What Rashmi did not know was that her father had more or less fixed her marriage with Avinash, a lawyer and a friend of the family. Rashmi never thought of Avinash as a potential husband, more as a friend of her elder brother and her parents. Avinash was also several years her senior.

After the death of her father, Rashmi's mother told her about her father's wish. Not only did Rashmi's family break tradition by holding the marriage within the mourning period, which typically lasted for a year, but after the wedding, Avinash moved in to live with Rashmi and her mother. The house was renovated in such a way that they, Rashmi and Avinash, had a luxurious place to themselves—a house within a house. And her mother had an entire floor to herself. Rashmi's brother, a successful lawyer, lived with his family in Bhubaneswar. While all this was going on, Rashmi, too, had little time for Asha.

After six months of secretly reading Anand's letters, a desperately lonely Asha poured her heart out to him. The day she did so was another of those days when she wished she had never been born. In the morning, she and Karuna had words. In the afternoon, matters got worse. In the evening, Karuna complained to Aditya about her. Asha was in the adjacent room, ironing a large pile of family laundry. She flinched at every word her mother said. Each pore of her body cried out at the unfairness of the allegations. Unable to contain her despair, Asha began to write in her journal that night. She was not aware at which point she moved on from writing in her journal to writing a letter to Anand. So great was her need to be loved, it never occurred to her she needed to find out more about Anand, if he was indeed the sort of man who would make her happy, before letting him into her innermost thoughts.

The next day when she gave her letter to Anand, concealed inside the book he had given her, she experienced a range of emotions—from elation to utter confusion. Her heart was beating fast, she was panic-stricken as if she had jumped off a stomach-churning ride on a plane, hoping her parachute would open up and she would have a safe landing. She was too excited to be able to concentrate on anything until she heard back from him. All day she was restless and apprehensive like a cat on a hot tin roof.

Anand wrote back the next day, "I am shocked to read your 'confessions' and cannot believe you have suffered so much for so long. It seems impossible. You appear so serene. Everyone thinks you are so blessed—the only daughter, beautiful, good, intelligent, you come from such a fine family. You are like the deep blue sea, appearing calm from a distance, yet churning inside. I don't know why you trust me, why you have so much faith in me. Has it not occurred to you that I, too, may betray you when the occasion arises?"

Instead of taking heed of his warning, her reaction was to trust him more. *If he were untrustworthy, would he express such noble sentiments? All the time he has been writing to me, has he not been confiding in me?* Asha thought. Besides, these letters were her lifeline, medication that kept her alive. Her attempts to find the right man had failed—prayers and fasts did not work. And God, she concluded, worked in far too mysterious ways for her to understand. Except, here was Anand, tall and handsome, sending her love letters in books. Perhaps this was going to be her *Love Story*? Perhaps God had finally heard her prayers.

Asha was so immersed in her world she barely got to grips with the real one. During this time, she made cryptic entries in her diary. "Words cannot express my love for Anand. He is my east, west, north, south, the sky, my world, the air I breathe. Just thinking about him makes me happy." Or "I could not live without loving Anand. Nobody in this family is happy or wants to be happy. High tension at home today, but I am secure in my love for Anand." On another occasion she wrote, "I feel so lonely at home, no one to share my unhappiness with—no one except Anand." She saw herself as one of the six characters in her family in search of happiness. Now she had found someone to share her search with; her love for Anand was going to save her.

They exchanged letters—'confessions' he called hers—without ever exchanging more than a few words in person. She was not yet eighteen when she pledged her love and her life to him. He did not exactly ask for her hand in marriage. In fact, they had barely spoken to each other until that afternoon, five months after she started writing to him. They were alone in the classroom, waiting for a tutorial.

They stood close to each other, lost for words, gazing into each other's eyes, when he said, "I'll always try to make you happy if you give me a chance."

She had heard him speak before, but listening to him utter the words she had been yearning to hear overwhelmed her. As if he had taken her up a beautiful mountain and asked her to jump off the peak with him. She looked at him, spellbound, ready to give up everything for him.

"Give me your hand," he said. And she did.

Holding her right palm with both his hands, Anand whispered, "I am yours if you want me. I will always be yours. Will you be mine?"

She nodded yes in reply, although she could barely move or

speak. Her lips and throat were dry; her whole body trembled. She could not even manage a smile, she was so filled with emotions, an intoxicating mix of fear and excitement.

In her sleep that night Asha dreamt that scene, everything was exactly the same except it was a dream. Even in her dream she knew it was not real, just a figment of her imagination. It felt unreal when she woke up—she knew it had never happened, not really, except in her dream.

When they met in class the next day, both had arrived early, she asked him, "Did you mean what you said yesterday? Did you *really* mean it?"

"Yes, every word," he said. Then he asked her, "And you? Have you changed your mind?" He smiled, waiting for her answer.

"No," she whispered. "I wondered if you had. I had a dream…"

"I had a dream too—we were getting married," he said, taking hold of her hand and gently squeezing it.

They could not talk any more as they heard footsteps approaching. By the time the other students walked in, Anand had returned to his seat in the back row. They continued to exchange long letters expressing their undying love. On her eighteenth birthday, he gave her a piece of A4 which simply said—*I love you.* It was written in blood. By the time Asha read the message, it had oxidized into a shade of rust. She did the same in return, pledged her love back in blood. Anaemic, she had to prick her fingers several times to squeeze out enough blood. Her fingers were sore for days. As she was willing to die for love, this was nothing.

The day Aditya learnt of his daughter's decision to marry Anand was also the day his blood pressure went berserk. He was hypertensive to start with, and life's drip, drip, drip of disappointments had to cause damage sooner or later. He was in his study going through some papers, filing away those that he needed to keep.

Asha had accidentally revealed to Karuna her decision to marry Anand. They were having one of their arguments in the kitchen when Asha blurted out, "I will no longer be a burden on anyone; don't worry. I will leave home for good, and you can live happily without me causing you grief."

"What do you mean you'll leave home?" Karuna asked.

"I will marry Anand," Asha replied.

"And who is this Anand you plan to marry?" Karuna enquired incredulously. "Your father needs to hear this!" And she marched off to talk to Aditya.

Immersed in work, surrounded by piles of papers, Aditya was going through one of the files when Karuna walked in. Without any warning she repeated the exchange between her and Asha, ending with, "Asha says she is going to leave home with some Anand! What have you all been doing? Your precious daughter has been carrying on with this boy in her class—and none of you know anything about it?"

The entire pile of papers slipped from Aditya's hand. He was meticulous about papers and files. Asha could not believe what had just happened. She had followed her mother; she now wished she had not opened her big, stupid mouth, wished her mother had not told her father. She wished many things now that her secret was no longer hers. Asha thought her father would explode with grief and anger. But all he did was slump back in his chair without uttering a word, as if he was experiencing a dizzy spell. He was crestfallen, the way he looked when he had received news of his father's death. Something precious had been taken away from him without his consent. As he closed his eyes his face registered his anguish.

"See what you've done!" Karuna said. When Aditya opened his eyes, she asked, "Are you all right?"

He shook his head as if to say he was in hell, and he closed his eyes again.

Mother and daughter stood there, quiet and tense, until Aditya opened his eyes and said, "Asha, I can't bear to see you or hear what you have to say. You go. I can't talk to you now. I must first talk to your ma."

Asha's heart was beating so fast, she went to her room and lay down in bed.

After Asha left, Karuna sighed, "What do we do now?"

"I don't know, but she cannot marry that Anand fellow," replied Aditya.

"We must find out what sort of a boy he is," Karuna suggested.

"I can ask Debasish babu what he thinks of him. Dr Biswal may also have some idea. But are you sure she is serious about marrying him? Not just saying this to annoy us?" Aditya asked.

"She is serious; that's what she said. I'll find out what Debasish babu has to say. As head of the department he must know Anand. You rest now as you are not feeling well. You can ask the principal, I mean, Dr Biswal, tomorrow."

That evening Asha overheard her parents discussing the matter with Abhay.

"Debasish babu seems to think Anand is not a bad sort; well, at least he did not say Anand was a drunkard, a thief, a womaniser or a scoundrel," Karuna reported.

"Did you ask him about Anand's family?" Aditya asked. "If you cannot trust your own child, how can you trust what anyone else says?"

"I don't think he knows the family. He just said Anand was 'all right' from whatever little he knows of the boy and the way Anand conducts himself in class. That's better than hearing he is a goonda or a lafanga," replied Karuna.

"I have no idea what made her agree to such a stupid match! She does not know her onions from her apples. Why does she think she is fit to choose a husband? Our culture is different. What does she know about him or his family? How will he support her; how will they live without any income? Has she considered all that? Is this what we taught her? She'll end up being a burden on me for the rest of my life." Aditya sighed.

The exact phrase in Oriya was 'hanging like a millstone around the neck'. Asha thought hanging round someone's neck like a pearl necklace was no bad thing, or like a child hanging playfully around the neck of a parent. But her father was not an optimist, he was a glass half-empty kind of man; worst-case scenarios plagued him. Asha was so affected by this remark she resolved never to be a burden on anyone.

"Try to see what he can become—through her eyes. If he can make her happy, if he really cares for her, he will make something of himself. Even if we don't know the family, if he is as Debasish babu says, a good boy, perhaps it will not be as bad as we fear." Karuna was a glass half-full sort of human being.

Asha was surprised to hear her mother. Why could she not be like this always?

"The problem with what you say, Karuna, is—if he can do this, if he can do that. What *if* he can't?" Aditya asked, shaking his head as if he could see the future of his daughter unfurling right before him.

"I'll find out whatever I can about this Anand. I've seen him on campus, he seems well-behaved, fairly tall, quite good looking, well-dressed," said Abhay.

"Manners maketh a man, they say," said Aditya. "But one must also look into a man's heart as much as his family background. Families matter."

Days after he learnt of Asha's decision, Aditya was taken ill. He suffered from severe chest pains and acquired a searing left arm and a swollen left foot. His blood pressure shot up. Even after a week of this dance with death, doctors had no understanding of his condition. His blood pressure remained high, the pain in his leg clung like a vice, and the swelling refused to abate. What cannot be cured must be endured, everybody said and prayed for him to get better. Asha was distraught with her father's illness and blamed herself for it. She would have given everything for her father to get well. But how could she renege on her promise to Anand? Her stammering returned. As she did not speak much during those troubled times, she successfully disguised her speech impediment.

News of Asha's choice leaked out the day after Karuna went to confer with Professor Debasish Pani, head of the English department. Karuna had requested that he keep the matter confidential. It soon became public knowledge when he told his wife, and she told her sister, in the strictest confidence. And she passed it on to her sister-in-law, also in confidence. Aditya and Karuna realised the cat was out of the bag when the spate of marriage proposals for their daughter trickled down dramatically. Tongues started wagging that Asha, who could have had her pick of husbands, was wasting her future on someone with few prospects.

When Karuna told Aja about it, his council was, "Let Asha study and complete her master's. She might change her mind."

Asha waited for her parents to change their minds; her choice of partner was not negotiable. "I will not have an arranged marriage. If you do not accept Anand, then I will not marry him. I will not do anything against your wishes. But I will not marry any other man." She made it clear.

As Asha did not waver in her decision, her parents agreed to Anand coming to meet her at home. They thought it was better this way, allowing him to meet Asha under their watchful eyes, rather than meeting somewhere furtively without their knowledge. Anand came under the pretext of study, every fortnight. Asha did not wish to push her luck. The evenings he came to see her, after the getting-to-know-each-other chit-chat with the family was conducted over tea and snacks, Anand and Asha retired to her room. They would sit there discussing the books they had read.

As all the doors and windows of the room were also left open, the family could overhear their conversation. Reassured, they would move on to attend to their various chores.

There were evenings when the young lovers found themselves alone in the house. On those occasions they disappeared to the backyard. Sitting on large cushions under the starry sky, holding hands, they would talk of nothing and everything. He would draw her closer, embracing her, kissing her. His hands would explore her body as if he was blind and needed to impress her features onto his memory. She was terrified someone might catch them touching, embracing, kissing. She thought they were breaking all the rules.

⁂

Aditya never wanted his daughter to marry Anand, but could not articulate his objections calmly, rationally. He got emotional and said the wrong things. Then father and daughter would stop speaking to each other for days. Asha was used to Karuna's legendary silences. When her father started doing something similar, she thought they had, at least, one thing in common.

Aditya had not asked Dr Somnath Satpathi to talk to Asha about her choice. As a good friend, and a professor of psychology at Harrison, Dr Satpathi sensed Aditya's unhappiness with his daughter's decision. Aditya was in good company as Dr Satpathi, along with the rest of the state of Orissa, thought Asha had made a terrible mistake.

"His family background is not similar to yours," Dr Satpathi explained to Asha one evening when he was visiting the family. "In all good marriages, it is important that both partners share similar values and have similar expectations from life. If backgrounds are radically different, the chances of success decline."

"Mousa, what you say is indeed right. But don't you think arranged marriages have their limitations. Love and understanding make people more equal. Arranged marriages are based on..." Asha was searching for the right word. "Well, arranged marriages are not always based on an equal partnership," she added.

How could he disagree—this modern, liberal, Western-educated man whose son went to study in America, fell in love with his classmate and married her, an African American. Imagining he was talking to his son, Dr Satpathi said, "Have you thought of the possibility that another man, more deserving of you, could love you as much if not more? Lack of a reasonable income, if not financial independence, will not permit you to live happily."

"Anand will find a good job, I'm sure," Asha replied.

"Then why not wait till he does before you decide to marry?" he said. "Asha, you possess a fine sensibility; you are capable of deep feelings. But, there is no substitute for experience," Dr Satpathi added as he got up to leave.

As Asha rarely mixed with people outside her circle, she never found out what others thought of her choice. If she had, the chances were she'd have dismissed them as frivolous, jealous gossip. Just the way she despatched Dr Satpathi. Being idealistic, she ignored what the world thought. She had resolved to marry for love and not for the usual reasons associated with arranged marriages—security, connections, status, prestige, wealth—which she thought of as demeaning. Trapped in her personal hell, like a fly butting against a glass window, she was unable to see the open space around her, the vast sky and the freedom it had to offer.

CHAPTER 12

Asha did not know what to make of her dream. This was the morning after she had a dream about the grades she had been awarded in each of her six papers in the BA Honours in English examination. It was barely a week before the results were officially due. She was accustomed to dreaming of events that later came true. These were not premonitions, but dreams she saw in Technicolour like movie trailers. But she had never before dreamt anything about herself, not in such depth or detail. On waking, she felt disoriented, unsettled, and could not get over her dream.

She could not make up her mind which was more surprising—knowing she had been treated unfairly or the fact she had dreamt every sordid detail. Her first-class academic record was set to be ruined by Mrs Priyambada Patnaik, who had assessed one paper, Paper Six to be precise. Asha had been awarded unusually poor marks in that paper. As if that was not shocking enough, she also dreamt that Mrs Patnaik had connived with another examiner to ensure that Asha's grades in English would disqualify her for the award of a first class. This second examiner had also rated her paper unexpectedly harshly. Asha had never received such poor grades for any of her papers before.

She could feel it in her bones; it was not a dream she could forget. She now knew how it felt to have a glimpse of the future, yet remain powerless to do anything about it. Being forewarned was not being forearmed. *What's the point of this dream, dear God, if I can't do anything about it? Why punish me with such knowledge?* Asha wondered as she joined the family for breakfast, but could not eat anything.

"What's the matter with you?" Karuna asked.

"I dreamt I've been awarded a second-class honours," Asha replied.

She then retrieved a piece of paper and read out the marks in all six of her papers. She had written them down, in case she forgot or got them mixed up.

Aditya, though blessed with a strong instinct for people and situations, considered himself a rational person, scientific and logical in his approach. When explaining something to his children, he would say, "Science ta bujhunu. Try to understand the way things work, appreciate the *science* of it." Like art or beauty, science for Aditya was a quality of mind that one needed to cultivate if one was unfortunate enough not to possess it. Naturally, on hearing about his daughter's dream, his initial response was, "Asha, it's only a dream."

Feeling utterly miserable, Asha said, "I know it's a dream, bapa. But I cannot accept a second class even in my dreams! You can understand that, can't you? Just consider for a moment—what if it's not just a dream?"

Aditya nodded and said, "I understand. But tell me, what can I do? On what basis will I complain and to whom? What will I say—my daughter dreamt she has been victimised, that her grades have been tampered with by Priyambada Patnaik, the professor and head of the English department in Vidya Vihar, and her husband, Prithviraj Patnaik, the director of public instructions? How can anyone take the matter seriously?"

He was not only referring to the inconvenience of dreams, but also to the fact that the university statutes did not permit the re-examination of papers. To make matters worse, the university did not have a vice-chancellor at the time. There was a deputy vice-chancellor, who had no power to do anything and never did much anyway. Everyone joked that was the reason he was appointed, not to do anything. He was nicknamed 'Vice'. Not only did he not do anything, whatever he did was no good. The man was thoroughly corrupt. Then there was the chancellor, the Governor of the State, who had mightier matters on his mind, such as devastating floods, political scandals and an impending election.

"What about talking to Prashant babu? He knows what the Patnaiks have been up to—trying to get you transferred?" Asha suggested.

She was referring to the Secretary of State for Education. He had been a student of Aditya's and had helped him foil the many attempts by Prithviraj Patnaik to transfer him from Harrison College. The fact there were no colleges offering courses in his subject did not make any difference to the Patnaiks. Nor was Aditya being transferred to set up a new department at another institution. No, they wanted him out of Harrison College because he refused to do their bidding.

"First they tried to transfer you, let me think how many times— was it three times in the past year? It's caused us so much grief, and all because of that laboratory assistant, Rabi Das!" Asha reminded her father.

"I can talk to Prashant, but he can't change the university statutes," Aditya explained. "I can talk to one or two others, too. But what can anyone do now? The results are due any day," he added, worried about his daughter's grades.

The trouble began when the couple, the Patnaiks, joined the Education Department in Orissa. Prithviraj was appointed director of public instructions while his wife, Priyambada, took over the English department at the newly established postgraduate centre,

Vidya Vihar. There was a move to establish a new centre of postgraduate education in Bhubaneswar, the capital of the State, thereby manoeuvring a shift in power and funding away from Harrison College to Vidya Vihar.

Bhubaneswar became the new capital of Orissa in 1948 soon after India's independence. Cuttack had been the seat of government in Orissa for almost a thousand years before the capital moved to Bhubaneswar, the Temple City of India, which in turn used to be a flourishing city long before Cuttack was founded as a fort city in the tenth century. After almost a century of being the premier educational institution of Orissa, Harrison College was slowly being dislodged from its pinnacle.

The changes ushered in by the ambitious couple initially proved beneficial to some members of Asha's extended family. Her uncles moved from Harrison College to Vidya Vihar and became professors and heads of their respective departments. Aditya, however, never benefited from these developments. Even at Harrison College a postgraduate centre was not established. He never became a professor, though he had built up the geography department from scratch and published books and academic papers in various journals. Under his tutelage, many geographers had emerged and gone on to achieve greater glory.

The rift between Aditya Guru and the Patnaiks began when Rabi Das, a laboratory assistant in the geography department, approached Aditya with an unexpected proposal. He wanted his son, who was going to sit for the Bachelor of Arts examination in geography, to be awarded a first class.

That evening when Aditya reached home he was visibly upset. Reporting the matter to his wife, he said, "That Rabi Das is a scoundrel."

"What has he done now?" Karuna asked sympathetically. Rabi Das constantly did things that annoyed her husband.

"He had the audacity to ask me to inflate the grades of all the students so his son can get a first class! Everyone knows his son is not the brightest boy in the mohalla. If he studied hard and took some private tuition, he might just scrape through with a lower second class. He's basically a third-class student, yet Rabi Das thinks he can buy me with a bribe. What's the world coming to?" Aditya explained.

When Abhay heard of it, he said, "I didn't know his son was studying geography. These days people have no values; they'll do anything." Abhay was also thinking of his own laboratory assistant, who was giving him a hard time. The man practically lived in the department, and Abhay found it difficult to evict him. "I fail to understand how laboratory assistants can have so much power!" he added.

The Gurus had not known of the friendship between Rabi Das and the Patnaiks. The dastardly plot was revealed when Rabi Das turned up again, as bad pennies do, with the suggestion, "If you cannot help me, Aditya babu, why don't you leave Harrison College for a few years? You can return once my son has completed his studies. What about becoming a principal in some college? The salary is more; you must need a dowry for your daughter. If you need any additional funding, that can be arranged too."

"Why doesn't your son leave Harrison College to study somewhere else?" Aditya replied, unable to curb his anger at the absurdity of the proposition. "Please do not return to my home to discuss such matters."

Not long after this exchange, Aditya heard through the grapevine that his transfer from Harrison College was imminent. With four children at various stages of their education in school and college in Cuttack, Aditya's blood pressure kept shooting up. As luck would have it, Prashant Mishra was at the right place at the right time. He did not support any of the transfer proposals, saying there were enough people capable and interested in becoming the principal of the college that Aditya Guru was being transferred to. The files left Mishra's office with his recommendation that 'Prof Guru should not be transferred from Harrison College, the State's premier institution, as that would leave the department without the benefit of his stewardship.' He had highlighted his reference to Aditya Guru as 'Prof Guru', emphasizing the injustice and humiliation already endured by Aditya Guru.

Prithviraj Patnaik was powerless in the face of such a recommendation from his superior officer. As Prashant Mishra and Aditya Guru were Brahmins and the Patnaiks were Kshatriyas, the incident was interpreted as an ongoing power struggle between the two highest castes. Aditya remained at his post in Harrison College. He and his family were immensely relieved their lives had not been turned upside down just because the megalomaniac Patnaiks wished it.

News of Asha's second class, albeit in the form of a dream, left the family stunned. Powerless to reverse the situation, Aditya asked Abhay, "Will the Patnaiks really sink that low? It'll be difficult to do anything after the results are announced."

"Papers are not officially re-examined, and even if one gets them re-examined unofficially, the original marks cannot be revised," Abhay confirmed, after a sip of his cup of orange pekoe tea. Normally, at this point in the family tea ceremony, he would say with supreme satisfaction, "Happiness is a fine cup of cha!" And everyone present would smile and nod in agreement. But today their thoughts were elsewhere. Nobody commented on the excellent quality of the tea that Asha had just prepared.

"What an unfair system!" Karuna gasped, thinking it could easily have happened to her.

"How can they get away with it?" said Vikram, knowing they would.

The family was sympathetic, but did not know what could be done to avert the disaster. A week later, the results were declared. Asha's position was second in the university, she had been awarded a second-class honours in English, with distinction in the other subjects. This fall from grace, from the first-class first position she had become accustomed to, riled her. The person who came first in English, Priyanka Mohanty, was the same caste as the Patnaiks. She was also a student at Vidya Vihar. To add insult to injury, Priyanka had never been awarded a first class before.

Asha admired her father for standing up to the Patnaiks. But to be awarded exactly the same mark as her father had given Rabi Das' son was more difficult to swallow. Aditya had gone out of his way to ensure he graded that boy's paper fairly. He had shown the paper to his colleagues to be doubly sure he was not being swayed by his own prejudices.

When Abhay saw it, he said, "Nana, if anything, you've erred in his favour."

One of Aditya's colleagues, also a Kshatriya, was more direct. "Sir, I would have given that scoundrel much less. You have been more than fair."

In his effort to be fair, Aditya ended up being lenient.

What would I have received if bapa had been fair? Asha shuddered to think.

When Madhav finally got hold of the names of the examiners of the six papers in English, they were all amazed to learn that the two papers in which Asha had received the lowest marks were also the ones allocated to Mrs Patnaik and a professor in English from Rajasthan. Handing over the piece of paper, where he had made a note of the names of the examiners, Madhav observed, "I cannot believe how accurate Asha's dream was! It is uncanny."

The family also learnt that Mrs Patnaik had submitted her papers late, which had enabled her to find out what grades Aditya had awarded Rabi Das' son. It was no coincidence that Asha received exactly the same mark in the papers graded by Mrs Patnaik. Had she assessed Asha's paper more harshly, Mrs Patnaik would have drawn attention to herself. Had she been smart and given Asha a few marks short of Priyanka, the misdemeanours of the Patnaiks would have gone undetected. But the Patnaiks wanted revenge—they wanted Asha to get a second class.

It was not possible to prove the Patnaiks had bribed the external examiner. Their involvement came to light after a third examiner, also a Kshatriya, confided to his classmate, Madhav Mishra, how the Patnaiks had approached him via a mutual acquaintance to find out if he might be willing to do the needful thing for a payment.

This examiner, a professor of English in Delhi University, told Madhav, "I was outraged. Giving Armita the highest marks gave me great pleasure; she deserved it. What sort of teachers do we have these days who work against their own students? The Patnaiks should be prosecuted for this!"

Learning she had a few supporters boosted Asha's morale. She had been terribly upset when her professor, Debasish Pani, a self-professed Gandhian, did nothing to help her. On the contrary, he hinted to Aditya and Karuna that perhaps Asha had neglected her studies as a result of her emotional entanglement with Anand.

"Armita should try harder for her master's," was all the support he offered.

Asha was quietly furious when she heard what Prof Pani had said.

"I'm not sure Gandhi would agree with Prof Pani!" Asha told her parents.

Anand did not say much during this whole episode except to reassure Asha that everyone knew she deserved a first class. Anand had by then moved to his parents' house. There was no opportunity to meet and discuss matters properly. He had been awarded a second class. Asha did not wish to find out more about his results; she had simply lost faith in the appraisal system. She spent days and nights in her personal wilderness, thinking she could not face such a blow again in a couple of years' time. Her parents did not think it would be repeated.

"Why are you so sure it won't happen again? Just because they've stopped harassing you now doesn't mean they won't try again later. Prashant babu may have moved to another post in a couple of years. What will you do then?" Asha asked her father. "Something must be done," she added, not knowing what that might be.

"Yes, something will be done when the time comes," Karuna said. It was another of those days when the maid had not turned up. "But now, I need your help in the kitchen. There is plenty of time to sort your problem. The world is full of problems, Asha. Our job is to learn to prioritize them."

"All I'm saying is that it'll be too late if I wait two years to deal with my problem," said Asha, following her mother to the kitchen.

"I agree, some problems are best nipped in the bud," Karuna replied.

While chopping the vegetables, Asha nicked one of her fingers.

"Be careful, Asha. You don't want to lose a finger on top of your first class. You can't change the world unless you save yourself first," Karuna said.

Asha applied an antiseptic dressing on it and carried on with her chores. So absorbed was she in her thoughts she almost cut herself again.

When Aja arrived and was apprised of the latest developments, he asked, "What can we do? What do you want us to do, Asha?"

"I don't know, Aja. I can't pretend nothing has happened. They'll do this again unless they are stopped. I cannot afford a second-class degree for my master's as well! Why does the university have such idiotic laws in the first place? Can you do anything about the university statutes, Aja?" Asha replied.

"I'm not sure what I can do," said Aja. "The university is ruled by its statutes, and it is up to the council to address such issues."

Asha could not imagine surviving another such calamity. Her family may have been willing to take that risk, she was not. Compelled to *do* something about her results, she could not rest till she had done everything in her power. Yet she could not think of anyone she could turn to for help.

Help finally arrived in the form of a stranger called Gyan Prasad. Asha overheard her father and uncles talking about the appointment of an administrator at the university. That was the first sign of hope. *When injustice and corruption reign supreme, sooner or later it leads to the collapse of the system, if not always of the perpetrators*, she thought. Vidya Vihar was on the verge of such a nemesis. *But will the troubleshooter being sent from Delhi do the right thing?* Asha wondered. That he was not someone from Orissa pleased her. She hoped he would have no axes to grind as a result.

Asha enlisted the help of a close family friend to arrange a meeting with Gyan Prasad. A request from someone within the academic community, including her family, would have resulted in leakages, delays, cancellations, compromises. Her instincts served her well. Within a month she was in Mr Prasad's office, explaining to him why she thought grave injustice had been done to her.

She told him the whole story and ended her petition with, "This year, I was the victim. Next year, it'll be someone else." Asha was not sure how Mr Prasad would respond. Seeing him nod gravely, she added, "You need not take my word for granted, though I assure you I am telling you the truth and nothing but the truth. Please make your own enquiries into the matter, and you'll soon discover what kind of corruption and nepotism has been going on here. I am not their first victim. Hopefully, with your help, I will be the last. I don't think my career will survive a second-class master's degree on top of a second-class bachelor's."

Gyan Prasad was listening carefully to every word of hers. Then he asked, "What do you want me to do? What do you think should be done?"

"Please ensure they do not have the power to grade exam papers when I sit for my master's in a couple of years. Nor should they have the power to influence others to do their dirty work. They should not have the means to harm others, not just students but other teaching and administrative staff. They have abused their power repeatedly. This is not an isolated incident," Asha replied.

"I will do all I can to help," Gyan Prasad assured her. When she held her palms together in a namaste preparing to leave, he added, "I'm very sorry about the BA results. It should never have happened. I will do my best for your MA."

"In light of what has happened, perhaps the university statutes can be amended?" Asha ventured to suggest. "If my grades could have been challenged publicly, they would have thought twice about what they did."

He nodded. "I'll look into that, too."

Gyan Prasad was true to his word. The Patnaiks were barred from grading the MA English papers the year Asha sat for her master's exams. The couple had quietly moved to non-academic posts outside Orissa. Asha heaved an almighty sigh of relief when she had her first-class first position restored to her. She was the recipient of the Gold Medal in English for securing the highest marks in the university. She received her medal, but the convocation ceremony was not held that year.

Asha did not even try to find out why that was the case; she already knew—her life had reverted to its original outliers. Orissa was bankrupt, financial prudence necessitated such cuts. She made another appointment with Gyan Prasad, this time she went with her father and took a large box of mixed sweet delicacies from Calcutta Sweets, gift wrapped, to thank him for his Godlike intervention.

"I am sorry about the convocation," said Gyan Prasad. "At least you've got your rightful position in the university!"

"We are immensely grateful," Aditya said.

Asha nodded in agreement, smiling.

"I'm glad I was there to help you. So what are your plans?" he asked. Then looking at Aditya, he said, "Hope you won't marry her off? By all means marry her, but you don't need me to tell you how gifted your daughter is. She must be allowed to do whatever she chooses to do with her life." Then he added, "If I can help in any other way in the future, let me know. Are you going to try for the IAS, or will you go into academia? Whatever you decide, I wish you well!"

This signalled the end of the meeting. Father and daughter thanked Gyan Prasad profusely for his help, their palms held in a long namaste. Asha could not fathom if the gossip about her choice of partner had reached Gyan Prasad's ears. If it had, he never hinted he had a view on the matter, except, of course, to let her father know what he thought of her academic achievements.

CHAPTER 13

Asha's life had changed irrevocably; no one disputed that. Her family regretted it. According to her parents, she was stuck in a rut, entirely of her own making, which was far from the desirable place she could be in. Life was full of problems; one did not add to the quantum of suffering by one's own actions. Aditya felt it more acutely than his wife. If he was not so completely shattered with her decision, if he could find the right words, he would have explained to her that human propensity to make mistakes is infinite, while our ability to undo them is finite. If we could learn from our mistakes, all was not lost. He was unable to say anything at all to his daughter. Instead, he shared his misgivings with his wife.

"Do you think Anand will really marry our Asha and make her happy? If he didn't marry her, it would be a blessing in disguise. I'm afraid he'll just ruin her life. Where is he these days? What is he doing? What is wrong with her? Why can't she see things for what they are? How can she be so blind?" Aditya could not believe how naïve his daughter was.

Karuna listened sympathetically. While they rarely agreed on anything, the world appearing in contrasting disguises to each, they respected each other as a parent and knew that each wanted the best for their children.

After giving the matter some thought, she said, "We can't force her to marry someone we choose. Also, how do we find someone who will marry *her* if she insists on marrying Anand! Is there a man with such a generous heart and soul? I have no idea what Anand is up to. Asha said he is preparing for the IAS. They've both lost a whole year with the delays—first with the MA exams and then with the delay in the declaration of the results. What a mess the educational system is in! What can we do but pray and wait?"

"Not just the educational system, the bloody country. The future of our daughter, too, is in no better shape. Anand won't get into the IAS, nor will he find a decent job," Aditya prophesied.

"Well, we don't know that for sure. If we knew, we could try to reason with her. There's no guarantee that if we find someone for her, she'll be happy. Nothing is certain. Asha, too, has no idea. You can tell by that look on her face. She is so unhappy. I don't understand the point of being in love and being so miserable?" Karuna sighed.

"She does not have to be unhappy. She can change her mind today. For an intelligent girl, she can be stupid and stubborn. She comes first in class, but does not know where her own happiness, her best interests lie. Anand is not going to make her happy. That much I can say with confidence. Love may be blind, but marriage will open her eyes. It'll be too late then," he said.

"We don't know that for sure," Karuna pointed out. "If her marriage turns out to be unhappy, it will not be of our making. Our responsibility is to find the right girl for Vikram. His marital happiness is in our hands, and we must do the right thing," Karuna reminded him.

"But where have all the eligible girls gone? I thought Dr Hota might want his daughter married to our Vikram. But he never came forward with a proposal, and now she's married to some engineer in America," said Aditya.

The world was slowly becoming incomprehensible to Aditya. He could no longer fathom the reason behind other people's choices.

"Perhaps we should've taken the first step. We'll have to see more girls. I agree it's not easy to find a suitable girl for Vikram," said Karuna.

"The proposal comes from the daughter's family," Aditya reminded her.

"That's not always the case—we had so many proposals for Asha before she decided to marry Anand. It's our responsibility to find the right girl for our son."

"Oriyas are insane," said Aditya, as if he had just realised he was not an Oriya and certainly not insane. "There is this crazy pecking order—first come the IAS, then men with jobs abroad or those going for studies abroad, third the IIT graduates. Doctors appear after engineers, or at best alongside them. By encouraging Vikram to become a doctor, we may have diminished our chances of finding a suitable girl!"

"That would be ridiculous if what you say is true. A good doctor is never out of work and is never poor. Do you know a good doctor who is not doing well? There is also the family culture to consider. You are in the teaching profession, so are Abhay and Madhav. Your father is a historian and archaeologist. The world has changed, I agree—people are after money. There is too much corruption. We cannot think like others, even if we tried to. So why compare ourselves with others?" said Karuna.

Looking back over the past few years of her life, Asha could not decide if it was a glass half-full or a glass half-empty situation. The MA examination, which was due to take place before the end of the academic year, prior to the summer vacation, took place in December—thanks to student riots and other civil disturbances in Orissa. It wasn't clear what the students were protesting about. The results were delayed for another six months. Events were spinning out of control. No one took responsibility for the shabby state of affairs in Orissa, though matters were significantly worse in Bengal, where universities had been shut for years, thanks to the Naxalite movement.

Asha's own life was held in limbo like an unfinished sentence. Cursed like Sleeping Beauty, she was waiting for Anand to find a job so they could get married. Until then life remained frozen. There was no prospect of Anand finding a job as he, too, was waiting for his results. When Anand moved to Vidya Vihar for his graduate studies, they could no longer meet as frequently. They kept in touch via letters, which is also how they had communicated when he was at Harrison College. But seeing each other was better than not being able to do so. They used to exchange books with letters concealed in them. The problem with posting letters was that they regularly disappeared in the post.

"I wonder who reads the missing letters," Asha confessed to Rashmi, whose life had also changed dramatically, though she seemed happily reconciled to the state of matrimony and was expecting her first child.

"What will you do after your results?" Rashmi asked as they lay side by side gently swinging in a hammock in Rashmi's colourful roof garden.

"I don't know—perhaps apply for an ad-hoc lectureship when it's advertised. With all the tamasha going on, my parents are worried how long it will be before I can get married. Can't blame them for thinking I've made a mistake," said Asha.

"What do you think? You can always change your mind, you know, and marry someone your parents choose. You have that choice," Rashmi reminded her.

"You sound like my father. Without Anand my life will be unbearable, incomplete. How can I leave him, especially when he is trying so hard?" said Asha.

Deep inside, she was far from certain when she would be able to feel complete; there was always something missing. She felt as if by saying those words she could make things happen, like reciting a mantra. She did not want to leave home, go to work and earn a living. Her home was her castle. She wanted to make a home just the way Rashmi had done.

"Does Anand feel the same way you do? Maybe your father has a point?" This was the first time Rashmi had asked Asha such a direct and personal question.

Asha looked at Rashmi for a moment and replied, "Do you know if your husband loves you the way you do?"

"We've had this conversation before. I don't; I never will. That's why I chose the safe path. But you have taken the riskier route. You have chosen love, but has love chosen you? As you know, even our Constitution does not guarantee us the pursuit of happiness!" Rashmi laughed, but she was serious.

Asha joined in. It felt good to laugh. She remembered the laughing game they'd played as children. Asha told Rashmi about it, and they laughed some more.

When a letter arrived from the Government of Orissa inviting Asha to an interview for the post of lecturer in English, Asha assumed that Anand had also received a similar letter. She had not heard from him for three weeks. The last time he wrote, he was at his parents' home. He seemed not too concerned about his joblessness. Asha, on the other hand, was going out of her mind worrying when things would fall into place and they could marry and start living together. Yet never did she waver in her decision and consider the prospect of marrying someone in a position to provide her with a comfortable life and perhaps moments of fulfilment and happiness. She had given her word, and she felt committed. They were as good as married—for better or worse.

The day she went to attend the job interview, Asha was far from happy with the way things had turned out for her. A job was not what she yearned for. She had come for the job because she did not wish to be a burden on her parents. She turned up thinking she would be the only female interviewee. And was looking forward to seeing Anand, not most of her female classmates, married and pregnant.

"What are you doing here?" Asha asked Shakti, unable to hide her surprise as she surveyed Shakti's rotund figure.

"The same reason you're here," Shakti replied sweetly. Then she asked, "Where is Anand? I can't see him."

"I, too, thought he'd be here," confessed Asha.

She did not expect him to deliver miracles; just a letter saying how he was and what he was up to would have been fine.

"Maybe he's attending the next batch of interviews. Where is he living these days?" Shakti asked.

"With his parents," Asha replied. "When are you due?" was all Asha could think of asking, though she felt like saying a lot of things. But didn't, realising it would make her sound, more or less, like her mother.

"Once I get the job, I'll join and then take leave. I can take some French leave too, if I need to." Shakti winked.

Asha was aghast listening to the cavalier way in which her classmates were planning to make use of the generous maternity allowance provided by the State, as if it was their personal dowry. Shakti had done everything Asha could never do—get pregnant first, then marry, get a government job and take advantage of all the benefits. Perhaps it was the only way Shakti could get her parents and her boyfriend to agree on the marriage. And now she was planning to take an extended maternity leave even before getting the job! Asha was flabbergasted.

Their employer, the Government of Orissa, would give Shakti and Asha the same salary. The fact that Asha was a Gold Medallist or that she would do a better job made not a jot of difference, except that Asha was posted at Harrison College, the premier institution for higher education in Orissa. Shakti would have shunned such a high-profile posting. It would have involved a lot of work and prevented her from taking all the leave she had in mind.

That night Asha started writing a letter to Anand, telling him she had touched the limit of her own sorrow, and wanted to know if he was ready to stand in the center of the fire with her and not desert her. Words came rushing out like a stream down a mountain, gathering pace, bouncing down boulders, disappearing into crevices, exploring the landscape of its birth. The river of her loneliness gushed forth from the mouth of the Mahanadi, where the sun sat smoking idly all day long, watching the world go by. The words rolled over scree, mud, clay, hills and falls, gathering momentum. They claimed her completely. Asha lived in a cloud, writing poetry.

She could not remember exactly when she had started to write. It seemed as if she had been writing forever, which may indeed have been the case. She wrote because it was easier to put her thoughts down on paper rather than utter them aloud. She feared those around her did not have the time to listen, listened without hearing, or perhaps heard without understanding. It reminded her of the madman in College Square who stood on a box across the road from the traffic policeman waving his arms as he blew his whistle loudly, trying desperately to direct the unruly traffic. The madman imitated the traffic policeman and waved his hands as he spouted words. Most passersby ridiculed him, a few shouted back, commanding him to get out of their way. He was as much of a nuisance as the policeman.

It is true that Asha wrote mostly for herself; she did not feel the need to tell others what was going on inside her head. It seemed simpler this way, yet she felt the need to write in riddles. Her poems were short, cryptic and abstract—speaking in metaphors and images. She never sent her poems for publication, unaware such a practice existed. The poems that first appeared in the college magazine were more by accident than design. One day Prof Pani had asked her for a few poems for the magazine. She had no idea how he found out that she wrote poetry.

But the day she heard from a major Indian poet that he would like to publish one of her poems in the forthcoming issue of his celebrated journal, Asha's joy knew no bounds. She'd asked her father to post the poems. Asha then forgot about it, as she never expected the letter to reach its destination or the editor to like her poems and offer to publish them. When a letter addressed to her arrived within a week, she went into a state of euphoria that lasted for days. When a copy of the magazine arrived, with her poem on the first page, her joy was limitless.

"What are you so happy about? Has Anand written with news about a job?" Karuna asked.

"Ma, wait..." Asha replied and ran to bring the magazine. "See, they have published my poem!"

After reading the poem, Karuna said with approval, "Yes, it is very good. When did you write it? Have you written more?"

Karuna was a writer and poet herself; she wrote in Oriya. Asha found her mother's style exceptional—moving yet muscular. But Asha felt she could never write as well as her ma. After the birth of her two younger sons, Karuna was unable to keep up with the competing demands of the world of writing and her own private world. Something had to give; it was her writing.

"I wrote this not long ago. The poem just came to me, demanded to be written, and here it is in print! I cannot believe it," Asha said ecstatically.

"I don't wish to burst your bubble of joy, Asha. But when you get a rejection letter next, will you feel as much joy?" Karuna asked.

"What do you mean?" a puzzled Asha asked back. "I'll be devastated, I guess, if I get a rejection. But I can't expect every poem to be accepted either."

"All I'm trying to say is don't get too excited when success shows its face; remember, failure is the same face with a mask on. Success and failure are like the two sides of a coin. If you meet one, just think of the other. It helps to keep your balance. When a poem is rejected, it's not because it isn't a good poem," said Karuna.

Asha nodded, taking in her mother's wise words. "You remind me of Kipling," said Asha. "Remember his great poem, 'If'?"

"Yes, but you haven't told me if you've heard from Anand?" Karuna asked.

"No, I haven't."

Karuna was upset that the joy of being published had disappeared from her daughter's face. But now that they had spoken about Anand, Karuna asked, "Do you think he really cares for you?"

"How can I know? How can anyone know? I think he does. It's a matter of trust, and I trust him," Asha said philosophically, resigned to the fact that human beings can never really know such things. "Can anyone ever know if they are loved or not. All I know is *I* love him. Maybe that is my punishment."

"How can love be a punishment, Asha? I love you, your bapa loves you, Aja loves you, your brothers and uncles love you—some kinds of love you know. And they bring joy to all of us. But whether Anand loves you, only God knows. Sometimes I wonder if Anand knows! Remember, it doesn't have to be a punishment; you can change your mind, if you're not sure. You have your entire life ahead of you," Karuna said. Then she asked, as an afterthought, "Do you like him?"

"What an absurd question—of course I do!" Asha replied.

"Not as absurd as you think. If you like someone, you can always enjoy their company. Love is complicated. It can be. You can love someone without trusting them. That's the worst kind of relationship..." Karuna could explain no further.

Asha felt fairly certain she liked, loved and trusted Anand. As there was no way she could know if Anand truly loved her, and from time to time that existential question bothered her, she kept writing about it, mostly in her diary. Occasionally they came out as poems, which eventually found a home in some journal or another. Every publication was so unexpected, it always tasted sweet.

The day she got her letter of appointment, Asha also got a letter from Anand. It was brief and to the point. He had not been invited for an interview for the Government of Orissa's ad-hoc lectureship posts. However, he was preparing for the IAS entrance examinations. He mentioned in passing a job offer from a private college. Jobs with private institutions were insecure, at the mercy of ruthless businessmen who hired and fired as they pleased. Asha hoped he would not settle for that. Anand also wrote he had applied for a research fellowship at IIT Bombay. The letter ended with a cryptic line, 'You must feel free to shape your life as you please.' Life had replaced the word destiny which he had crossed out. He'd added, 'PS: I love you.'

Asha was not entirely sure what he meant. How was she to shape her life as she pleased without him? Did he not know that *he* was her destiny? She wanted to know if he could live with his own failure, stand in a ditch and still look up to the stars and the moon and say yes! She wanted to hear that he would make something of himself—first and foremost a good human being. She wanted so many things—wanted God to build a bridge for her to walk across the sky and storm, fire and water, to love. If he loved her, he must know all this, she thought.

She showed her letter of appointment to her parents and reported the gist of Anand's letter to them. Aditya nodded, knowing anything he said about Anand would come out wrong. Reading the appointment letter, he asked, "When will you join? The letter does not specify a date? Shall I ask Dr Biswal?"

Karuna spoke for both of them when she said, "At least Anand is trying—let's hope he qualifies for the IAS."

"I hope so too," said Aditya. "Ma, remember when you are older, as old as we are now, you will have regrets. But you don't want to regret things you could so easily have done differently. Nor do we want to think you could've lived a better life, that we could've done something about it. You have a choice now; make good use of it. Choices don't remain forever... You know what they say about time and tide."

"Bapa, I, too, hope the choices I'm making will bring me happiness, not regret," Asha replied.

"Are you sure? You went off and found someone without our knowledge. You know what a conservative society we live in. By simply making such a choice, you prevented us from finding the right man for you," said Aditya.

"Well, none of us know what the future holds—whether your happiness lies with Anand, or you'd been happily married already with someone we found for you," Karuna observed.

"No one knows the future. We can only try to do the right thing now!" said Aditya. "The chances you have now will not be there in the future, remember that. Our society does not offer too many choices; it is unforgiving if you make a mistake."

Within days Asha joined Harrison College as a lecturer in the department of English. She was expected to spend time in the staff common room chit-chatting with other staff members. She found that the most challenging part of her job. Asha was not good at small talk. That she was the only female member of the faculty, the youngest, and the only lecturer who was the recipient of the university Gold Medal made her stand out among her colleagues.

Teaching was also a drama in several acts. When Asha was a student, the boys in her class were always up to some kind of mischief. Difficult to blame them, as some of the lecturers were so incompetent they should never have been appointed in the first place. The roll-call, the first act, was a farce. Yet teachers persisted in wasting time, often spending half the allocated class time on the futile exercise.

While the lecturer poured over the register, calling out the numbers and ticking them off, students who had 'presented' themselves slipped out through the back door. Others excused themselves after the roll-call saying they were feeling unwell or drumming up some incredible excuse. Once a student, who turned up dressed like Gandhi, said he had to go and save the nation! On another occasion, the only students who had not walked out of the class were the girls, who watched with amusement the shrinking-class syndrome. When the teacher finally looked up, noticing the empty benches, he said, "We better go as well," and he shuffled out!

On another occasion, the teacher had a speech impediment. He started the roll-call with, "Thee thirthee?" He was referring to roll number 330.

The student, who was very much present but suffered from a similar speech impediment, replied hesitantly, 'Yeth, thar!'

The lecturer was upset, thinking the student was making fun of him. So, he corrected the student with, "Say yeth thar, not yeth thar!"

"Yeth, thar!" the student repeated respectfully, at which point the entire class burst into irrepressible laughter.

The lecturer, losing his temper, commanded, "Say yeth thar!"

Finally, another student stood up and explained, "Sir, roll number 330 has a speech impediment—like you. He is not mimicking you!"

The students tried their best not to giggle and laugh after that.

It was customary for female students to sit in the front benches. Thanks to the rise in the female student population, and to English being a compulsory subject, women occupied one half of the class. During Deepavali, the men brought fireworks to the classroom. During the lecture, someone would light a firecracker. Hearing the sizzling sound of a matchstick lighting the nozzle of the firecracker, the girls sitting at the back would plug their ears with their fingers, anticipating the firecracker going off. Some of the girls were so terrified they looked like the three monkeys—see no evil, hear no evil, speak no evil—as they sat with their eyes closed, ears covered and mouth zipped up. Those nearest to the firework demonstration slowly crept away from their seats. Rows of students disappeared while this hullaballoo went on.

What if my students treat me like that? Asha worried, determined that her classes should not turn into such farces. She came prepared and did not waste time telling the students what a lousy profession teaching was or that they should all aim to join the IAS. She made her own rules and started with dispensing with the roll-call.

"I don't wish to waste your time or mine," she announced. "I don't know all of you—there are over a hundred roll numbers in the register. I see about seventy or at best eighty present here. I also know that some of you are quite capable of saying 'present' even when the person, whose roll number it is, is not present. I have no idea who Arvind Das, Roll Number 120, is," Asha said referring randomly to a name and number on her list. "If I have to verify your identity and then take the roll-call, I cannot do my real job— which is to teach. So everyone will be marked present. If you wish to leave, please do so now. If you stay, you cannot disrupt the class. If you do, I will walk out and report the entire class to the head of the department and the principal. Is that clear?" Asha asked loudly.

She was half-expecting half the class to walk out. After all, she had given them permission to do so. When no one did, she was relieved and surprised. The students, too, had not expected to be presented with such an option. Initially, they stayed out of curiosity and inertia. For Asha it was an opportunity—what else was literature for if not to make you think, ask relevant questions, and have fun in the process? She shared with the students her view of the world, encouraging them to find out who they were and could be. Her classes were packed, attracting students who did not belong to the class.

CHAPTER 14

It is true that preparations for Asha's wedding began the day she was born. Karuna had been buying things for as long as she could remember. She would mutter to herself, "This is for Asha's wedding," or, "This is for Vikram's wife," as she invested in a gold bangle or a necklace. Yet the most basic of necessities for the two marriages were still not in place—a bride for Vikram and an income for Anand. As she could do nothing about the latter, Karuna focussed on what was achievable. She had been diligent, considered almost a hundred proposals for Vikram, seen more than a dozen girls, but had not yet found one she thought 'suitable'.

As Karuna and Aditya also saw the world through completely different lenses, life did not always run smoothly in the Guru household. With the two pulling in opposite directions, they often found themselves standing alone, at a tangent, far away from where they had started. It was not unusual for them to return home not talking to each other and then complaining to the children of the unreasonableness of the other.

"Your father never listens to me, says the wrong things—at this rate, we'll never find the right girl for Vikram," a frustrated Karuna informed the family one evening after returning home from an expedition to meet a girl and her family.

"I did as asked. Then your ma changed her mind! Somehow

I'm to blame," Aditya said in self-defence. "What did I do wrong? I'm tired of it all."

"Why did you eat all those sweets and sit there enjoying your tea when you knew well we could not possibly choose that girl for Vikram?" Karuna complained.

"What was I to do? It was a long journey, and I was hungry. There was no time to eat before we visited them. We were already late. Why did you not say something to me then? We both knew there was no chance of an alliance, but what is the harm in accepting their hospitality? Perhaps we should not travel such long distances just to see a girl. Aren't there any decent girls in Cuttack?" Aditya replied.

"If there were, would we be foolish enough to go all the way in search of one—incurring all that expense, spending so much time and energy?" said Karuna.

When Abhay arrived, Aditya complained, "It is surprising we can't find a reasonably attractive girl, from a good family background with no hereditary diseases, who is a graduate! I simply cannot believe it. How can it be that difficult?"

"And we don't want a dowry!" Karuna added. "Can't imagine if we wanted a dowry what sort of a girl we'd have to settle for!"

"Probably a good one. You see, sometimes people think that if you don't want a dowry, something is wrong with your son," said Asha.

"Don't listen to her. Asha is playing the devil's advocate. She does that to annoy me," said Karuna. Then she added, "Suresh used to say when he was looking for a son-in-law, 'Boudi, I just want a boy who has an income and has no hereditary diseases.' We have a prospective son-in-law with no income and no daughter-in-law in sight! I believe our children are blessed with all the attributes we are looking for. Asha has even gone and done the unthinkable, taken up a job! Yet we can't seem to find a girl for Vikram, and God alone knows when Anand will secure an income!"

"Perhaps it has something to do with families wanting sons and not daughters. There are simply not enough girls around?"

Asha suggested as a possible explanation for their inability to find a suitable girl.

"You maybe partly correct, but I must say, you come up with some curious ideas. I know every family wants a boy, but I do not know anyone among our reasonably large network of friends and acquaintances destroying a female foetus simply because they do not want a girl! Take our extended family; we would not dream of doing anything of the sort. I've not heard of anyone doing anything unusual either to have a son. Children are God's gift. You accept whatever you are given," Karuna said philosophically.

"Taking into account the perennial shortage of girls, let alone girls who will meet your exacting standards, perhaps you should have arranged nana's marriage a long time ago as they did in the past," Asha suggested.

"We have to look at the situation today and can't go backwards," Aditya said. "If we could, I'd have arranged both your marriages at birth. There was clearly a reason why they had child marriages before! Look at the mess we're in now."

"We'd have a different kind of mess if we had done so," Karuna remarked. "There's a good reason why child marriages no longer take place, at least among educated people. We can't always be responsible for what others do; we can only try to do the right thing. We've been looking for a girl for Vikram for some time now. But I agree finding the right girl is proving harder than I imagined!"

"I should've handed over the job of finding a suitable boy for me, so you would be begging me now to find a boy myself!" Asha observed.

"You see, that's where you're completely wrong. There were many good proposals for you—Indian Administrative Service officers as well as from the Foreign Service, engineers with good jobs in America, and doctors too. There were plenty of good suitors for you. We thought you should complete your studies, but then you went off and chose Anand, and look at the state we're in now!" said Karuna.

"I never knew you had so many proposals. No one told me!" Asha remarked.

"How could we when you insist on marrying Anand? Even now, I dare say, if you changed your mind, we could find a suitable boy for you," Aditya added.

Trying to mask his disappointment, Aditya still hoped his daughter would see her mistake and change her mind.

"You're looking for the perfect girl; there is no such person. You're not happy with me—someone you gave birth to and spent your life training. You're always telling me I'm not good enough. How can a girl from a different background fit in? No man, I think, would also be good enough for me," said Asha.

"You amaze me—I don't criticize *you*!" Karuna replied. "I just want you to be the best *you* can be. But you never listened—you went off and found someone, never even asked us for our opinion. As if we were your enemies! What can we do but hope he'll make you happy? That is all we can pray for—because what you've done has not made us happy or proud. If you end up unhappy, don't blame us." Karuna held back her tears. "As parents we will always want the best for each one of our children. If I went around saying how great or wonderful you are, how would that sound? Also, how would it have helped you to be the best you can be?"

"Ma, you criticize me as much as you want," said Vijay.

He and Vivek were back home by then, and had gravitated to Aditya's room.

"Me too," Vivek added. "I understand why you tell me off. Nani knows too, but everyone needs to hear how extraordinary they are, sometimes."

"Being extraordinary can also be a problem," Vijay said. "Then all the ordinary folks will fail to understand you, be jealous of you, and end up hating you."

"I thought you knew how special you all are—to your father and me. Maybe I should tell you more often than I do," said Karuna.

"I wouldn't do that, or we'll all get so swollen headed you'll have a hard time cutting us down to size. Also, we wouldn't recognize you if you went around praising us. Who would we turn to for criticism then?" Vijay joked.

"Admit it, ma; no daughter-in-law will rise to your expectations," Asha said.

"How can they? They are brought up differently. Arranged marriages took place between families that knew each other and when the children were young, young enough to adapt. Women these days marry late. How can they be moulded by the mother-in-law, especially when she is seen as the bad, evil one?" Karuna sighed. "The world has changed, but not all change is always good," she added.

"*Plus ça change, plus c'est la même chose...*" said Asha.

Karuna replied, "It's Tamil and Malayalam to me!"

"The French have a saying—the more things change, the more they remain the same," Asha explained.

⁂

Regardless of her lack of faith in arranged marriages, Asha did not decline the invitation to join the family delegation to see another girl for Vikram. Aditya and Karuna had seen the girl once, unofficially, at a wedding. Though not ecstatic about Tanuja, they had not rejected her, although her formal education had been interrupted due to her father's illness. Karuna thought if Tanuja was willing to continue her education, it could tip the balance.

As Vishu had a habit of turning up unexpectedly, it was no surprise when he arrived that morning. It turned out to be a happy coincidence. Asha accompanied her parents, Vikram, Sadhana, and her uncles, Abhay and Vishu, to meet Tanuja. They travelled in Vishu's jeep; it was a two hours' drive from Cuttack.

Once they settled into the journey, Sadhana asked, "Mausi, why has Tanuja not carried on with her education? Did you not want a graduate for Vikram?"

"Oh yes, we would definitely prefer a graduate, but it is difficult to find one with the right family background. The parents of such girls want to marry them off to IAS officers. Not all families are like ours, you see," Karuna explained.

Sadhana was the kind of girl Karuna would have liked as her daughter-in-law.

"I don't understand this craze for an IAS!" Abhay exclaimed.

Sadhana nodded as if to say there was no accounting for other people's tastes.

"Why not when you get a large house, servants, and all kinds of facilities?" Karuna pointed out. "Nani was not looking for a doctor husband for you. But when the proposal came, she recognized the advantages of marrying a doctor." No one pointed out that Sadhana's in-laws were well off. Karuna then said, replying to Sadhana's original question, "You see, Tanuja's father was ill for some time before he died. Her elder sisters were all married. It fell on Tanuja to look after her father."

Remembering her own childhood after the death of her mother, Karuna had concluded that Tanuja, too, did not get the right breaks in life. Given a chance, she would also become the best of what she could be.

"I see, but when did her father die? Could she not have studied after his death?" Sadhana persisted.

"Her brother said she was embarrassed all her classmates were now her senior, so she refused to go to college," Karuna replied. "If Tanuja is willing to study after the marriage, we should consider the proposal seriously."

"Look at bohu," Vishu said with pride. "She studied after the children were born, and now she's a graduate! I have to give credit to nana, but mostly to bohu."

Vishu's wife had never been to college, but he was not fussed about it. He did not enjoy studying, but excelled in sports. He never completed his bachelor's degree.

"What did her father die of?" Vikram asked.

"I'm not sure, but we need to find out." Karuna made a mental note, thinking of enquiring about possible hereditary diseases.

Once they arrived at the Mishra family home, Tanuja's brother, Arnab, was surprised to see the entourage. It seemed like a good sign that so many of the Guru family had turned up. *They must be interested in the proposal*, he thought, ushering his guests into the sitting room. His mother joined them. Tanuja arrived with a tray full of sweets and savouries only to disappear after placing the tray on the table.

She's attractive enough, but what is she like as a person? Vikram wondered why she did not stay to have a chat.

When Tanuja returned with another tray laden with several cups of tea, Karuna said, patting the seat next to her, "Come and sit down. You've been busy since we arrived. We haven't had a chance to talk to you."

"Oh, she is very shy," said her mother as Tanuja went and sat next to her.

Karuna assumed she sat there so they could face each other.

"Please try the samosas. They've been freshly made by Tanuja," her mother said as she passed the cups of tea around.

Everyone was temporarily engaged in sampling the sweets, samosas and namkins. They made appreciative noises, but there was not a lot of conversation flowing. Then Karuna excused herself to wash her hands, and the ladies decided it was time for a bathroom break. Soon they found themselves sitting in another room while the men carried on talking in the other room. Tanuja sat quietly taking turns smiling at Karuna, Asha and Sadhana. But she never opened her mouth.

Then Karuna asked, "Your ma tells me you're a good cook. What do you like to cook, Tanuja?"

Tanuja looked at her mother, who replied, "She'll cook anything you want her to. She was looking after her father; she did everything."

Karuna took the opportunity to enquire, "How did Mishra babu die?

"He suffered so much, I cannot tell you. Without our daughter here, I could not have managed, he could not have survived…" and she broke down in tears.

Karuna looked at Asha and Sadhana, wondering what to say next. Recovering her composure, Tanuja's mother said, "My daughter will do everything you ask her to. She will make you proud and happy! Her father's blessings go with her."

Reasonably tall, fair, and smooth-skinned, Tanuja was not unattractive. She may not have been slim, but she was not fat, slightly on the plump side, perhaps.

As conversation among the women remained subdued after Tanuja's mother's emotional outburst, Karuna suggested, "Perhaps we should go back and join the men? Tanuja, come with us— they've all come to meet you."

The ladies joined the men, but all the questions directed at Tanuja were answered by either her brother or her mother.

Until finally an exasperated Vikram asked, "Tanuja, what do *you* enjoy doing—cooking, reading, music, painting?"

After a long pause, looking a bit confused, Tanuja said shyly, "Everything."

Everyone laughed.

Then Karuna said, "It's good to be interested in everything."

Vikram wished he had heard more directly from Tanuja. He could not help wondering why she did not speak for herself.

⁂

As they drove back home, Karuna was eager to hear everyone's views. She asked Sadhana first, "So what did you think?"

"She is attractive enough—maybe a bit plump…but…"

Sadhana had not finished her sentence when Karuna interjected, "She'll lose weight after marriage—most women do."

"Or she might become fat once she's pregnant and then remain so after having a child?" Asha offered an alternative view.

Vikram smiled but didn't say anything. Everyone else was silent.

"Sadhana, I interrupted you. You said Tanuja is a bit on the plump side, but...but what?" Karuna reminded her niece.

Before Sadhana could reply, Vishu offered his view. "Bohu can teach her yoga. You don't want too skinny a girl, such girls always fall ill."

"True, she has good child-bearing hips," Sadhana pointed out. "And as Vishu uncle says, if you teach her yoga and she is more active, she will look trim. Tanuja probably does not do much now, after the death of her father. Sitting at home, cooking and eating can make anyone plump. We got slimmer and fitter after marriage!" Then turning to Vikram, Sadhana asked, "What did you think? You saw her for the first time. What's your view?"

"Difficult to say...as you all said, she's not unattractive, but as a person, what do we know about her? I have no idea what she likes, dislikes, what makes her laugh or cry? I did ask, but she said she liked everything! The few words that escaped her lips did not give much away," Vikram said, unable to hide his disappointment.

"It's a good quality in a woman not to speak her mind, especially in the company of people she does not know," Vishu pointed out.

"I agree," said Aditya. "Your ma did not say much when we were married, but now I can't get a word in. It's generally a good thing to keep one's own counsel, don't you agree? Calmness is a good thing in a woman."

"Perhaps, but what's the point of my meeting her if all I can say is she is not bad to look at! You could have told me that," said Vikram.

"Speak and you lose, keep silent—you also lose. A woman can never win—flip-over double-strike like our rupee coins. In any case, how can anyone know another human being after one brief encounter?" Asha chipped in.

"All the more reason to find someone from a decent, cultured and trustworthy family," Karuna said.

"What is your view, Abhay?" Aditya asked.

Abhay, who had been sitting quietly in the back, replied, "Women change a lot after marriage. What you see today is not what you'll get tomorrow. After a year with the family, she'll shape up. Bohu, Sadhana and Asha will influence her positively."

"What if she doesn't change, does not want to change?" Vikram asked.

"All women change after marriage," Karuna and Sadhana said in unison.

Unsure of what her mother and cousin actually meant, Asha said, "One thing you can be sure of is change—whether you like it or not. Even you will change."

"I can help Tanuja. She'll learn, I think," Sadhana said. That was the least she could do for her favourite cousin.

Vikram sensed something was not quite right with Tanuja's responses, but could not quite put his finger on it. Sometimes he felt he could not trust his own instincts and concluded he was getting cold feet. Tanuja's lack of engagement was mistaken by the Guru family for modesty, shyness and a desirable quality in a woman.

Aja, who had not met Tanuja, on seeing a photo of hers remarked, "Silence is a good quality in a woman."

Unable to find the perfect girl for her son, Karuna thought that if Tanuja was willing to study and widen her horizons, there was no reason why they should not bring her home as their daughter-in-law. Under their care and influence, she could become the person they wanted her to be. After all, a girl with strong views of her own could not be moulded similarly.

Karuna and Aditya went to meet Tanuja again. This time Karuna specifically asked her if she was willing to study after her marriage.

"Vikram will be busy preparing for his medical exams. It will be an ideal time for you to study as well. Are you happy with that? He may also go to study abroad. Do you have any problem with that?" Karuna asked.

Unsurprisingly, mother and son replied, "Tanuja will do whatever you want her to. She will bloom under your guidance. You will not regret your decision."

Karuna directed her question again to Tanuja, who nodded her consent and whispered a barely audible, "Yes."

Karuna, who had struggled to study all through her childhood as a result of her mother's death, assumed Tanuja had faced similar challenges in her life with the loss of her father. Given the opportunity, she thought, Tanuja would bloom into the woman she would like her daughter-in-law to be.

CHAPTER 15

That summer Asha received an all-expenses paid invitation to a conference at the American Institute in Hyderabad. When Karuna heard about it, she said, "Asha, how can you travel alone; is anyone else we know attending the conference?"

"I don't know, ma. This is a conference by invitation only and not one to which any academic can apply to attend. It's an honour to be invited! I'm probably the only one invited from Orissa. Please can I go?" Asha pleaded.

"I'll ask bapa. I take it Anand has not been invited? Which reminds me, what's his news?" Karuna asked. "Now that we've settled Vikram's marriage, it will be a good idea to have both the weddings together. But how can you marry a man without a job? Why did you choose a penniless man as a husband? We are not rich. We can't give you a dowry—does he know that? And you, do you know that without money love cannot survive either? It is all very nice to marry the one you love, but why choose someone who has no means of looking after you?" Karuna complained.

It made financial sense to have a joint reception for both weddings. Aditya and Karuna could have secured a reasonable dowry for their son, which would have paid for both weddings. But they did not want a dowry, nor did they offer one for their daughter. When they got married, no dowry was exchanged.

They wanted their children's marriages to be free of the curse of dowry as well.

"Last I heard from him, Anand wrote he'll be coming to Cuttack soon. Maybe he'll have some good news then," Asha replied. "But can I please go to Hyderabad?"

"Hyderabad is not important, your marriage is. The question is how long will you wait for Anand to find a job?" Karuna sighed.

"As long as it takes," Asha replied. "Like you, I think my marriage is important, and that's the reason I *have* to go to Hyderabad."

"What a ridiculous idea! What's the connection?" Karuna remarked, feeling sorry for her daughter's plight.

"You won't understand," said Asha.

"You keep saying that every time I say something you don't want to hear. We are only saying what we believe is for your good. You don't seem to be thinking clearly at all. Love can do that; you think you can overcome everything," said Karuna.

They were sitting in the front veranda, sipping their mid-morning cup of tea. Their conversation was interrupted when the postman arrived. On seeing their pet mongoose standing upright as if at attention and the postman hesitating to open the gate, Asha went to collect the post.

"Rikki is quite harmless, really. He's chained, as you can see. You can come in," said Asha as she approached the gate.

"Harmless? He's ready to attack, can't you see?" replied the postman, looking warily at the mongoose. "What did you call him?"

"Rikki..." Asha said with a wave of her hand as if to say it was a long story and he did not have the time to hear it.

Recognising Anand's handwriting on one of the envelopes, she tore it open as she walked back from the front gate.

"Anything important?" Karuna enquired.

"Hmm...hmm..." Asha muttered as she read the letter.

She could not help thinking how her parents used to check the post first before handing hers over. So many things had changed. A few years ago, she was not allowed to go to the movies, although they could not prevent her from hearing every sordid detail, especially the sex scenes, from her friends. Asha never sneaked away with her friends to see a film. For a start, it was impractical to do so. Hindi films were so long it would be impossible to lie one's way out of it. Even with Rashmi's help, it would not have worked. Besides, Rashmi lived under similar prohibitions at her home, though her family was on the whole more relaxed about films. After Rashmi got married, her husband took her to practically every movie. Asha could not bear the prospect of being a gooseberry tagging along with the newly married couple. "What, go with you and be a kebab mein huddi?" Asha would say, declining Rashmi's invitations to accompany them.

"What is taking you so long—haven't got all day!" Karuna complained as Asha kept reading the letter.

"Now who's being impatient? Anand has written that while he narrowly missed being invited for the IAS interview, he has received a research fellowship at IIT, Bombay. Says he will try for the IAS again next year," Asha said, her voice trailing off at the end as she tried to digest the unpalatable news.

"I don't understand," Karuna observed, mulling over the matter. "He never got invited to an interview for the Orissa government lectureships, and now the IAS. Yet he's got a research position at IIT? As long as he tries for the IAS again, that's some consolation. God knows if he'll get through next year. What if he doesn't? How long will you wait? Finding a job can take time; that's why one marries a man a few years older—when he's settled and a bit mature." Karuna was lost in her own train of thoughts that hurtled into the future without any sense of direction or purpose. "What's the point of marrying if his job keeps him in Bombay and yours is here?"

It was more of a rhetorical question as the prospect of Asha being in two places at the same time was a physical impossibility. Giving up her job to be with him did not seem sensible, either.

"As I'm going to marry Anand, we may as well go ahead with

the wedding. It'll make life easier for all of us. And you can have one big reception for both weddings," said Asha.

"In which case, we have to go to meet his parents and finalize the wedding. Are you sure this is what you want?" Karuna wanted to be sure herself.

"As sure as one can be. I had not realised you and bapa need to meet his parents. I've never met any of his family members," said Asha.

It had only just dawned on her that after the wedding she would have to deal with Anand's family. She felt strange even thinking of his family. *Will there be enough time and space for 'us'*, she wondered, *let alone 'me' after the wedding?* Asha tried to picture her life after marriage, which at that precise moment seemed as unimaginable as life after death.

<hr />

"Vijay or Vivek will have to accompany Asha to Hyderabad if she really wants to attend that seminar," Aditya told his wife. "I can't take time off, nor can Abhay."

"Vijay has his inter-university and State cricket tournaments," Karuna reminded Aditya. "These days children are busier than their parents. Perhaps they can fly her there?" Karuna mused aloud as she poured tea.

Aditya laughed and said, "Even if they had that sort of money, they won't pay for her flight. She is just beginning her academic career."

He found it difficult to believe his daughter had been invited to participate in such a high-profile event.

When Asha walked in, Karuna informed her, "No one is free to accompany you to Hyderabad."

"All I need is someone to see me off at the train station here. Isn't Abhay kaku's friend, Gupta uncle, coming to receive me at Hyderabad? Surely, I can manage the overnight journey on my own without anyone having to accompany me? I can't sleep on trains, anyway," said Asha. But she, too, could not help wondering what if something untoward happened on the train?

"Better to have someone with you. What if you need help? These days, people don't help each other, especially if you're in trouble. On the contrary, a woman on her own might be seen as a target," Karuna observed.

Soon Vijay arrived and, on hearing about Asha's invitation, said, "There'll be people we know who will be travelling to Hyderabad on that train. It's simply a matter of finding out who they might be! I'll make a few enquiries."

"You can't make such speculative plans. They might have seats in completely different compartments. It'll be better if Vivek goes with Asha," Aditya pointed out.

"I'll ask Vivek," said Karuna.

When Asha mentioned in passing to Rashmi that her trip to Hyderabad was being scuppered for the lack of an escort, she immediately said, "What a coincidence, Avinash's sister, Manju, and her husband are going to Hyderabad at that time! I'll find out exactly when. They will be your chaperones. Wish I could come too; it would be such fun!" Rashmi's eyes glistened with the prospect.

"Can you come? It'll be fantastic!" a delighted Asha asked.

"Wishful thinking." Rashmi sighed.

Asha sensed a hint of sadness in Rashmi's voice.

As luck would have it, Rashmi's husband's sister, Manju, was travelling to Hyderabad on the same day. Everyone was relieved that Asha would be travelling with people they knew. But her parents still worried about all the things that could go wrong, and they wouldn't be there to help.

"Look after Asha. She has never travelled alone before," Aditya requested of Samir as he shook his hand firmly before they disembarked from the train.

"Don't worry, uncle. We'll look after her," both Samir and Manju said.

Looking at her father and brother standing on the platform as the train pulled away, Asha felt a pang of loneliness she had never felt before. This sudden surge of affection for her family surprised her. She had insisted on attending this seminar. That was her way of escaping from the family hothouse, where the only topic of conversation was marriage. Yet she was already missing them.

Noticing her discomposure and moist eyes, Manju remarked, "You've never left home before, have you? Mousa looked so worried—his only daughter. Fathers and daughters—what will happen when you get married?"

"I've never travelled on my own," Asha said. "That's why they're all worried. To be frank, so am I."

"It'll be fine," Manju said, taking Asha's hand. "You're going to attend some seminar, right? Rashmi said, but I forget. My memory is like a sieve these days. This is what happens after a few years of marriage and family life; your brain starts to work in ways you cannot understand!"

Asha replied with a smile, "Yes, I'm going to attend a seminar at the American Institute. Then I'll be staying on for a week to do some research. To be invited to such a prestigious seminar makes me nervous—especially all those professors from the US and from the best universities in India."

"Rashmi told us how talented you are, a Gold Medallist too!" Samir said.

Asha smiled again and replied, somewhat embarrassed, "Rashmi is so intelligent herself. I've no doubt she'd have been invited had she..." Asha stopped, realising that what she was going to say might sound the opposite of what she meant. Then she said, "I mean, unless we're placed in certain situations, we do not always find out what we are capable of. I suppose that's what we call *bhagya*, destiny."

Samir and Manju nodded. Samir said, looking at his wife, "What did I tell you? Armita here is no ordinary girl. She topped her class in MA, best all-round student as well. She'll go places. Just don't forget us when you're famous. You are a thinker, a philosopher; anyone can see that!"

Apart from an elderly gentleman who was quietly reading a journal, they pretty much had the compartment to themselves. Asha and Manju were chatting away when Samir announced he was going to have a lie down.

"Wake me if you need anything," he said as he climbed up to the top berth. "Manju, call me if you need anything," he repeated as he adjusted the pillow and spread the blanket, both courtesy of Indian Railways.

"I will," she replied. Turning to Asha, she said, "I, too, feel tired, didn't sleep a wink this afternoon. Thankfully, we can all go to bed early tonight after dinner."

Asha was partial to her afternoon siestas; she, too, had missed hers. "There was so much to do today, I missed mine. But I can't sleep on a train," she explained.

"Don't tell me this is your first train journey as well?" Manju asked.

"No, no. I love trains and have been to several places with my parents, but not on my own. I can't sleep in a public place like a train; anyone can walk in. It's not as if you can lock yourself in from inside."

At the next stop, they were joined by a couple who occupied the two remaining empty seats. Asha moved to the window seat when she saw them hesitating at the entrance. After the train resumed its journey, a waiter dressed in the uniform of Indian Railways arrived to take their orders for dinner. He looked so old and decrepit, with bushy eyebrows, a drooping and unkempt moustache, and hair growing out of his nostrils and ears, that Asha could not help staring. He was already staring at Asha and Manju as if he had discovered two apsaras trapped on his train.

"We'll have the vegetarian thali," Manju said, trying not to smile at the man's extraordinary face and dazed expression.

"Me too," said Asha.

"How many thalis do you want?" he enquired, looking at Samir.

"Three," Manju answered.

"Do you want anything else?" he asked.

"No," said Manju.

As the waiter stood there as if she hadn't answered his question, she said, "Just a moment." Turning her head upwards, she asked Samir, "Did you hear that? We are having the vegetarian thali."

When Samir did not reply, Manju got up and nudged her husband gently. Still Samir did not respond. She gave him another nudge, harder this time. "He is fast asleep!" she whispered to Asha with a scandalised look on her face. "I thought he was just having a lie down! Hope he's not coming down with something." The second poke woke Samir up, and he turned to face her. Manju practically jumped and screamed, "You were all right when you went to sleep!"

Samir could barely open his eyes, his eyelids were swollen; he was suffering from one of his allergies.

"I feel pretty awful," he said in a hoarse voice. "I don't want to eat anything."

"I have some bananas and biscuits. You can have that," Manju suggested.

"Yes, don't worry about food for me. I'll have something from your thali if I feel like it. The bananas and biscuits will be fine," he mumbled, going back to sleep.

"We'll have two thalis," Manju informed the waiter.

He nodded vigorously and looked at Samir with concern. He just stood there looking at the remaining passengers as if he was surprised to find them there.

"He's so prone to allergies. It looks pretty bad," Manju informed Asha. Then she stood up and asked Samir, "Do you want to take the medication now?"

"After the meal," Samir's muffled voice could be heard from above.

"Two thalis," the waiter said as he made a note of their seat numbers and shuffled sideways to take the other orders.

Dinner was a silent affair. Samir was feeling no better, and the food was much too spicy. By midnight, Samir and Manju were both ill. Samir's allergy got worse after dinner. Luckily, the medication knocked him out. He was soon snoring away along with the other men on the train. Manju could not sleep. She suffered from severe stomach cramps and lay on her berth, writhing in pain. The painkillers she took did not seem to work.

Asha felt lucky not to have been stricken by any ailment, except she felt permanently exhausted. She was surprised when she saw all the medication that Manju carried with her, virtually a mobile pharmacy. Asha had brought nothing of the sort with her. All through the night she kept dosing off, but could not fall asleep thanks to the off-key ragmala of men snoring all around her.

Then around 3am, Manju said, "Asha, can you please get some water at the next station? We've run out of water. Samir, as you can hear, is fast asleep. Thank God, otherwise his allergy would get significantly worse."

Asha was concerned the train might leave while she queued in the platform to fill their bottles with drinking water.

"Can you manage with tea?" she asked.

"Unfortunately not, it'll make matters worse. I need water," Manju pleaded.

"If I can't buy water from the vendors and I have to go out to get it from the station, then you must pull the chain if the train leaves and I'm not back," said Asha.

"I promise. How can I possibly leave you?" said Manju. "We're supposed to be looking after you! Now you're looking after us. I am so sorry."

"I never meant you'd leave me stranded at the station deliberately. I just mean that you're not well and Samir bhai is asleep. If the train leaves without me at this hour in a strange place, I won't know what to do," Asha explained.

"I'll pull the chain, promise!" Manju reassured her. "I can't sleep either. I'll be watching you like a hawk."

At the next stop, Asha was surprised no vendors were selling water. Those were tense moments when she ran to fill the water bottles. She could barely stand still in the queue and kept hopping as if standing on live coals. Her nervous restlessness protected her as the man behind her was doing his best to press himself against her. Finally it was her turn at the drinking-water tap, and Asha sprinted back safely to her carriage. The train whistled and was off again, reminding her of men who let out low wolf-whistles when they saw a woman they admired and wanted her to know. Not like the lecherous man in the queue trying to rub himself against her.

"You are such a good person, and you ran like a professional. Rashmi told us you were an all-rounder, good at everything! I can see that now," said Manju.

The couple who had boarded the train later slept through it all, so did the elderly man who had only spoken a few words when he placed his order for dinner. The next morning when the train reached Hyderabad, a bleary-eyed Asha searched for coolies to unload their luggage. The platform was crowded; there were so many people milling about, it was impossible to move. As Manju and Samir were feeling poorly, it was settled they would wait in the platform for their hosts to find them. It was not practical to wade through that jungle of people with their suitcases.

Samir finally spotted his sister standing at the opposite end of the platform. He waved at her until he caught her attention. Asha did not know Dr Gupta, nor what he looked like. The thought had not crossed her mind as to how she would locate him once she reached Hyderabad. As luck would have it, when Samir's sister and her husband arrived at the station, they ran into Dr Gupta, a neighbour, who explained that he was there to receive a friend's niece from Cuttack. Samir's sister remarked it was such a coincidence as they, too, had come to receive family from Cuttack.

The introductions took a while; there were six people who had to be introduced to each other.

Then Asha said, "Gupta uncle, I am Armita, Abhay uncle's niece."

"That's a coincidence!" said Manju. "How did you know?"

"Just an educated guess," Asha said. "What are the chances of another Dr Gupta from NGRI coming to receive a friend's niece from Cuttack?"

"Asha told us about you. She even predicted you'd know my sister," explained Samir. "The funny thing is we were supposed to be looking after her. But she ended up looking after us—my wife and I both fell ill on the train. Without Asha we could *not* have managed. She has not slept at all last night!" Samir filled in the details.

"Maybe we can all meet up before we return to Orissa?" Manju suggested.

"Yes, why don't we all get together when you're both feeling better?" Dr Gupta said as they made their way out of the station and followed each other in their separate Hindustan Motor cars to the National Geophysical Research Institute.

❦

The next day Dr Gupta took Asha to the American Institute, which was not far from his home. He left her with Prof Paramjit Singh, the director, who seemed to know Dr Gupta. Asha wondered if this is how the world works—she saw herself being passed like a parcel from one pair of hands to another. But this game of passing the parcel was far from simple—one ran the risk of being dropped, mishandled or destroyed at any point. So far she had been in safe hands. *What if my luck runs out?* Then she remembered her Aja telling her how God carries us during the hard times.

"You should've informed us about your arrival. We could've arranged a pickup," Prof Singh said, bringing Asha back to the here and now.

"I wasn't aware I could've done that, Prof Singh. But Dr Gupta has been very generous," Asha said, looking at Dr Gupta.

He seemed like the kindest man on earth she could think of, outside her family, needless to mention. His wife, daughter and son were delightful. They lavished their affection on her. Asha could not believe how attached the two children became within a day. The daughter was barely three, and the older son about six. They insisted she stay with them, not at the institute. It was agreed that Asha would come and stay with them after the seminar.

"I'll come and collect you next week. In the meanwhile, if you need anything, just let us know," Dr Gupta said as he stepped back into his car.

"We are here, too, to look after our visitors, Guptaji! But I'll make sure she calls you even if she doesn't need anything," said Prof Singh.

After shaking Dr Gupta's hands, Prof Singh turned to Asha, "By the way, Armita, call me Paramjit. Tell me, how do you know the Guptas?"

"He's a friend of my uncle who is also a geologist," Asha explained.

"Your family is in education, right? I looked up the Commonwealth Directory of Universities and noticed a few Gurus," he observed.

"Not all my uncles are Gurus—for example, my maternal uncle and the husband of my mother's youngest sister. They are also professors and heads of their departments," she said.

"I'd guessed you belong to the academic mafia in Orissa," Paramjit joked.

"On the contrary. Considering I ended up with a second-class BA (Hons), I'd say my family wield no power at all! What sort of a mafia would put up with such humiliation and injustice? The true mafia in education were the Patnaiks. Thankfully they could not operate while I took my master's."

"Didn't you get the Gold Medal for your master's?" he asked.

"Yes, I did. But for my BA (Hons) I was awarded a second class, though I passed with distinction in the other subjects. I was not awarded my rightful position in the university," Asha explained.

"How extraordinary! You must tell me more when we meet for dinner tomorrow. I've invited a few friends to my home; you must come. For now, let's settle you down at the institute." And he led her away, introducing her to other members of staff and the seminar participants.

⟡

The following morning Joshua Hart, a Harvard professor, launched the seminar with his inaugural lecture on American Transcendentalism. During the discussion that followed, he asked the participants what they thought was the most important characteristic of that group of writers. He wanted an answer in one brief sentence.

Asha said something along the lines that these individuals were in search of an American identity, and she quoted Emerson's phrase 'an original relationship with the universe'. It was sheer coincidence she had read Emerson's essay, *Nature*, not long ago, and those words had stuck.

Over dinner, Paramjit quizzed Asha about her views with regard to the speakers and the overall arrangements at the conference. He also asked her about her BA exam results. When he heard the story, he remarked, "It's incredible. But you'll be pleased to hear Joshua, Professor Hart, thinks highly of you. Your answer impressed him—what did you say? I had to leave the class briefly, unfortunately."

By then Asha had forgotten what exactly she had said. She was trying to remember when the Harvard professor came over with his plate of habshi halwa to join them. The conversation veered off in a completely different direction when he asked, quite casually, if she had considered coming to study at Harvard.

It seemed like such a wild idea, the only thing Asha could think of saying was, "From where would I get the money to go to Harvard!"

"If that's your only problem, a scholarship can be arranged," he said.

Asha had no idea that Harvard's admission policy was blind to financial need. But money was not her only concern. As one did not go around telling perfect strangers about one's personal life, she could not find a way of telling him there were other considerations such as marriage. It never occurred to her to accept his offer, go to Harvard, and marry later. However, when Asha returned to Cuttack, she felt differently about many things. She could not explain what they were, even to herself. She assumed it had to do with her marriage, just about everything did.

Her parents and Abhay went to settle matters with Anand's parents. While they were away, Asha wrote to Professor Hart, enquiring if his offer would extend to Anand as she was soon to be married. She never received a firm yes or no answer. He implied it might be possible, but his letter did not convey the same level of enthusiasm he had expressed in person. He ended his brief letter with, "Some people have strange priorities."

A couple of months before the wedding, Vikram had serious doubts about his. One evening, finding Karuna alone in the kitchen, he confessed, "Ma, I cannot marry Tanuja. During the brief encounter I had with her, I sensed a complete lack of warmth on her part, of any emotional connection. I feel she has agreed to the marriage because of her family situation. It may be an arranged marriage, but she should feel some desire to marry me. What if she does not feel anything for me?"

Karuna was right in the middle of her cooking. She sensed her son's need to talk. She had heard it before and thought the matter had been settled. As Vikram raised it again, she said, "Let's have dinner first, and then we can all talk about it. Can you call Asha? She's never around when I need her."

"That's not true," said Asha as she walked in. "I'm here, though not for long as you are so keen to marry me and send me away!

What do you want me to do?" Asha had arrived towards the end of their conversation.

"Lay the table; remember Aja and your uncles are here," Karuna said.

"Yes, I can count, ma." Asha smiled and looked at her brother. "Is everything okay?" Asha asked, sensing everything was not.

"Nothing you need to worry about," said Karuna.

"If nana has a problem, it is also my problem, our problem."

"We'll talk after dinner," Karuna said, feeling overwhelmed with problems.

Unfortunately, Karuna's dinner did not turn out as good as expected. She was a good cook, and Aditya was indeed a connoisseur of her cooking.

"Something has gone wrong with the cooking today. Normally, Karuna's fish curry is beyond compare," Aditya pointed out.

Vikram and Karuna exchanged glances.

Vikram said, "Ma cooked exactly the way she cooks this curry every other time. So the outcome should not have been different. Einstein once said that if you do the same things over and over again, you cannot then expect to get different results."

"Einstein was clearly wrong," said Karuna, "You can do the same things and get very different results—every time! He was no cook, or not talking about cooking."

"You could not have done exactly the same thing this time as before. It is not possible. But will someone tell me what we are talking about?" Aja asked.

"Vikram is having doubts again about marrying Tanuja," Karuna replied.

"Yes, he told me." Aja nodded.

"We've given our word; how can we break it now? I thought we had discussed it and decided to go ahead?" said Aditya, surprised.

It was a sentiment Asha had heard many times, the importance of keeping one's word. My word is my bond! She, too, gave her word to Anand and felt she could not break her promise. The family never once thought what might happen if their son's marriage failed. Such an outcome would not have been considered possible. Once committed, you worked at your differences. A marriage was to last a lifetime, not like the shoddy goods made in India, which did not last a few months.

"She's the girl for you," Vishu said.

Aja had never met Tanuja, only seen a photograph, just the way he had seen his wife's photo when he married, and that was that. He loved his wife for the rest of his life. Aja asked, "What do you not like about her? Education does not turn a woman into a good wife or mother."

Asha was surprised that while her Aja believed in God and thought the kingdom of God was within us, he did not admit the possibility that it might be God urging Vikram not to marry Tanuja. But then perhaps Aja had a point, she concluded. If we listened to all our inner voices, there would be anarchy! Also, she could not help wondering if being well-educated, which she suspected she was, meant she might not turn out to be a good wife and mother.

"She can continue with her education after the marriage. Your ma completed her formal education after she was married and all of you were born," Abhay said.

All these arguments had been made before. It was as if everyone was reminding themselves why they had agreed to the alliance in the first place.

Then Karuna said, "We'll call off the wedding if that is your final decision."

Everyone looked at Vikram, expecting a firm answer. But he still could not pinpoint exactly what was bothering him. It was just a premonition, albeit a strong one, of a lack of engagement, warmth and understanding on Tanuja's part.

CHAPTER 16

A month before the wedding, Asha found herself alone with Anand at the All India English Teachers' Conference in Bombay. This was the first time they were together without any chaperones. At the evening reception, they ran into Anshu, a good friend of Anand's. The conversation meandered, interrupted by brief interludes with other guests, several of whom recognized Asha by name. Her academic and literary publications were clearly making their mark.

During a brief lull in the evening's proceedings, Anshu asked, "So, Anand, what are your plans?"

"We are officially getting married next month. But we're as good as married already," Anand replied as he gently squeezed Asha's hand.

They stood close to each other, secretly holding hands. A table laden with flower bouquets revealed only the upper half of their bodies.

"Congratulations! I was enquiring after your career plans. As you are a research scholar here, can you not become a lecturer?"

"The head of the department doesn't like me. I don't think he will support my application. I'm thinking of applying to another IIT," replied Anand.

This was news to Asha. He had not mentioned any of this before.

"What will you do, Armita, continue to teach at Harrison?"

"Yes, until we know what the future holds," said Asha. Then she casually mentioned the offer from Harvard, career and finances being uppermost on her mind. "Would've been wonderful if we had both been accepted!" she added.

"Hmm, indeed!" said Anshu thoughtfully. Then addressing Anand, he added, "Love is like a rare orchid. It needs nurturing. Armita has been putting a lot into the relationship-kitty. You *must* pull your weight."

Anand's body stiffened; he let go of Asha's hand, moving away slightly. Asha thought she was imagining it, but Anand's gesture felt terribly hurtful, his imperceptible shift of weight from one foot to the other and the sudden unclasping of his hand. She would have done the opposite and demonstrated her commitment had she been in his position. *If Anshu could see it, why not Anand? Have I really made a mistake? The wedding is in four weeks. Invitation cards have gone out. How can I change my mind now? Society will not forgive me; no other man will have me.* Her own responses rattled her. They were uncannily similar to those of her parents when Vikram had raised his doubts about his marriage.

As if all this was not confusing enough, Asha was intoxicated with the previous night's lovemaking when she had tasted the elixir of life. She did not know such happiness existed—her ecstasy like a thousand suns rising. She had wanted the orgasmic feast to last forever. In fact, Anand said after the third time, "You are unique!" She had no idea what he was talking about. For her, it was just love—this giving and taking, this inseparable embrace of milk and water, the climbing of a tree, the twining of a creeper, and marriage spreading a shamiana of pure pleasure. Asha wanted to hear wedding bells, not warning bells.

She found a thousand and one reasons to have faith in love. She told herself complete understanding between men and women was a myth. *Love is not love which alters when it alteration finds.* She saw herself as the fixed point of the compass, the lodestar, steadfast in her love for Anand. Besides, it was no longer just her and Anand, the families were now involved. How could she let everyone down? A double wedding had been arranged. The wheels of destiny had started moving, and she felt powerless to slow down, let alone stop the juggernaut.

After returning from Bombay, her premonitions intensified. She could not help thinking something terrible was going to happen. *Double, double, toil and trouble*, the words kept dancing in her head. The double wedding seemed inevitable, something destined to happen. Like her exam results, she had no control over it. She wrote in her diary just days before the wedding, 'I feel panic-stricken. I cannot marry.' The next entry the following day was, 'I have sacrificed so much in the name of love. How much more will I have to sacrifice? Will I be able to live with myself if I find out Anand does not love me, not enough? How much is enough; how does anyone know? Am I capable of giving up everything for him? Does true love make such unreasonable demands?'

Praying before she went to sleep did not protect her from nightmares, one of which involved a ferocious snake with fangs spouting streams of fire that threatened to destroy her. Every time it struck, Asha jumped higher and was miraculously saved from being consumed by the flames around her. If her subconscious was trying to warn her against the wedding, she had no idea of the depth of its portentous tidings. The night before the marriage ceremony, she woke up with night sweats and panic attacks, feeling like a lamb being led to slaughter. She steadied herself thinking of her night with Anand when her sky had swirled like the aurora borealis.

Yet she knew something was wrong, that the morning would bring her grief. Like her brother she could not define it, nor did she know what to do with her premonition. She kept a record of her thoughts in her diary. 'I am apprehensive. I feel scared. I am falling, sinking, collapsing. Why am I getting married? Nothing makes any sense to me! When the gods wish to change things, they make us see things differently. What am I to do now? What can I do?' She did nothing.

On the day of her wedding Asha was woken up at dawn. The men in the family, who had gone to attend Vikram's wedding the day before, had just returned. The house was already humming with activity. Everyone was busy with last minute preparations. But there was no sign of Anand or his family. The house was full of guests who had come early to bless Vikram and his bride. Everyone waited in varying states of exhaustion and apprehension for the groom to arrive, for the wedding to take place. The family elders abandoned all hope of the ceremony being completed within the auspicious period. As nothing about Asha's marriage had gone to plan, everyone was reconciled to the wedding knot being tied after the sacred period had passed.

By the time Anand's entourage arrived, it was well past lunchtime. Asha had not had anything to eat since dinner the previous night. Even that she could not eat as her stomach had been churning away, unable to let the poison out. Brides were expected to fast before the ceremony. When the bridegroom's party finally arrived, Asha was so anxious she passed out on hearing Vikram blow the conch shell. Her brothers took turns blowing the conch shell as the women ululated their welcome. While Asha was having her fainting spell, there was no one there with her. She had been temporarily abandoned as everyone ran to watch the fanfare surrounding the groom's arrival.

Asha had no clear recollection of what happened during the next few hours when the marriage took place, except that she had gone to the bathroom to throw up and then fainted. Everything that took place after that was happening to someone else; *she* was there merely as an observer. She went through the rituals hypnotised and did not have to say or do anything. All through the ceremony she felt paralysed. The fumes from the ceremonial fire and the faint smell of turmeric from her sari, which had been blessed and purified by being soaked in turmeric water, left her nauseous.

At one point, through her veil, she caught a glimpse of Anand's face. He caught her eye too. She did not recognize the look on his face. She could have been getting married to a complete stranger. The wedding veil obstructed her vision when the knot was tied. The tiara on her head gave her a fierce headache. They were as good as two strangers circling the fire seven times as the priest chanted the mantras. And then they were married.

After all these years of feeling unloved and misunderstood, complaining bitterly to God and her diary how miserable she was, Asha was unprepared to leave home. Becoming a wife did not make her less of a daughter. On the contrary, the idea of leaving home for good made her feel more of a daughter than ever before. When the time came for her to leave, she felt all energy sucked out of her. Someone had switched off the lifeline that had kept her ticking, but she was not dead.

The tears of the family spoke in one voice—we wish you happiness in your new life, we pray your new family will love you as much as we do. Each member of the family was coming to terms with the loss, even the servants were weeping openly. Vikram abandoned his attempts to blow the conch shell when it was time for his sister to step across the threshold of their home. Vijay tried unsuccessfully and left the conch shell behind. Vivek was wiping his tears long after the train pulled away from the platform.

Asha could no longer see their hunched silhouettes receding through the flood of her own tears. Her limbs felt numb, her head light; someone had injected her with a hallucinogenic drug. She looked at Anand, his father, and the faces of strangers in the train compartment. They all appeared far removed as if she was on the moon or on some distant planet watching her own self and the spectacle of human suffering unfurling around her. At the same time, she experienced a rising wave of tenderness for the family she was born into when her eyes rested on her uncle's profile.

Abhay crouched on the floor of the carriage, adjusting one of her suitcases beneath their seat, securing it with a padlock. He was accompanying Asha to her in-laws' home. This was another family tradition—an adult male family member accompanied a newly married daughter to her in-laws. Marriage was a full service, door to door, to ensure nothing went awry in transit.

Thus began a lesson for Asha in discovering how much the family she was born into really mattered to her. Although from now on her family was supposed to be the one she was married to. Days before the marriages took place, a strong bond descended upon the Guru family like an invincible web binding them forever. As if her father in the process of giving her away in *kanyadan* was taking her closer to his heart. There was a coming together of forces, a tidal wave of goodwill, a state of blessedness; her parents agreed on everything. Never was a family so tightly knit, feelings brimmed over, and every action was touched with love and compassion.

Marriage may have been a girl's best career, but no one had prepared Asha for the vagaries of such a choice or warned her of its pitfalls. No one mentioned how she would feel entering the Promised Land. Nor had anyone instructed her on what she should do to make her journey a success. She had not prepared herself either, thinking she had achieved the most difficult task—of loving Anand, unreservedly.

So when she walked towards her in-laws' house and a sense

of belonging did not descend upon her, Asha wondered why her innermost self was playing tricks at such an inappropriate moment, like a best friend behaving unexpectedly badly. Uneasiness descended upon her as she walked unescorted, trying not to trip on her sari. There was no front veranda, no compound wall or pavement leading up to the house. She was left standing at the threshold of her in-laws' house. There was no one there to receive her. She felt numb; her limbs no longer obeyed her command as if her body knew instinctively what her mind refused to acknowledge. She took one slow faltering step and lurched forward to the door for support. *It's only a fainting spell. It'll pass once I've had something to eat.*

When Vikram arrived with his wife, the Guru family, along with relatives and close friends, were waiting to receive the newly wedded couple. Karuna was ready with her thali for the traditional welcoming arati. Asha had escorted the new bride in. The pavement leading up to the house, the long veranda in front, and the entrance to each of the rooms were decorated with intricate, symbolic chitta patterns painted by hand using rice paste. Marigold flower braids, Pipli shamianas and other decorative hangings adorned the passageways. Brass pots, decorated with sandalwood paste, turmeric and vermillion, filled with water and crowned with leaves of bel-patri and coconuts, stood on either side of the main entrance, keeping a watchful eye on proceedings. Earthen pots similarly embellished stood in a row along the main entrance as the bride and groom were welcomed with the pomp and circumstance reserved for deities.

The sound of conch shells spread across the neighbourhood; prayer bells rang out announcing the bride's arrival as the women of the house ululated. Children ran around screaming "The bride has arrived," as if anyone could have missed the hullaballoo. Neighbours, all dressed up and ready for the signal, ran out of their homes to participate in the welcoming ceremony. On their special day, bride and groom are feted like gods, exempted from all the usual duties that govern the life of a householder, including touching the feet of elders as a mark of respect. For those four days a newly married couple are treated like divine beings.

Asha's reception at her in-laws could not have been more different. There was no arati, no welcoming ceremony. First, she waited in the taxi while her uncle supervised the unloading of the suitcases and the various gift boxes. Both Anand and his father disappeared with a couple of the lighter boxes each, and never returned. Abhay paid the driver once all the luggage was arrayed in front of the house.

The lack of any welcoming ceremony surprised both Abhay and Asha. They looked at each other. He shrugged his shoulders. She felt ridiculous standing at the entrance, waiting to be invited in. When no one appeared, Abhay entered. Asha followed. She felt slightly sick the moment she stepped into her in-laws' house as if someone had placed some food in her mouth that did not agree with her. How on earth could she spit out her marriage? Asha wondered why her parents had not picked up any of the vibes she was getting. Unable to unlock the significance of her premonitions, she attributed her feelings to hunger and tiredness.

Eventually, a woman appeared who Asha assumed was Anand's mother, though there was no discernible resemblance between mother and son. Asha bent forward expecting her mother-in-law to intervene and prevent her from touching her feet. But she never did anything of the sort. *Perhaps their customs are different*, Asha thought. Then a younger woman arrived, but did not greet Asha. She simply stood there as if someone unknown had arrived unexpectedly. Nobody seemed to notice Abhay either.

After an uncomfortable silence, Anand's mother led Asha to a room with a double bed and a Godrej almirah, both gifts of her parents. Three of the large suitcases were hers too. After all, she was going to spend a month with her in-laws before returning to her job in Cuttack. Anand then led Asha to pay her respects to Maa, the spiritual disciple and collaborator of Sri Aurobindo, and the spiritual guru of Anand's family.

Every Brahmin home has a private shrine where family members do puja, light a joss stick or an earthen lamp, individually or collectively, depending on the occasion. Asha's family shrine consisted of a collection of deities from the Hindu pantheon. They prayed to various gods and goddesses, but worshiped only God, the nameless One. "You are beholden to no one but God; all our gods are mediators." Her parents and grandfathers had told her so—independently, on different occasions, expressing exactly the same sentiments. It had never been a problem for Asha to pray in church to Christ or Mary. They too, like the Hindu gods, were mediators.

When asked to pray to Maa, it was not a problem for Asha. Except, after such a long journey, she needed the use of a bathroom. Some nourishment, even a glass of water, would have been welcome. Did Lord Jagannath not allow his devotees to attend to their bodily needs first?

"Can I please wash my hands first?" Asha said, hoping that would enable her to use the toilet.

Anand pointed at the washbasin in the dining area, which was practically where they were standing.

Asha had to think on her feet. "I wash my feet as well before I pray."

He showed her the bathroom. The bathroom was small. It had a no-nonsense air about it—a tap, a bucket and a mug. Asha was used to bathrooms with toilets and separate bathing areas, not to mention accessories such as mirrors, shelves, towel stands, rails, hooks for clothes, a selection of soaps, oils, shampoos, toothpastes, towels, etc. With a bladder ready to burst and a growing sense of claustrophobia gripping her, she had no choice but to urinate there and then. She opened the tap, thinking there would be no water supply, but was pleasantly surprised to hear the gurgling sound of water rushing out, muffling the sound of a steady stream of pee. She heaved a sigh of relief and let go!

The first night Asha was left to sleep on her own. She did not mind; she needed a good night's rest. In the morning, she was still in bed when Anand opened the door and walked in without as much as a knock.

"It's 6:30 already," he said. "Why don't you get ready, have a bath first."

Asha could not believe it—not a kiss, an embrace, no sign of endearment, not a cup of tea or a glass of water. She had gone to bed after midnight, so what if it was six thirty in the morning! She was still full of sleep.

At home she was used to long baths. Karuna often complained, "How will you look after your home and family if you take so long to bathe?" Asha would explain that it was simply not possible to rush through the manifold stages of bathing—first she had to wash her clothes, which would have been soaked in advance. Then she would have to massage her body with special oils, apply the home-made revitalising, cleansing herbal concoctions to her face and body, and wait for fifteen to twenty minutes for the application to work its magic before bathing. While waiting, she would read. She had read several novels in the peace and quiet of the bathroom.

The days when Asha washed her hair, the ritual was slightly different. She applied specially treated oil to her scalp an hour before, followed by a herbal pack for half an hour. A proper bath could easily take a couple of hours if one added the various post-bathing rituals, including the application of various lotions and potions while the skin was still tingling fresh.

That was not the end of the matter. One had to put on fresh clothes and make-up, and hang out all the washed clothes neatly on the clothes line and secure them with wooden pegs before picking whatever flowers were in a state of readiness to be offered to the gods. The flowers had to be washed before the puja could be done with the lighting of joss sticks and lamps, followed by prayers, seated in lotus pose on a prayer mat, before one was ready to face the world. By which time one was, of course, invariably exhausted, hungry and in need of food and sleep!

As a result, mother and daughter never washed their hair on the same day at the same time, though once in a blue moon their bath times coincided like a partial eclipse in the skies. The rare occasions when Karuna and Asha ended up washing their hair on the same day, it caused a crisis in the operations of the household. It was certain the postman would call during that jinxed hour with a special delivery that needed signing, or someone well known to the family, but not close enough, would drop by with an invitation to their son's or daughter's wedding, expecting to be invited in, offered a drink, or hoping to use the toilet. Asha noticed how the various repairmen turned up precisely at the moment she was set to bolt the bathroom door. These men would arrive to fix the leaking tap, the blocked drain, the blown mains, or something one could not afford to be without, which needed fixing the day before!

As Asha prepared for the day, her past seemed unreal, something that had happened to someone else. Here, life could not be more different. Bathing was not the sort of artistic accomplishment it was back home. She was expected to complete her morning rituals in less than half an hour before she started cooking, which used up the entire morning and a good part of each evening. The rest of the time Asha spent attending to the demands of her in-laws, their relatives and guests. As she had never stepped into Anand's parental home before, there was no way she could have known how much of a stranger she would feel there.

The afternoon Abhay returned to Cuttack, Asha was sorely tempted to accompany him, but felt her family would find it baffling. She could not fully understand it herself, nor could she cope with her growing sense of panic, of being adrift. She told herself things would look brighter and better in a few days while acknowledging this was not a promising start to married life.

On the fourth night, when marriages are traditionally consummated, Asha lay awake the whole night, watching the flames of her heart leaping across the ceiling. As she did so, she ruminated on the ritual of the couple tending to the earthen lamp, making sure it kept burning all through the night. It probably began as a means of providing the couple with some light so they did not have to make love in the dark, she concluded. After all, these ceremonies pre-dated the discovery of electricity. But there appeared not a spark of light in her marriage.

"Don't let this lamp burn itself out." Asha's mother-in-law left with these instructions, assuming her educated daughter-in-law knew nothing about earthen lamps and wicks.

Anand soon fell asleep, leaving Asha to tend to the lamp. *So much for sharing and caring,* she thought, lying wide awake beside him as he snored lightly. After watching him and the lamp for over an hour, she wondered what on earth she was doing in that strange room with a strange man sleeping next to her. He was definitely not the Anand she knew. Lying beside this imposter, she felt disloyal to 'her' Anand.

Her sense of alienation did not get any better in the morning. If anything, it got progressively worse as her sensitive nature was daily violated by idle gossip about her family. Her jewellery was meticulously examined by the relatives and guests of her in-laws. The women felt no embarrassment, uncovering the sari from her head to scrutinize her ornaments. They whispered snide remarks to each other in front of her, deprecating the quality and value of her necklaces, bangles and earrings. Asha ignored their remarks just as she ignored the way they dressed, smelled and behaved.

But when Anand and her in-laws carped about how her parents had failed to give her a 'proper dowry', as they put it, she could not bear that ignominy. The never-ending talk of gold and dowry she found depressing, not merely cheap and insulting.

Then one day, while they were getting ready for bed, Anand said, "Your parents did not give you anything."

Asha snapped back, "I thought you married me because you love me and not for the dowry! Tell me, what did your family give you for your wedding?"

That night she could not sleep. He lay there next to her, snoring. What saddened and surprised Asha most was that she could no longer talk to Anand. He had transmorphed into someone whose character bore no resemblance to the man she knew and loved. The thought she could have had an arranged marriage and saved herself and the family all the angst kept gnawing away inside her all night.

Apart from Anand's mother, no one said what they meant—especially his father and sister. His sister, who was called Jhia (daughter) at home and Ina (mother) outside the home, was not someone Asha could talk to. An attempt at a joke fell flat on its face when Asha asked Ina when her sister-in-law was getting married.

The day before Ina's wedding, she showed her saris to Asha. "Do you like this one?" Ina asked, spreading it on her extended arm as she posed like a model.

"Yes, very fetching!" said Asha.

"When bhai got his first salary, he bought this for me," said Ina.

It was an expensive *maniabandhi* sari. Smiling back at her sister-in-law, Asha wondered why Anand had not given her anything when he got his first salary.

On the day of Ina's wedding, her family were anxious to impress their son-in-law and the few guests who had accompanied him. The groom's father and other close relatives were not present. Asha knew nothing about Ina's in-laws or why the groom was there with only a couple of his friends, not the usual entourage of family and relatives. The wedding and reception was a modest affair.

The next morning, Ina and her husband, Sudhir, left. There was no plan for anyone from Ina's family to accompany her. As Asha's uncle had escorted her, Anand decided at the last minute it was part of his family tradition that he should accompany Ina to her in-laws'. Asha was upset. Ever since their marriage, Anand's focus had been on his sister and his family. *Nothing has really changed*, Asha thought bitterly and regretfully, realising she had swapped her status at home for an inferior one at her in-laws'! Luckily, Sudhir insisted they needed no escort, and he left with his wife.

That night Anand made love to Asha for the first time since the wedding. After their passionate lovemaking, lying in his arms, Asha asked him why he had not touched her before.

Anand replied, "Well, our first night was in Bombay, remember? If you must know, I was worried about Jhia's wedding. Now they are married, I can relax. And, now that *we* are married, I don't have to worry about you either."

"What do you mean?" Asha asked, thinking, *these can't be the sentiments of a young man in love.*

Anand had never courted her madly, nor lavished her with gifts. She had never expected the kind of whirlwind romance one saw in films or read in books. She did not have unrealistic expectations from a man who was still struggling to make his way in the world. All she'd wanted was to be an integral part of his life, his innermost self. After all, he was always on her mind; he was the centre of her universe.

Starting to kiss her all over her body, he began to make love to her. "You are now all mine," he said as he rolled over, balancing her on top of him.

"And you—are you all mine?" Asha asked.

Anand never replied, but as he started making love to her again, she thought she had received her answer.

CHAPTER 17

The month Asha stayed with her in-laws was spent mostly cooking. She could not imagine her sister-in-law doing anything similar in Cuttack. Nor could Asha comprehend why her mother-in-law left for the temple before her father-in-law left for work. She did not work at the temple; the temple activities would not cease without her. Asha was puzzled why she did not go to the temple after her husband left home. Did the worship of the Divine, like charity, not begin at home? Asha would have appreciated a guiding, if not helping, hand in the kitchen. She had not expected to spend so much of her time in her in-laws' kitchen immediately after marriage.

Asha found it difficult, if not ludicrous, to imagine her ma disappearing first thing in the morning to a temple, leaving everyone at home in the lurch! She had not fully appreciated the true extent of her mother's dedication to the family, her unflagging service, her deep involvement in her home and family—something Asha had taken for granted. She had grown up seeing her ma looking after everyone, day after day, year after year. It seemed as if that is what mothers did.

Here, Asha was left to sink or swim. She got up early to prepare breakfast for her father-in-law. Until one day it dawned on her how religion was indeed an escape for women such as her mother-in-law, who woke up at dawn, bathed and left home, returned for lunch, and had an afternoon siesta before going out again in the evening to the temple for kirtan and gossip with other women like her. The temple seemed like a wonderful social club for women such as her mother-in-law.

But who prepared breakfast? Did Ina do the honours? Asha wondered as she served her father-in-law a freshly cooked breakfast, more or less, in complete silence. Anand had made it clear that she should speak only when spoken to. Asha found the lack of conversation in the morning conducive. The last thing she wanted was to carry on a conversation with her father-in-law. She needed a lot of time to think, and her new role in life did not change that aspect of herself.

Then there was the maid, Kumari, who had to be supervised. Asha let the maid get on with her chores. No point in spoiling her with a pep talk like her ma did with their housemaids. While Asha was engaged in the kitchen, Anand slept. He usually got out of bed after his father left for work. Then he had breakfast with Asha around 9am. Sometimes breakfast was delayed if he overslept, which he did every other day.

This meant Asha did not eat anything for over three hours after she woke up. Soon she began to suffer from acidity, a condition she knew nothing about. On one occasion, she was so nauseous she threw up and had to go to bed after her father-in-law left the house. This elicited smiles from the maid, who, discarding two okras that were joined like twins, declared, "If you eat this, you'll have twins."

Asha was on the verge of explaining the physical impossibility of having twins by eating the forked okra if she was already pregnant, as Kumari seemed to think. Asha stopped short on seeing the maid's rotten black teeth. The smell of biddis that emanated from her mouth also made Asha feel faint. Struck with the state of Kumari's teeth, Asha felt compelled to teach her some basic dental hygiene.

"Do you brush your teeth, Kumari?" Asha asked.

A surprised Kumari replied warily, "Yes, sometimes!"

Asha's sudden interest in her teeth convinced Kumari that Asha was indeed pregnant. After all, did women not do strange things when they were with child?

"Why only sometimes? Why not every day? How do you clean your teeth? Do you clean your tongue or not?" Asha enquired, trying to get to the bottom of Kumari's dental habits.

"Ashes, twigs…" replied Kumari, adding laconically, "Toothpaste no good for teeth…teeth fall off."

Asha did not have to suppress a smile as Kumari gave one of her fulsome laughs, displaying all her blackened buck teeth. Asha remembered the times she used a neem twig to brush her teeth when they visited the village where her father was born. Each morning she would run across the field with her cousins, chewing a twig of neem. She was particular about finding one that was smooth. She washed it thoroughly before sticking it in her mouth like a lollypop. The neem tasted bitter, but when she washed her mouth later, it left a sweet aftertaste which she relished. In the afternoons, when they ate sugar cane, tearing the scales off greedily with their shining teeth, everything else tasted bitter, failing to match the tingling freshness of sugar. All that chewing was meant to keep the teeth clean and strong.

"Do you use neem twigs?" Asha carried on with her investigation.

"I use whatever twig I can find. Sometimes, I find a neem tree." Kumari giggled as if she was cheating in class.

"You must brush your teeth every day and clean your tongue. Stop smoking those biddis. They are not good for you." Asha gave her a lesson in hygiene.

"Bohuma, I smoke pica," Kumari corrected her and added, "Everything is bad for you—even marriage!"

Having realised her mistake, Kumari stuck her tongue out, raised her eyebrows and opened her eyes wide, giving a pretty good impression of the goddess Kali. Assaulted again by the odours from Kumari's mouth, her acrid breath a toxic mix of pica and halitosis, Asha could barely breathe.

"Why do you think marriage is bad? Kumari, are you unhappily married?" Asha asked when she recovered.

Kumari was younger than she looked. While her teeth were falling apart, her body was firm, her breasts incredibly pert under her sari. She did not wear a bra and probably thought wearing one was not good for her breasts either.

"My marada," Kumari replied, referring to her husband, "beats me up every night. He comes home drunk, does not know what he is doing."

Asha had a vision of Kumari on the cross, her husband impaled on another. She was thinking who the third person might be when her reverie was interrupted by the image of Anand framed in the door.

He said disapprovingly, "Why are you gossiping with the maid? Father is waiting for breakfast." Then lapsing into a mix of tongues, he added, "*Jaldi* serve *kara. Bapa kamaku jibe*, important meeting *achi.*"

Asha had prepared upma, having found cauliflower, carrots, and tomatoes in the morning's shopping done by Anand. As she carried the breakfast tray to her father-in-law, she wondered why Anand, who had made a brief appearance that morning offering to do the shopping, had disappeared again. She did not much like the imposter who had taken, more or less, permanent residence since their marriage!

This new Anand was exhausted all the time. It felt like one of life's many little ironies that she, the anaemic and permanently exhausted, had energy left over for a chat and a cuddle after a full day of household chores. While Anand, a perfectly normal, healthy man, who did little at home or elsewhere, fell asleep the moment she lay down beside him. He would start snoring, disrupting her chances of a decent night's rest. As if that was not frustrating enough, all through the day the conversation was about dowry and pregnancy! This was not what she imagined married life to be—it was exactly what she did not want it to be.

One morning Asha found herself alone. The maid had not turned up; her father-in-law had gone to work. Anand, too, disappeared after breakfast with the cryptic message, "I'm going out!" Between cooking and cleaning, Asha was savouring a quiet moment with a cup of tea. She was missing her family, wondering how they were getting on with Tanuja. Absentmindedly, she moved aside a pile of old magazines and newspapers to make space for her teacup. As she did so, Asha noticed a letter that uncannily resembled her own handwriting. She looked at it again and realised it was indeed her own. When she rifled through the pile of papers, she was startled to see several of her letters, all addressed to Anand, lying there in full view!

Asha experienced a sequence of emotions—disbelief, puzzlement of the this-can't-be-true-must-be-a-mistake variety, followed by outrage, anger, disappointment and a deep sense of violation. She could hear the wild palpitations of her heart and was afraid it might leap out of her body, which was also quaking like a leaf in a storm. When she stopped trembling, Asha began to retrieve all her letters on the table. Wondering how many of her letters were left lying around the place, she resolved to rescue as many as she could find. She examined every accessible nook and corner of the house, searching for her letters, which in her view had been abandoned like defenceless victims, violated and left for dead. She could not help crying as she scoured her in-laws' house for pages where she had poured her heart out to Anand.

When she could not find any more pieces of her heart lying around, she sat down and prayed. Asha prayed for a miracle—for the abandoned letters she had not found. She wished the words in all those letters would come alive and simply walk away free and safe, no longer trapped in a cage like animals in a zoo. If anyone found one of her letters, they would see a blank sheet of paper; her words, as if written in magic ink, would simply have vanished.

That night when she was alone with Anand, by which time he was half-asleep, Asha wanted to tell him how he had broken her heart by so callously leaving her letters lying around. But then she thought, *If he had any discretion, would he have treated my letters in such a cavalier manner?* She kept his letters safely in the locker of her almirah. Asha was so distraught, she could not even lie down.

Waking up from his stupor, Anand complained, "What's taking you so long?"

Silently she lay down, stretching her body across the bed without touching his. He turned towards her; soon he was on top of her, crushing her with his weight.

Pushing him aside, she cried, "Why did you not keep my letters safe in your personal custody? Why do I find them lying around the house?"

Anand's answer, without an iota of embarrassment or guilt, upset her further. "My sister must've left them there. She used to copy from your letters when she wrote to Sudhir. I think that's how she got him to fall for her. Wish she didn't throw them around." He then dismissed her concern, making light of the situation with another bombshell that his sister had in effect trapped Sudhir. Asha wondered if she too had been trapped.

"What I don't understand, Anand, is how your sister got hold of my letters in the first place?" Asha asked.

He was sucking her breasts, his eyes closed as if tasting ripe Alphanso mangoes. He never answered. Asha was in no mood for lovemaking.

"Why did you give them to her, and if you didn't, how did she get hold of *my* letters? Why didn't you stop her from reading them, let alone allow her to copy what I wrote? They were private—from me to you," Asha cried, trying to extricate herself from his embrace.

He laughed as he pinned her down firmly and said, "What does it matter? She is now married to him, and we are married too."

"How can you say such a thing? What do you mean she trapped Sudhir? Are you saying you trapped me too?" Asha asked.

His words had dredged up all the past doubts from the bottom of her heart. They now floated like dead fish in the sea. Anand did not reply, just carried on heaving and sighing over her. Asha's humiliation was complete.

As the days passed, Asha stumbled across more lies. Since the day she discovered her letters, she developed a habit of examining any paper or pile of papers she found lying around. She could not bear the idea of her letters lying in such a state of disgrace. She would have preferred if he had burnt them. Asha made it her job to rescue her letters.

One day she came across an examination certificate that stated Anand's age. He was two years older than her, yet Anand had told her he was a year older. Not that it mattered in the least. It was just the shock of realization that she had been lied to yet again. Their horoscopes, where the birth date is mentioned, had never been matched. In any case, a horoscope is only as trustworthy as the person it belongs to. Horoscopes were consulted in Vikram's case. It was an arranged marriage, and all the formalities were observed. In Asha's case, none of the traditional customs were adhered to.

Then she found out that Anand had received a third class in his intermediate exams, the one prior to the bachelor's. He had told her he got a second, a good second at that. Asha now understood why he was not invited for the government lectureship interview, his grades were simply not up to scratch. It was as if she had opened a cupboard and all the skeletons had fallen on her. She would perhaps not have attached too much importance to any of it had she been told the truth right from the start. But finding things out the way she did days after the wedding was hard to stomach.

Anand took Asha for a short break to a hill station near Sambalpur. The place, surrounded by a low range of mountains, had a tranquil, picturesque quality. Its quiet simplicity appealed to her. During the day, the hills changed colour—starting with shades of crimson to blue, then gold to green. At night, everything was charcoal black. Walking back to the guest house after their first meal at a local restaurant, Asha could not see beyond a few yards around her. But she could see the stars shining brightly. She thought she could hear the hum of the universe. They saw a spectacular meteor shower, which took her breath away. Lost in the hillside forest, the wind howled a haunting melody. The frogs croaked as if there was no tomorrow, and the cicadas went crazy. When Anand took her hand, she gave it a squeeze.

Every time there was a rustle in the undergrowth, Asha froze, thinking they were being stalked by some wild animal. Snakes did not sleep at night, she knew from her family's several encounters with these creatures. Her parents had spotted snakes several times in the garden as they sat outside taking in the cool summer breeze. The reptiles were drawn to the white blossoms of rajnigandha, jasmine or lily. Their heady and intense fragrances would drive any animal round the bend. Once, a cobra couple appeared in the garden. Abhay was the first to spot them. He signalled to Karuna and Aditya to be perfectly quiet and remain still like statues until the cobras slithered away. Mercifully, they did not raise their hoods as they glided past.

Another time, on a scorching summer afternoon, Asha saw a snake enter the house. It went straight for the storeroom, which was filled with so many household gadgets and baskets of fruit and other consumables, it was impossible to guess where the snake had taken cover. It took hours to remove every single item from the room. Vivek brought Rikki, his pet mongoose, secretly hoping for an epic battle, expecting Rikki to tear the snake into pieces. Rikki puffed as he sniffed around. Then he settled down to enjoy the fruits ripening in the baskets. The snake was curled up, perfectly camouflaged, in the basket filled with black, white and coloured electrical wires. When the servant boy emptied the basket in the backyard, the snake disappeared like a dream. All the men waiting with their lathis ready to strike could not even touch it; the snake slinked away, ghostlike, from their sight.

Asha was worried about running into the local tribals, whose skin was so dark and smooth they melted into the night. One could touch them without seeing them, except the whites of their eyes, and their teeth dazzled like so many moons. Anand placed his arms around her as they walked back to the guest house. It was difficult to tell if he was feeling romantic or was afraid; he kept on talking about ghosts and other supernatural beings. He thought the bungalow was haunted, said he could feel the evil spirits that resided in their room. Asha was grateful they left her alone.

When they reached the bungalow, Anand said he was tired and fell asleep. Within a couple of days they had exhausted the entire repertory of local cuisine. There was not a lot else to explore in that neighbourhood. It was in many ways an ideal location for a newly wedded couple. But Anand's restless fatigue and unpredictable moods meant Asha could not relax. The moment she dozed off, he would wake her up to make love, and when she was feeling amorous, he showed no interest. The passionate lovemaking she had imagined simply did not materialise.

On the contrary, the things that did happen were far from amorous or entertaining. The first morning, for example, Anand said he did not wish to see her in a nightie. She had to be 'properly' dressed in a sari the moment she woke up, certainly by the time tea was delivered. She could not be seen in her dressing gown.

"Your edicts," Asha joked, "are longer than those of King Ashoka's." Then she said, "Can I not disappear into the bathroom when the tea is delivered?"

"Who will open the door?" asked Anand.

"Well, you can—you don't have to change," Asha replied.

"No, you must be ready to open the door."

"But why, and why on earth do I have to be ready first thing in the morning?"

The night before he had insisted she should not wear anything at all in bed. Then, he had hogged the blanket, leaving her shivering in the cold. When she got out of bed to put on her dressing gown, he woke up, insisted on making love, and removed her nightdress.

Anand glowered at her and said, "Because I said so."

Asha salaamed and replied, "Yes, huzoor!"

She gave up trying to figure out what was really going on inside his head. They returned to his parents' home and to more incomprehensible rules of conduct.

The day after their return, Ina was also back. The conversation was all about how happy she was at her in-laws', how rich her in-laws were, and how wonderfully they treated her. *What on earth are you doing here, then?* Asha could not help wondering. The interminable chatter about gold, money, land, and houses was unbearable. She was also fed up of cooking and serving her in-laws round the clock and then having to listen to such drivel. What upset Asha most were Anand's constant jibes against her parents, that they had not given her a large enough dowry.

One night, as she was getting ready for bed, Asha burst into tears when Anand repeated a litany of allegations against her family.

"I asked my parents not to give me any dowry," Asha began. "They did not listen to me, of course, and gave me so much more than I expected and you deserve. They raised me, educated me. I have a job, and I love you. *I* am your dowry. They arranged a fine wedding ceremony and reception, gave me all this gold jewellery, not to mention dresses and gifts to all your family, this double bed, mattresses, linen, my trousseau, your wedding suit and other dresses, and kitchen utensils. Do you want me to list everything?"

"Your parents did not do their *duty*," he replied.

"What exactly do you mean? Have you done your duty, your parents theirs? Do you mean my parents did not give *you* a substantial amount of cash in dowry, in addition to everything else? Then I am truly deceived," she said.

"You can say whatever you like, but I am speaking the truth," he said.

"I have no idea what truth you are talking about. Let me remind you, as you seem to have forgotten. When we met, you said you never wanted any dowry. What's changed? Why all this talk about dowry now?" Asha asked.

Anand looked at her and smiled as if to say 'How naïve can you be?' The truth hit her like an unstoppable lorry in whose path she had suddenly found herself. Contrary to what he'd said, he had always expected a large dowry.

When he never replied, Asha said, "I can only feel sorry for you—you always thought my parents would give you a large cash dowry on top of everything else!"

It was her Aja who had warned her parents against doing just that. "What if he and his parents spend it and leave Asha with nothing? You'll have nothing more to support her with. It has taken you a lifetime to save a small amount; from where will you get more? Aditya babu will retire soon. Your two younger sons are still in college. And all these things—furniture, clothes and ornaments—Asha cannot eat if she is hungry. She does not have a home of her own. She has to work because her husband cannot provide for her. The furniture you've given *her* will stay in Sambalpur. Do you think her in-laws will give it to her when she makes her home, and God only knows when that might be?"

Asha had never ever heard her grandfather speak so plainly and harshly to her parents, so annoyed was he with Karuna and Aditya for squandering their meagre savings. Asha had taken up a job so she would not have to depend on her husband or her parents. She herself never wanted a career. Her dream was a happy home. But if the path to happiness was through work and sacrifice, so be it.

"We should never have married until you were financially independent and capable of looking after a wife. None of the women in my family work, as far as I know, none of the women in yours do. Why do you expect the impossible from me? Why are you not happy with what you've got? I can't see you being happy, ever!"

"You don't care for my parents," said Anand.

"What makes you say that? I've been slaving away for them since I came here. Would I do so if I didn't care for them? How much do *you* care for my parents? Apart from blaming them for everything, what have *you* done for my parents? I don't go around accusing you of not caring for my parents?" Asha pointed out.

"Well, let's not get started about your parents. If they really loved you, they'd have given you a proper dowry," Anand repeated angrily.

"If you wanted a 'proper' dowry, you should've married someone else. You knew the score right from the start," said Asha.

"Maybe I should have!" Anand muttered under his breath.

Asha was grateful that by the end of the week she would be back in Cuttack. She wasn't sure what problems awaited her there, but somehow the problems at home seemed preferable to the ones here.

CHAPTER 18

Before she got a chance to have a heart-to-heart with her mother, Karuna took Anand and Asha aside and told them, in confidence, that all was not well with Vikram's marriage. Asha was stunned. She had not imagined her mother saying anything of the sort. Nor had she told her mother about her own marital problems. They had arrived only a couple of hours ago and had not yet unpacked. Preoccupied as Karuna was with her son's marriage, she never thought of asking her daughter if she was happy, if her in-laws had been kind to her. She took it for granted her daughter was happy. Asha had posted home a card saying all was well. *No point in upsetting the family*, she thought. She also feared Anand would read her letter before posting it.

Asha could not help thinking how utterly different their two families were. His family never shared any confidences with her, nothing about their daughter's wedding, why their son-in-law's family had not come. All Asha heard was how 'wonderful' everything was at Ina's in-laws'. She knew that was far from the truth. Yet her mother trusted Anand unquestioningly. She had gone all the way from opposing her daughter's marriage to admitting him as part of the family. After that conversation, Asha found it difficult to tell her mother the truth about her own marriage. Also, she secretly hoped to find her way back to the Anand she knew and loved. Thus, never have to tell anyone about the stranger she encountered in Sambalpur or how unhappy she had been at her in-laws'.

The evening Asha and Anand were invited for dinner at Abhay's home turned out unexpectedly badly. Anand arrived late and then spent the whole evening contradicting Asha. It was not a friendly banter, not a-taming-of-the-shrew kind of drama by any stretch of the imagination. At first, everyone smiled, a bit confused, thinking Anand was trying to be funny but not quite succeeding.

By the end of the evening, the snubs and jibes aimed at her made it difficult for Asha to pretend otherwise. She could not keep up the pretence of a Laurel and Hardy exchange, could not remain calm while Anand's snide comments landed on her like flying knives. After dinner, Abhay excused himself, and Priti kept herself busy in the kitchen. Anand pretended as if nothing was the matter, carrying on with his rude remarks. Asha sat silently, too shocked and humiliated to acknowledge how fast the entire edifice of her life was collapsing. Unable to ignore the way in which Anand persisted in verbally abusing his niece, Abhay returned to the dining table. Like Lord Krishna, Abhay's presence held back the volley of word-arrows landing on Asha.

Finally Asha said, "Kaku, I'm tired and must go home."

Taking leave of her aunt, she thanked her for the splendid dinner.

Anand said nothing, not even a thank you, let alone apologise for his appalling behaviour all evening. He simply walked out of the house. What hurt Asha most was she could no longer pretend about her marriage. Her pride in her choice of partner was shattered by the man she had loved all these years. Abhay and Priti were left stunned.

"I cannot believe it!" Abhay told his wife the moment he locked the door.

Even Priti, who excelled in double entendres, could not help smarting. She was upset enough to say, "Had she not chosen this man and fought endless battles for him? Did all that amount to nothing more than this?"

"Do you think he'll do anything to her in the rickshaw?" Abhay asked several minutes later. The thought had just crossed his mind.

It had not occurred to Priti that anything of that nature might transpire. They both panicked.

"Should I go after them on my bicycle? Hopefully, the rickshaw-wallah's presence will deter him," he said.

"I don't think you can catch up with them now. But you must go to nana's place tomorrow and tell them what happened. They need to know," she said.

"I cannot believe two such gifted children could have such bad luck! You cannot make this up!" said Abhay.

❦

The following morning after breakfast, Anand announced he was leaving for Sambalpur. No one said anything. A grown-up man was free to do as he pleased as long as he behaved responsibly. Though in Anand's case, no one really knew what the latter translated to. Asha, already worried about the paltry state of her finances, thought all this travelling would be expensive, and she would end up paying. At that moment, she realised why her father had been so concerned when he first heard of her decision to marry Anand. Her father *knew* that he would be the one picking up the bill. However much she disliked having to earn a living, Asha felt immensely grateful for her job.

For the first couple of days, with the daily tensions temporarily alleviated, Asha found Anand's absence peaceful. She needed the time to rest and recover. By the beginning of the following week, she began to wonder why she had not heard from him. She waited every day for his letter. Then at the crack of dawn on the sixteenth day, she was woken up by raised voices. It took her a moment to notice Anand standing on the other side of the mosquito-net, peering down on her.

"Your mother should've opened the front door!" he complained.

"What's the matter?" a bewildered Asha asked. "Why did you not write and let me know you were coming? You'll feel better when you've rested. Get out of those clothes and come in."

Anand stood there grumbling, "Your mother didn't open the front door."

"What are you talking about?" Asha asked, still full of sleep.

"She asked me to come round to the back door," he said.

"We all do that," Asha replied. "My uncles would've done the same had they arrived at this hour! If you'd let us know you were coming, I would've waited for you at the front gate with a garland! What does it matter which gate you had to use to enter the house? At least you didn't have to climb electrified, barb-wired walls or enter through the roof!" she added, trying to lighten the mood.

As Anand had arrived without any notice, no one was expecting him. Karuna, being a light sleeper, woke up when she heard someone trying to open the front gate, which was kept padlocked at night. On seeing Anand, she signalled to him to use the gate that wasn't locked, and make his way to the back entrance of the house so she could let him in without disturbing the entire household.

"Your mother is very mean," Anand said, unwilling to let the matter rest.

"Where does meanness come into all this? Ma asked you to come round to the back entrance because she now considers you part of the family. I'd have been asked to do the same, so would my uncles," Asha explained patiently.

"She did not give me enough money to pay the rickshaw-wallah," he added.

"You asked her for the fare! Why did you not pay it yourself?" Asha was so surprised she rose and sat lotus-posed on the bed, fully awake.

"I did not have any change," he said.

"You *knew* you were coming here. *You* also *knew you* were going to arrive at this unearthly hour—why did *you* not carry sufficient change with you. Why do you expect ma to have the right change when *you* didn't? That, too, at four o'clock in the morning! She gave you what she thought was the right fare. If you wanted to pay the rickshaw-wallah more, you should've asked her for more. Better still, you should've paid the fare yourself. As far as I can make out, she was only being helpful."

He disappeared into the bathroom, murmuring, "Like mother, like daughter!"

"I heard that," Asha cried. "First you come and disturb my mother. Had it not been for her, you'd still be standing outside. You wake her up, then ask her to give you money for your rickshaw fare. Instead of appreciating her help, you complain she did not treat you right!"

Anand had already locked himself in the bathroom.

A week later, they were getting ready for a family photograph when Vijay knocked on the door and announced, "Nani, Sadhana nani is here. Come when you're ready."

"Yes, I'm coming," Asha replied. Turning to Anand, she said, "You better get dressed. I'm going to talk to Sadhana nani."

When Asha returned, Anand was still lounging around in his pyjamas. On seeing her surprised look, he complained his shirt had not been ironed. Asha had ironed the shirt that morning. So she said, "Do you want to iron it yourself?" Thinking that if he felt it was not done properly, he could do it fresh to his satisfaction.

Rumbling with suppressed anger, like thunder before lightning, Anand snapped, "Shut up, you bitch!"

Karuna and Sadhana were talking just outside the room. Like Abhay and Priti on the night of the dinner, they were dumbfounded. The genie was now out of the bottle, though the women did their best to pretend that nothing was the matter. Anand sulked for the rest of the day. He went through the motions of the photographic session. Asha sensed it was the calm before a storm. That night he was nowhere to be found. Everyone waited for him for dinner. It was during the waiting she overheard her parents and her Abhay uncle talking in the next room.

"I simply would not have believed it unless I saw it myself. He is not the boy we thought he was!" Abhay said, shaking his head in disbelief.

"He cannot live here," Aditya said, unable to supress his anger.

"But what will happen to Asha?" Karuna cried out in despair. "He is able to survive anywhere, under any circumstance, but our Asha cannot."

Frustrated and outraged, Aditya said, "Nobody listens to me— I've been saying all along he's a good-for-nothing laphanga! She insisted on marrying him. Let her suffer. No one else will marry her if her marriage fails."

"That's why he has been going around with that face, long as a fiddle!" Karuna said as if she had understood something that had been bugging her for days.

"He takes no responsibility for his wife, abuses our hospitality. He is like a cuckoo, a parasite, a dung beetle..." Aditya's fury failed to find the right words.

"Don't upset yourself. Your blood pressure will get worse; you'll fall ill. It won't have any effect on him," Karuna reminded her husband.

"I don't know how this situation can be resolved if he persists in behaving the way he does," Abhay said, without expecting anyone to offer a solution.

For the first time, Asha saw things from her family's point of view and felt immensely guilty for landing everyone in such a fine mess.

Anand returned after midnight, smelling of alcohol. Not wishing to precipitate matters, Asha did not even ask him where he had been. *Things are always better in the morning,* she told herself. Instead of falling asleep, Anand cuddled up to her after he tucked himself inside the mosquito net. Then he suggested they move to a place in the outskirts of the city. His uncle had arranged it for them, he said.

Could this be a way out? Asha wondered, but could not see it working out, even in the short term. She remembered visiting such bungalows as children, accompanying Aja on his official duties, but only for a morning or an afternoon.

"Is that not meant for government people on duty?" Asha asked.

"*We* are government people on duty." Anand chuckled.

"I meant like the administrative officers," she said. Though Asha did not find the prospect appealing, she was in no position to resist. Not at that precise moment anyway. "We can spend the weekends, but commuting daily makes no sense. What about food—where do we eat? The room won't have any cooking facilities. We need to find a small place in town. Finding one in the campus will be impossible."

Asha knew how difficult it was living on a government salary. Money, or the lack of it, was a big concern. She got paid once every six months, and the amount was far from adequate. Since her marriage, her admiration for her parents for raising their family had increased multifold.

"We'll sort all that later once we move," Anand said as he started to kiss the nape of her neck.

She yielded to his caresses. He had not been that gentle and passionate recently. She responded to his embraces, their lovemaking ecstatic that night. A couple of days later, Asha left with Anand to spend the weekend away.

Holding her daughter close, Karuna said, "God be with you. Be patient. Everything will work out."

Aditya, not very good with words, held his daughter when she bent forward to pay her respects. He wiped his eyes once the rickshaw pulled away. No one could see his helplessness, how difficult it was for him as a father to relinquish the care of his daughter to someone he could not trust! He stood there, his frustration and anger blown away like ashes in the wind.

The ride from her parents' home to the bungalow took over an hour. They passed the railway crossing and the shanty dwellings beyond it. Finally, she could see the sun setting across the majestic Mahanadi. Asha's heart lifted; she was happy. She touched Anand's hand gently, but he moved his away. He had been silent all this time. Then he began to accuse her parents for failing to find a place for them to live. Asha could not believe that the unmissable beauty of the sunset had failed to move him, that he could not reciprocate her feelings, directing his energy instead against her parents. She found his accusations unfair and felt immensely sad he was not happy to have her by his side. Their thoughts could not have been more divergent.

Recovering her composure, she said, "Why do you expect my parents to find a place for us? It is *our* responsibility. My father raised a family of six. He looked after his sisters and brothers—not to mention the many students who came to him for help. If we can't manage between us, how do you expect him to support us? Besides, if my parents do not love me, as you keep saying, then I would not accept a paisa from them. Only where there is love and respect can one accept any help."

"You talk nonsense, all this hisab-kitab!" he said, his face reddening.

"You used to agree with me once—you said we would not be like others. *We* would be different, set an example, share every burden, and not accept any dowry. I don't know where that Anand *is* these days—what happened to *you*, *us*?" Asha asked, grieving for the man she knew and loved.

"You don't understand," he said, bristling.

"I do and thought marriage would make it easier for us. I was wrong."

Dismissing all negative thoughts, Asha told herself—*Be patient, all will be well*—as she entered the bungalow. She uttered a prayer like a female priest at a griha pravesh ceremony, asking to be blessed with happiness during their stay there. Later, humming an old Hindi film song, *ajeeba dastan hai yeh, kahan shuru kahan khatam*, she put away the few things she had carried with her.

Anand went off to have a bath. He was not exactly the domestic type, but Asha was a born homemaker. She transformed even the humblest dwelling into a welcoming palace. It had been up to her to do whatever shopping was necessary. In reality, she borrowed everything from her parents. He did not even carry the luggage, the rickshaw-wallah did.

Anand emerged from the bathroom, half-wrapped in a towel, water dripping inside the room, and he announced, "You can use the bathroom now."

Before entering the bathroom, Asha took off her sari and put it carefully on a chair. She was wearing the cotton slip traditionally worn under a sari and the blouse. Anand grimaced as she walked the few steps to the bathroom. She locked the door without asking what was wrong. Discarding her clothes, she turned on the tap. Sitting beneath it, she lost herself in the warm, revitalising embrace of water. Momentarily, all her troubles were washed away.

She came out of the bathroom in a fresh slip and blouse with the bath towel flung over her, wondering what had brought on his expression of disgust before. At home, she was accustomed to wearing the sari inside the room, the bathroom floor being too wet for draping oneself in six yards of cloth. The lower edges of the sari got wet and soiled, and took longer to be cleaned as the dirt seeped into the fabric. All the women in her family did so.

On seeing her, Anand said, "My mother would never come out naked from the bathroom like you. She gets dressed in the bathroom. You have no shame at all, no lajya. You say you are from a khandani family, yet you have no culture!"

"I'm not naked!" Asha could not help laughing. "The bathroom floor is wet. There is no need to wear the sari in there when I can wear it comfortably here. What's your problem? What I am wearing is perfectly decent. In many parts of the world, it would be considered quite decent to appear like this in public. I'm definitely *not naked,*" she said calmly, but was upset enough to consider asking him to get dressed in the bathroom, not wander out like a bull pissing.

She began to comb her hair, but was so angry with his remark, she needed to breathe deeply. Then she lay down on the bed and closed her eyes for a few moments. She hoped Anand might come over, make up, and stop quarrelling with her. After all, they were now in a place *he* wanted them to be in.

Sitting in the armchair at the other end of the room, Anand bellowed, "Get up. We have to go and meet Mr Lenka."

Mr Lenka was the man in charge of the place.

"Let me lie down just for a moment. I have such a headache, even my feet ache! But are they expecting us? Will Mr and Mrs Lenka be prepared to receive us? Should we not go another time after giving them some notice? Have we been invited? We don't have a gift for them either," Asha said.

Anand did not reply. Then Asha dozed off briefly, but was woken up by a steely jab on her chest.

"If you don't want to come, I'll go on my own," said Anand.

That remark did not upset her; on the contrary, she welcomed it. But then he suddenly turned on her. "Don't think you have done me a favour by marrying me." And he stomped out of the room, banging the door loudly behind him.

She heard him pacing in the front veranda like some wild animal. *Why can't he go to see Mr Lenka if he wants to? Can he not explain that I'm tired and resting? Most husbands happily do so. Why does he take pleasure in hurting me? Why is every act a mini-battle for him? How can things unravel so fast?* Asha agonized.

Anand came inside and shouted, "Why are you making a show of yourself? People can see your half-naked body on the bed."

"Perhaps your pacing up and down the veranda is attracting the attention of passers-by? Nobody lives in the bungalow. Seeing a stranger walking up and down in an agitated state is a spectacle worth watching. It's not for nothing these bungalows are called inspection bungalows!" Asha joked, trying to make him laugh.

Orissa may have been the kind of place where life was full of care, but its people always found the time to stop and stare. Asha knew how easy it was to rustle up a crowd by just standing somewhere, anywhere, without being in anyone's way or obstructing anyone else's business, simply by staring at the sky or your navel. A very curious lot, the Oriyas.

Anand was clearly in no mood for light banter. When Asha got up to shut the window on her side of the room, he grabbed her by her shoulders and said, "What do you think of me, you haramzadi? Just because you are paying for me, you think I'll do as you wish, you bitch? Why don't you commit suicide? Go, get a divorce. I'll leave you at your parents' place tomorrow. You bloody bastard, how you humiliate me."

Taken aback by his attack, Asha took shelter in the bathroom.

"Don't think I care if you cry," he shouted, banging the door. "Why don't you go and drown yourself in the Mahanadi?"

When she did not respond, he yelled, "Open the door, you daughter of a fucking mother-of-a-bitch. You wanted to marry an IAS; why didn't you? Why didn't you marry a rich man?"

"How many times do I have to tell you I never wanted to marry an IAS or a rich man? I could've done so if I wanted to. But why did you marry me if you feel the way you do? No one forced you to marry me," she cried.

Thinking he had gone to Mr Lenka's house, as it had gone awfully quiet for a while, Asha came out of the bathroom. Anand was there, waiting like a panther.

Grabbing her by her arm, he shouted, "Must've bloody sinned

to have married you; committed the greatest mistake of my life. You're not the kind of girl I wanted to marry. I never loved you, you stupid bitch." And he laughed like one possessed.

Asha was saved by three steady, loud knocks on the door. It reminded her of the way her brothers knocked. *But surely they couldn't be here? They do not even know where I am,* she thought.

Anand released her and went to open the door. The bungalow's resident peon announced dinner was ready as he dexterously put one foot inside the door and did not budge until Asha was out of the room. The peon then followed Asha at a respectful distance all the way to the dining room.

Drunken, abusive husbands were all too common. The husband of their housemaid sometimes came home drunk. But he was pretty harmless, more a mouse than a tiger. He shouted at the sky and threw a few things around, especially kitchen utensils that made a lot of noise, but rarely committed any acts of violence against his wife or children. One evening Vikram, Vijay and Vivek gave him a visit and told him in no uncertain terms that he and his family would have to leave their employment if he carried on in such a manner. His drunken performances stopped after that.

Asha had never imagined her own life would descend into such a drama. When she had first spoken to Anand that fateful afternoon in college, she had not done so because he reminded her of Mr Darcy or looked like the matinee idols of the day. Asha had approached him simply because he happened to be there. She'd have asked the same question to any other person standing there. How was she to know that her innocent query would have such devastating consequences—that it would encourage him to climb the proverbial mountain? How was she to know that she, the cynosure of all eyes, was a trophy worth winning? Or that this was the sort of thing that aspiring young men did? Her brothers were nothing like Anand.

Since the wedding, she had heard so many derogatory remarks from Anand about herself and her family, she had lost count.

She could not reconcile the Jekyll and Hyde aspect of Anand's personality. What puzzled her was how within days of her marriage she had discovered his other self, something he had kept hidden from her all those years. Had the transformation not been so dramatic so soon after the wedding, she would have assumed that in time all marriages descend into some version of hell, though she had never seen her father treat her mother in such a manner! Compared to what she was going through, her parents' marriage seemed perfectly happy.

After dinner she stopped outside Mr Lenka's house to pick some flowers. She loved the smell of jasmine; the flowers were delicate and beautiful like filigree ornaments. *No wonder the Goddess Saraswati is described to be as fair as jasmine,* Asha thought. Mrs Lenka joined her and said loudly enough for all to hear, "Please take some flowers." Then she whispered, "Don't worry. We're here."

Asha nodded gratefully. It was just one woman looking out for another. *Why is it that those you love fail to understand you while complete strangers do?* Asha mused, returning to the room, her palms full of fragrant jasmine flowers. She was hoping to spread them on the bed and make up with Anand. But he had separated the twin beds and was sprawled on one. On seeing her, he pulled the sheet over his face and turned away. Asha went to the bathroom. By the time she returned, he had already switched off the light.

As she groped her way back to bed, she remembered the games they used to play as children. But this did not seem like one. Unable to sleep, she wondered if he had been like this all along and somehow she had failed to notice. *If I was to marry a stranger,* she thought, *I could've had an arranged marriage and made my parents happy. How foolish was it of me to imagine I could regain my lost world of childhood happiness through the love of a man. What have I done!*

She was a moth caught in the jaws of a lizard. The dawn did not bring any hope. The pain she was experiencing was the most intense feeling Asha had ever known. At the same time it was the most private and least communicable.

CHAPTER 19

Woken by the touch of cold fingers on her crotch, Asha was surprised to see Anand squatting over her, spreading her legs apart.

"Not now," she said, turning away.

"Sex is best in the morning," he said, fondling her breasts and kissing them.

"Use a condom," she murmured, half aroused by his passionate embrace.

"It's not the same," he whispered as he began to make love to her.

Later, when they woke up, he was in a good mood. They even managed to have a conversation. He said he felt neglected by her family, especially by her mother.

"What has my family got to do with the way *you* are behaving with *me*?" Asha asked. She did not wish to start a fresh argument, so she said, "Please don't make *our* time together unhappy. *I* am not neglecting *you*." She did not think it would be wise to remind him how she'd felt when she was at his parents' home.

That morning, the newspapers were full of the Janata Party's success in the general elections. The Congress (I), Mrs Gandhi's party, was decimated. Anand was delighted with the outcome and asked Asha what she wanted.

She appreciated the gesture, knowing he did not have the means to buy her gifts. "Your love and understanding is enough!" she said.

He gave her a crushing embrace and carried her back to bed. Asha was happy. The rest of the day passed relatively uneventfully. 'Never let the scramble for having enough to live obscure your goal of having something to live for,' she noted in her diary that night.

The ride back to her parents' the following morning went smoothly. As the rickshaw-wallah pedalled them across the long Mahanadi Bridge, she admired the landscape, the red fertile soil. People attended to their daily chores—some washed their clothes, spreading them out to dry on huge boulders, while others bathed, almost naked, in the river. Women scrubbed their utensils; men their cows and buffaloes. It was warm, promising another hot summer. The wind touched their faces with its invisible fingers. Asha and Anand smiled as if they had been blessed by the gods.

Anand chatted excitedly about the state of the nation—how things were going to be different from now on, change for the better. Asha hoped it would be the same for them too. It was then he slipped in the news that he had been posted at Harrison College. Though surprised, Asha thought her ship had come in as he gave her a kiss. A young man cycling by, whistling as if he had won the lottery, smiled at her and sang, *"Tu cheese hai masta, masta..."* Asha turned her face away, blushing.

As they neared her parents' home, Anand said, "Why don't you give your mother some money for the living expenses?"

"Yes, I'll talk to her. No need to worry about it at the moment," she said.

Earlier, Anand had mentioned in passing that he had only Rs 200 on him. Asha was not sure if he expected her to give him some money. As she did not have any spare cash either, apart from the fare for the rickshaw-wallah, she did not offer any. When they reached her parents' home, Karuna opened the door and greeted them warmly. She seemed to be in a happier mood too. Asha was pleased and thought things were finally falling into place.

Then Anand, turning to Karuna, said, "As we are staying here, can you keep this?" And he offered her a hundred-rupee note.

A surprised Karuna said, "Can't my daughter and her husband stay in our home without having to pay?"

Anand felt he had been slighted yet again by his mother-in-law.

Asha did not think her mother had said anything offensive, so failed to guess the direction of his thoughts. After some tea and snacks, they left together for college.

Anand did not tell her he was going to join that day. Later, when they were supposed to return home, he casually informed her that he was not returning home with her. Asha assumed he was going to see some friends and celebrate his new job. Not wishing to turn into a nagging wife, she did not ask what time he'd be back. He thought she did not care enough to ask.

Asha only began to worry about Anand when he was not back by the time her father began to lock up. She could not go to sleep, afraid of another encounter between him and her mother, and knowing how prone he was to misinterpreting whatever she said or did. Asha lay awake till the early hours of the morning, wondering why her marriage was unravelling stitch by stitch.

The next morning when she dragged herself to college, she saw Anand chatting away in the staff common room. Immensely relieved to see him there, she smiled. The SCR was no place to discuss their private affairs. The office peon remarked how lucky it was they were both posted in the same college, same department. It then dawned on her he had already joined. Asha had a lot of questions for Anand, but could not possibly ask them, not then and there.

Anand did not say anything, instead he left the SCR. When she saw him again in the library and wanted a word, he simply shushed her and moved away. Before he left, he whispered sarcastically in her ear, "You go home, little princess."

Asha was so miserable she went to see Rashmi. Not finding her at home, she went to Sadhana's and, much against her will, confessed her woes to her cousin. Sadhana calmed her down before accompanying her home. By the time Sadhana left, the entire family was worried about Asha's marriage.

"Look into your own health and happiness," Sadhana said when she left.

"Only God can help us." Karuna felt helpless, faced with so many unexpected disasters. "How can both marriages fail?" She wanted an answer from God.

Aditya was so frustrated, all he could think of saying was 'I told you so', but refrained from saying it in the presence of his father-in-law.

The rest of the family sat in stunned silence.

"We are not here without a purpose," Aja said. "If we understand our purpose in life, our destiny, we will also understand the reason for our suffering. Only the brave and patient understand the meaning of life by surrendering to God."

Aja's words provided a spiritual anchor for the whole family.

Trying to understand life and her destiny, Asha accompanied Anand to the inspection bungalow the following weekend. Once again Asha found the beds separated when she came out of the bathroom.

"Why must you do such a thing, Anand? Why should I come here if you won't talk to me and do not wish to share a bed with me? If we can't work out our problems, what's the point of being married?" she asked.

He pretended he had not heard. Unable to get through, frustrated, angry and desperate, Asha hit the wall with her bare hands and cried, her body taut with grief, "Why are you punishing me? What have I done?"

If she was hoping her sorrow would elicit a sympathetic response, she was sorely mistaken. Anand continued to ignore her, and she continued to feel an inner throbbing pain, as if her heart was going to explode. When she accidentally banged her head against the wall, trying to switch off the light, he began to laugh hysterically.

Then he got up, went to the bathroom and returned with the belt from his trousers, which he had left hanging there. Asha could not think of a reason why he needed his belt at that hour. He began his litany of accusations against her. When she turned away, he whipped her with his belt, smashing her glass bangles and cutting her forearms in the process. She yelled in pain. He only stopped when he heard voices outside. The lashes left her back badly bruised. She kept seeing flashes of light when she closed her eyes. She lay on her stomach, unable to lie on her back, sobbing. It was dawn when she was finally rescued by sleep.

The next morning he made passionate love to her, over and over again, whispering, "I love you. I'm so sorry I hurt you. I will do anything for you, my love."

She had no idea what had triggered this. Asha learnt, slowly but surely, that *she* had little to do with his outbursts. He was responding mostly to his inner demons. She failed to understand why these demons surfaced so soon after the wedding. The question uppermost in her mind was—*If this is the price of love, can I afford it?*

Her back ached as he made love to her. All the tenderness in the world could not take away the pain he had inflicted the previous night. He began to lick the lash marks on her back that stood out in relief, sore and angry. Every time he did so, it hurt so badly she had to bite her lips to stop herself from screaming. In between lovemaking, he applied whatever creams and lotions he could lay his hands on to her wounds. It left her squirming and writhing.

But he kept kissing her and spent the whole day making love to her. When he came for the final time, he said, "Remember this moment. We have set a new record."

Asha was confused; what record was he talking about?

He reminded her of a conversation they'd had, before their wedding, about a cousin of his whose husband had made love to her seven times in one day during their honeymoon. "I've broken that record," he said proudly.

She wished he applied his competitiveness in other ways.

That night he made love to her again. And as he did so, his head in the air as if he was riding a horse, his face lifted up so he did not see the look on her face or the pain he was causing, he said, "You've not sacrificed anything for me. Prove you love me—have my child."

His words sparked an angry ember that spread through her body like wildfire. How could he think of bringing a child into their precarious world?

"We'll have a child when we have a home, when you can be a responsible husband and father," Asha said, struggling to disengage her body from under him.

Anand pinned her down as he continued to thrust himself harder and deeper. She finally extricated herself from his grip and escaped to the bathroom. It was then she noticed the condom stuck inside her. When she took it out, it was leaking. She noticed clearly visible pinpricks. She began to wash herself furiously.

She could hear him yelling, "I want a divorce, you bitch…"

Returning to bed, she lay down, exhausted, convinced she could not face this any longer, let alone for the rest of her life.

"Go ahead! Don't keep threatening me with a divorce. I can't bear this any longer," she said calmly. "I will *not* bring a child into this wretched world you've created for me. If you want a child, mend yourself." She turned away from him, her tears flowing uncontrollably.

"You don't think I am responsible? I'll show you responsible, you bitch!" He went on repeating the word BITCH with increasing ferocity. She found his new litany of abuse so extraordinary her tears dried up.

Unable to bear his accusations, she said, "Anand, everything you say is untrue. But, if you had such knowledge, why did you marry me?"

"I made a bloody mistake," he said, slapping her hard first on one cheek and then the other.

As she cried out in agony, he started to throttle her. She tried to push him away without success. Pinning her body down with all his might, he forced himself on her. She kept repeating, "No, no, no," as she pushed him with all her strength, but realised she was no match for him. Until that moment, Asha had harboured a belief that she could fight off a rapist. But Anand weighed down on her with all his might, this time without a condom, and raped her.

Her sense of outrage blazed all through the night. Every pore of her body cried out for justice. She could not bear to look at him snoring there beside her. *God, what have I done? Do not abandon me. If I forgot you in the midst of my troubles, why have you forgotten me?*

The journey back to her parents' place the following day was a sombre affair. She had nothing more to say to Anand. After the previous night's tempest, he was calm. They passed the same landscape and scenes in silence. There was something reassuring about the solidity of the earth. The flowing river offered hope of change, of suffering passing like the clouds, and the sky promised things unknown. Yet Asha knew something inside her had changed, died, forever.

Anand dropped her off at the front gate and did not come in. Asha had a bath before crawling into bed. Her body was sore, her head throbbed, and she shivered involuntarily. Bright lights kept flashing when she closed her eyes. She was in no state to go to work. If her family had misinterpreted her sleeplessness at the beginning of her marriage, now they knew why she needed her sleep when she was home. But no one knew the true extent of her suffering. Asha, too, could not face the truth, let alone tell her family what had really been going on while she was with Anand. The weekends were a different country.

Asha needed to sleep, but was scared of sleeping as she kept seeing a terrifying snake in her dreams, a vicious creature intent on killing her, striking her with a stream of fire that emanated from the volcano of its mouth. Death was certain. Yet every time it struck, she jumped away from its path and was saved. The dream only ceased when she woke up in a sweat, breathless, crying for help. She stayed in bed all week. Anand never came to see her.

⁓⁕⁓

Aditya did not much relish the idea of Asha staying with them, worried that Anand would leave her there. He would have liked her living with her husband. Asha would have liked that too, but the way things turned out, she had nowhere else to go. Her body was a wreck, her soul was in pain, her financial situation was precarious, and she felt lonelier than she thought was possible.

Her appointment as a lecturer was on an ad hoc basis, coming top of her class in the university counted for nothing. Asha knew that being confirmed in her job on a permanent basis was a matter of time. But time was her enemy. Ad hoc appointees received their salaries irregularly; she received hers every six months. Getting paid involved her father or uncle having to contact someone in the State Administrative Offices, as if the State of Orissa was doing her a favour by paying for services rendered over the past six months.

When Asha got paid in arrears, she contributed towards her living expenses at home and paid off her debts at the bookshop and the sari shop. These days she no longer had any money left to buy anything from D.P Sur and Sons, the bookseller, or Ramananda Lal, the textile merchant. Anand constantly needed loans, which he never paid back. Often he emptied her bag, helping himself to whatever money he could lay his hands on. Asha learnt not to carry too much cash in her purse. The precariousness of her existence took its toll. A large income may be the best recipe for happiness, but a meagre one certainly helped her in understanding the limitations of human nature.

Cash-flow problems aside, her main concern was Anand's new avatar. Not only was there no light at the end of the tunnel, she had no idea how long the tunnel was. They may have had the kind of problems any young couple faced, but the way their relationship had crumbled under the weight of the new reality was a revelation. *Is it not in times of great distress that we discover the truth about our self and others? Perhaps God is trying to teach me a harsh lesson,* she concluded.

Despite the myriad ways in which her expectations had been shattered, Asha could not destroy her feelings for Anand. She felt as if she'd lost an arm and a leg in an accident, but the ghost of her limbs haunted her. Her habit of loving lived on in her. In a state of constant mental and physical trauma, she could not eat or sleep, losing twelve pounds in a month. Her blood pressure shot up. She suffered from high fever, delirium, panic attacks, and exhaustion. She woke up several times each night with one thought on her mind: *How was I so deceived?*

When Rashmi called on Asha, finding her friend in bed looking frail and defenceless, she said, "I can no longer bear this."

"What do you mean?" Asha enquired in a feeble voice. "What's the matter?"

"I don't gossip, but I've been hearing such rubbish about you and your family, I had to warn you." Rashmi was on the verge of tears.

On seeing her friend so upset, Asha leaned forward, trying to sit up. "You mustn't listen to rumours! Come here," Asha said, stifling the shooting pains that wracked her body when she stirred. "You know what people are like. Remember the first time we met? You told me the rubbish you'd heard. People don't change."

When Rashmi gave her a hug, Asha recoiled in agony. "Ahh!" she cried out as a lightning flash of pain passed through her spine.

"What's the matter?" Rashmi asked. Then she noticed the bruises on her arms and neck. "Mausi and mousa must be shattered," she said.

"They will only worry if..." Asha stopped.

Rashmi, who was sitting on the edge of the bed, started to stroke Asha's back gently as parents do when consoling a child. When Asha flinched again, Rashmi examined her back. On seeing the bruises, she ran out of the room in a flood of tears.

Returning with Karuna, Rashmi said, "Mausi, see what that bastard has done to Asha. He's been going round telling people all kinds of nasty stories about her and your family. I am so sorry I never saw any of this coming."

"Why did you not say anything, Asha?" Karuna asked, appalled at what she saw. Before Asha could reply, Karuna said, "I should've known better."

"I didn't wish to add to your problems. I'd insisted on marrying him. Bapa never wanted it, nor did you. This can't be God's will, but why else would I suffer like this?" Asha could barely speak. "I have brought this on myself."

"I don't know about God's will, but you cannot carry on like this. What sort of a man does this to his wife?" Karuna observed incredulously.

"I will tell others what that bastard has done to you. To add insult to injury, he goes spreading lies against you and your family! What is wrong with people these days? Just leave him. How can a husband do this to his wife?" Rashmi asked, aghast.

"I can't carry on like this," Asha confessed.

As Rashmi applied amrutanjan on Asha's back, the smell of camphor made them cry. "It reminds me of temples and prayers, but I no longer know what to believe in. You should've said something before." Rashmi sighed.

"Take this now. I'll give you another dose later," said Karuna, handing Asha ten drops of Arnica tincture in a small glass of water. "Asuras like Anand should be kept behind bars," she added.

"Men beat and rape their wives, yet there is no law to protect us," said Rashmi. "Never thought Asha would have to experience this..."

"Something must be done," Karuna said. She had no idea what that might be. Karuna left the room, chanting the Durga mantra.

The family nursed Asha and counselled her to be patient, to pray, and have faith in God and the healing power of prayer. They lavished their love on her and urged her to be strong. They believed in her ability to overcome her problems.

"Be positive. Good things will happen," said Vijay, holding her hand.

Asha could not believe her younger brother could be so calm and sensible!

Vivek cried when he heard what had happened. His world seemed to have fallen apart with the two marriages. The only thing he could say to express his deep sorrow was, "I'll never get married."

"Do not precipitate the matter," Sadhana said. "Give it time. Time will heal."

"Look after yourself; health is wealth. No children. The state of your health and finances will not permit it," was Vikram's advice.

"Save money; no unnecessary expenditure, and don't finance Anand any longer. And don't neglect your job," counselled Aja.

Vishu was so upset, he swore, "That swine, what does he know the worth of our pearl, Asha? I pray life treats him the way he has treated his wife."

"It is not easy to know a human being. It is indeed a tragedy you were so deceived. You know what they say—to err is human," Abhay consoled Asha.

"I don't know what to think. Everything is falling apart," Aditya said when he could not see a way out of the disastrous situation.

"Life sends us trials. We did everything in the right spirit, what we thought was right and good. What else could we have done? We mustn't fall apart when God sends us unexpected trials," Karuna consoled Asha and her family.

Three weeks later a letter arrived in the post addressed to Prof Armita Guru. It was from Anand. He did not say why he had not visited her, nor did he wish her a speedy recovery. Instead, he'd written he expected her to fulfil her duty as his wife, that he was being denied his conjugal rights. He also mentioned in passing that he never meant the things he'd said. The letter ended with, 'You said you loved me, you'd do anything for me—why don't you prove it by having my child?' He had not said anywhere that he regretted his behaviour or that he loved her, needed her, missed her, and wanted them to be back together.

As Asha shed more tears, she remembered the times he used to declare his eternal love and loyalty. It seemed a lifetime ago, as if she had imagined it. Only the other day he had reminded her, "I never meant the things I said or wrote before. It was just—what do they call it? Ah, sweet nothings! Now we're married, I mean every word I say." Then he'd laughed in a way that frightened her. Reconciling his contradictory personas was hard, like being at sea and not knowing the exact position because the trusted compass was giving erratic readings. It was as disconcerting as reading your favourite book only to discover that your understanding of it was deeply flawed. After five years of courtship, she thought she knew him. But after her marriage, she had no idea who he really was.

When Asha missed her period that month, she thought she would also lose her mind. She had been counting the hours since that tumultuous night. Every single day had been a day spent in hell, and every night she lay in bed praying for her period. Unable to tell others her predicament, trapped in a lattice of conflicting emotions, she kept battering away at the walls that imprisoned her. A week later, when there was still no sign of her period, Asha broke down and could not stop crying.

When Karuna heard her sobbing and asked what the matter was, Asha confided, "Ma, I might be pregnant. But I'm not ready for a family. Anand is not the man I fell in love with. He is trying to trap me with a child. How can I bring a child into such an unhappy, traumatic marriage? It won't be fair—certainly not to the child." Asha could not bring herself to tell her mother that Anand had raped her with the sole intention of leaving her pregnant.

Karuna made an appointment with the family homeopath. They went to see him the next day. She explained to him their predicament. "Her husband is not financially settled. That is why she is living with us. If she has a child, how will she cope? She has a job to do as well. Once her life is settled, they can have a child."

The homeopath was a practical man; he appreciated Asha's dilemma. He may have also heard the gossip. In Cuttack, everybody knew everybody else's business.

"Yes, it's always better to plan a family," he said, nodding sagely. "But why did you not use contraception?" he asked.

"I did, tried to," Asha said, filled with despair.

The homeopath gave her a tiny glass phial with white pills and told her to be more careful from now on. "Take this tonight before you go to bed," he said. Turning to Karuna, he added, "Madam, let me know how she gets on."

That night before going to bed, Asha examined the slender glass phial and could not believe those tiny, white pills would save her. Having grown up with homeopathic remedies, she trusted them. She said her prayers before tipping the pills on her tongue and let the sweet crystals dissolve in her mouth.

The next morning she had her period. The bleeding was heavy—dark clusters of jelly appeared when she urinated. She had to change her sanitary pad every half-hour. She felt faint with the sight of so much blood, but was immensely relieved she was no longer pregnant. It was a devastating realization she did not want Anand's child.

CHAPTER 20

The day Asha received an invitation to attend a seminar in Madras, courtesy of the United States Information Service, Anand turned up at the house, unannounced. He wanted her back. Though the Guru family was deeply disappointed with him, no one was ready to accept the dissolution of Asha's marriage. She too believed, like some determined scientist, that if she tried harder, one last time, she might succeed in finding the secret to a happy married life.

Asha interpreted Anand's arrival as a good omen and determined to salvage her marriage. People undertook hazardous expeditions to save what they valued most. Nations sent entire battalions to war, who then perished in the struggle, she reminded herself. She reckoned if they could spend time together in Madras, without being burdened with the responsibilities of a household, including the distractions and demands of their respective families, they would possibly be able to save their marriage. She wrote to Prof Singh at the American Institute, requesting that he recommend Anand as a participant.

The evening she left for Madras, Vijay accompanied her to the railway station. Anand was already in his seat. Making sure his sister's luggage was carefully padlocked under her seat, Vijay took his leave, wishing them a safe journey. Anand ignored Vijay, who waved at them as the train pulled away from the platform.

Asha's brothers had not objected to their sister marrying Anand.
Like Asha, they thought he would make something of himself and
would want to be taken in, shaped and mended by the people who
cared for him. Anand had done nothing of the sort. Instead, his
behaviour had shocked them all. Had he really changed, or was he
always like this? They had all felt let down, more than they thought
possible.

Asha blamed herself for what she thought of as her failure to
inspire Anand to change himself. She believed in love, thought love
would ultimately triumph, that their problems were mere trials in
the path of true love. She knew the importance of having a path
in life—a path was something you could return to. A good person
is one who is good even in times of great distress. She was certain
she would find her way to the man she thought Anand was, and
believed he could be. She thought of many such things during the
overnight journey to Madras.

The moment they checked into their hotel room, Anand
wanted to make love. Asha, on the other hand, wanted to have
a wash and eat something. All through the long train journey he
had behaved as if she did not exist. While he kept snacking away,
he'd offered her nothing. When the hawkers came by with tea,
coffee, peanuts, and pakoras, he bought whatever he fancied and
astonishingly consumed it all, handing her the leftovers from time
to time. Asha did not wish to say anything to him in public. Nor
did she buy anything from the hawkers, thinking he might take
offence if she did so. It was not until lunchtime the following day
that she had the inedible railway lunch. On reaching the hotel, a
ravenously hungry Asha wanted a shower and food, making love
was not uppermost on her mind.

When she tried to explain, he complained, "You keep saying
you love me, but I can't even make love to my wife. Let alone have
a child."

She held on to the belief that with the grace of God everything,
yes, absolutely everything, could be mended. She believed if she

surrendered everything to God, love would lead her to happiness. Why it left her in this state of confusion, devoid of all that is good, wholesome and redeeming, was beyond her understanding.

Asha's journal, her confidante, was where she confessed all.

***

Journal entry, Madras, 10 May:

Anand left the seminar room without as much as casting a glance at me. When I returned to the hotel, he was fast asleep. Careful not to wake him, I lay down at the opposite end of the large double bed. When he woke up, I asked him if he wasn't feeling well. He never replied. I must've dozed off after that, for I was woken up by a loud bang. I realised Anand had just slammed the door shut.

I went out to the balcony to see where he was heading. I don't know why I did that, nor why I can't be more detached. I spotted him in the crowd. After a while, he looked back in my direction. I waved at him, but he turned and walked on. After walking a few paces, he looked back again. Our room was on the ninth floor. I could not see his face. I came in disappointed and stayed in bed.

He was back soon and started shouting. "Are you a prostitute? Do you want sex?" he yelled and said I was showing off my body like a *veshya*. There is nothing I can do right these days. He does not like the colour of my lipstick, my clothes, not the way I talk or walk. It was pointless telling him that I'd stepped out onto the balcony because he left without telling me where he was going. And the reason I want to know such things is because I love him.

Journal entry, Madras, 12 May:

Anand accused me of going to Hyderabad on my own to have fun with the men attending the course. Unable to bear his constant taunts, I said it would be better to commit suicide than have to listen to him. "You always feel like committing suicide," he said and laughed. How can he accuse me because I went to Hyderabad?

What about all the girls who attended with me? Why are men above suspicion? What about him—he disappears for days without telling me where he goes or what he does! Even when I am not with him, I am not free of him. I love the man I thought he was, but I cannot live with the man he is. Society will not allow me to live without him. Even in my sleep I am not alone. I have lost *my self*, my identity. I am no longer *me*. I don't know who *I* am, what is happening to *me*, or *why I* exist!

Journal entry, Madras, 19 May:

This morning Anand returned from Delhi. There was no time to talk as we were late for the seminar. In the evening we went for a walk on the beach with some of the other participants. Reena left her handbag in our room. The plan was to return to the hotel after a walk, then take a taxi to Chitra's for dinner. Anand and I returned to the hotel. I asked him about Delhi, but he never said anything and kept reading the newspaper. I suggested we go back to the beach to return the handbag. We found them, Reena and Rupen, lost in each other's company. I was so jealous.

Anand was no longer in a mood to go to Chitra's. It would have taken another half-hour to get there. So we returned to the hotel and had something to eat. When we went to bed, he said he could not make love to me, that something prevented him from doing so. He spoke as if I was to blame. Before he went to Delhi, he was like a sex maniac, even on the night I had that terrible stomach pain. It was so intense I could not stop crying. Instead of asking me what was wrong, he behaved like a spoilt child. It is not that I deny him sex. But he uses sex as a means of punishing me.

Journal entry, Madras, 20 May:

The organizers had arranged a trip to Mahabalipuram. First thing in the morning Anand declared he did not want to go. I suggested he stay in and relax in the hotel. He then changed his mind and came along. I had the distinct feeling he did not want me to go and enjoy myself. When we went to the beach, he said, "Why don't you go and drown yourself." He was not joking.

The girls had gone into the sea. They stood knee-deep in the water, their saris hitched up, their shalwars folded. Anand said bitterly, "Go, drown yourself, you bitch!" Every word of his was like a snake bite, and poison seeped into my veins. I needed the ocean to churn the poison out. I kept walking into the sea and stopped when the water reached my hips.

The girls warned me not to go further. They had no idea what dark thoughts were disturbing me, how capable I was of walking into oblivion. There was a huge wave, which came crashing down on me. I was thrown back towards the beach; someone was trying to knock some sense into me. I was saved from the powerful undercurrents dragging me out into the sea. God had taken me in His hand and reprimanded me for turning into a twenty-four-carat fool! At that moment, I realised Anand was not worth dying for. Later, Chitra said, "You gave us such a scare."

Journal entry, Madras, 23 May:

I am at my wits' end. I've no idea what I can do to remedy the deteriorating situation. He flares up for no reason, none that I can fathom. Last night, he was bad-mouthing my family, said he wanted to blow us all up! These days my tiredness is limitless—wish I could sleep forever. His shouting and my exhaustion together proved explosive. I started packing. I had no idea what I was doing or where I thought I might go at that hour. Listening to him spouting venom was unbearable. It would have been easier to look into the mouth of a volcano.

He switched off the light and did not invite me to join him in bed, nor did he ask me why I was packing my suitcase. I switched the light back on. I was in the middle of folding a sari. He got up. I was expecting him to switch off the light again. But I felt the fist of Muhammad Ali descending first on one cheek and then on the other. I saw a flash of light; then everything went dark. I thought he'd switched off the light. I crumpled in a heap on the floor, narrowly missing the sharp edge of the bed.

When I recovered, I saw his foot coming down on my face. He yelled, "Stop whimpering, you bitch. If I divorce you, people will spit in your face." I should have kept silent. But unable to contain my outrage, I said, "Nobody will spit in my face; instead they'll tell me—*we told you so.*" Then he spat in my face.

I wanted to get out of that hell when he began to strangle me. I started to choke; eventually he let go. I lay there remembering bapa's warning that he would kill me if I went back to him. Yet everyone also wanted me to try to rescue the marriage. I mumbled to myself that bapa had been right all along.

He shouted, "What did you say?" When I did not answer, he lashed out with his belt. When I regained consciousness, I could not move. I was writhing in pain. I had a throbbing headache and did not think I was going to survive the night.

The next morning I couldn't get out of bed. I had to miss the seminar. Don't know what Anand told everyone. Chitra came to see me when Anand was out. Taking one look at me, she said, "I must call the doctor." I persuaded her not to. We agreed if I was not feeling better the next day, I would see a doctor. Chitra realised that calling a doctor would precipitate matters. "You *must* leave him if you want to live," she said. I nodded. It was not possible to carry on like this. The day we left, Chitra told me she knew what I was going through, she'd been there. I'd never have guessed.

Journal entry, Cuttack, 24 June:

From Madras, we went to Pondicherry, then to Sambalpur before returning to Cuttack. In Pondicherry, Anand's violence and anger calmed down a bit. But his mood swings continued—making love to me one moment and behaving atrociously the next. Returning to his home made me see clearly that I could never be part of him or his family. His father is not a good man. In a letter to Anand, he had written that I needed to be taught a lesson and deserved to be beaten. I cannot imagine bapa writing such a letter to nana. Instead of counselling his son to love and care for his wife, he stokes the flames of discord.

My mother-in-law is better. Even her brother who visited once seemed nice. His youngest son, barely four, climbed on to my lap and said he would marry me, look after me, and buy me a gold comb for my hair. When I gave the child a hug, he was thrilled and would not get out of my lap. I do not know how my mother-in-law lives with my father-in-law. Is that why she spends so much time in the temple?

It was she who told me how foolish I had been to tell Anand how unhappy I was in my home. "We are all unhappy adolescents. What makes you think you were the only one?" She said it was up to the husband to make a home and then take a wife. "Why did you marry him when he had no income or the means to keep you in the style you are accustomed to?"

Aja had told me the same thing. Then why did everyone put so much pressure on me to marry? I had a job. Could I not have gone to Harvard? Was it so important to be married? Why did I listen? Did I deserve all this suffering? I know women are killed every day for not bringing enough dowry. Must I be thankful for not being burnt alive or strangled to death? I may be pregnant again and have not had my period as expected. I can't bear living like this—always afraid of Anand, unable to trust him, not wanting his child.

He comes out with insane pronouncements like 'a wife must be subordinate to her husband'. What a difference between the man who spoke of equality between man and wife when we were in college! I'd never have believed all this if it was not happening to me. Ma said even Rama went after a golden deer. Mere mortals like me are fallible, easily deceived.

Journal entry, Cuttack, 6 July:
Anand has been selected for the Allied Services. He is happy. But marriage has opened my eyes. Was this the only way of finding

out the truth? My good news for the day is that I got my period. It was extremely painful, but I am happy and relieved. I do not want a child with someone I cannot trust. He beats me, rapes me, slanders me—expects me to surrender totally to his wishes. I know bringing up a child involves sacrifice, but to sacrifice everything for a grown man? What if Anand turns violent against the child? Who will protect us?

Journal entry, Cuttack, 10 July:

I went to spend the weekend with Anand. He kept saying his life was full of sorrow. What about me? I am not lying on a bed of roses in a palace with an attentive emperor of a husband and slaves fulfilling every desire of mine! Last night he forced himself on me without any condoms, said he was being spontaneous. He accused me of never being spontaneous. How can I be if I can't trust him? I pushed him away, saying, "No condom, no sex."

"What will you do? I am stronger than you." He laughed, taking pleasure in overpowering me. He was serious, not saying it in jest.

Seeing me in tears, he withdrew and went to the bathroom. He took a while, at first I thought he was sulking. But he returned wearing a condom and made love as if he was a condemned man. He kept going long after the condom was torn and leaking.

Journal entry, Cuttack, 13 July:

It was Anand's birthday today. He was in a funny mood. I'd suggested we spend his birthday together. He said it was not possible. When I returned from my class, the department was empty, except for Anand. "If you want to come with me, let's go immediately. Otherwise, I'm off," he said gruffly. Having told me he didn't want me to come with him, I was not prepared. I suggested we go for a meal locally. If he had changed his mind, that was fine; we could've taken a rickshaw. What was the hurry—particularly when he had no specific plans? I wanted to go home to collect a few things for the overnight stay. Instead of coming with me, he left in a huff. Before leaving, he whispered, "Bitch," in my ear. Think he is going mad, driving me insane.

Journal entry, Cuttack, 23 July:

Today is my birthday. I have been suffering from a high fever for the last nine days and have not been to work. Anand has not come to see me. He sent Anshu to see me, and he said that I should go and live with Anand's parents in Sambalpur. It infuriated me so much I left without saying anything. I could not believe it was the same Anshu I had met in Bombay. I accepted the card Anand had sent.

Later when I opened it, it contained a birthday message, written in blood. "Happy Birthday," and scribbled in pen below, "I love you." If he really loves me, why not come and say so himself? Is it so hard? I do not want him to write in blood that he loves me, then rape me and beat me up when I am with him!

Journal entry, Cuttack, 30 July:

I do not know why I went with Anand last night. I know I'm clutching at straws, but what can you do when you're drowning? He said when he becomes secure financially, he will no longer allow me to see my family. "You have to choose between me and your family." Then he said he would divorce me and destroy me and my family. All my anger and frustration came out like water from a burst pipe.

"Go ahead. File a case instead of constantly torturing me with such threats. Nothing else is left for us, is there? You beat me, spit in my face, rape me, starve me, lie about me and my family, steal and cheat—the list goes on. You have no intention of making a home for us, however modest. Yet you wish to trap me with a child. What sort of life will that child have? You want my father to provide for you. We both have jobs. Bapa is to retire soon; he has two more sons to educate. What sort of a man are you? We have everything, yet we are not happy, cannot make each other happy. I love you, yet all

I receive is abuse. The few days we spend together are intolerable. You've ruined my health. You have no respect for me. You are far from being a good husband. You are not even a good human being. All the things I now know about you are killing me. I do not know why God did not prevent this marriage. I do not know what God has in store for me, but I am done with you."

Anand just sat in the chair and did not rise to beat me, nor did he contradict me. Maybe I turned him into a stone, myself into a mountain instead of an ocean.

Journal entry, Cuttack, 5 August:

Last night I dreamt Anand and I are at a conference, which turns into a Ram Lila. There is a huge crowd surging towards the area where the performance is to be held. I hear a public warning announcement that there are poisonous snakes in the grass, at which point I sense a snake near my feet. I leap high into the air; I reach the stars. I've had this dream before. But this time the snake also stands on its tail and raises its hood at me, but cannot touch me when it strikes. I am just out of its reach. It hisses at me, emitting fire. I retreat beyond the fire and escape by the skin of my teeth. It was a terribly frightening dream. I woke up in a sweat, screaming.

Journal entry, Cuttack, 25 August:

Today I complete seven months of marriage and two years of lectureship. The marriage has been a wreck. I made a catastrophic mistake. People make mistakes all the time, but their lives do not fall apart! Teaching has given me moments of satisfaction; it has given me some independence. If love is too much to expect in marriage, then I expected a lot. The love I've known in marriage is not the kind I can live with. I did not know there are so many kinds of love, some as poisonous as hate. My *need* for love blinded me. Now that I can *see*, I also see the damage I've done to myself. I've been my own worst enemy. Was it for this that Aja asked me to pray to God to 'help me, guide me and protect me'? What is the best path for me now? I married him for love—not for any other reason. I thought he loved me too. As love is lacking in the marriage, the rest does not concern me. Without love there is nothing to hold on to. Bringing a child into my world would be nothing short of criminal.

Journal entry, Cuttack, 11 September:

A soul-destroying day! It has been raining cats and dogs; it was declared a rainy day. I did not have to take leave to go to hospital this god-forsaken morning. Ma, you are doing all this for me now; why did you not *show* me your love when I needed it most? Maybe there would've been no Anand in my life, no deception, no abortion? God does not provide much evidence of His existence, either. It is painfully humiliating to have your insides wrenched out. No anaesthesia was used during the entire process. It was sheer torture. The excruciating pain released all the hatred that lay suppressed in me for the man who put me there. Everything he had said before our marriage was lies, nothing but lies. I never imagined love could be so treacherous. I know it is not love that is so, only human beings. I try to pray, but cannot. I've always been on the side of good, yet I've suffered. I am no more God-intoxicated. There is nothing more I want from God. I can no longer say *my* God.

Journal entry, Cuttack, 12 September:

Last night I was awake all night listening to the rain. Everything has gone wrong in my life. The rain cannot wipe the slate clean. Loving someone does not make things right. Yet I have little to offer—except my love. I thought that was enough. I feel empty, looted, a country raped like Bangladesh. That was the price of war and freedom. Is it also the price of love? How can men rape their wives and get away with it? I calmed down when I began to count my blessings—how ma has been looking after me, how it is not illegal to have an abortion as it is in some parts of the world, that I did not have to go to some quack and risk all sorts of complications, including death, how Hinduism is enlightened enough to let me live without making me feel stigmatised, though society may not always be as kind. I do not know how many women in my country are raped, get pregnant and need an abortion. I do not know anyone who has suffered like me, but then what do I know about the world? I've lived in ignorance. Ma said medical termination of pregnancy for married women is common. How many are a result of rape within marriage?

Journal entry, Cuttack, 24 September:

Yesterday, I woke up and thought everything that had happened to me was a dream. For a moment I thought the nightmare of my life was over. But who can wipe out the past? What does not kill you makes you stronger, they say. Lies, all lies. I have no strength left to live. I remember the day I gave my hand to Anand, promising to belong only to him. I'd experienced something similar that day. When I woke up, I'd thought it was also just a dream, the commitment we had made to each other. Later that evening, when I was playing my guitar, I stood up and broke my bangle, the *sankha* on my right wrist. It was a bad omen. The next day, when I saw Anand in college, I asked him if he had changed his mind. He said, "No," and asked me if I had. I replied, "No," as well. And when I'd opened his letter, it said: '...deeds cannot dream what dreams can do—time is a tree (this life one leaf), but love is the sky and I am for you.' I'd cried tears of joy!

The other *sankha* bangle I had kept with me all these years broke today. Both my wrists are now without a *sankha chudi*. My life is bare.

If your happiness depends on others, you can never be truly happy. When you give, you have to give without expecting anything in return. But how does one live with such violent love? I will learn to live without love. When the gods make you different, they also make you unhappy. I was born with many gifts, with many ways of enjoying life and of suffering too. Human beings are born to suffer. They say God helps those who help themselves. I ask God for help as I can't help myself. I seek light. I am in the dark. It is all dark, dark, dark...

Journal entry, Cuttack, 3 October:

Indira Gandhi was arrested today. Dramatic changes are taking place in my country. The Emergency she'd declared in 1975 was withdrawn by her in March this year. India's sixth general election was held, and the nation's first non-Congress-led government came to power. The Janata government swore in Moraji Desai as its PM. These are major developments in the life of a young nation. I've been so immersed in my personal problems I have not noticed how the world is changing. The price of freedom is eternal vigilance. I was not vigilant enough in my personal life, and I paid a heavy price. Mrs G could not trust anyone, and that is how she landed in this mess. I know how that can happen. But that was no reason to declare an Emergency and deprive the nation of its hard-won freedom.

Life had been good to her. She had sons, and she did not have to leave her husband because he was cruel to her. She just loved her father more. No woman can love more than one man and be happy, except when they happen to be her husband and her young sons. Within most marriages women find a way of loving and living. Why did I fail? It is not for want of trying. Perhaps women acquire strength after they have children? But I can't think of bearing his children.

I cannot think of any reason why I loved him, and can see no reason to stay in this marriage, nor have his child. I feel anger, outrage, humiliation, sadness. I feel many things—all negative. I try to find my way back to goodness, but cannot. When Pandora's Box was opened, all that was left was Hope. I can't find Hope.

CHAPTER 21

It is difficult to say precisely when Asha finally gave up on Anand. It was something everyone, including Asha, realised retrospectively when she no longer went to spend her weekends with him. The family were relieved she had accepted the things she could not change. They prayed and thanked God for giving her the serenity to do so.

Asha could not fathom why everyone had made such a big deal of marriage; was it some kind of a collective hoax? She knew marriages were about a lot of things—security, money, power, land, alliances, advancement, and sex, of course. But these were not the kind of things she had sought for herself, not in her marriage.

"What about marriages based on love, respect, understanding, kindness, honesty? Isn't a *swami*, a husband, akin to God—someone who loves you unconditionally?" Asha asked Rashmi, though she could have been talking to herself.

"No, that's what your parents do or are supposed to. A husband doesn't love you that way, not usually, anyway," replied Rashmi.

She told Asha about a cousin of hers who had doused herself in kerosene and set herself alight one afternoon when she could no longer bear the brutal treatment of her in-laws. Her husband was at work, the mother-in-law had gone on a pilgrimage to Kasi, and the servant was on leave.

"Why did she not return to her parents?" Asha asked, astonishment written large on her face.

"Her parents did not want her back. I offered to help and said she could stay with us. I suppose in the end, she couldn't find the strength to go on. Society is worse than a prison. Divorce is not an option for a woman, not in our society," said Rashmi.

"In a good prison, like the ones they have in some countries in Europe, you can live reasonably well, even hope for a better life one day, and don't have to kill yourself," Asha observed. Then she told Rashmi how Anand had taunted her the last time they were together, saying she went back to him only for sex. "I didn't know it was our last time together. Our relationship did not end because he said that. I'd heard a lot worse. I suppose, in the end, I ran out of everything. I had nothing more to give."

"Is it such a terrible thing for a wife to want her husband? Most husbands would be pleased," Rashmi said. Taking Asha's hand in hers, she added, "Come, come...he's not worthy of your tears. With a face like yours, you should smile; it lights up your eyes. Everyone knows how very beautiful you are, but your real beauty only your true friends and family know. Now, give us a smile?"

Asha made a feeble attempt, but her face distorted again, and she cried, "Every time I returned to him, it got worse. Even when he was at his most passionate when making love, as that seemed the only way he could express himself, it was inextricably linked to violence. The violence, the taunts, his cruelty seemed to arouse him. I was stupid and desperate enough to put myself in a vulnerable position. How futile was that! I've learnt my lesson, learnt to value the gift of life."

"You are a fighter," said Rashmi. "Not everyone is blessed with your kind of strength. Most women would not have survived what you've been through. It speaks a lot about our society that a man can beat and rape his wife, yet she can do nothing about it legally. The law does not protect her; the police don't do a thing. Yet people blame her, and it is the woman who pays the price. At least we no longer have sati, but it was the British who banned it!"

Asha sniffed and said, "Lately, Anand's terms of endearment hurt me terribly; they alienated me, even disgusted me. They say when you love someone, love lives on after the object of that love dies or disappears. My love for Anand had taken hold of me—like some dreadful illness. Sometimes, it takes years to see what's been staring at you all along. Maybe it took all that violence for me to see the truth. Had Anand died in a freak accident during the first week of our marriage—worse things have happened to new brides, you know—I'd have loved him to distraction for the rest of my life," Asha added, wondering if that would have been a better option.

"You'd never have known the Anand who made a loathsome appearance later. It's like Jekyll and Hyde, his contrasting personalities before and after the wedding," Rashmi remarked. "Most men do change after marriage, but Anand had actually concealed his true self before. At least, now you know. You won't wonder in twenty years' time what sort of a marriage you'd have had!"

"I was so good at deceiving myself. There had been signs before, but I ignored them and told myself nobody is perfect. Everyone knew he had no money and did not come from an established family. That never bothered me. I really thought he loved me, and that we would be happy, if nothing else. Thought he would find a good job eventually. But was there any cause for the way he treated me?" Asha confessed.

"We all thought he would make you happy and do something worthwhile with his own life. How can anyone imagine he'd turn out to be such a brutal man?" Rashmi said. "You must think about your future. Leave the past in the past."

"What future? I'm in this mess because of my own actions! Walking away from my marriage was my only option. I could not stay in it and change it—God knows I tried. The more I accepted whatever filth was doled out to me, the worse it got. How was I so deceived? I thought he was a good man. I've destroyed my future."

"Come on, Asha. How can you even think so? You are

intelligent, sensitive, strong, beautiful and good—a decent man will consider himself lucky to marry you. Next time, you'll know how to judge a man better. You were so young when you made your promise to Anand. How could you possibly know anything about men? Maybe this is your path to a happier life and true love." Rashmi consoled her.

"I'm not sure about anything any more," said Asha.

Asha's health suffered after the abortion. She was on sick leave for a month. Anand took a transfer to Sambalpur and moved in with his parents. The first letter Asha received from Anand threatened to get her job terminated. Knowing he could do no such thing, she ignored it. But when he initiated legal proceedings for the restoration of conjugal rights, Asha had had enough. She had no intention of being raped and going through another abortion. He had not visited her during her illness, nor did he send any messages, not a word to say he missed her, loved her, hoped she was well.

Orpheus loved Eurydice so much, she thought, *he was ready to follow her to the underworld. Having found Eurydice, he couldn't bear not seeing her face while bringing her back to earth. He could not resist looking back. And here is Anand, demanding his conjugal rights!* An outraged Asha conceded it was time to divorce him. Her family had come round to that conclusion some time ago—divorce would be the only way for her to make a clean break and hopefully a fresh start.

"Otherwise, he'll keep coming back to harass her," Aditya said.

Asha agreed with her father. There was a time when she, like Savitri, would have followed Anand to the end of the world and negotiated with Yama for the life of her husband. It was hard for her to accept how swiftly everything she believed in had come crashing down. *Better to fail by sticking to one's principles,* she thought, *than succeed by not having any.*

Returning to live with her parents was not what Asha had

in mind after doing her best to leave. But life had turned into a continuous process of coming to terms with all the things she had rejected. *If only I had agreed to an arranged marriage and made my parents happy,* she reprimanded herself. As the losses and liabilities in the balance sheet of her life kept rising, she did not know where she would find the mountain of hope to keep her balance.

<hr />

The fact that Vikram's marriage was also not faring well aggravated Asha's plight. It was as if some malevolent spirit was playing havoc with all their lives. She was not alone in this desolation of dreams—the entire family was stranded in this dangerous island that threatened to destroy their world. It was hard for Asha, as she no longer had the use of her old room. Her parents were not being thoughtless. Now that Vikram had a wife, there was literally not enough space for Asha.

Vijay remarked one day, completely out of the blue, "After marriage a woman's place is with her husband."

Asha was so flabbergasted, she said, "How can you even think of such a thing, Vijay? You *know* how Anand treated me."

"I don't know, but this is no longer your home," he said.

"How can I afford to rent a place and manage with Rs 500 per month, which is doled out to me by the government once every six or seven months? If I do so, people will criticize our family. I will most likely be attacked one night, if not robbed, raped and killed. This is my home, Vijay, as much as it is yours. I am as upset as you are with the way my life has fallen apart!" Asha said, on the verge of tears.

"You made your choice. Nobody forced you to marry him. You should've stuck it out with him," Vijay said, angry and hurt.

"God knows, I tried. I wanted my marriage to work; that's why I kept going back to him. It was not humanly possible to carry on. Yes, I made a mistake choosing Anand. But you can't correct one mistake by making another. One day you'll regret your words. I don't believe you mean it!" Asha was so upset, her body trembled.

"First there was all that unhappiness because you insisted on marrying him. And now all this pain because you can't stay with him. Why can't you get anything right in your life? All we wanted, want, is to see you happy," he said as he stormed out of the room like a bat out of hell.

"So did I, but life has a way of not turning out as we expect it to. I know I can't live here forever. I just need some time to sort out my life," Asha said, raising her voice so Vijay could hear her.

Both her parents had mentioned on separate occasions that she should not think of living with them as a permanent solution. They may have expressed such sentiments out of sheer frustration, but it did not hurt any less. After her experiences with Anand, living at home, albeit against her family's wishes, seemed like the safest option—until she found a more lasting solution. What that might be she had no idea.

"Of course you can stay here till you're sorted. But what can we do?" Karuna intervened. "We have to live here, in this society. We have to consider the family's position. Even Rama had to agree to Sita's *Agni parikhya*. Do you think he ever doubted her or wanted to test her? He was the king and had to lead by example."

Aditya nodded in agreement and said, "You may not agree, Asha. But family and society can be a source of great strength, especially the family."

"I'm not denying it. But unless good people stand up for what they believe to be true, decent and honourable, how will society change? We also create society. Rama should have defended his wife and set an example," Asha replied.

"Perhaps, but *we* are not Gandhi or Jesus Christ," said Aditya. "That requires a lot more sacrifice than we can bear. We are doing the best we can."

"We agreed to your marrying Anand," Karuna said. "We are not saying you can't stay here. We don't know what to do either!

Maybe it would be good for you to go abroad for further study? You've always wanted to do so."

"There's no guarantee if I'd had an arranged marriage, I'd have been happy," Asha pointed out without mentioning her brother's marriage. "I'm applying for scholarships and research positions in America and Canada, and have been offered a research fellowship from the University of Ontario. I'm waiting for the other applications. Let's see what happens. I should've considered that Harvard professor's offer seriously. But would you have allowed me to go alone, if I hadn't got married and gone through hell first? You wouldn't even allow me to go alone to Hyderabad!"

"Going out alone in our country is not safe for a woman," said Aditya. "What can we do? I can't change the world for you—even if I wanted to. Don't you think I would if I could?"

"Then how do you think I can live alone?" asked Asha.

"We don't want you to live alone!" Aditya replied. "We always wanted you to live happily with your husband. Vijay is upset. Don't take his words to heart. We tried to protect you and did what we thought was right for you."

"Marriage seemed like the right thing. No one can say what might have been. Life for a woman is unthinkable without marriage and family. How many single women do you know?" Karuna added.

"Exactly—and that's the reason I can't live alone!" said Asha.

"Can't you write to the Harvard professor? Surely, a year does not make a difference? If you were eligible then, you should be eligible now?" said Aditya.

"You keep trying. Something will work out," Karuna added.

"Your academic work is being recognized nationally, Prof Pani was saying," Aditya added. "I'm sure you'll get financial support for studies abroad."

"God takes away something and gives us other things. We must learn to accept our failures, or what we see as our failures. There is no other path to happiness. That is why they say God's ways are inscrutable," Karuna reminded Asha.

"If we accept everything, nothing will change!" said Asha.

"Some things we can change, I agree. That's why we need to know the difference between what we can change and what we can't," replied Karuna.

"Yes, ma, but how can you be part of a society that does not give you the choice to survive on your own terms—with or without a man?" Asha asked.

"Those things we can't change, we must leave to God. One can only keep trying, but remember some things take a long time to change, sometimes not in one's lifetime. So know your limitations. The person who does and knows the difference between what can be changed and what can't is blessed, indeed," Karuna explained.

***

Asha's new head of the department, Mr Mishra, added to her problems by making things unnecessarily difficult for her at work. It is true the previous head, Prof Pani, had not done anything to fight the machinations of the Patnaiks. But he had been a good teacher, and when Asha joined the department, he was supportive and did not go out of his way to complicate her life. The new head was neither a sound scholar, nor a good teacher. He was by no means a fine administrator. One had no idea what his views were about society, culture or literature. Being old, he depended upon the so-called Young Turks, though these young men were all older than Asha. She delivered her lectures, took her tutorials, spent her spare time in the library, and returned home. Keeping to herself did not make Asha popular among her colleagues.

On Ganesh Puja day, in the early evening, the whole family was having tea when Hari, the peon from the English department, arrived with a letter. He excused himself as soon as she signed for the letter as if to say, 'Madam, I had absolutely nothing to do with this. I'm just the messenger.'

Reading the letter, which summoned her to a disciplinary

meeting the following week to answer charges relating to her dereliction of duty, confused Asha. *This cannot be real*, she thought, not knowing whether to laugh or cry. However critical Asha's family may have been of her choice of partner, they appreciated her dedication to her job.

When she read out the letter, Aja asked, "Is this true? Were you unable to attend to your job because of problems in your marriage?"

"Aja, I've never missed a class. This is the work of some of my colleagues. I can't understand what Mr Mishra stands to gain..." She began calmly, but stopped, unable to complete her sentence, overcome with emotion.

Aditya said agitatedly, "That Mishra babu is a useless fellow. Nobody likes him. You can't depend on him to do the right thing."

"Her colleagues are jealous," Vijay pointed out. "The students like nani—she is well regarded; the students think she is a good teacher."

"Her research articles and poems are also getting published widely. Her colleagues must be envious," Abhay added. Having been appointed professor at a young age, he knew all about the envy of colleagues.

"What sort of a man would do this, particularly when she is having such a difficult time in her personal life? I cannot believe it." Karuna sighed.

"This is harassment. She is on sick leave. Sending a letter home on Ganesh Puja day, a holiday, is incredible. I think Anand is behind all this," Vikram observed.

"What will you do, Asha?" Aja asked.

"I'll reply to the letter and attend the meeting," she replied.

"Mishra babu needs to be summoned to a disciplinary hearing himself. This is his pre-retirement posting. The least he could do is *do* the right thing, not go trumping up false charges against the only woman in the department!" said Aditya.

"Don't worry. He'll get his just dues when he's exposed for victimising nani. Wait till the students find out," said Vivek.

"That's a good idea," said Vikram. "Why don't you invite the entire department to the meeting next week and expose the traitors?"

"They may make her life even more difficult," said Aditya.

"Attend the meeting. I'll be surprised if they go ahead with it," Aja advised.

Going through the dates and times when she was supposed to have not taken her classes, Asha was not entirely surprised to learn her conniving colleagues had got the facts wrong. Two of the dates cited were non-starters—the college was officially closed. On the third occasion, all classes were suspended for some administrative reason beyond her control. On the fourth occasion, she was ill and had sent in a sick note. The fifth charge was baseless. She had taken the class; the register would prove that unless they had doctored it.

Asha knew a copy of the charge-letter would have been sent to the principal. When college reopened, she went to meet Dr Biswal, who on seeing her, dismissed her with a wave of his hand as if to say, 'You don't have to worry about the charges.'

Dr Biswal suffered from a terrible stutter and communicated extensively with his hands and facial expressions. This impediment, however, had not prevented him from heading the premier educational institution of Orissa. An able administrator and scholar, he was widely admired. Students loved and respected him. He never chastised them for joking at his expense. One of the funnier episodes that circulated at the time was how he sang the national anthem, *Jana gana mana*. Towards the end—*Jaya Hey, Jaya Hey, Jaya, Jaya, Jaya, Jaya Hey*—as the story went, he would get stuck on the first *Ja* like a record player, never progressing beyond that syllable.

Seeing a piece of paper in her hand, he summoned her in. Asha handed him a copy of her reply to the HoD. As he read her response, he suppressed a smile. She had tried to disguise her sense of outrage at being falsely accused, but could not completely let go of it. She had written how it had not been possible to take a tutorial class on such-and-such date as the college was closed, or it was a holiday and none of the students were in attendance, etc.

Dr Biswal then said, "N-never f-forget you are a t-teacher. You were l-late once for invi-vigi-l-lation. I told you that day not to be l-late again. I also sp-spoke to A-Anand. L-life is life. W-work is w-work. N-never f-forget that." He dismissed her with a wave of his hand.

"I remember, sir," Asha said, nodding. "I am always punctual, almost always. That day you know what happened. It was beyond my control."

"I w-will t-talk to Pro-professsor M-Mishra," he said.

Dr Biswal not only knew the names of most of the students and teachers in the college, he also knew their families. Blessed with boundless energy, he walked the length and breadth of the campus every day. As he walked, he would speak to students about which class they had come from, which class they were going to, the name of the teacher, if the teacher arrived on time, whether they were satisfied with the teaching. Every evening, he went for a walk that encompassed the campus. Along the way he spoke to staff, students, administrators, peons, cleaners—he had his finger on the pulse of the college. Nothing escaped him.

While Asha was waiting for things to happen, anything that would change her life, she was invited to an interview for the award of a national scholarship to study abroad. When she arrived at the Ministry of Education, in Delhi, the large waiting room was already crowded. What unsettled her was the way in which the men, most of the candidates were men, bragged about their chances. Several of them were from Delhi's better known universities. They behaved as though they had already been awarded the scholarship and the interview was a mere formality.

When Asha was called in at around teatime, she had more or

less given up hope of success. *I must finish what I've started*, she told herself, entering the room.

The first interviewer, a lady in her late forties or early fifties, asked questions of the 'who do you think wrote this passage?' variety. The second interviewer's questions were marginally less irrelevant. *At this rate, I will definitely not qualify*, Asha thought as her desperation mounted. The third interviewer asked about the blip in her academic record. But first she wanted to know more about Asha's marital status. The scholarship did not extend to the spouse. As Asha had indicated in her application she was married, the choices being restricted to single or married, that panel member wanted to know if Asha was in a position to accept the award. It was a valid question. A married woman from Orissa, or anywhere else in India for that matter, was not necessarily free to pursue her personal goals in life.

When Asha said her marriage was in the process of being dissolved, there was a loud, collective gasp. Divorces were rare in India, let alone in Orissa. There was concern that someone so young and beautiful should face such misfortune. But there was an equal measure of curiosity. The body language of the panel members said it all—they suddenly came alive, straightened up, adjusted their collars and the folds of their saris, and leaned forward, not wishing to miss a word. Their facial expressions changed, too, as their eyes lit up with anticipation of a juicy tale. They wanted to hear the gossip directly from the horse's mouth.

"We think we know what's best for us, but we don't," Asha said as diplomatically as she could, by way of an explanation as to why her marriage failed. "I did not want an arranged marriage and thought I could find Mr Right myself. I was wrong. I was betrayed. I should've had an arranged marriage and made my parents happy. But how was I to know I would be so deceived?" she concluded.

"What happened? Did he cheat on you, want a large dowry, was he violent, beat you?" one of the panel members enquired, unable to restrain her curiosity.

"He was not the man I thought he was. I only found that out after the marriage. I tried to make it work, but it was unworkable. It was the violence…" The words stuck in her throat. After a pause, Asha said, "So you see how important it is for me… This scholarship will truly change my life!"

Embarrassed at their own reactions, they changed the subject. Another member reminded her about her second-class BA considering she had a first-class record. They smiled with relief when she answered that question. At least, they did not have to feel guilty about it. People like happy endings. Even the lady who had been asking her the most difficult, albeit irrelevant, questions softened and said, "Just as well Mr Prasad arrived to your rescue. You wouldn't be here, otherwise!" The tone of her voice suggested it was a good thing she was.

Asha was relieved, too, and wanted to tell them it was chance that brought her there. When the letter inviting her to the interview arrived, she was in Hyderabad. No one in the family had checked her post, though not long ago her post was vetted regularly. It was luck that had brought Asha back to Cuttack. She almost did not see the letter herself; it was hidden under a pile of post. She could not believe no one had bothered to open a letter from the Ministry of Education, Delhi.

In Hyderabad, she was being urged to delay her departure and attend another conference. She could easily have stayed a few more days; it was the summer vacation. There was no great rush to return home to all the angst surrounding her failed marriage. Yet for no apparent reason, she had declined the institute's generous offer. Only after she was home did she realise how fate had played its part. She had one day to organize her affairs. Vijay accompanied her to Delhi the following day.

It was dusk by the time Asha emerged from the interview room.

Vijay, who had been patiently waiting, asked, "Nani, how did it go?"

She shook her head as if to say, 'I'm not too hopeful.' When they reached Cuttack and the family wanted to hear how her interview had fared, Asha replied, "I have no idea. Frankly, I'm not optimistic. The Delhi-wallas will probably get it."

Aditya said, "You keep trying. Something good will work out."

Karuna added, "Yes, your turn will surely come."

When another envelope arrived from the Ministry of Education, Asha did not open it, so convinced was she that it contained bad news.

Noticing the unopened letter, Aditya enquired, "Why have you not opened the letter, Asha?"

"Why don't you open it, bapa?" she suggested.

When Aditya opened the letter and read its contents, keeping a straight face, he said in a serious tone, "Well, you better read it."

Karuna asked impatiently, "What does it say? Has she got it or not?"

Asha stood there, smiling from head to toe. "They've selected me! Good things can happen to unlucky people," she cried, unable to contain her joy.

"What has luck got to do with it? You deserve it," said Aditya.

"Bapa, my BA results were tampered with—*that* was bad luck. I had done well in both those papers. I won't mention the marriage. But getting the national scholarship—who would've thought I'd be awarded one?" exclaimed Asha.

"The truth is you created your luck—you met Mr Prasad about your BA results." Aditya smiled. "We did not do that, you did."

"Bapa, I still consider myself lucky that Mr Prasad helped me," said Asha.

"I accept that, but remember there is a difference between struggling for something, preparing for it, making yourself worthy of it, and things that simply fall on your lap and you've done nothing to deserve it," Aditya said.

Asha wasn't sure if she had earned the national scholarship. It was her marriage she had struggled for, made herself worthy of—yet that failed.

As if he could read her mind, Aditya added, "Ma, I'm not denying you could've been luckier in your marriage. The sad truth is Anand did not deserve you. What I am trying to say is—had you married someone more deserving of you, then you would've been luckier in your marriage too."

"Some people are born lucky, some earn their luck, while others have good luck thrust upon them. Maybe I was just born unlucky..." said Asha.

<hr />

As a student of English literature, Asha felt compelled to apply to Oxford. Her scholarship would support her at any university of her choice. She filled in her name, address, and enclosed her publications just in case—three articles published in academic journals in India. The rest of the questions in the application form were left blank. She had no idea whether she wanted to go to Christ Church, Somerville, or Magdalen. Nor did she know anyone who could have helped her make that choice. Most of the form was left blank as she did not know any better.

Any application for study abroad by a lecturer in a government college in Orissa had to be sent through what was referred to as the 'proper channel', not unlike food passing down the oesophagus to the stomach and not down the trachea. Except, in this instance, the papers would travel up the hierarchy. Not only was the process cumbersome, it rarely worked unless progress was monitored assiduously like a patient in the Intensive Care Unit. And its peristaltic passage through the Kafkaesque system was facilitated with patience, diplomacy, good humour, bribes and whatnot.

In Asha's case, the application would first have to be approved by the head of her department. Then it needed the approval of the principal of the college, followed by the director of public instructions. Finally, it needed to be sanctioned by the secretary of education. Incapable of dealing with the shenanigans in the academic and administrative world, Asha simply sent off the application directly to Oxford, making sure the man at the post office counter franked the stamps.

The rest one had to leave to God. Growing up in India without trusting God was not an option. She routinely sent off letters and forgot about them, as most never reached their destination. And those that did and were fortunate enough to elicit a response never made their way back. The postal system was in stark contrast to the reproductive system. A sperm had a significantly higher chance of fertilising an egg than a letter reaching its destination and the sender receiving a reply. As Rashmi put it, "Apply, apply—no reply." Then, there was the cost associated with applying. American universities, ahead of the rest of the academic world in financial acumen, required an application fee. Enterprising applicants from India requested a waiver of all fees. It was common practice to apply for a study grant, in addition to travel costs and any other costs one could think of.

When Asha received a letter of acceptance from the Tutor for Admissions, Gloucester College, Oxford, and was assigned John O. L. Jones, the Thomas Wharton Professor in the Faculty of English Language and Literature as her supervisor, she had a pretty good idea how luck had played its part. Granted, it was not entirely a passive outcome. If she'd not sent in that application, she'd never have been lucky. If truth be told, it had taken her three years and a small fortune in rupees to get lucky. No, she did not apply to Oxford for three consecutive years. Oxford was one hit—bull's eye. Since her marriage broke down, Asha had been applying and receiving offers of places at various universities in America and Canada. She had not felt confident enough to accept any. By the time Asha was admitted to Oxford, she had also had the time to reflect on her new status and learnt to appreciate what was on offer.

CHAPTER 22

Asha was not the only one in her family adjusting to life's vicissitudes. The state of Vikram's marriage was a grave concern. Now that Asha had officially filed for a divorce, there was tremendous pressure on the family to ensure Vikram's marriage did not end similarly. At least with Asha's marriage they consoled themselves saying that they always had their doubts, they had strongly advised her not to, but she'd insisted on marrying him. It was not the same with Vikram. They had left no stone unturned to find a suitable girl for him.

While many incongruous relationships bloom and several unsuitable alliances flourish, Vikram's marriage showed no such signs. Ironically, Asha's separation may have laid the foundation for the eventual dissolution of Vikram's marriage. It no longer appeared like the end of the world. On the contrary, living with the wrong partner seemed more like it. Despite tradition and society's fierce disapproval of divorce, Asha had been slowly winning support from unexpected sources. The sheer force of her character—her integrity, loyalty, and courage—had impressed many.

Tanuja, though not a great beauty or a woman of many talents, would have made a good wife to someone. Unfortunately, her brother and mother were not honest brokers. They turned a blind eye to their daughter's shortcomings, promising on her behalf things they knew she was incapable of delivering. They got greedy and married Tanuja off under false pretences into a family where she did not belong. Perhaps they thought matters would not reach a breaking point. Divorce was unheard of.

After Tanuja's father died, her family were keen to marry her off. Keeping an unmarried, uneducated daughter at home was unwise. It was perhaps not surprising they were economical with the truth. However, the truth is that when people lie, they begin to believe in their lies. Instead of making up for the lie by doing the right thing, they slide down the slippery slope, unable to take control. Lies give birth to more lies.

The world is full of people who are not interested in education or culture, nor are they members of Mensa. Yet they go on to live perfectly ordinary lives. It would be foolish, too, to blame her family for choosing Vikram. He was a fine catch—a doctor with excellent career prospects from one of the most outstanding families in Orissa. Tall, slim, handsome, well mannered—what was there not to like about him?

As far as Vikram's family were concerned, they never suspected Tanuja's family of camouflaging the truth. The Guru family genuinely believed Tanuja would grasp every opportunity to shape herself into a more desirable woman. Karuna and Sadhana were convinced that would be the case and Tanuja would begin to blossom under the loving care of her in-laws. And the men—Aditya, Vishu, Abhay and Aja—never considered it a serious obstacle to the alliance.

That is the reason when Vikram said he was not sure about Tanuja, the family did not break off the engagement. They never doubted their decision—had their wives not turned into more desirable creatures after marriage? The family acted honourably. They had given their word and believed Tanuja and her family would be true to theirs. People change, everyone thought, so too will Tanuja, given the right circumstances. She will become more like the woman they wanted her to be.

They never thought they were deceiving themselves with false expectations. How were they to know that Tanuja would turn into her own worst enemy? Their trust would be trampled upon because Tanuja was unwilling to be moulded. It would have been fine had she made it clear from the beginning, before the wedding. They would've called the whole thing off.

Karuna failed to understand her daughter-in-law, assuming everyone wanted to be better. Sadhana could not fathom Tanuja's lack of interest in doing anything to make herself a more attractive, interesting person. People would count themselves blessed, Sadhana thought, to be given such a chance. But Tanuja stuck to her mulish, self-defeating ways and refused to change course. The fact that her family had given their word that she would study, educate herself, and learn the customs of her husband's family and their way of doing things did not bother Tanuja.

After a year of applying sticking plaster to a marriage that needed extensive reconstruction, under conditions where no one was sure the edifice would survive such major renovation and not collapse and crumble into dust, it was clear something had to give. After trying and failing, trying again and again, and failing as many times, everyone was exhausted with repeated attempts to hold falling ramparts together. The Guru family, in various stages of confusion, irritation and frustration, did not know how to rescue the situation.

They could not believe people no longer kept their word and felt no dishonour in doing so. They were baffled that doing the right thing was no longer enough to secure their world. Any number of things could destroy it—from naivety and lack of experience to lies and bad luck. They all played their part in the termination of Vikram's marriage just as they had done with Asha's.

The afternoon Tanuja left her in-laws' home, she let it be known that she was going with her brother to visit her mother, who was ill. It was a run-of-the-mill event. Asha thought her sister-in-law was going to have a short break with her mother, as daughters do. She even escorted Tanuja to the gate, carrying some of her bags to the car. It never occurred to her why Tanuja was carrying so many bags if she was only going away for a few days.

Karuna was having a nap. Tanuja asked Asha not to disturb her. "Please let her rest," she said. "Ma needs her sleep. I'll be back before you begin to miss me."

Tanuja had taken all her jewellery, including the ones given by her in-laws, along with the best saris, Karuna was to discover later. When Tanuja left that afternoon, everyone at her in-laws' assumed she would be back within days. In fact, most of them did not know she had left with her brother.

It was Vikram who first enquired when he returned home in the evening and could not find his wife. "Ma, where is Tanuja?"

"She's gone to see her mother, who is unwell. Arnab came in the afternoon and took her. I thought you knew. I was asleep then, but I didn't ask when she'd return, just assumed she told you," said Karuna with a confused look.

"She never told me anything about her mother not being well or her plans to visit her mother," Vikram said, betrayal written all over his face.

"She only told me this morning, after you'd left. I just assumed she'd told you," Karuna added, unable to digest her daughter-in-law's deviousness.

"Maybe she'll write," Aditya said. He, too, was not at home when Tanuja left.

It dawned on them that Tanuja had yet again been economical with the truth.

A week later, when no letter arrived, Karuna asked Aditya as they were having their morning tea, "Why would she leave just like that? I doubt her brother will want to keep her. What a silly girl!"

"But she thinks she's very smart. That's the problem—she is incapable of rational thought, forget humility, consideration or compassion! You simply cannot talk to her. All you hear is lies, lies and more lies. How can one knowingly build a life on lies?" Vikram said in a manner that startled everyone. He was a patient man, rarely raising his voice. He had overheard the conversation and could not help giving vent to his deep frustration.

"That's why they had asked her not to open her mouth when we went to see her. We did not realise it. But did anything happen recently between you two?" Karuna asked, her tone of voice suggesting that nothing would surprise her.

"She is a congenital, pathological liar," Vikram said. "She does not know the meaning of the word honesty or integrity. It's not as if the world appears differently to her—no, no, no. That I would understand. But she is manipulative, compulsively so. At first I thought after she had lost her father, maybe no one listened to her, so she got this way. But she twists everything you say. The more I gave, the more she took—without a thought to what *I* might want. How can you live with such a person?"

Karuna and Aditya looked at their son and each other, aghast. They had never seen Vikram so upset.

"Maybe the marriage went to her head. She thought she had won the lottery," Aditya observed.

"I found it impossible to teach her anything—she was not receptive to anything. On the contrary, she was determined to have things her own way," Karuna added. "Why agree to study and learn if she did not want to? People these days will say anything to get what they want. No scruples, no values—no responsibility."

"She told me when she has a child she will turn the child against me and our family—'put everybody in their place' were her exact words," fumed Vikram. "I've no desire to bring her back. We should've called off the engagement when we had the chance— better late than never."

"How could we end up with two crazy people—first Anand and then Tanuja?" Karuna gasped.

"Seems like carelessness..." Asha said. She had just walked

in and heard the tail end of the conversation. "We are a family of idiots! Too trusting and naive, expecting others to be like us. We were never dealing with equals. We had little in common. They both despised us and did not love or admire us. How can you change yourself if you don't wish to? We pegged our dreams to the hope they might!"

Aditya was so worried he did not know what to say. He put his right hand on his heart as if to say he had played his part in good faith.

A stunned Karuna observed, "How can anyone expect this to happen—both marriages to fail together?"

"She would've been the perfect match for Anand—their notions about everything are so warped," Vikram said. "It is impossible to live with such people!"

"I agree," said Asha. "Genuine differences in viewpoints can be bridged, but values—essential values like trust, loyalty, honesty, integrity and understanding—these cannot be compromised. It's as if both of them are from a different planet."

"We thought they were like us when in reality they could not have been more different," Aditya pointed out.

"Yes, we projected *our* self, *our* expectations on to them. Unfortunately, we were let down. It's our fault. Lucky we found out sooner than later," Karuna said.

Vikram nodded and said, "Tanuja left of her own accord; nobody asked her to. She didn't even tell me her brother was coming to take her away. Her leaving may be a blessing in disguise. I'm not prepared to spend the rest of my life with someone I cannot trust or respect. She seems to possess no moral convictions of her own that are worth having. We all went out of our way to admit her into our fold; no further sacrifices are necessary. Enough is enough! Just because we made a mistake doesn't mean we should keep paying the price for the rest of our lives."

"Let's see if she returns—of her own accord," replied Karuna.

"Not after such jiggery-pokery," said Asha. "And all that pride, do you think people like her and Anand ever admit they are wrong?"

"Then we must, and not let us be deceived any longer," Vikram said firmly. "Maybe I should pursue my plans to study abroad."

Over the next few months it became clear that Tanuja had no plans to return. Vikram, already deeply disillusioned with his marriage, made it clear he did not want her back. The marriage was definitely over. Within months, Vikram was offered a job in a reputable teaching hospital in the National Health Service in the UK. The family, though delighted with the unexpectedly attractive job offer, were totally unprepared for such a development. They had gotten used to Asha's snail's pace and presumed it would be years before Vikram would leave home.

That summer, when Asha returned from Hyderabad—by then her research trips to the American Institute had become an annual affair—she was not greeted with the usual hustle and bustle of household activities that was directed by her mother. The house was alarmingly quiet and felt empty. She did not wish to ask the servants which member of the family had gone where. By early evening, everyone was back, but still no sign of her mother. Instead, her father handed her an envelope, saying, "Ma has gone to Aja's for a few days."

Asha opened the envelope and found a letter from her mother.

Ma Asha,

My leaving home will make things difficult for you, but I cannot stay. What am I to do? We are all victims of circumstances beyond our control. You knew that returning to live with us after your marriage would cause us grief and pain. But were you able to bear your suffering and stay away even for our sake? It was when your anguish exceeded your highest level of tolerance did you decide to return to live with your parents, knowing well that would be the last thing we would want. Similarly, I've gone past the threshold of my inner turmoil. No longer can I think of you all, my children, and carry on as before. No longer can I face life drawing on hope when I look at your faces. Do not expect me back, and do not come to plead with me to return. I cannot return.

You will be leaving for Oxford before long. Until then I know you can manage without me. If you can't, then think your mother is dead. God will look after you. After all, what more can I do for you now? May God bless you and make your life, so full already with suffering, a happier one. I have been praying to God for a long time now to grant us all happiness. When God will listen to my prayer, I do not know, but I keep praying. One day God will, I know. I hope it will be sooner rather than later. I love you more than I can express. Ma

Asha could feel her mother's anguish. It pained her to read the letter, which offered no explanation about what precipitated such an avalanche of grief. All Asha could glean from talking to her brothers was more or less what her father told her. Had Karuna gone to Aja's for a rest, it would have provided a sensible explanation. The family was exhausted—emotionally and physically. Everyone needed a break.

It baffled Asha how her parents, who lived under one roof for such a long time, managed to grow into such different people. If their father thought something was white, it was quite possible the same thing appeared black to their mother. The world just appeared distinctly different to them. That was a reality—like the existence of the sun and the moon. No wonder we all turned out completely different from one another too, she reminded herself when she witnessed the rainbow of opinions within the family. The Guru home was like a mini Galapagos Island—they were not different species, just different manifestations of the same.

The children saw the universe in its glorious diversity. Reality had that rainbow quality—the same things appeared differently to them. What was even more fascinating was the same things appeared differently to the same person at different times. *How did our parents not get round to living happily together while agreeing to disagree about most things? Or maybe they did and just gave the impression of not doing so?* Asha wondered. The differences between them were ancient history. Why did ma give up now? It was one thing to go to Aja's place for a rest, quite another to say she could never return! It simply did not make any sense. When Asha investigated the matter further, her brothers were as clueless.

"I was angry and said a few things I shouldn't have," confessed Vijay. "But I'm not sure why that upset her so much. It's not the first time I lost my temper. I'm always losing my temper, saying the wrong things," said Vijay, genuinely surprised, contrite and upset. "I will never open my big mouth and say things in the heat of the moment," he apologised, adding, "I'm sorry I told you some terrible things too. It was rather thoughtless of me."

Asha replied, "Maybe it was the last straw? But I agree it doesn't make sense. Something else must have made her terribly unhappy. But you must learn to curb your tongue, Vijay. If you say something hurtful to someone when they are down, it can tip them over the edge. You can say the same thing to them when they are feeling stronger, and they can take it. Also, words have a way of living on in memory."

"I didn't think," Vijay admitted. "I hope she didn't go because of me."

"I don't think so. It was just everything—it became unbearable," Asha said.

"I hope ma will come home after a few days' rest," Vivek said, unable to bear his mother's absence.

"I'm sure she will." Asha nodded.

Lunch was a sombre affair. They ate in contemplative silence.

In the evening when Abhay arrived and said he was going to Aja's, he asked if he could take anything for Karuna. Asha sorted a few things for her mother and insisted on accompanying him. Karuna's personal belongings were ferried back and forth by anyone who visited her. And someone visited her every day. Aditya had gone to see her the day before, but Karuna was not ready to return. Nor did anyone know when she might be back.

When Abhay and Asha arrived at Aja's, Karuna was not there. Saswati had taken her out. Nobody seemed sure where the sisters had gone—to the temple, to see a doctor, shopping or to visit someone? All these options seemed unlikely, though plausible.

"Is ma unwell?" Asha asked Aja.

He assured her that her mother was fine. Asha spent at least an hour discussing possible reasons why Karuna may have decided to come to Aja's. He listened to her patiently, but had no answers.

Finally, he said, "We all need a break from our day-to-day lives. Running a home and looking after everyone can be very demanding."

When Abhay said it was time to leave, Asha asked for the umpteenth time, "But why did she leave? What happened, Aja?"

"I don't know, Asha. You must be patient and trust in God!" Aja said as he laid his hand on her head, blessing her.

This made Asha feel worse, and she broke down completely, thinking if the only option is to leave everything to God, then things must be really bad. Tears flowing down her face, she cried, "Why is everything falling apart?"

"You're crying like a child," Aja said. "I'd give you some Threptin biscuits, but I've run out!"

Asha could not even manage a smile.

On their way back, she complained to Abhay, "Kaku, why did ma go away with Saswati mausi if she knew you were coming?"

"Well, she didn't. I didn't say which day I'd come or at what time. Besides, she didn't know *you* were coming. Your ma will be very upset when she returns and finds out she missed you," he replied.

"Why leave home in the first place?" she asked.

"The same reason you went to Hyderabad—she needs a change. Remember, your mother is at home all the time. The rest of us go out every day; you do when you go to college. We all get a chance to be distracted, not her," Abhay explained.

"Then we should take ma out more often," Asha said, somewhat puzzled because she thought her ma was happiest at home.

"It's not as simple as that. When bad things happen to your family, it can destroy you. Maybe your ma blames herself for all the things that happened to you and nana," Abhay offered an explanation.

"Kaku, are you saying ma blames herself for our marriages?" Asha asked.

"I don't know. It's not as simple or specific as that. It is most likely to be a combination of things that upset her. Remember, we don't fully understand ourselves—certainly not the mind or the soul. Perhaps we aren't meant to. Otherwise, God would have given us a clue about a lot more things, including his own existence! Some things simply cannot be explained and have to be accepted," Abhay said.

"Are you saying we can't understand what ma is going through, or that ma doesn't understand herself?" Asha asked. "I know we cannot understand God. But it isn't God I'm trying to understand—just ma! Is ma having some kind of a breakdown? If she's depressed, then we need to help her..." Asha said, thinking of the agony she had herself been through and which still haunted her. She felt guilty that, immersed in her own sorrow, she had not noticed her mother's.

"Would you not have a breakdown too if everything you've invested in is destroyed? Your parents have lost more than you can imagine. It's not easy to accept the things that happen to us," Abhay said. "Asha, none of us is meant to understand God, but even human beings are difficult to understand."

"Who took her to Aja's?" It had just dawned on Asha that someone must have escorted her mother. *Why did that person not reason with her, dissuade her from going in such a state of mental turmoil and unhappiness?* Asha wondered.

"Aja had come to your home. I don't know what happened. I don't think anybody knows. Bapa doesn't know; he wasn't at home. To be frank, your ma may not know either. When you're caught in a whirlwind of suffering, you are the eye of the storm. You lose perspective; it takes time to regain your inner calm. You heard what Aja said, your ma needs a break from everything—to rest and recover. It's been an extremely difficult time. You don't need me to tell you that," Abhay said.

Asha knew nobody could understand the human mind, but the heart? Was the heart not easier to delve into? "I don't understand anything any more," she said.

Abhay, taking hold of his niece's hand, said, "Asha, you must think positively. Once you go to Oxford, your life will change in ways you can't imagine. Your marriage may have fallen apart, your life has not. If your parents had said, 'Asha, live here with us always,' you wouldn't have applied for that scholarship. Don't think they don't love you. Your parents will always love you. Your family will always be there for you. Not many people have been blessed with as much. These troubles will pass like clouds in the sky. Remember even clouds have a silver lining."

"Bapa thought he was burdened with me for life. I could never make ma happy. Everything I did was not good enough. Anand betrayed me, was cruel to me. Now I have to go away alone to a place I know nothing about, where I have no family or friends to fall back on. As if that isn't bad enough, ma is saying she cannot return home. She and bapa always had their differences, always quarrelled. Why leave now? If she doesn't return, who will care for Vijay and Vivek? Bapa can't look after himself. Ma can't live at Aja's forever. Who will look after ma? Without her, there will be no 'home' for any of us, not even for ma." Asha poured her heart out.

"Remember what Aja said—be patient. It won't come to that! What you call quarrelling is part of life. You need someone to bicker with. Unless you've been married for a long time, you cannot know what real love is. Your ma and bapa know it, but everyone needs time to be alone. Even the most devoted of couples. Every marriage goes through difficult periods. You simply have to find a way of working it out. It is sad in your case it was not possible. That's why you had to leave Anand. If he really loved you, do you think he'd have let you go?" Abhay said.

"He did not let me go. I had to escape—just to survive," Asha replied. "There was no love..." Asha faltered and could not find the words to describe her loss.

"If he really loved you, he would've changed, realising how much he hurt you. And about bapa saying you are a burden and ma never being happy with you, you mustn't take these things to heart. It is like the moon; none of us can see the other side of the moon. Try to see the other side of your parents' love," said Abhay.

"Why must I have to leave home and go away all alone to a place I know nothing about?" Asha asked.

"Sometimes, we have to focus on the good things in life—going to study in Oxford, for example. Don't take it for granted. My father and your Aja had to struggle immensely to get an education. Their families never supported them. Bapa had to cycle miles to go to school. Aja often did not have enough to eat when he was studying. Everyone goes through problems—sometime or the other. Suffering is like the clouds in the sky, they disappear just as they appear," Abhay explained.

The next evening, Asha saw an envelope on her study table. She recognized her mother's handwriting. The house was quiet. Through the window, she could see the sunset, the blaze of colours so striking her heart ached. She could not ignore nature's indifference to the human condition. She opened her ma's letter and began to read it.

Asha Ma,

You have experienced one of life's greatest sorrows with fortitude, patience and courage. If you break down now like a branch plucked off the tree, I will suffer immensely—my soul will be in pain, my body will be sick. You too will experience these things, but to what purpose? I cannot come back.

Vivek is a child; he does not know what grief is. He will be truly hurt, yet I cannot see a way back. You thought that I never loved you, why? I had and still have no idea till today why you felt that way. I never believed it when I found out. I am now reaping what I sowed. I did not realise what you were going through; could I have prevented anything?

You told me not long ago I had turned Anand against you by telling him things about you. You may have said all that in anger and frustration, but you could still contemplate such a thing. It breaks my heart to think so. It is my bad luck I've had to experience all this. I never knowingly did anything to hurt you or anyone, never wished to teach you a lesson by inflicting pain. I loved and love you—all. And will do so as long as I live.

Other women have borne so many children and have experienced the joy of having them. I gave birth to only four—and have seen more pain and suffering than I ever imagined. You have witnessed your nana's bhagya and survived yours—both marriages were beyond endurance. Vijay's grief and agony you can see yourself. And Vivek is just a child, what does he know of suffering?

I am atoning for my sins. I pray to God every day to rescue us all from suffering. You are my flesh and blood, and I know you will be able to weather this storm in your life.

With my love, Ma

Asha went to visit her mother again, this time with Vivek. "I need to spend some time alone with ma," she explained as they set off.

"Fine, you talk to her. I'll go upstairs and talk to Aja," Vivek said, thinking his sister was in a better position to talk to their mother and persuade her to return home. "I'll come and talk to ma after that," he said.

Karuna was delighted to see them. After the initial exchanges, Vivek said he would join them after he'd spoken to Aja. Mother and daughter went to the kitchen to make tea. Karuna asked Asha about her trip to Hyderabad and her preparations for Oxford. Asha finally got a chance to ask her ma why she'd come to stay at Aja's. But Karuna would not tell her much, nor was she ready to return home.

"I don't wish to talk about it," Karuna said.

"Ma, you can stay here for as long as you wish. But do you know how long you want to stay?" Asha asked.

"No, I don't," Karuna replied absentmindedly.

"Remember how bapa, Vijay and even you complained that I could not stay at home, that I should go and live with Anand?" Asha said.

Karuna interrupted her. "My situation is entirely different."

"I agree," said Asha. "That's my point. *You* have a home. I never had one. Staying here is fine, but this is Aja's home—it is your home too, I know. But it is also Saswati mausi's home, Madhav mamu's and Kamini mausi's home. However, *your* home will remain yours forever. You know that, don't you? I never had *my* home…never had anything that belonged to me and Anand. You have so much. Do you really want to walk away from everything?" Asha asked.

Karuna was silent for a while. Then she said, "I cannot go back…"

"Why can't you return to your home? Tell me because I don't understand. If you're here for a change, a rest—that's fine. Stay as long as you need. Otherwise, I'm lost. Bapa may not be perfect, but he's a lot better than a lot of other men I can think of. Your life has been very hard, but is living here the answer?" Asha asked.

"You always take bapa's side," Karuna complained.

"That's *not* true, and you know it. I'm not taking anyone's side! And this is not about bapa. I am only thinking about *you*," Asha said.

"You will go away to Oxford. What difference does it make to you where I live? Change, uncertainty and suffering are all part of life," said Karuna.

"It is because I have to go away that I'm worried about you. If you live here with Aja, tell me, who will look after Vijay and Vivek?

Vijay, as you wrote to me, is suffering in his own way, who knows what problems he'll have once I'm gone. And Vivek, how will he cope? I cannot imagine you want them to suffer, what have they done? Besides, who is going to look after *you*? As you and bapa don't want me to stay with you, I can't look after either of you. Please tell me what is wrong, why you can't come home? Life will get a lot harder for you if you don't return to *your* home. If there's anything I can do, I need to know," Asha said, holding her ma's hand.

Karuna looked at her daughter helplessly, thinking how young and innocent she was, how even her ruined marriage had failed to take that away. How could she shatter her daughter's dreams by displaying the tattered chador of her life, show every tear and hole, every painful stitch that repaired its frayed canvas, every gash that had finally reduced her to rejecting her world? Her entire life— the death of her mother, marriage soon after puberty, children, housework, life's endless disappointments, her struggle to be a good mother, the breakdown of her children's marriages, having to see them leave, go away to places she knew nothing about—flashed past her.

Before Karuna could say anything, Aja arrived with Vikram and Vivek, the three of them laughing and talking, clearly in a good mood. Asha greeted her grandfather by touching his feet.

"Asha, I didn't know you were here. When did you arrive?" Aja greeted her, adding, "Have you had anything to eat or drink? Would you like some tea?"

How much Aja has changed! Asha thought. Once upon a time they did not drink tea in his presence, nor listen to film songs. She smiled, acknowledging the extent to which her Aja had grown to accommodate the world as it changed. While Karuna chatted to her sons, Asha answered Aja's questions.

Soon the cook arrived and Aja instructed him about dinner. Govardhan, now old but not yet ready to retire, greeted Asha. She asked him how he was faring.

"With God's grace, all is well. I see God is looking after you too, though you look a bit thin. Come and stay here with Karunama. I'll feed you both properly. Don't leave without dinner! I'll make something special tonight," he said.

"How can we miss your special cooking?" Asha said.

When they left that evening, Asha told her ma in private, "We are all very unhappy without you, especially bapa. He can't express himself, as you know—but he is truly alone, completely lost without you. Don't you think he, too, might be having a breakdown? We are all suffering...like you. But we need to be together to get through it. Otherwise, who is going to hold the family together?"

Karuna again looked at her the way she had done before and blessed her daughter as she bent and touched her mother's feet.

On their way back, Vikram and Vivek carried on with their conversation. Asha could not help thinking how lost her mother looked—for those few moments before her brothers and Aja arrived, and just before they parted—as if Karuna wanted to tell her something and then could not find the words. Asha felt they were all lost and needed each other to find the way. Looking at her brothers laughing and chatting, enjoying each other's company, she realised they had instinctively found the answer to life's unfathomable problems. As long as you can laugh and talk, there is hope.

After almost five weeks at Aja's, one evening Karuna returned home. Asha had no idea her father had gone to see her mother. She was delighted that whatever transpired between them had persuaded her to come home. Her father could not stop smiling. Karuna, too, seemed happier. She certainly looked rested.

The next morning Asha woke up to her ma complaining to the servants how dirty and uncared for the house looked. "I go away for a few days and return to see the house in such a dire state. I can't believe it. What have you all been doing?"

Asha knew her mother was back for good. She stayed in bed, savouring the moment, pulling the blanket like a sky over her head.

CHAPTER 23

The flow of visitors—uninvited and unexpected—kept rising as Asha's departure drew closer. The family had no idea how people found out, but they came lamenting the misfortune of such a beautiful and gifted girl having to leave home alone. "What is a woman without a husband and children?" they lamented. "Who'd have thought the marriage of the granddaughter of Amitava Guru and Siddhartha Mishra would fail?" they cried. "How will she manage alone in a foreign country?" they wondered. Asha noticed the names of her grandmothers were rarely mentioned, though it was women who usually made such remarks.

There were lone voices who admired her, one of whom was Suniti Sen, a colleague at the Women's College, where Asha was now teaching. She had been transferred from Harrison just a few months before she was due to leave for Oxford by the Patnaiks, who were back in Orissa and causing more havoc in the education department. Mr Gyan Prasad had returned to another post in Delhi. The university and the state of Orissa were reverting back to their old ways.

One afternoon, when Mrs Sen walked into the staff common room, the place was buzzing with salacious gossip about the newest member of staff, Armita Guru.

"They say he beat her up regularly, that's why she left him. But he's so handsome! God knows what awaits her in England," said one unmarried lecturer, giggling like a star-struck teenager imagining the wicked ways of the Wild West.

"I wouldn't mind some rough you-know-what," said another.

She resembled a large swaying teapot as she placed one arm on her hips and held the other up like a spout as she wriggled her bottom. Giddy with all that wriggling, swooning with loud laughter, she sat down in a capacious chair, which she had claimed for herself. The other members of staff were known to vacate the chair the moment she entered the room if they had accidentally taken possession of it. It was difficult to say whether they pitied her for not being able to squeeze into the other chairs, or that she was such a bully they did not wish to invoke her wrath.

"What is the world coming to? We had to put up with our husband's beatings," murmured a third lady, older than the other two.

The congregation nodded, acknowledging the world had indeed gone mad.

"You can't end a marriage just because your husband beats you—we'd all be without a husband, home, and children!" a fourth lady declared with astonishment at Asha's utterly unreasonable behaviour.

And laughter broke loose like a snapped, quadruple-stringed necklace of well-rounded Hyderabadi pearls bouncing down marble stairs.

"What an example to our daughters! The girls look up to her. She is setting such a bad example. What if our daughters emulate her, choose their husbands, and then walk away from their marriages on such flimsy grounds! Society would fall apart," added another with three daughters to marry off in the not-too-distant future.

Similar remarks continued to ricochet around the staff common room. The women, who could not teach properly, gossiped expertly.

"How could she stay with him if he ill-treated her? In any case, he was not a suitable match for her." One young lecturer dared raise her voice.

"Are there any other kind?" asked the teapot, still convulsing with laughter.

"Why did she marry him, then?" another pointed out, hoping to ingratiate herself with the staff, most of whom thought Armita was getting away with murder!

As head of the English department, Suniti Sen did not relish such discussions among faculty members. She silenced the whispering crowd with, "It took courage to do what Armita did. She loved him and went against her family and society to marry him. What do we know why she then decided to end her marriage? How many of us are qualified to judge her? This sort of talk brings us no credit at all."

With a few words, Mrs Sen ensured her colleagues would not gossip in her presence. Getting friendly with juniors in the workplace could spell trouble. Also, in an all-female college, everyone would expect favours—my mother-in-law is not well, my son needs to be taken to the doctor—the excuses would never end. It was no concern of hers if, in her absence, conversation sparkled with juicy gossip, hysterical laughter, innuendo and more. After all, women had little else to entertain themselves with, apart from such tittle-tattle.

Privately, she could not help wondering why Armita—cynosure of all the eligible men in the state, the bluest of blue-chips in the 'marriage market', the jewel in the crown of Orissa—had not settled for someone more deserving! Oh, the frailty of the best of us, she sighed.

One blistering summer afternoon, the heat and humidity of Cuttack at its peak, when it was an effort to stir, when even the crows and lizards took shelter from the sweltering sun, Asha made her way to college in a rickshaw. She had a lecture to deliver. The tarmac threatened to melt. The rickshaw-wallah reeked of garlic, his dark, glistening body streaked with salt. She felt sorry for him, his straw hat no protection against the murderous temperatures.

When Asha appeared in the staff common room, it was quaking with venomous laughter. She walked in, tall and slender, wearing a crisp white, cotton sari. The laughter stopped abruptly as if Ma Durga had appeared. The bitter tongues, bilious and buzzing a moment ago, fell silent. Asha felt an overwhelming desire to leave the place for good.

⚬

The officer at the British Consulate in Calcutta took less than five minutes to terminate the interview with Asha for her visa. After barely glancing through her application, he declared, "You don't have the necessary papers."

Asha had turned up with all the documents she had been asked to produce—the letter of admission from her college in Oxford, proof of financial support, i.e., the letter confirming her scholarship, ticket from Delhi to Heathrow, and a valid passport. In fact, she had written twice to the British Consulate to make sure that was all they needed. The reply sent to her the second time underlined the four items.

Showing him the two letters from the Consulate, Asha said politely, "Sir, I have all the documents I was asked to bring to the interview."

"Where is the letter of no objection from your employers?" he quipped.

"Sir, if such a document was required, why was it not mentioned in either of the letters sent to me? I made two enquiries just to make sure." She pointed to the letters in front of him. "How was I to know such a letter was necessary? I can send the letter on my return. I have here with me all the documents that were requested. It will be an additional expense for me to attend another interview. I am a national scholar; can you not show some consideration?" Asha felt breathless after her little speech.

The officer sat there with his lips pursed, his eyes focused on something on the wall at the opposite end of the room, his face frozen, resembling a papier mâché puppet. Then he spoke in a staccato voice as if someone had suddenly remembered to pull a string. "Come back with the correct papers."

This being Asha's first encounter with British bureaucracy, the inefficiency of the system astonished her. Not that India was better, but no Indian would do anything as mindless as that—take the trouble of sending two letters saying one thing and then denying it! *I am here with all the documents they asked for, and still they will not honour their word. How did the British build an empire?* She could hardly imagine.

"I hope your friend in the *Brutish* Council will be able to help you next time," Rashmi said when she heard of Asha's wasted trip. "Why are you going to that country, anyway? They think they still rule us, can't you see? Great Britain—my foot! Why not America? Go to Harvard. Get in touch with that professor who invited you."

"How was I to know I'd be dealt with so unfairly? Had it not been for Oxford, I wouldn't go to England either. How can I turn down an opportunity to study at Oxford? I can go to Harvard later. Also, one must give credit where due—just think of all the great British writers, inventors, thinkers," Asha reminded her friend.

"Years of living in India, dealing with Indians, has *Indianised* the British," Aja remarked when he heard about the visa business. Aja's boss, in pre-Independent India, was an Englishman. He was honest, intelligent, and decent. They respected each other and got along fine. "The English today are not the same. The best ones died in the wars," added Aja.

On her second visit, Asha was first subjected to a humiliating physical examination. The doctor at the British Consulate prodded, squeezed and kneaded her stomach so assiduously she was in tears. Being extremely ticklish, she could well imagine what it would feel like to have rats running and gnawing all over your belly. She was then interviewed by another officer, who wished to know more about her marriage. Was her husband going to accompany her?

It transpired that Anand had written to the British Consulate, requesting them not to grant 'his wife' a visa. This interview Asha did not mind. The man simply wanted to hear her side of the story. She told him about her marriage and that she was waiting for the divorce. He examined her papers and noted she had a scholarship, an offer from Oxford, and was travelling alone. He had no objection to granting her a student visa. It was the doctor's pummelling of her stomach that outraged Asha.

When she went to Calcutta for her first interview, she had not contacted her friends in the British Council to help her out with the visa. The process seemed straightforward. She was asked to provide specific documents; there seemed nothing arbitrary about the decision-making process. *Why should I bother my friends for unnecessary favours?* She did not even contact them, as there was not enough time to meet anyone during her flying visit.

But when she was turned away, she contacted Sujit Bhattacharjee. Asha could not risk another mess-up by the blundering British authorities in Calcutta. She made it clear to him that if she was turned down again, she would have no regrets about not going to Britain. She would go to America and let her college in Oxford know why she was unable to accept their offer.

"You should have no trouble this time," Sujit wrote back.

When they met after she was granted the visa and she told him in passing about the doctor, he explained, "Giving birth to a child in England is the surest way of receiving financial support from the state, the welfare system, and then staying on in the country. You could say he was doing his job, albeit very insensitively. Must've been an older man, eh?"

"Why would anyone want to be pregnant without a husband, Sujitda? After all these years in India, haven't they learnt anything about our culture? Besides, how will I manage alone in a foreign country with a child and study for a degree? It's bad enough going there alone without anyone to fall back on!" Asha replied, bewildered at the prospect of arriving pregnant in Oxford.

"Unfortunately, some people have done exactly that," replied Sujit. "Often we pay for the sins of our ancestors. Sometimes we also suffer for no reason at all—because someone somewhere has the power to do so. You know what they say—power corrupts, absolute power corrupts absolutely. You better be prepared for more of this sort of thing. Racism is pretty common in England. They may be lucky that *you* want to go to Oxford, but will *you* be lucky there? As a national scholar, you could've gone to study at any Ivy League university in America. I told that to my friend at the British Consulate when I complained about the way you were treated before. I hope that the people you meet in Oxford will not let you down," he added.

"Sujitda, I know in our country men grope, harass, attack, rape women, and the woman is held responsible for what happens to her. But I thought in Europe women were more liberated—human rights, privacy, not to mention feminism. But the English doctor has opened my eyes. It appears it is quite acceptable for an Englishman to pummel an Indian woman's stomach under the pretence of doing his job. And the woman can do nothing about it!" Asha observed.

Sujit looked at her sympathetically and said, "Let's hope you meet a few good men and women in Oxford."

The reality of leaving home and the land of her birth, perhaps for good, crystallised in Asha's mind after she was granted the visa. Her distress manifested itself in various forms—heart palpitations to passing fevers, wandering aches and pains to sleepless nights. There was little she could do to mitigate the symptoms, which were exacerbated by having to organize her affairs—secure study leave, sort out her divorce, pack her books, dispose of her other possessions, not to mention prepare herself mentally for the inevitable departure.

As Aja had predicted, all the things her parents had given her as dowry remained at her in-laws. The few possessions she had at her parents' home she stored away with great care—especially her books, her best friends. Asha bought a new Godrej almirah and arranged her books in alphabetical order. In each shelf, she placed one square block of Odonil and a sprinkling of naphthalene balls as if she was casting a spell to preserve her books. She also kept important documents and papers relating to her job, studies and the scholarship for future reference. When she gifted one of her favourite saris to a younger cousin, who then complained that she had not been given a new sari, Asha made a trip to the temple to donate her clothes to the beggars.

Among the hardest of all her self-imposed tasks was getting rid of her personal memorabilia. She resolved to let go of the past and make a fresh start. She had no plans to reinvent herself. She knew in life nothing disappears; everything leaves a mark. The marriage had so cauterised her she could no longer bear to look at the wedding photos. It had taken many days and nights of tears and heartache to get to this state of preparedness. Yet it took only one agonizing afternoon to make a bonfire of her past—photographs of her wedding, her letters to Anand, his letters, her diaries.

Watching the edges of photos and papers curl up in flames and crumble into ashes was like attending her cremation. Asha sat in the scorching sun, in one corner of the sprawling backyard, not far from the spot where she used to sit with Anand during the days of their courtship, watching her life burn to cinders. The heat left her dazed. She felt faint seeing a trembling haze rising from the burning earth. The more we die, the more we live. *It will take a bit longer for my body to burn*, she thought.

"What would you do if you had nothing—no society, parents—to hold you back?" Rashmi asked while they were having what she referred to as their 'last supper'.

"Are you planning to betray me?" Asha asked in jest.

"What are you talking about?"

"You referred to our 'last supper'—will you betray me like Judas?"

"Certainly not, but answer my question first."

"I don't seem to know my inner *self*; who *I* really am. How can I know what I must do with my life? I must first find out who *I* am so I can be the best of me. I thought love, in the form of marriage, was my vocation. But woman proposes and both God and man dispose," Asha replied.

Rashmi laughed and said, "I thought you'd say you want to meet a handsome, rich man and travel the world with him before settling down to having lots of children and live happily ever after! But this is too deep for me. Is that why people travel—not to explore another country, but to return home refreshed, bearing new perspectives of who they are? Well, go to Oxford and return an enlightened person!"

"If you believe we have a soul and the soul's journey ends with becoming one with God, whichever way you define God, then, yes, we are all returning. But I don't really know enough about these things. Why did you ask me such a question? You must be the last person in need of an answer to such a dilemma," Asha asked.

"We are all in need of answers. Life is offering you a chance of a lifetime to break free of chains." Rashmi gestured as if she was all tied up in silken cobwebs and was unable to remove them. "I can't wait to find out how you will use this unique opportunity. Don't you want to be the person you always wanted to be?"

"You mean different from the person I am today? Do you have such a need—to be someone you are not? The only thing I *know* is whatever circumstance I'm placed in, I'll end up being myself—the same as I am now. Is that too boring for you? What else can one be?" Asha replied.

"So, like millions of Indians, you believe in *fate*, what will be, will be?" Rashmi started to sing *"Que Sera Sera"*.

"The song, may I remind you, is not Indian. Besides, it depends on how you define fate. Buddha left his kingdom in search of enlightenment—was that fate or an act of choice? I feel life is pushing me one way while what I want, you already have—a happy marriage. This is the problem with life, misallocation of resources. Someone wants a child, and they can't have one. Another couple, terrible parents they may be, end up with six! What a crazy world we live in?" Asha laughed.

"A happy married life is a mirage. Don't be fooled by appearances. Like you, we should all be granted the opposite of what we desire. When the gods wish to punish us they answer our prayers, remember? I'm delighted you're going to Oxford, but I'll miss you dearly—with whom can I have such stupid conversations?"

It had been months since Asha began saying farewell to friends, family, cousins and acquaintances. It was not the same with her immediate family. There was no path that could lead her away from them. She had been having conversations with her brothers, her father, grandfather, and uncles about a lot of things. But they were not farewells, perhaps fare forwards. Having seen their expectations adjusted so radically within such a short time, the family had accepted the destiny of their children was not in their hands. They were pleasantly surprised that Asha was going to Oxford. All they could hope for her now was that life would treat her kindly.

Mother and daughter had been so busy preparing for the twin departures, they had not been able to sit down for a proper heart-to-heart. Then one afternoon, a few days before Asha was to leave, they found themselves alone at teatime.

"Ma, do you remember that evening at Aja's when I asked you about why you could not come home?" Asha began. "You were on the verge of saying something when Aja, nana and Vivek arrived, and we got distracted. I've been meaning to ask you since then—what were you thinking of saying?"

Karuna had not forgotten that moment either when her life had flashed past her like a corpse floating down the Ganges. She still did not know how to share her thoughts with her daughter.

"Ma, I know you are finally leaving home. I am proud, happy, anxious, sad, angry, disappointed—all at the same time. If your marriage had been happy, we'd have had some idea of what to expect. Now, we have none. In our culture we attach too much importance to marriage—for good reason, perhaps—but there is a price to be paid for everything," said Karuna.

Asha looked at her mother, astonished. "What do you mean, ma?"

"Look at my life—my mother died when I was just a child. I did not have a proper education as Aja was always transferred from one rural posting to another. There were no schools in most of those places. After puberty, I was married, barely fifteen. Our backgrounds couldn't have been more different—your father's and mine. I had no experience of managing a household. Looking after four children is not easy. I tried to be the best mother I could, but where did it get me? You grew up misunderstanding me, thinking I did not love you. The marriages failed—and now I'm losing two of my children. You and nana are going to places I know nothing about...What sort of life is this? What is there left for me?" Karuna replied.

Seeing tears in her mother's eyes, Asha's eyes moistened too.

"Ma, please don't be despondent—we cannot change the past, but we can shape the future. All those years I suffered thinking you did not love me—not as much as nana. *He* is the apple of your eye. I felt as if this was not *my* home. Now I know that anywhere I go, I have to find a place elsewhere," said Asha.

"Women are like rivers that flow, nurturing the land around them. If they stop or dry up, they die and are forgotten," said Karuna.

"We must believe that the best is yet to be, that happiness lies ahead. Otherwise, it will not be possible to carry on. So never think your life has no meaning—you've brought up four children. We love you more than we can ever express. I've said hurtful things to you, so has Vijay—but you know we couldn't live without you, not for a day. I cannot say how much I love you," said Asha.

Wiping her tears, Karuna added, "Married life has been hard. Bapa does not understand me..."

"I know you'll say I'm defending him. Bapa, too, says you don't understand him! It hasn't been easy for you, I know. But after what I went through, your marriage seems happy to me, ma," said Asha.

"Bapa has never been physically violent, I agree. But when someone you share your life with does not understand you, it is very lonely. You know that. Maybe you've got a chance to find your own happiness now that you'll be alone—left to make your own decisions. You tried once to live for someone else and you failed. Maybe living for others is not the way. I don't know why they say it leads to happiness. We need to live for ourselves too," Karuna said.

"We just need to keep trying—trying to learn to be happy," said Asha. "Bapa is lonely too. I wish you could find happiness in each other. Can't you find *your* own happiness by being yourself and realising *your* potential?" Asha asked.

"I don't know any woman who has. Even happily married women remain unfulfilled. You sacrifice everything at the altar of marriage and family, and then find you've nothing left when the children grow up and leave." Karuna sighed.

"It's never too late to do all the things you'd like to," said Asha.

"It is too late. There is a time for everything..." replied Karuna.

"Have you spoken about any of this to bapa? Does he feel the same, I mean, as if he too has not had a chance to do all the things he wanted?" asked Asha.

"He doesn't understand. How can I speak to him about such delicate matters? Even you did not understand me," Karuna said. "I gave birth to you, looked after you and still failed to get through to you. You suffered too as a result. What is the point of bringing children into the world if it is so full of pain and suffering? Sometimes, I think we give birth to atone for our sins," Karuna replied.

"I remember you once told me—pain and pleasure walk together; can't have one without the other. I think the choices open to women are limited. We both feel that somehow life has cheated us! Life has to mean more than this?" Asha asked.

"I'm afraid that's what it is—an illusion. Life is maya..." Karuna said, rising from her chair on seeing Aditya and Abhay at the front gate.

"We must learn not to stand in the path of our own happiness," said Asha.

The week before Asha left, her family went into a state of shocked resignation—not unlike soldiers returning home after prolonged action on the frontline, individual action having lost its purpose or meaning. God's ways were inscrutable, human beings placed on earth for reasons beyond comprehension. Yet, it was this disconnection between God's ways and our understanding of it that was the reason for our unhappiness. As every living being was part of God's creation, whatever life offered was also God's will.

Hinduism understood human nature and made it easier to accept injustice and unfairness by arguing that as we sow, so we reap—albeit over many lives. The key was time. You never ran out of hope because you never ran out of time. You could at any moment change your destiny by right action, the interpretation of 'right' being left to individual discretion. Once you change, the world around you changes. Even with such knowledge, of God's majesty and infinite forgiveness, the Guru family were unable to accept their sudden fall from grace.

When children leave home, families go through changes that

appear insurmountable. Happy families may all be alike, and every unhappy family is unhappy in its own way. But here was a family that was both happy and unhappy at the same time. It brought them closer just like the days before the weddings when everyone agreed about everything. Love flowed from each heart moving through the grief of parting.

The two older children were leaving home, not to study at one of the best universities in India. No, they were leaving for places their parents knew nothing about. God had cut off both their limbs and expected them to swim across the river of sorrow with its deadly currents. Why would an omnipotent, benign God do such a terrible thing? They consoled themselves thinking this suffering was sent to them for a reason. How else could anyone bear such injustice? Aditya and Karuna were so wrapped up in sorrow that their own helplessness in the face of such calamity, the extent of their vulnerability, escaped them. Sometimes there is no choice but to survive first, reflect later.

Thankfully, the two younger sons were there providing a reason to carry on. They were innocent and had nothing to do with the family's tragedy except to be touched by it. How could they not be affected by such events? How could they find their way through this quagmire of suffering? And who would have thought that Vijay and Vivek, born several years later like a conversation between friends that had never been concluded, would provide a reason for holding the household together? It was as if God had offered them to Karuna and Aditya as compensation for what He would take away. God's ways were inscrutable indeed.

It was harrowing to lose a son. It is on the eldest son the burden of hopes, dreams and aspirations of parents descend upon. From a daughter there was no such expectation. They knew from the moment of her birth that their Asha would be married, lost to them forever, becoming part of her husband's family. But a son—to lose the eldest son was like being asked to offer their hearts to the gods. How would they survive such a sacrifice?

Well-wishers who had reassured Karuna when she fretted about her daughter's future saying, "Don't worry, Asha's wedding will be the celebration of the century!"—stood silently by, unable to explain how such disaster struck. No one could explain why Asha's marriage, cracked open like a coconut and the milk of her desires spilt at the feet of the gods, was not blessed by them. Why was God indifferent to her plight?

"How can it be just?" Karuna complained to her father. "You give birth to them, look after them, love them, how can you just let them go? When will I see them again? Why should I be punished like this, have to bear such pain—bring them into the world and then lose them?"

"Even Rama had to leave his kingdom," Siddhartha consoled his daughter. "Ma, you have to think of their future and be strong for them."

He knew of one's right to action, never to the results of action, success or failure being retrospective.

"Sita went with Rama," Karuna protested.

She knew her father meant well. It seemed like the other day the children were born. Before she knew it, they were leaving home. *Mahabharata* was all but over.

CHAPTER 24

All my life I've been waiting. All the things that happen to me and those that do not, all the people I meet and those I don't, keep defining me inexplicably. Life is what happens to us while we wait for things to happen. Asha paused. She needed to think between her thoughts. "Good things come to those who wait"—her mother's voice rose up an elegant staircase of light rising skywards. Instantly, she could hear her father's voice—"In the long run we are all dead." *Must learn to live amid uncertainties, contradictions, remain open to possibilities...* Her thoughts scampered around like dragonflies in a pond.

The flight had been delayed a couple more hours since the rescheduled departure time was scrawled illegibly on the notice board, which was barely visible, placed as it was behind a massive pillar near the entrance to the airport. Flights to Delhi from Bhubaneswar were not scheduled daily. When a flight took off, it was an event. Delays, cancellations, and postponements were common in all aspects of life. If anything happened on time, it was more by accident than by design.

In the distance a man cleared his throat and spat noisily before shooing away a street dog that snarled back at him scuff-shuffling the dust. Crows fought over a dead lizard, or was it a field mouse? A mynah took off lustily with its trophy—a fat, writhing worm dangling from its beak. The cacophony of human voices, barking dogs and chattering birds provided the background accompaniment to a song from the *Geeta Govinda* playing full blast from a radio in a tiny tea stall near the government-owned Orissa Handloom shop that had the pride of place inside the airport lounge. The voice of Raghunath Panigrahi cast a spell, *Hari ne kara sum, Hari ne kara sum.*

Lounge would be too grand a word for the space in question. The airport in Bhubaneswar—the capital of Orissa, India's second poorest state—was an airstrip not larger than a cricket pitch, a place where people waited as at a bus station. The airport had a hands-on, do-it-yourself air about it. You could see the luggage being carried to the aircraft and observe it being unloaded.

A punctilious, punctual person, Asha was grateful for the delay. Her farewell party, though, was beginning to exhibit signs of restlessness—the pain of losing a daughter, granddaughter, sister, cousin, niece slowly assuaged by other demands. Nature's way of reasserting order. She stood there split between the child that never wanted to leave home, and the daughter who could no longer stay. She had not moved from her place, but felt as if she had left and returned.

"Sar, flight ready now, everything is fine. Armita can now board," announced an airport official, an ex-student of Aditya's, whose head moved with such excitement it threatened to fly off its hinges.

All the young men in that particular conclave of humanity were in love with her, or thought they were. Asha had many suitors, yet it had come to this. Betrayed by the one she chose, *she* was the one leaving.

Daughters traditionally left the Guru family cloisters with their husbands. The wedding ceremony a way of ensuring a smooth transfer of responsibility—from one man, the father, to another, the husband—the arranged marriage being the best example of parental due diligence, safer and more rigorous than any mega corporate merger. Everything was scrutinized, structured, ordered. Marriage was no place for mistakes, divorces, abortions. Asha was well-trained for this changing of the guard, initially grieving and dreading the arrival of such a day when she, too, would leave home. Yet, here she was leaving home, without a husband, to build her world elsewhere. That's the way dreams are shattered, the variance between our desire and the world's.

Just when she abandoned hope of seeing Rashmi before boarding the aircraft, Asha heard her unmistakable voice. Alighting from the rickshaw with unceremonious haste, Rashmi failed to notice her colourful, polyester sari making its way up over her calf, revealing a shapely leg. The jingle-jangle of her gold and glass bangles and the tinkling of her silver anklets turned several heads.

Not realizing what the hoo-ha was all about, Rashmi said somewhat out of breath, "I've been praying all the way to get here in time. You cannot imagine my plight—everything that could go wrong did go wrong! The driver reported sick, I couldn't get an auto, had to come in a rickshaw, the roads are terrible not to mention the traffic..." She stopped. Clearly this was no time for her usual pronouncements on the deplorable state of the country.

Addressing Asha's parents, Rashmi said, "Do I see tears in your eyes? Hope these are tears of joy. It's not every day a daughter of Orissa goes to study at Oxford. How many Oriyas have the honour of being national scholars and going to Oxford? The Chief Minister should've been here to see our Asha off. One day the whole world will recognize her worth. Go, girl, and show them what you're made of. We may be from India's most backward and poorest state, but our culture is rich, we are no less than the best in the world. So never be backward in putting yourself forward!" Rashmi said, warmly hugging her friend.

When it was time for Asha to finally board, Vijay and Vivek were the first to touch her feet in farewell. Asha embraced them, holding back her tears, unable to imagine how she would live without her family. Her parents placed their hands on her head as she leaned forward for their blessings, tears streaming silently down their forlorn faces. Seeing their daughter leave home and country alone left them distraught. They had not brought her up to survive in some foreign land on her own.

"From now on God will look after you," Karuna said. She believed prayers like thoughts travel the world.

Holding her face in his hands, Aditya whispered, "God be with you always."

Asha bowed down to take the dust from her Aja's feet. She had not seen her Aja look so desolate, his grief-stricken face reminding her of a funeral in progress.

"Asha ma, may God help you, protect you, and guide you," said Aja, placing his right palm on her head. "Write when you reach Oxford."

The look on the faces of all her family members confirmed a shared sense of helplessness. Later, when she saw the photos neatly arranged in the farewell album, her face, too, acknowledged the end of her world, not a single face wore a smile, each a tableau of grief.

Making her way to the aircraft, lips quivering, eyes moist yet burning, Asha had a premonition she could never return to make a life for herself in the place of her birth, nor raise a family in the land that nurtured her and gave her everything before taking it all away. Stepping inside the aeroplane, having crossed the Rubicon, she waved a last long goodbye, taking in every detail. It may not have amounted to much to a casual observer, who would perhaps have dismissed the whole scene as sentimental. For Asha, it was her world.

Once settled in her seat, the practicalities of flying demanded attention. Every moment was a crisis waiting to happen, and each cell of her body alert like camels standing to attention during the 'Beating the Retreat' ceremony, which marked the end of the Republic Day celebrations in Vijay Chowk with the stately Rashtrapati Bhawan in the background. Asha could barely see anything through the oval-shaped window, the glass scratched and dirty. When the plane lurched and moved forward, the floodgate of emotions lifted and the world dissolved before her. The ghostly faces in the window were the first to disappear, the profiles of temples silhouetted against the late afternoon sky followed. The lush green and brownish-red plots of land, the rivers that fed the rich landscape lingered the longest, reluctant to let her go.

As the flight took off, the aircraft, three-quarters full, roared and shuddered. She closed her eyes, terrified the wings would burst into flames, the moment she noticed sparks from her window seat. What a way to die, to be cremated in such a manner! She had never begun anything with more misgivings. Silently reciting the Gayatri mantra, *Om bhu bhubah swah*, did not help. She tried all the other mantras in her repertoire. It kept her busy for several minutes. Yet she could not get rid of the vision of her family standing at the airport watching her plane's flaming descent. Thinking of her family wiping their tears leaving the airport once her aircraft was no more than a speck above the horizon, Asha wiped her tears. Since the day she received the letter confirming the scholarship, she had been crying privately. Now she could weep openly. She had shared with Rashmi her dread of this day of reckoning. Rashmi consoled her as Lord Krishna had counselled Arjuna, "Be true to yourself; everything else will fall into place." The two friends had wept copiously, knowing there was no choice in the matter.

Asha imagined her family having to go through another wrenching farewell and letting go when Vikram would leave home a week later. He had been offered a post at Newcastle General Hospital. It was a prestigious start for both the children. But the family could not reconcile themselves to the injustice of their loss. In one fell swoop two of their offspring had been snatched away.

They had invested everything in their children. If their daughter had married a successful man abroad or their son had left with his wife to enhance his career, it would've been different. Such a model of loss and forbearance existed.

But this was unimaginable—the children paid the price by leaving, their parents by having to stay. If they had left together or stayed together, they could have endured their losses better. They had no peer group, no family member or friend who had gone through similarly shattering experiences, to provide guidance or support. When the gods wish to punish you, they send you experiences not shared by others.

Never having stepped outside the home without an escort, travelling alone to England was an act of faith. Never having been encouraged to stand on her own, Asha now prepared to face life alone. *Preparedness is all*, she reminded herself, leaning back on her seat. When you have no choice, you do what has to be done. The problem lay in not knowing what exactly needed to be done. She continued with her thoughts—sometimes, all we are left with are our memories.

Knowing she had to live no matter how many skies had fallen, Asha felt utterly miserable, more than she thought was possible. Memories rushed in like angels. She remembered her mother describing the night of her birth. Karuna was massaging her head, oiling her hair. Asha had heard the story several times before. Each time it was a slightly different story, different strands of memories inserted, deleted. Asha wanted to hear it all over again, as if hearing it for the first time.

She remembered her ma's words. "The nurse ignored my pleas for help, asked me to go to sleep! 'But what if I give birth in my sleep?' I cried. The pain would not allow me to sleep." Asha was falling asleep; a head massage had that effect. In fact, any massage made her feel drowsy. And thinking about it now, immersed in her mother's reverie, had a similar effect. She recalled Karuna's words as she combed her hair and whispered, "How are you, Ma?" Asha was not sure—not then, not now—if Karuna was speaking to her mother or her daughter. It did not matter—perhaps she was talking to both. It happened many lifetimes ago. Mother and daughter realised separately, together, the eternal presence of the past. Imagining herself inside her mother's belly, sitting in the aeroplane with her eyes closed, made Asha feel secure. She felt cradled in the consciousness of the universe—everything existed in a latent state of potentiality, as if her life was waiting to begin.

⁕

Before Asha left for Oxford, people had shared confidences that opened her eyes. The rules that glued society together were stretched and bent if not broken! None of these people had any experience of life outside India; some had never left Orissa. Yet they advised her on how she should conduct herself abroad, the advice reflecting the speaker's unmistakable personality. Some envied her, saying she had escaped the chains that bound them. Others pitied her for having to fend for herself in exile, like Sita in the Dandaka forest, but without Rama by her side.

Elders, friends, relatives, even relative strangers, enlightened Asha about her future, Vilayat, England, Oxford, America, the West, There—the simultaneously attracting, repelling *Abroad!* Words of wisdom were bequeathed gift-wrapped to mark her departure. She had stored these mementos in the back drawer of her memory. Keep a thing by you seven years, and it'll come in use though it was the Devil. Seemed like the perfect time to unpack them now.

"Learn to *see*, not just look—as if you've never *seen* anything before. Follow your heart; trust yourself. Do not look at yourself through the eyes of strangers, Asha. Do not measure your achievements by their standards. Be yourself. Go explore, dream, discover…"

"Leave your personal nightmare behind you. Expose yourself fully to all that your new life has to offer. When you return home, you will be equipped to face everything. Remember, Armita, your roots are here."

"You are one of us, Armita. You will not find happiness in a foreign land. You may become rich, even famous, but you will never feel at *home there.*"

"I greet you, Armita, at the beginning of a great career," she recalled Paramjit echoing Ralph Waldo Emerson's response to Walt Whitman's *Leaves of Grass.*

The world was divided into those who called her Asha, or any variation of it, and those who knew her as Armita. Not that those who called her Armita did not care, it was just a different kind of caring, a different way of seeing the world. Sometimes it was as different as waking and sleeping, silence and speech, day and night.

Paramjit's greeting was for her alternative career as an academic, its favourable prospects in light of her scholarship to Oxford, especially after her *real* career in life had suffered such an unexpected setback. What these well-wishers were referring to was the highly expected not happening, events that alter lives for ever. Two such events had connived in recreating Asha's world—the breakdown of her marriage and her winning a scholarship to Oxford.

When Asha had rejected traditional arranged marriages, she had no idea where her search for love might lead. She could not have imagined it would leave her broken hearted, or that she would find herself leaving alone for Oxford! It was as if she had been preparing all her life to walk through one door, then suddenly it had slammed shut, severing her arms and legs. She felt lucky crawling through another that opened unexpectedly, but it still left her at a disadvantage like a dancer without legs, a pianist without arms. That's how she felt making her way through her alternative life, which bore no resemblance to what it was promised to be.

She steadied herself, thinking, *If I can't make it through one door, I'll go through another door—or I'll make a door. Something terrific will come no matter how dark the present.* She could not remember whose words she was falling back on. It did not matter. Leaning back on her seat, resting her head on the headrest, she closed her eyes and let her mind wander as it emptied itself like an hourglass. She had a vision of herself soaring high in the sky above elegantly imposing spires and domes gleaming in the sun, a new world beckoning her.

GLOSSARY

Agni parikhya: Trial by fire. Agni in Sanskrit means fire and parikhya is a test or trial. In the Hindu religious epic, *Ramayana*, Sita's chastity was questioned after she was abducted by the demon, Ravana. To prove her chastity, she went through a trial by fire.

Aintha: Oriya word for food that is considered defiled. Hindus, especially Brahmins, are particular about their food—not only what they eat, also how it is cooked. If the cook or anyone else tastes the food with the spatula and stirs the dish using the same spatula, the food is defiled. There are many such restrictions.

Alakhani: The root of the word Lakhani is linked to Goddess Lakshmi. Alakhyani translates to a female who is not a Lakhyani, or one who does not adhere to her dharma, and is undeserving of the blessings of Lakshmi.

Arati: The worship of gods with lamps. Devotees typically circle the lamp three times before the image of the deity they worship.

Asura: Contemporary usage of asura refers to an evil, godless person.

Bada Danda: Main Street

Badmash: A rogue, ruffian, bad or evil person.

Bakshish: The tradition of charitable giving of gifts or money during festivals showing gratitude or respect. An offering to the gods may also be considered bakshish. A faqir or holy man may ask for bakshish without thinking of his action as begging. A bakshish, like a tip, is also offered to someone who delivers a service for which the person may not be paid for appropriately.

Bel-patri: Refers to the trifoliate leaves of the medicinal plant, the Bael or Bilva tree, whose fruit is variously known as Quince apple, Stone apple, Wood apple, Elephant apple. The leaves are used in the worship of Shiva. The tree is considered to be holy, and its worship is mentioned in ancient Indian writings.

Bewakoof: In Urdu, it refers to a foolish person or a simpleton.

Bhagya: Luck, fate, fortune

Bhai: Brother

Bhajan: Religious or devotional songs

Bhalloo: Bear, the animal

Bhasana: On the tenth day, the clay idols made for Durga Puja are taken in a procession to the river for immersion.

Bhoji: Feast

Biddi: Refers to the short, thin, handmade Indian cigarettes filled with tobacco and wrapped in the locally grown tendu leaf tied with a string. Inexpensive and without a filter, the risk of smoking a biddi is significantly higher than conventional cigarettes.

Brahmana: A Brahmin; also refers to an enlightened human being.

Chaat: Savoury, spicy snacks

Chador: A sheet, bedspread, blanket or piece of cloth

Chakra: Derived from the Sanskrit word for wheel, it refers to various kinds of chakras—from the Ashoka Chakra in the flag of India to the chakras of the human body. The Sudarshana Chakra is a spinning, disk-like super-weapon used by Vishnu.

Chandi: Silver

Chor: Thief

Chorani: A female thief

Chowkidar: Watchman or gatekeeper

Chudidar: Tight fitting trousers worn by both men and women in South Asia, traditionally a kurta or kameez is worn over the chudidar.

Dakshina: The term originally described the payment made for the services of a priest. Pilgrims habitually give dakshina when they visit a temple. Dakshina also means south, southern; it can also means right-handed, able or clever.

Daku: Dacoit

Dari: Carpet or mat

Darshan: An opportunity to see or an occasion of seeing the image of a deity or a holy person. Hindus attach great importance to a darshan, or a view, of a saint or holy image.

Dilli: In various Indian languages Delhi is pronounced as Dilli.

Durga Puja: Worship of the Goddess Durga

Dussehra: The ten-day Hindu festival widely celebrated in India. The word, Dussehra, is derived from the Sanskrit Dasha-hara meaning the remover of ten. It refers to Lord Rama's victory over the ten-headed demon, Ravana. The day also marks the victory of Goddess Durga over the demon Mahisa.

Eve-teasing: Euphemism used in India to describe sexual harassment of women, especially unwanted sexual remarks or advances in a public place. Eve-teasing often turns into violent public attacks.

Gada: Indian mace

Gangajal: Holy water of the Ganges used in pujas. The term is also loosely applied to any water that is used in worship. When visiting a temple, the priest pours the sacred water into the palm of the worshipper as blessing. The common practice is then to sip the water or touch the holy water with one's lips and then sprinkle the rest on the head.

Ghee: Clarified butter used by Hindus in worship and cooking. Ghee is applied to the wicks of lamps. It is also used to light the lamps. It is used in sacrificial fires, including weddings.

Goonda: A hooligan, thug or bully

Gotra: Refers to a clan or lineage within an Indian caste. Marriage between a man and woman of the same gotra is traditionally prohibited as it is thought they are descended from a common male ancestor. The practice of discouraging marriage between members of the same gotra was intended to keep the tribe free from inherited genetic traits that were considered negative, as much as to broaden the influence of a particular gotra by wider alliances with other lineages.

Griha Pravesh: Hindu ceremony, traditionally performed on the occasion of one's first entry into a new house.

Gup-shup: Gossip, chat, conversation

Haramzadi: Term of abuse referring to an illegitimate, female child.

Hata: Oriya word for an open market

Hathi: Elephant

Hisab-kitab: Keeping account

Jejebapa: Grandfather

Jejema: Grandmother

Juhar: In Oriya, refers to the custom of touching the feet of elders.

Kaku: Uncle or father's younger brother

Kanyadan: Kanya is a young girl and daan refers to the act of giving or donating. Kanyadan is the gift of a daughter. The idea behind kanyadan is that a daughter, especially a virgin, is a father's most precious gift. He seeks to give her to a worthy recipient. The act is therefore compared to making a gift to the gods.

Karai: Wok used in Indian cooking

Khandani: Noble, high status, cultured

Khus-Khus: An indigenous cooling device adopted by the British in India from the Mughals. The installation of tatties made of khus-khus grass over windows, doors, verandas of a house proved an effective method of keeping cool.

Kriya: Last rites

Kshatriya: Also spelled Kshetriya refers to the second highest in ritual status of the four varnas, social classes or castes, in Hinduism. Historically, it referred to the warrior or the ruling class.

Kutcherry: Office, the word originally referred to the Court of Law

Labha: Gain or profit

Lafanga: An ill-bred, unprincipled, man, especially one whose behaviour towards women is dishonourable, a cad.

Lagna: Sacred period during which religious rites are performed

Lathi charge: Lathi refers to a stick or baton. In India, police often resorted to baton charges during riots and violent demonstrations

Leila and Majnoo: Love story popularized by the Persian poet, Nizami Ganjavi.

Mahabharata: One of the two major Sanskrit epics of ancient India that define the core of Indian culture and philosophy; the other being *Ramayana*. The *Bhagavad Gita* is the philosophical treatise that forms part of *Mahabharata*. The story of *Mahabharata* also contains an abbreviated version of *Ramayana*.

Mahalaya: Mahalaya heralds the advent of Durga Puja, the worship of the Goddess of supreme power. It is observed seven days before her puja when the Goddess is invited to descend to earth. This invocation is done by the chanting of mantras and slokas. Since the early 1930s, Mahalaya has come to be associated with the broadcast of a radio program at dawn, called "Mahisasura Mardini" or "The Annihilation of the Demon." This All India Radio programme consists of a recital from the scriptural verses of "Chandi Kavya" and Bengali devotional songs.

Mahamantras: Maha means great, mantras are prayers or religious chants

Mamu: Uncle or mother's brother

Mataji: Mata means mother in Sanskrit, and ji is a respectful and polite form of address. Mataji is also used to address a holy woman. When Vikram addresses his younger sister as Mataji, he is being playful, and is teasing her for her piety.

Mausa: Uncle or mother's sister's husband

Mausi: Aunt or mother's sister

Medha: The structure displaying the Goddess Durga with other deities, usually lavishly decorated with gold and silver ornaments.

Mohalla: Refers to a community, housing block, town or village

Moksha Patam: Snakes and Ladders, an ancient Indian board game, emphasizing the role of karma or fate in life.

Nabami: Ninth day of the festival of Dussehra

Namak-haram: An untrustworthy person, traitor, betrayer. Namak means salt and haram refers to that which is forbidden.

Namaskar: Customary word and gesture used in India when meeting or parting. The greeting, derived from Sanskrit, is said with folded palms held in front of oneself, a bow expresses reverence. Namah in Sanskrit means adoration or obeisance, and kar means do. The word te means you; namaste is I bow to you.

Nani: In Oriya, nani means older sister. It also refers to father's sister.

Paan: Betel leaf, coated with edible calcium carbonate, wrapped around shavings of areca nut and other spices such as cardamom, cloves, depending on the personal preferences of the eater. Paan serves as a digestive and a mouth freshener.

Pasapalli: Handloom sari woven in Orissa. The name is derived from pasā or gambling. These saris have intricate check patterns of contrast colours resembling chess boards.

Peon: Derived from the Spanish word, a peon is an office attendant, an orderly, a person hired for odd jobs, a person with little authority, often assigned unskilled tasks or an underling.

Petromax: Petromax is a brand name for a pressurized kerosene lamp, with a mantle, used in India. These lamps were similar to paraffin lamps used in Europe, Tilley lamps in Britain, and Coleman lamps in America.

Pica: Similar to biddi, pica is unfiltered tobacco rolled in tendu leaf.

Puja: Worship

Raga: Raga is the basis of compositions in the Indian classical musical tradition. Ragas are associated with times of the day, moods and seasons. In Sanskrit, rāga is defined as the act of colouring or dyeing. It refers to the creation of a mood or feeling of love, desire, delight, anger, loss, etc.

Rakhyasuni: Female demon

Ramayana: The great Hindu epic, describing the life of King Rama

Rama Lila: Rama Lila is a dramatic re-enactment of the life of Lord Rama as narrated in the Hindu religious epic, *Ramayana*.

Ratha Jatra: Annual Chariot Festival, also called Car Festival, associated with Lord Jagannath and traditionally held in Puri, Orissa. Puri is considered to be one of the four most sacred places in India.

Sahib: Arabic word, meaning master, used as a respectful form of address for one's superior of a bearer of high office. It was a term used to refer to the colonial masters in India. It is still used in traditional circles as a form of address. It also refers to the European race, or someone of Caucasian origin.

Sala: Brother-in-law or wife's brother. Occasionally used as a term of endearment. It is also a common term of abuse.

Sankha: Conch shell, sankha are white bangles worn by married women

Sarba mangala mangaley: The first three words of the Durga mantra, a prayer for universal good. Sarba means universal and mangala is good.

Sasura: Father-in-law

Sattvik: Literally means pure, divine or spiritual. In Vedic philosophy, it refers to a state of mind that is calm and peaceful. Sattvik food refers to a diet bestowed with such qualities.

Shamiana: A marquee or ceremonial tent used for outdoor events ranging from marriages to business conferences. The history of the shamiana dates back to the Mughals in India.

Sherwani: A coat-like dress, similar to a doublet, worn over the kurta and chudidar.

Sloka: Slokas like mantras are prayers.

Sudha: Interest: charged when making a loan

Suna: Gold

Swadhin: Independent

Swarga: Heaven

Swayamvara: Refers to the ancient Indian practice of a girl choosing a husband from among a list of suitors. Swayam means self, and vara means choice or desire, vara also means bride-groom.

Tamasha: A show, pageant, or theatrical performance; could also refer to a prank or making a huge fuss.

Teen Devian: Three divine beings. Teen means three, and Devi refers to the female manifestation of divinity. Teen Devian also refers to a 1965 Bollywood film, starring Dev Anand, about a poet falling in love with three different women.

Tu cheese badi hai masta, masta: In Hindi, the phrase translates approximately to—you are extremely attractive, your beauty is intoxicating.

Tulsi: The sacred Indian basil

Veshya: Prostitute

Zari: Refers to embroidery made with gold and silver threads

ACKNOWLEDGMENTS

I wish to thank the many individuals who encouraged me to write a novel. As it has taken me over two decades to come out with my first offering, most of them would have forgotten their role in making it happen. I am, however, indebted to their collective faith in me and express my deep appreciation of friends who have walked alongside me in this venture.

I am immensely grateful to those who read *A World Elsewhere* in its previous incarnations, and offered comments, criticisms, encouragement, praise and guidance. My thanks are due to Dr Alexandra da Costa, Prof Jaysinh Birjépatil, Peter Hodgman, Amita Khosla, Lamia Kronfli-Walker, Lance Lee, Melissa Marshall, Anita Money, Pauline Nolet and Julia Pike.

Without the support of my family this novel could not have been written. My mother and brothers read parts of the novel and offered feedback. Special thanks to my brother, Sanjay, for the photographs and the cover design, which was implemented by Lalit Kanhar.

A World Elsewhere is dedicated to my family and to the memory of my father who died in January 2001.

AUTHOR BIOGRAPHY

Shanta Acharya was born and educated in Orissa, India. She studied at Oxford and Harvard before working as an investment manager in the City of London. The author of nine books, she has been published in fields as diverse as poetry, literary studies and finance. *A World Elsewhere* is her first novel. www.shantaacharya.com

Lightning Source UK Ltd.
Milton Keynes UK
UKOW04f0041160915

258690UK00001B/23/P